THE FACILITATOR

Jack Larsen

&

James Haynes

THE FACILITATOR

Jack Larsen

&

James Haynes

INKWELL BOOKS
Writing·Publishing·Printing

ISBN: 978-1-939625-04-5
Library of Congress Control Number: 20160229632

Published by Inkwell Books
10632 North Scottsdale Road, Unit 695
Scottsdale, AZ 85254

Tel. 480-315-3781
E-mail info@inkwellbooks.com
Website www.inkwellbooks.com

Printed in the United States of America

PROLOGUE

Washington, D.C
February, 2009

PRESIDENT LIFTS BAN ON OFFSHORE DRILLING
By Washington Post Staff

Washington, D.C. - In a stunning policy reversal, Interior Secretary Jackson Delamater today lifted the ban on offshore oil exploration and drilling. After less than one month in office, the President, an ardent opponent of offshore drilling, has apparently changed his mind on the subject.

"The President feels that, despite his own personal reservations about offshore drilling, energy independence is absolutely critical to the security of the United States," Delamater said in his statement....

The President, a relatively young man, had come literally out of nowhere in the last eight years, rising from an Oklahoma state legislator to a surprise election to the United States Senate and now to the pinnacle of power. He had been a criminal defense lawyer and political activist in Oklahoma City before running for the state legislature.

The President's rise to national prominence and eventually to the Oval Office had been accomplished with the help of a well-oiled campaign by a variety of liberal-to-moderate organizations and groups whose only aim seemed to be to undo all the policies and practices of the previous Administration. The President's meteoric rise was all made possible by his extraordinary public speaking ability.

He could mesmerize a hall full of college students or a convention center full of party delegates. He sometimes exuded a messianic fervor for his core issues and causes. And his causes were an eclectic collection of the old left, progressive and new – some said inspired – goals.

For one, he favored a policy of reaching out to the Islamic world. He seemed to genuinely feel that the United States had become obsessively anti-Muslim in the wake of the September 11 attacks on New York and Washington, D.C.; feeling instead that Islamic fundamentalism was simply an outgrowth of U.S. imperial policy in the Middle east, of U.S. support of Israel and of the invasions of Iraq and Afghanistan.

The President's new-found energy independence stance seemed to many to be in conflict with his level of comfort, support and trust of the Arab world. In the wake of the reversal on off-shore drilling, his background and policies once again would be examined and dissected by the talking heads on CNN, Fox News and other assorted pundits, paid "experts" of one stripe or another.

A commentator on Fox pointed out that the President's record fundraising for last year's campaign included over $50 million in contributions via the Internet – contributions which could not be verified as to source, as Federal law required. The commentator speculated further that a major portion of this funding was thought to be from well-heeled citizens and corporations of Saudi Arabia and other "friendly" Arab states, which is also prohibited by Federal law. MSNBC, predictably, called this just another Fox News hatchet job on the President.

The President's staff – many quite perplexed at his policy about-face - searched for an appropriate forum at which he could espouse his energy independence policy and explain why, reluctantly, he had concluded that off-shore drilling must be part of such a policy.

The Sierra Club, Greenpeace, Pure Earth International and other activist environmental organizations were strangely quiet. To be sure, each issued a terse news release deploring – in one form or another – the Administration's action. But that was it. No outraged press conferences, no real follow-up. They referred to "the Administration," not "the President," as if it were possible that some idiot who had slipped through the cracks and onto his staff had perpetrated this dirty deed.

CHAPTER 1

OFF THE CALIFORNIA COAST NEAR SANTA BARBARA, CALIFORNIA
MAY, 2009

Just after 4:30 p.m., with rain beginning to fall, Captain Mike Ryan, master of the Royal Energy Company's ocean-going tug, Barona, felt the cable tighten, signaling that his boat had the barge, *Wheeler*, under tow. The *Wheeler* was a 60,000-barrel oil barge, and it was fully loaded, bound for the company's refinery in Richmond, across the bay from San Francisco. It would, as always, be a long, slow trip.

The *Wheeler* made this trip every ten days, sometimes bound for Long Beach and sometimes for Richmond. On each trip, she was towed by either the Barona or the sister tug, the Cortina. Each trip began at the Ellwood Marine Terminal, where she was loaded with 60,000 barrels of her black cargo.

The Ellwood Marine Terminal was supplied by undersea lines from, among others, the oil platform, Holly, which floated 211 feet over the floor of the Pacific two miles west of Goleta, a town just north of Santa Barbara. The Holly had been producing this precious cargo every day since it was installed in 1965, except for the days it was closed for routine maintenance or repairs. The Holly, the barge and the tug had been a very nice investment indeed for Royal Energy shareholders.

Soon after leaving the terminal, as the Barona towed the *Wheeler* at five knots northwest and toward the open sea, the storm intensified, the winds whipping the sea into rough swells and the rain coming down harder. The tug had only a four-man crew, with Ryan serving the combined roles of Captain, helmsman and radioman. He also had a chief engineer, who was primarily responsible for the proper functioning of the engine and the winches, and two jack-of-all-trades deck hands. As he stared through the rain pelting the windshield of the pilot house, Ryan watched the three men scurry around the deck doing the things necessary to prepare for rough seas. Equipment on the deck was lashed down tighter; everything not needed was stowed.

Ryan liked what he saw, especially the work of his newest deck hand, Floyd Wheeler. He had thought it amusing when the Royal Energy personnel office – what they called Human Resources these days - had sent him a replacement deck hand with the same name as the barge they towed. But the man seemed capable and unafraid of work. Deck hands came and went. They were the lowest-paid seamen and drifted into and out of his life like the flotsam washed ashore by the sea each day.

Ryan lit a cigarette and watched his gauges, making sure his heading was true. A short, stocky man with the weathered face so common to men who lived on the sea, he had made this trip a couple of hundred times in his 15 years with Royal Energy, but he was always careful. He knew that since 1969, the pressure on oil operations in the Santa Barbara coastal area, from drilling to transportation, was enormous.

On January 29, 1969, for reasons unknown to this day, a Union Oil Company platform in that area had blown. When it was capped, the resulting pressure had resulted in five breaks in an east-west fault on the ocean floor. In the eleven days it had taken to cap the ruptures, 80,000 barrels – some 3,360,000 gallons – of oil had bubbled to the surface. Incoming tides had swept the thick tar ashore along 35 miles of some of the most scenic beaches in the United States, and eventually formed an oil slick of 800 square miles. The slick moved with a mind of its own, eventually sliding south to foul the beaches of Anacapa, Santa Cruz, Santa Rosa and the San Miguel Islands.

This incident, Ryan knew, was generally recognized with starting the environmental movement in the United States. The fact that it happened in California gave that start added energy. Ryan loved his job, loved being at sea along this gorgeous coast. He just hated the fact that he had to live in

California to experience it.

He was a Memphis native who learned the tug-barge business at an early age on the Mississippi River, and had adapted quickly to pulling his cargo, as he did with the seagoing oil barges, rather than pushing it. On the smooth waters of the Mississippi, tugs almost always pushed the barges rather than towing them. Those were real people, the ones who live and work along the Mississippi, Ryan thought. Californians were just weird. One of his favorite t-shirts, which he loved to wear when shopping in his local Safeway supermarket, had, on both front and back, the legend,

CALIFORNIA IS LIKE A GRANOLA BAR
WHAT'S NOT FRUITS OR NUTS ARE FLAKES

The Barona dived into a deep trough. The seas were getting rougher, even though they were still in relatively protected waters. Suddenly, as she crested a wave, the Barona lurched forward, her speed accelerating. Ryan knew instantly what had happened. He had not touched the throttle. The sudden acceleration could be caused by only one thing.

The thick steel cable attaching the *Wheeler* to the Barona had broken. Just as Ryan was processing this alarming turn of events, a second jolt to his mental processes occurred. The Barona's big, reliable Cummins Marine diesel engine coughed twice and died. Ryan grabbed his radio microphone and called his base at the Ellwood Marine Terminal to report that he was dead in the water and the laden barge was drifting free in the water. He knew that with the wind velocity and current direction, the *Wheeler* would drift in the direction of the platform, Holly.

Fortunately, the sister tug, the Cortina, had arrived at Ellwood just after he had departed, so Ryan was assured that help was on the way. The base operations officer instructed Ryan to communicate directly with the Cortina on a second radio channel. Ryan switched the channel selector on his radio.

On the Barona's deck, Floyd Wheeler scrambled as quickly as he could toward a hatch. When he reached the engine room, the chief engineer was frantically trouble-shooting the possible causes of his engine quitting.

"This happened to me once on a tug in Puget Sound," Wheeler shouted to be heard over the wind that whistled through the boat. "It sounded the same. Two coughs and it died. Let's check the fuel line."

Sure enough, a thick substance of some unidentified origin was found in the main fuel line. Once it was blown out by a high-pressure air nozzle and reattached, the engine fired right up. Cummins Marine, the chief engineer thought to himself, really did produce the most reliable product on the market.

Ryan felt a wave of relief when he heard the engine come to life. He became further impressed with his new deck hand once his chief engineer reported the man's quick thinking. Now it was time to go to work. Ryan called the Cortina on the assigned channel and heard the calm and reassuring voice of his old friend, Arlen Allen, master of the Cortina. They were running at top speed - about 12 knots - through the heavy swells in the direction of the Holly. Allen's plan was to get there first and, if necessary, block the path of the *Wheeler*. Ryan wheeled his boat around and headed off at top speed in the same direction.

Ryan and Allen could see the same thing on their radar screens: the *Wheeler* was on a collision course with the Holly. And the barge, for an unpowered vessel, seemed to be making alarming speed in the heavy winds and currents. As the two tugs closed on the barge, both men could now see in the rainy distance that their radars had not deceived them. The *Wheeler* had a very good chance of striking the Holly.

Ryan was closer – and the *Wheeler* was, after all, his responsibility – so he took charge. "Let's circle around her and get between her and the platform," he told Allen on the radio. Two clicks on the radio told Ryan that Allen had heard and acknowledged his message. The plan, both men understood without it having to be said, would be to push the *Wheeler* away from the platform before attaching a tow line to her.

The tugs made several attempts to circle the barge and get on her south side without risking hitting the Holly themselves. But the winds and the waves conspired to thwart their efforts. By now, both deck hands were in the pilot house with Ryan, awaiting instructions. The chief engineer, as usual, was below tending to his own business.

Ryan and Allen were both getting desperate. Each time they tried to circle and ease up to the barge to start nudging her away from the platform, a wave would rock the barge, heaving her side into the air and making a nudge impossible. Wheeler watched the strain increase on Ryan's face. "I'm not sure this is going to work," Ryan muttered at length. "The fucking sea is just too rough."

"Why don't we just head for her stern and ram her off course," Wheeler suggested quietly. The barge was sliding sideways toward the platform. Ryan considered the suggestion and could think of no better ideas. He told Allen on the radio what he was going to do and asked him to head west to get between the barge and the platform's south side while Ryan tried to muscle the barge south of the Holly. Again he got two clicks in reply. Allen was a man of few words but one of enormous skill with a tugboat.

The Barona struck the *Wheeler* just right of center on her stern. Ryan felt something give as contact was made, but his mind was on the immediate task at hand. He pushed forward on the throttle and the huge screw of the tugboat dug harder into the water. He could feel the speed pick up. Never taking his eyes off the rolling stern of the barge, he saw with satisfaction through his peripheral vision the platform, Holly, slide by on his right.

As he put distance between himself and the Holly, Ryan returned his attention to the sensation he'd felt through the wheel as his tug contacted the barge. He directed the two deck hands to the bow to check what they could see, taking care, of course, not to get too near the bow. The sea was still pitching both vessels up and down like corks. He was desperate to maintain the contact he had with the barge lest even a tiny bit of separation cause the vessels to crash into each other. He didn't even want to think about the result of such a happenstance.

Wheeler raced up the steps to the pilot house to report a tear in the *Wheeler's* hull. He estimated it was about four feet long and just above the waterline. Yes, oil was leaking. Barges like the Wheeler, Ryan knew, were simple single-hull vessels, and any breach in the hull could result in a leak. That is but one reason why these barges were towed, not pushed. Still, the fact that the tear was relatively small and that it was above the waterline meant the leak might be small. He reported the discovery to Allen and asked him to approach the barge on its starboard side and try to get a tow line around one of the davits near its starboard bow.

Once the Cortina had accomplished this very tricky task, Ryan would back his tug off the barge's stern and move up and try to duplicate the feat along the port bow. Then, the two would work together to tow the barge farther away from the Holly.

While he was waiting for Allen to report that he had secured his tow line, Ryan called his operation center and inquired about the availability of an oil tanker that could be dispatched to offload the barge's oil at sea. He knew the crazies would castrate him and everyone else at Royal Energy over so little as a pint of oil being spilled in the Santa Barbara Channel. Despite the fact, he thought bitterly to himself, that between 100 and 170 barrels of oil per day seep naturally from the seabed in that channel. But still, it is what it is, and he was determined to get this barge as far away from land as he could. The weather was finally cooperating. The wind was dying down, the rain had stopped and the seas were calming.

Ryan's radio squawked and he was advised by operations that the non-profit group – supported by all the oil companies operating in the area – Clean Seas was on its way. Clean Seas was an oil spill cooperative and they would work to minimize the spread and to clean up the oil that had so far escaped. He was also advised that *Prime 10*, a tanker belonging to the rival Prime Oil Company, was at that time 15 miles southwest of their location, en route from Long Beach to Alaska. It was diverting immediately and would rendezvous with the barge.

Ryan was to keep operations posted continuously on his GPS coordinates, which would be much more precise than having the *Prime 10* try to track them by radar. Operations would relay the coordinates to *Prime 10* until the rendezvous was affected. When it came to incidents that would rile the environmentalists, all oil companies were on the same side. Competition could wait for another day.

Once the *Prime 10*'s pumps had drained the *Wheeler*, it sailed off for San Francisco Bay, reporting that it had taken 54,600 barrels aboard. It would offload that amount in Richmond before continuing to Alaska. The

Cortina detached from the *Wheeler* and set sail for the Ellwood Marine Terminal. Meanwhile, the Barona, which had reattached a steel tow cable to the barge's bow, was to tow the damaged vessel directly to the San Diego shipyard for repairs.

Once the tug docked in San Diego, after having handed off the barge at the repair pier, Ryan and the crew went ashore for a bite to eat before meeting back at the boat for the return trip in four hours. All seamen had their favorite hangouts in major ports like San Diego. The tug would be refueled and resupplied by then.

"Captain Ryan," Floyd Wheeler said, "I need to change out of these clothes or I'll get grease all over the restaurant. I'll catch up to you in a few minutes." Ryan assured him he would save him a seat at the table.

While waiting for Wheeler, Ryan pondered the strange events that had started this whole episode. He distrusted coincidences, but of course he could never have known that Floyd Wheeler had attached a small device that used a slow-burning but very intense heat to eat through the steel cable that lashed the barge to the tug. Nor could he have known that Wheeler had also injected the thick substance into the tug's fuel line, and done both in such a way that their effects were timed perfectly.
Ryan never saw Floyd Wheeler again.

Clean Seas did a remarkable job, cleaning up the oil that had leaked from the *Wheeler* before any of it reached land anywhere. Nor were there any reports of birds or other wildlife being affected by it in any way. Still, the environmentalists went ballistic. They needed a cause, especially since "their" President had declared open season on new off-shore drilling.

Ryan seethed the next day as he sat in his apartment and read – for perhaps the tenth time – the headline over much of the bottom of the front page of *The Los Angeles Times*.

60,000 BARREL OIL BARGE RUPTURED
IN SANTA BARBARA CHANNEL

Santa Barbara, CA - The oil barge Wheeler, under tow from Santa Barbara to San Francisco with 60,000 barrels of crude oil aboard, broke its tow line and reportedly was rammed by its own tug, the Barona. The contact crushed and ruptured the hull of the barge, which is believed to have spilled its entire load into the Santa Barbara Channel. The extent of the environmental damage has not been determined, but is expected to rival the 1969 spill in the same area...

"Jesus Christ," Ryan exploded to himself. "The bastards can't get anything right." He stomped out the door to head to the Ellwood Marine Terminal to debrief the entire incident with Arlen Allen and a half-dozen operations and public relations honchos from Royal Energy.

CHAPTER 2

JACKSON HOLE, WYOMING
FEBRUARY, 2009

The ninth long-range private jet of the day, this one a Gulfstream IV, touched down at Jackson Hole Airport and taxied to the FBO, or fixed base operator, essentially a service station for private aircraft. There, the multi-million dollar Gulfstreams and Lears – and even the odd Cessna 172 – were hangered, serviced and refueled. This FBO, use to handling the aircraft of the rich and famous, also provided complimentary limo service into the town of Jackson for those who wished it.

None of the planes, of course, were identified save for their FAA tail numbers. In fact, all nine now at the Jackson Hole Airport were owned by ShareJet, a company which offered a sort of air taxi service for those who did not have the funds or the inclination to either own or use their own jet.

Since the Rockefellers and others of the moneyed gentry had discovered this idyllic setting at the foot of the Grand Teton Mountains, Jackson Hole had been a favorite haunt of the wealthy. They were attracted to hunting, fishing and whitewater rafting in the summer and skiing in the winter. Private jets at the airport were not an uncommon sight. Still, nine of them landing on the same day was a bit unusual, but the always-discrete employees of the FBO took it in stride and accepted the tips as they drove the visitors – precisely two people from each plane – to the lodge in town.

This Gulfstream IV was the last of the nine to arrive, but was in plenty of time for a dinner meeting, scheduled to start in one of the suites at 8:00, a meeting that would be attended by nineteen people, seventeen men and two women. Before that, some of the men would stop in the bar for an early cocktail and to check out the selection of ever-present working ladies. The ladies seemed to have built-in early warning devices that told them when corporate planes were inbound.

The dinner had been purely social. The next morning, the nineteen men and women were seated around a large square table in a first-floor conference room. The chief executive officer and one trusted lieutenant from nine of the largest American oil companies and one Saudi, well-known to the Americans.

Now, as they sipped coffee and chatted among themselves in the conference room at 9:00 a.m., they would get down to business, although only one person in the room knew at that time just what that business was. It was a measure of the respect, and perhaps apprehension, the others held for the Saudi that they were here at all, in view of the sketchy information they had been given about the agenda.

Of course, it helped that the Saudi had met privately with each of them during the prior two months, hinting at his plan and encouraging them to attend this important – and secret – meeting. Enlightened self-interest, as always, played a major part in their individual decisions to attend. Also playing a part was the knowledge that most, if not all, of the others would be there, and how would it affect their business if they were the only ones who were invited and chose not to attend.

Akrum al-Kahtani, 55, was one of the hundreds – maybe thousands - of cousins in the Saudi royal family. He had served for many years as his country's oil minister, before being honored by the king with the rank of Ambassador at Large. It was during his oil ministry that his guests had become acquainted with him. Known to be a shrewd custodian of the one resource that made his country a player on the world stage, he had earned the respect of his guests as a practical businessman and as a man with keen political instincts.

He knew that without its oil, Saudi Arabia, as with much of the Middle East, would be little more than a sun baked sand dune that was worth nothing to anyone other than the Bedouins who have scraped survival – and nothing more – from the land for centuries. He also knew that because of the complex political and military alliance with the United States, Saudi oil was being pumped from the land at – to him, at least - an increasingly alarming rate, given the current price per barrel.

As he sipped his strong Guatemalan coffee, al-Kahtani surveyed the people around the table. Mark M. Mazurka III and his son, Matthew were the Chairman of the Board and President, respectively, of the relative-small $10 billion-per-year Mazurka Oil, Inc., a family-owned Houston company with only 3,000 employees worldwide.

Paul Diles was a 68-year-old certified public accountant and was CEO of Largess Petroleum Products (LPP), an $18 billion-per-year, public oil production and petrochemical products concern based in the trendy Houston suburb of The Woodlands. He was joined at this meeting by his Vice President of Development, Dennis Guthier.

Nicholas C. Mansourian, 52, was CEO of Shale Oil and Lubricants Corporation, a $50 billion-per-year Philadelphia-based public company active in oil and gas operations as well as petrochemicals. He'd held that position for six years. Brent Burtman, Shale Oil's Executive Vice President, sat next to Mansourian.

Daniel Mirza, 61, was CEO of Mossy Oil, Ltd., another Houston-based oil, gas and petrochemical concern, founded in 1895 and now publicly-traded, with $65 billion in annual revenue and 16,000 employees worldwide. His childhood friend, Arthur Pariga, now a vice president, sat at his side.

Kristina Vandam was an enigma. Vandam was the only woman at the top of a major oil company, the Chairman and CEO of Prime Oil, Inc., a Los Angeles-based public company with $100 billion in revenues from oil, natural gas and petrochemicals. Prime Oil's Vice President of Corporate Communications, Sally Schultz, sat next to her boss, mentor and friend.

Rodney O'Connor, for the past 41 years had toiled at publicly-traded American Energy in Houston and been the CEO for the past 15 years. He was accompanied this morning by Arnold Thawley, a well-paid "yes man."

Fleming D. Worthy was CEO at $400 billion-per-year Petroleum Exploration and Refining, Ltd., or PERL Oil, as it was known. PERL's

Executive Vice President of Strategic Planning, Russ Vosselman, was with his boss and friend today.

Gord Waters was CEO of the privately-held and Wichita-based Cosmos Oil Products, or COP Oil, as it was known. The company dealt in petroleum, natural gas and chemicals and had annual revenues of $100 billion. He sat next to Allan Eibner, COP Oil's Senior Vice President of Finance and a personal friend as well as subordinate.

Robert Beck had been CEO of San Francisco-based Royal Energy, Inc., for nine years. During that time, he'd almost doubled Royal's annual revenues from $120 billion to close to $230 billion. Beck was joined today by Ed Herdt, a longtime friend and confidante.

Akrum al-Kahtani looked around the table and lightly tapped his coffee cup with his spoon to get their attention.

CHAPTER 3

SPRINGFIELD, ILLINOIS
MAY, 2009

The Honorable Homer G. Deeds was an unremarkable-looking man. At two inches less than six feet tall and 210 pounds, he had the overfed look of many southern Illinois farmers. He also looked like he would have felt more at home in bib overalls than in the three-piece suits which made up almost his entire wardrobe.

But Homer Deeds wore three-piece suits because that was what his constituents expected of a Member of Congress who had recently been elected to his ninth term. With the help of a dutiful and efficient staff, and with the symmetry afforded by his last name, he had long been known in Washington, D.C. and in southern Illinois, as Congressman "Good" Deeds.

"Good" Deeds was appropriate because, as he reminded his audiences whenever he stood behind a lectern with a microphone in front of him, he was a man of the people. A man dedicated to good deeds. A man who did the right thing. And he did. Especially when the good deed involved was something desired by a company or an organization or even a single person who was in a position to contribute to his reelection campaign fund.

More than anything else, Homer Deeds now realized that he could never return to the southern Illinois farm he and his wife owned. It had been in her family for four generations, and it still produced crops with the help of a foreman who was his wife's cousin. But after tasting the intoxicating power and prestige of Washington, the farm would be a suffocating symbol of failure, for the only way Homer Deeds would be exiled back to the farm was to lose a reelection bid.

Now, he was awaiting the arrival of a woman who had helped avert that disaster the previous November.

Sarah Cotton had burst into his life ten years earlier, when she had first appeared in Washington as an impossibly-young lobbyist, interning for one of the blue-chip K Street firms. She was tall and trim, with jet-black hair set off by deep blue eyes and shapely legs. Within months of her arrival in the capital, her title changed from Intern to Vice President. She picked up clients and contacts – Members of Congress, Senators and key committee staffers in particular – like a bum picks up cans and bottles. In both her personal and professional lives, Sarah was smart and resourceful. Professionally, she had been called a quick study, and she knew the art of leadership, compromise, teamwork, loyalty, manipulation and perfidy. She seldom used the latter, but when she needed it, it had proven a deadly skill. But she had never allowed herself to become some man's toy. Oh, she had her affairs. Two of them were rather intense and ended only when she let it be known that she was not prepared for marriage or anything else that might interrupt her career. But a man's toy? Never!

Now, Congressman Homer Deeds was waiting for Sarah Cotton, who had agreed to meet him in his Springfield "district office." It was unusual for a lobbyist to come to Springfield to see him. Most simply waited until he got back to Washington. But the two had an unusual relationship. She needed the Congressman's vote or support on any number of legislative or regulatory matters, and the Congressman needed her because she was smart and connected to financial resources and was a brilliant strategist who helped him in his re-election campaigns. Moreover, Martha Deeds, Homer's wife of 40-plus years and a no-nonsense farm girl who had been hardened by that upbringing, genuinely liked Sarah.

In fact, of all her attributes and skills, the one for which Sarah was most thankful was her uncanny ability to get along with women as well as men. She well knew that many women with her appearance were immediately disliked by other women, especially married, who saw beauty as a threat. Martha Deeds might have, too, except that Sarah talked with her as well as with her husband when they were together, and Martha knew instinctively that Sarah was "their" friend and was no threat to her.

When Sarah was ushered into the Congressman's office, she hugged him, as she always did, but only in private. She knew the speed of wagging tongues, as well as the damage they could inflict on a politician.

As usual, she was dressed in what she had come to call her "lobbyist uniform:" straight black dress, a single strand of very white pearls, tan blazer and black pumps. As always, "Good" Deeds marveled at her beauty and briefly thought, as usual, *"If I were just 20 years younger..."* The thought never lasted long, but was impossible for him to completely suppress.

"Thanks for coming to Springfield," Deeds said after his secretary had poured coffee for both of them. "I take it something couldn't wait until I got back."

"Actually, Congressman, it may have waited, but then I'd have missed the chance to have dinner with you and Martha at your favorite restaurant." Deeds' broad smile told her that, once again, she had said just the right thing at just the right time.

"Well, it's always good to see you, whether here or in Washington. But before you start, let me tell you again how much Martha and I appreciate your work in the last campaign."

In the first week of October the year before, with the election just a month away, Deeds found himself tied in the polls with his opponent, a relative political newcomer who railed against Washington "insiders" such as an eight-term, "entrenched" Congressman named Homer Deeds. Sarah Cotton had met with the challenger, a relatively young married man with a wandering eye.

Sarah had told the challenger that she had several clients who potentially were prepared to back the challenger with a very large independent expenditure campaign that would send Mr. Deeds back to his farm with his tail between his legs. The challenger was panting with excitement. Some of his excitement was over the independent expenditure campaign.

The challenger was invited to a preview of the potential campaign. It was to be set up in a hotel suite in Washington, where he would also be able to meet some of the supporters. Of course, he was able to rearrange his busy schedule, even though it was against the campaign finance laws for a candidate to have any contact with an independent expenditure campaign. That was why they were called "independent." But only the stupidest and most politically naïve actually believed those campaigns were ever truly independent.

When the challenger arrived at the suite, there were several men in business suits and four very beautiful young "hostesses" to serve them drinks and snacks of the finest variety. He was quite drunk in a little over an hour and forgot completely about the screening, occupied as he was with a stunning green-eyed blond who was seated with him on a sofa and seemed intent on sticking her tongue through his ear and into his brain. And, should he misread her intentions, she was also animatedly rubbing his thigh, her hand distractingly close to his crotch. The young man did not even notice when the television came on with the screening of the "campaign." Actually, it was a series of hit pieces from other districts and other campaigns around the county, and the other men had, one by one, left the room, but once again, the enthralled man did not notice anything but the hand and the tongue of the green-eyed blond.

At the properly-timed moment, the green-eyed blond whispered to the challenger that she wanted him right now, and that she had a room on the next floor of the hotel. Without saying anything to anyone else, the two disappeared and rushed to the elevators. Once in the blonde's room, she suggested that he make himself comfortable while she went to the ladies' room to freshen up.

He was soon sans clothing and lying proudly atop the bed. Then, the door to a large closet swung open and two completely nude women, one white and one black, jumped on the bed and encircled him, their hands all over him. This was followed very shortly by the reappearance of the green-eyed blonde, now holding an expensive high-definition camera with which she snapped over a dozen photos in quick succession.

The fact that a small packet of cocaine, with accompanying implements, was photographed lying on the nightstand next to the bed would be of significant interest to the police, if the man decided that calling the police was desirable in any way.

The challenger withdrew from the race the following day and Homer Deeds was reelected in a landslide. Miracles did happen, the Congressman was convinced, although he never knew the real reason for the man's withdrawal from the race. He had only mentioned something about "family considerations." Once again, Sarah Cotton's skill at the art of perfidy had been proven to be the stuff of miracles. Of course, Deeds would never know whether she was behind this particular miracle, but he had strong suspicions.

When the congressman asked her how he could help, Sarah got to the point of the meeting. "My client, American Pharmaceuticals, has developed a revolutionary new drug, Congressman. It's called AMHD-1. Their tests show it promotes regeneration of bone tissue in the knees and hip joints. Based on their tests, they feel it will virtually eliminate the need for many of the hip and knee replacement surgeries required today."

"Fascinating," Deeds mused. He knew several people who had gone through the surgery and the agonizing rehabilitation required afterward. For some, he knew, the surgery did not go well and they were worse off afterwards than they were before the surgery. "Is there a problem?"

"Well, the Food and Drug Administration has been dragging its feet on approval of expanded trials. As you might imagine, the orthopedic surgeons and their suppliers are not thrilled with the prospect of virtually being put out of business. They're making unfounded claims and lobbying the FDA hard, claiming AMHD-1 doesn't work, it causes harmful side-effects, that sort of thing. Nothing less than what we'd expect. But American Pharmaceuticals disagrees, based on its own tests, and all it's asking for is approval of expanded trials."

The Congressman's brow knotted. He was not known as a great admirer of the FDA, which was the main reason Sarah had come to him. "I'd be happy to help any way I can, Sarah. Can you get me whatever documentation you have on the American Pharmaceutical tests and the arguments of the orthopedic surgeons?"

Sarah smiled brightly as she reached into her briefcase and extracted a thick file, which she handed to him. He was not surprised that she had come prepared.

"I'll confer with a few of my colleagues," he said. "I know some who believe as I do that the FDA is too prone to pressure from 'traditional' medicine. We'll see what we can do about suggesting to the FDA that expanded trials hold little risk and might make certain senior members of

Congress more amenable to FDA budget requests."

Sarah stood. She had three hours to get to her hotel, shower and rest a bit before meeting Homer and Martha Deeds for dinner at the Congressman's favorite steakhouse. Again, she hugged him before opening the door and leaving.

In fact, her hotel was a short walk from the office building in which Homer Deeds' district office was located. She shed clothes while her laptop booted up. She checked her email before showering. One email was from Jared Welch, another Washington lobbyist, albeit with a wholly different type of client than hers. It confirmed their meeting next week at his office.

The dinner went splendidly. Sarah's prime rib – end cut – was superb and with business over, she was able to relax and enjoy the company of friends. Martha brought her up to date on their grandchildren and the farm. Sarah was always amazed at how current the woman was with the crops that were growing successfully and the ones they had trouble with. Martha gossiped a bit about some of the Congressional wives. There were a few – from California and New York, especially – that she disliked intensely and she loved to point out any damning story she heard about them or their husbands.

After dinner and almost two bottles of wine, Deeds suggested they skip dessert and head home. The Deeds must leave for Washington the next morning, he said, because he had some important business to take care of regarding the FDA. He winked at Sarah as he said that, and Martha beamed. He had obviously shared at least part of Sarah's "problem" with her before dinner. The Congressman's car was parked right in front of the restaurant, and even though it was only a block away, they insisted on dropping Sarah at her hotel.

Sarah's flight was the next afternoon, so she would have half a day to rest and clean up emails before getting back to her office. She called the bell desk and had them pick up one of her outfits for cleaning. In her work, she must always look fresh and her clothes new. Sometimes, she admitted to herself, it was a real chore to make that happen.

CHAPTER 4

WASHINGTON, D.C.
THE NEXT WEEK

Sarah Cotton bounded up the steps of the Capitol Building as if she owned them. Sometimes, she thought wryly, she did. She and the thousands of other lobbyists who spent so many hours hurrying up and down them.

Members of Congress, of course, were seldom seen on the steps in front of the magnificent building, unless it was to address a gathering of the press or some group of constituents; a high school championship football team, a church choir on a field trip or a bus load of senior citizens. Normally, the members entered and left the building by means of the underground tram which whisked them back and forth to their various office buildings where they and their staffs spent most of their time.

Now Sarah was hurrying to make the 10:00 a.m. subcommittee hearing on the French-developed so-called "day after" pill known as RU486 on behalf of a pharmaceutical client. It was nearing FDA approval, but, because it was a form of birth control not involving abstinence, its approval was mired in political warfare. Sarah, both personally and professionally thought FDA approval should be pro forma, given that the product had been legally and safely on the market in France and several other European countries for over two years.

The hearing did not last long – by the normal standards of Congressional hearings - and went quite predictably, with three fundamentalist clergymen from obscure and indefinable denominations railing against the drug as a product encouraging young women of no moral footing to engage in fornication against God's laws without any fear of consequences.

One of the blow-dried men of God pointed out that it was appropriate that the French – Godless whoremongers that they are – would have developed such an evil antidote for procreation. Sarah managed, with considerable effort, not to laugh aloud at some of the absurdities these men of the cloth uttered in the Lord's name. In the end, the hearing adjourned with no vote, some of the members of the committee paralyzed by the fear of political retribution.

Sarah had just enough time to hurry two blocks to the Hyatt Regency to sit in on an open meeting of Citizens for Responsible Growth, or CFRG, which she had heard from several people was an up-and-coming conservation group based in Monterey, California. It was, she had heard, much more centrist and forward-thinking than a group such as Greenpeace, which she thought was more interested in armed revolution and creating a new world order than in protecting the environment. Sarah was, at heart, a conservationist, which she saw as entirely different from what many called an "environmentalist."

By the time the hour-long presentation ended, Sarah had become even more interested in CFRG. The group's President, a tall, ruggedly handsome man named Boone Malory, had presented CFRG's goals in an orderly and businesslike manner, without the strident rhetoric of so many in the environmental movement.

But after the meeting ended, when she had made her way to the front of the room to talk to the man, she learned he had hurried out a side door. Another meeting, she had been told by one of the young helpers from the hotel, who was busy packing away the laptop from which Malory had made his PowerPoint presentation.

Later that day, Sarah was sipping a Campari and soda at Domenico's on K Street with fellow lobbyist and sometime lover Jared Welch. "I've got a good shot at RU486," she said. "It may even make it through this session, although it didn't come to a vote today. Those fundamentalist assholes almost made my case for me, their testimony was so preposterous.

Even our favorite subcommittee nay-sayer, the Bible-thumper from Mississippi, had a hard time keeping a straight face." Jared knew who she was talking about.

Sarah filled him in on the highlights, if they could be called that, of the opposing testimony. "Sounds like you wrote their speeches for them," he said with a wink.

"I wish I could take credit for it, but, honestly, Jared, I don't think even I could have dreamed up some of the crap they threw around today."

"If you get RU486 though this Congress, you'll be able to write your own ticket," he said. "You'll become the lobbyist every well-dressed special interest will have to have." She grimaced.

"Don't tell me you're still thinking about getting out of the business," he said quickly in response to her facial expression.

"I'm just tired of it, Jared. I'm bored. This was fun last year, but now I need a change. I want to do something…meaningful."

"God, I wish some of those people on the Hill could hear you say that. But I've got an idea. Why don't you marry me? That, my love, would be meaningful."

Sarah gazed at Jared as she extracted from her purse and lit a Turkish cigarette. It was a habit she allowed herself to indulge in occasionally. "Maybe to you, Jared," she said, looking him in the eye. "But I'd be bored with you by next year and looking for a new model. And you know as well as I do that it's true. You're a sweet guy and a fantastic lover. Really fantastic. But I like you now and then, not every day. I don't think I could like anyone every day."

"So what do you mean by something meaningful?" Jared asked, trying and not quite succeeding not to sound as defeated as he felt. "Whatever you decide to do that's 'meaningful,' won't you just be bored with it in another year, too?"

"Fair question. Maybe. Perhaps even probably. But in the year or whatever before I get bored, maybe I'd have accomplished something I can look back on with pride." She paused, eyes focused far away. "Anyway, I want to see myself as useful instead of just greedy."

"Greedy?" Jared almost gasped. "You really see yourself as greedy? I know I'm greedy and I see it in damn near everyone else on the Hill. But you? I see you just doing your job. You aren't living the dream like the rest of us. You're better at what you do than most, but you don't live the high life. Your condominium is simple. You don't even own a Benz or a BMW like everyone else has to have. The last thing you seem to me is greedy."

"I guess it's just the nature of the job. I know I get paid well and I usually manage to convince myself that I believe in the causes I get paid to promote. But then I have to ask myself why I continue to work for some of these slime balls. When I think about that, I think I must take it because I'm greedy."

Jared sipped his scotch and water. He always felt exhilarated in the company of this beautiful woman. Now he felt almost suffocated. He could not bear the thought of Washington, D.C. without her around, even if he only saw her occasionally, and on her terms. He signaled to the waitress that another round of drinks would be appreciated.

"So back to meaningful. Do you have anything in mind?" he asked.

"As a matter of fact, yes. I sat in on a meeting at the Hyatt this afternoon. It was a group called Citizens for Responsible Growth. I was really impressed. They have an ambitious agenda and they stressed their style was to approach environmental issues sensibly, working inside the system. None of the radical crap like Greenpeace and the others that do more damage to conservation causes than they could ever do good."

"Do you really think they'll get anywhere with that approach?" he asked.

"I don't know, but I think they need a good lobbyist. Someone who knows how this town works and who can get their positions heard. They're based out in California, and while I like everything I heard today, one thing I didn't hear was that they had any real presence here."

"And you're just the one to give them that," he said, a statement, not a question. "So what's stopping you?"

"The lead guy, Malory? I tried to introduce myself after the presentation but he'd already bugged out. I think he's a Washington outsider and knows it, but doesn't know how to go about getting on the inside."

Jared smiled. "Boone Malory." It was a statement, not a question.

Sarah nodded, her face showing her shock. "You know him?"

"I know him. Known him since college. Really nice guy, but he's not very outgoing. And he's scared to death of women, always has been. Didn't date that much in college when everyone around him was fucking their brains out. But I like the guy. He finally met the right woman, just before we graduated. They had a son. Then I heard the wife and son got killed in some kind of accident three or so years ago. A boating accident, I think it was. We'd stayed in touch before that, but then he became kind of a hermit. I couldn't even remember the name of his organization until you mentioned it. I just knew it had something to do with the environment. I'm surprised he made a presentation at the meeting today. I'd have thought he'd have left that to others."

"So you haven't talked to him for three years." Sarah muttered.

"No, I haven't, but in the coincidence of all time, I had a phone message from him at the office this morning. The message said he was in town – just for the day – and that he'd try me again if he had the chance before he left for the airport. He left his number in California. Or maybe it was a cell phone number."

Sarah brightened immediately. What an incredible coincidence! "Can you call him for me, Jared?"

"I can do that but I hope your interest in him is just as someone to work with. He's a good-looking guy and I don't need any more competition for your affections, as shallow as they are."

"Touché," she said. "But I've never mixed romance with business. You'll notice you and I have never worked for the same client. That's not by chance."

"Okay," Jared said with a grin that Sarah felt was just a tad forced. "I'll call him tomorrow. I'm sure I can talk him into meeting with you. But I think you'll need to draft the agenda carefully. Why he needs you without pointing out that he doesn't have the skills or knowledge to do his job without a lobbyist, that sort of thing."

Sarah put her hand over his and gave him the sort of smile that could turn a man into a puppy. "You're too good to me," she said as she stood. "And that's enough business talk. What does the rest of your evening look like?"

Jared bit down hard on the hook she had dangled. More quickly than she thought possible, he paid the bill, hailed a cab and they were on their way to his apartment.

CHAPTER 5

It had been an engaging and exhausting evening with Sarah. One of the best he could remember, and there had been some memorable ones. Sarah had a healthy sexual appetite and had honed her bedroom skills accordingly.

Jared was in his office, as usual, at 8:00 a.m., but waited until 11:30 to call Boone Malory. It was three hours earlier in Monterey, California. He punched in the number Malory had left on his message the day before.

"Boone Malory," came the deep voice when the call was answered.

"Jared Welch, Boone. Sorry I missed you yesterday. You're up early considering that your flight must have got in awful late."

"It wasn't all that late, local time" Malory responded in a professorial tone of voice. "I pick up three hours coming this way. I know you never got the hang of time zones and all. Anyway, how are you, Jared?"

"I'm good, Boone. Most of my big issues this session are moving along well. How did your presentation go yesterday? Find any new money? Or new converts to the cause?"

"Hard to tell at this point," Malory responded. "Nobody dropped a check on me yesterday. Maybe in a day or two the mail will bring us some good news."

"How's CFRG doing, Boone?"

"Still a struggle, probably always will be a struggle. But we're going about things the right way and it will take time. We'll get there."

"Well, it's going to be a hell of a lot harder to get there from Monterey. It's kind of off the beaten path as far as establishing a presence in Washington is concerned."

"Jared, you know why it was set up here. The west coast is the home base of the environmental movement. And I think it's important to take on the Sierra Club and the others on their turf."

"Boone, if you don't mind me saying so, Greenpeace and the Sierra Club have a bit further reach than California. Greenpeace is worldwide and the Sierra Club is all over D.C. like a bad rash. You can't compete with them by flying into Washington, giving a one-hour presentation, then hightailing it back to Monterey. You need a real presence here. Real and ongoing."

"And I'm sure my good friend Jared Welch can tell me how I do that," Malory said, both wary and with a touch of sarcasm in his voice.

"As a matter of fact, old buddy, I just happen to have a very good idea of how to do that."

"And that is…?" Malory was expecting Jared to pitch him as a prospective client.

"A lobbyist friend of mine was at your presentation yesterday and was impressed. That's a compliment to both you and CFRG. I've known her for years and she's got a great track record and smells bullshit from miles away. Whatever bullshit you were spreading yesterday, she liked the smell of it. She's been very successful and has made a lot of money. Now she wants to do something for the environment. Something constructive. She saw constructive in your approach and wants to go to work for you."

"She? Who is she?" Malory's voice was on the very edge of hostile.

"Be cool and let me explain, Boone. I think you know me well enough to know I wouldn't waste your time with something that didn't make sense for you. Her name is Sarah Cotton. As she tells me all the time, she's a conservationist more than an environmentalist, and she liked your message because of that."

"Well, it's pretty simple, Jared. Whoever this Sarah Cotton is, you know I can't afford her. I can barely afford to pay myself a salary. Our staff is down to me and a secretary. And there's another thing; if she's an old Washington hand, how the hell do I know I could control her? That's an important consideration for me."

"With her client list and track record, I don't think the control issue is even something for you to waste time thinking about," Welch responded. His voice too, was heating up now. "And I don't think you'd have to gamble a single dollar of CFRG's money on her. Not only is she a top-notch lobbyist – one of the very best in this town – but she's a great fundraiser. She's got what we refer to as an 'A list' rolodex. In other words, you hard-headed Irishman, I think she'd raise her own salary, and then some. As in 'a lot' some."

Malory did not respond for a long fifteen seconds. Just before Welch asked whether he was still there, Malory said, "So she'd work off the 'come' line?"

"I think she would be willing to do just that," Welch said. "Assuming she still likes what she sees when she meets with you. She asked me to set up a lunch or dinner for next time you're in Washington."

Malory hesitated again. "I don't know," he muttered finally.

Welch fairly exploded. "Jesus, Boone. Give me a break. You're running an organization that wants to reshape the environmental debate in the United States. You and your staff of one – repeat, one – other person are holed up in some strip mall on the coast when all the action is here in D.C. You've got no presence and no voice. And you never will have if you keep going the way you're going now. What the hell do you have to lose? You can't take a couple of hours to talk to her?"

"Okay, okay," Malory said, his voice soothing or resigned. Welch couldn't tell which. "I have a meeting two weeks from tomorrow with the chief of staff to Congressman Martinez." Marty Martinez, Welsh knew, was a veteran Democrat from Southern California, fairly conservative, very reasonable and realistic and always interested in finding ways to tone down the rhetoric on any issue. A perfect fit with CFRG on environmental issues.

"Good," Welch said, "Let's have lunch on the 16th then. I'll set it up with Sarah. We can talk about our college days if she scares you."

"Jared, I'd rather not go the lunch route." He consulted his calendar. "Can I just borrow one of your conference rooms for fifteen minutes on the 16th around 2:00?"

Welch's voice came with considerable heat. "Boone, you're being a real pain in the ass, especially to someone who's trying to help you. But if that's your deal, okay. I'll have Sarah here at 2:00 on the 16th and I'll have a goddamn conference room for you."

Malory agreed in a somewhat apologetic tone and after muttering farewells to each other, they hung up.

Sarah picked up her phone on the first ring.

"You're all set to meet the great man on the 16th at my office at 2:00," Jared announced. The sarcasm was hard to miss.

"I take it he wasn't wildly enthusiastic," she said.

"Another of your classic understatements, Sarah," Welch replied. "His tone was about what you'd expect when he's confirming a meeting with his life insurance agent or an appointment with his dentist."

Sarah had been there before, many times. "At least you got a meeting for me. That's more than I really expected at this point. I can't thank you enough. And speaking of that, I really enjoyed last night. See you on the 16th, if not before."

"Wait!" Welch said before she could put down the receiver. "Don't hang up yet. I had another thought. There's a reporter in town from San Francisco who's an old friend of Boone's – older friend than I am, in fact. She grew up with him and went to elementary and high school with him, if I recall correctly. Why don't I set up something with her while she's here?"

"A she?" Sarah asked skeptically. "You know I do better with men than with women, especially reporters."

"Jesus, you sound too much like Boone to be able to work with him," Welch said evenly. "But I think you'll like her. Amanda Baines is her name. *San Francisco Chronicle*. She also strings for a couple of magazines. She's done a couple of very nice pieces on Boone and his organization and is frustrated by the lack of traction they're getting here. I bet she'd help you with Boone. And she's working on another environmental story. You may be able to help her by getting her connected to a congressman or senator. That would be big for her."

What the hell, Sarah though. Can't hurt. "Okay, set it up. I'll make th time. And, Jared, thanks again."

When she hung up the phone, Sarah asked herself, not for the first time, "What would Jared do for me if I spent more time with him? Hmmmm?" Also not for the first time, she marveled at the wonderful simplicity of men.

Coincidentally enough, Amanda was staying at the Hyatt Regency Capitol Hill, scene of Sarah's first exposure to Boone Malory and CFRG. Dinner was set in the hotel's Article One American Grill. Sarah arrived ten minutes early, dressed as usual in her lobbying uniform: black dress, pearls, tan blazer and sensible black pumps. When she was shown to the table, she was surprised to see a very attractive, dark-haired woman in her late 20s or early 30s already seated. Sarah was early, but Amanda Baines was earlier. She looked more like one of the TV anchors than a newspaper reporter. After they had introduced themselves to each other, Sarah thanked Amanda for taking the time to talk with her.

Amanda smiled and stunned Sarah by saying, "Well, Jared was sure right about you. You are very attractive." Sarah actually blushed, not a common occurrence for her. Under other circumstances, Sarah might have been put on guard, ready to fend off a pass from another woman. It had happened before. But if Amanda were gay, Jared would certainly have told her that. So she took the compliment as genuine, all the more so given Amanda's own looks.

Amanda said, "So Jared tells me you want to give up fame and fortune and go to work for CFRG. I assume you know it's based in California?" Sarah nodded. "Well, you're going to put old Boone in a panic, I can tell you that. He doesn't do well at all with women, especially attractive ones." There it was again. A level of candidness she was not used to, especially in this town or from reporters. But she had long ago learned that, when they talked, people's eyes told her much about the person's character. In Amanda's eyes, Sarah saw both sincerity and integrity. Sarah, after maybe ten minutes, already liked Amanda. And that, God knew, was unusual for her.

Sarah asked whether they should order drinks.

"Well, Jared told me your favorite wine," Amanda responded. "That brand of chardonnay also happens to be one my favorites, so I already ordered a bottle." At that moment, the wine steward appeared at their table with a bottle and an ice bucket.

Sarah was impressed. Amanda was out-lobbying her.

After the wine was poured and the steward departed, Sarah said, "I understand your curiosity about why I'd want to give up a very nice lobbying practice to go to work for an organization that's so small and under-funded it's almost non-existent."

"The question had occurred to me," Amanda nodded.

"It's really quite simple, even though it will sound a bit corny, I'm afraid," Sarah began. "I've made a lot of money from my practice – more than I ever imagined before I came to Washington. I'm financially secure, but to this point I've done only what was good for Sarah, if you know what I mean. But now I'm bored." She paused to take a sip of her wine.

A waiter appeared to take their dinner orders. When the waiter departed, Sarah went on. "As I said, I'm bored. I go to the Hill and pitch whatever argument I'm being paid to pitch. I'm sick of pills and clinical trials. I want to do something for my country and for the planet. Conservation has always been a passion of mine, and even in my lobbying practice, where we're accused of being whores and hired guns – not without good reason – I've never taken a client I thought was bad for the environment. I heard your friend, Boone, speak a few days ago, in this hotel as a matter of fact,- and I was struck by his approach. I am more certain by the day that this may be the kind of fit I'm looking for."

"How long do you see yourself doing this?" Amanda asked. "I mean, is this an urge brought about by frustration that may wear off, or do you see yourself making a long-term commitment?"

Sarah admitted she did not know. She told Amanda that she had always been easily bored, but she thought the hurdles facing CFRG were enough to maintain her interest for a good long while. She told her about her fund-raising skills, as well as her famed rolodex. It wasn't really a rolodex, of course, nobody used rolodexes any longer, but what the hell? She was comfortable on Capitol Hill and thought she could help CFRG move its agenda forward. And, she told Amanda in a conspiratorial tone, she was equally sure Boone Malory – given his reticent personality – would never be able to move his agenda on his own.

"Some people are dreamers and planners and can visualize the future," she said. "That's Boone. But other people are the doers who work to make that vision of the future happen. That's me." She smiled at Amanda. "I hope that didn't sound as conceited to you as it sounded to me."

Amanda laughed. "I've known Boone since first grade and you have him pegged perfectly," she said. "But will you be able to adjust to such a radical change?".

"I don't think it's radical at all," Sarah said. "I'd be doing the same work I'm doing now, just for less money but for a better cause."

"Well then, here's to CFRG and its brighter future," Amanda said, raising her wine glass.

The entrée was served and they made small talk while they ate.

Over coffee, after the plates had been removed, Sarah said, "I really want to hear your take on Boone Malory and CFRG. It's important for me to know as much as there is to know about both, since I've only been given fifteen minutes for my interview."

Amanda stared, her mouth open. "He's only giving you fifteen minutes? That's bullshit," she blurted, then blushed. Sarah waved her off, told her that in Washington a word like that was as common as they came. Amanda continued. "Boone's doing what he does best; being a scared jerk. What do you want to know?"

"What is CFRG operating on now? I got the feeling it's pretty financially insecure? Does it have a contributor base that can sustain it, even at the present level?"

"Nothing, yes and no," Amanda said, her face tight. She was obviously fond of Boone. "Boone's not strong at fund-raising and he's not comfortable with it. His strength, as you so well said, is visualizing the future and the future consequences of actions today. He's not a good lobbyist, either. He can almost never meet with a Congressman or Senator, nor does he really try. He's more comfortable with their staffers".

"But like I said, he's uncanny at analyzing issues, determining the problems and developing solutions. And he can explain the issues and solutions convincingly – if he's comfortable with his audience. He's passionate about our stewardship of the environment, he has integrity and he's consistent in his beliefs. He doesn't blow around in the wind."

Sarah nodded. She could help Boone Malory with what he wasn't good at. They could make a great team. He could take care of the ideas and she could handle the fund-raising, the strategizing and the lobbying. "What else about Boone should I know that would help me understand him better," she asked.

"Like I said, Boone is passionate about the environment," Amanda said. "He wants to reduce the use of fossil fuels and develop alternative energy sources. I also told you he's got integrity. He knows we can't get off oil and into solar or wind or geothermal power overnight. So he's willing to work for gradual solutions while Greenpeace and the Sierra Club are storming the gates demanding immediate changes. He's too smart for that and I agree with him".

"You sound like you like him, and admire him, too," Sarah said softly.

"I do. He a very dear friend. As I said, we grew up together, went to grade school and high school in Scarborough, Maine of all places. Ever heard of it?" Sarah shook her head. "We never dated but were friends and involved in a lot of school activities together. We kept in touch after high school. I suppose that at one time I had a crush on him, but he was always shy around girls. I don't think he dated because he was afraid of how he'd react if he was turned down for a date".

"In any case, he got married right after college and they had a son. About three years ago, they were killed in a freak boating accident. I don't think he's over that yet, and I'm quite sure he hasn't dated since they were killed. He was in the Navy between high school and college – he went to the University of Southern Maine in Portland, studying business. That's where he met Jared. Jared wasn't from Scarborough, but I met him through Boone.

"He tried the business world for a year or so but got disillusioned with the culture of corporate America. He then worked for a couple of different environmental organizations and ultimately found himself on the west coast. That's where we reconnected. By that time, I'd gone to *the Chronicle* and he saw my by-line and called me. We've talked from time to time from that point to today".

"Then a guy named Heimer Myerhoffer, hell of a name, huh, heard a presentation Boone made somewhere and approached him with an offer to become CEO of CFRG. The first few years were easy because Myerhoffer, he was a big-time real estate developer who had to fight Friends of the Earth and all the other California crazies every day, was providing whatever funding CFRG needed".

"Then, the real estate market tanked and a painful divorce was followed by an even more painful stroke and Myerhoffer's philanthropic days were over. Boone has barely been able to keep the doors open at CFRG, begging for crumbs here and there. He desperately needs someone like you, Sarah. I don't want to see him fail. I don't like to even think about how he'd handle the failure of CFRG."

Sarah paused, absorbing all that Amanda - who, she was convinced, was quickly becoming a new friend - had told her. "I guess I'll just have to pull off a subdued dazzle in my allotted fifteen minutes," she said.

"Yes, you will. You must." Amanda's voice, like her gaze, was intense. Sarah was convinced that Amanda had feelings for Boone Malory. Love? Probably not, after all these years of being his friend. But strong feelings nonetheless.

Sarah was also surprised at her own feelings. She'd never had a really close female friend before and thought that Amanda might well become the first.

The waiter brought the check and Amanda insisted on signing it to her room, explaining that *the Chronicle* could afford it. Amanda assured Sarah she would keep their conversation from Boone and asked Sarah to call her as soon as her allotted fifteen minutes were over.

Sarah suddenly remembered that she had forgotten one thing Jared had mentioned.

"Oh, one other thing, Amanda," she said. "Jared mentioned that you might need some help setting up a couple of interviews with congressmen or senators on a story you're working on".

"Can you help with that?" Amanda asked excitedly. "It's sometimes so difficult getting through all the gatekeepers they have to get an interview, especially if they're not from California."

"Let me see what I can do," Sarah said. "Give me your cell phone number." Amanda did and Sarah gave hers to Amanda as well.

CHAPTER 6

Sarah was in her office early, as usual. She knew that Congressman Homer "Good" Deeds would be, too. He always was, if he was in Washington. She called him, as usual using the private line that rang directly on his desk and went unanswered if he was not there. He had once told her that only Mrs. Deeds, his chief of staff, the President of the United States and Sarah Cotton had that number. She suspected that there were others, but probably not many.

"Good morning, Sarah," his cheerful voice came over the line. Caller ID told him it was she who was calling.

"Good morning, Congressman. How did your meeting with your colleagues go yesterday?"

"Fine, Sarah, just fine," he responded, almost jovially. "All three Schaefer, Siedler and Piergallini are on board and we've got a meeting with the deputy director of the FDA next Wednesday." Sarah knew all three of the colleagues to which he referred. Jim Schaefer of Colorado, Sam Siedler of Wisconsin and Tim Piergallini of New York were all members of "Good" Deeds' subcommittee and, once they had committed, would back Deeds to the hilt. Or until the political shit hit the fan, but that was the inevitable way of life in the nation's capital.

"That sounds very promising," Sarah said. "But I never had a doubt that you'd know what needed to be done. Please thank your colleagues for me and ask them to let me know if I can do anything for them, besides the usual. Is there anything else you need from me to help you get ready for the FDA? More info on AMHD-1, or do you have everything you need?"

"I think I'm set, Sarah," the soothing voice intoned. "Call me Thursday and I'll fill you in on the meeting. Meanwhile, you have a good day, young lady."

"Thank you, Congressman, I will." Sarah paused just perceptibly. "Oh, and Congressman, there is one other thing I wanted to ask you about. I met a reporter for the *San Francisco Chronicle*, a woman named Amanda Baines. She's working on a series on the environment and the environmental legislative agenda. She doesn't have a lot of contacts on the Hill and asked if I could recommend a senior Congressman she could talk to about this. I thought of you, of course. I checked out on the coast and she's got a good reputation. I thought maybe if you had the time to meet with her, it would help raise your profile out west."

"Sarah, that's very nice of you," Good Deeds said. "I'd be happy to give her whatever time she needs. Have her call Mary to set up a time". Sarah knew Mary, who was Deeds' executive secretary, confidante and scheduler, quite well. Sarah had once had to go through Mary to get time on Congressman Deeds' calendar, but those days were behind her.

"I'll do that. Thank you once again, Congressman. I think you'll enjoy talking with Amanda. She's very sharp."

Sarah called Amanda Baines' cell phone. There was no answer so she left a message. She assumed Amanda was downstairs having breakfast. Or in the shower. She didn't know whether Amanda was an early riser like she was.

Thirty-five minutes later, Sarah's phone rang.

"Hi, Sarah, it's Amanda. Sorry I missed your call. I was in the shower."

Sarah smiled to herself. "Good morning, Amanda," she said. "I had a great time last night and wanted to thank you for shooting straight with me about CFRG and Boone."

"I had a great time, too," Amanda said. "Boone is a complex guy and, partly as a consequence of that, CFRG is a complicated subject. I hope I was helpful."

"I also had a chance to talk with a senior Congressman, whom I know well. He and his wife, as a matter of fact. I think he'd be a good place to start on your project on the environment. He's not a nut job on either side of the issue, comes from rural Illinois. He's also honest and a straight shooter."

Amanda gushed her thanks and Sarah went on. "Homer Deeds is his name. You may have heard of him. Ninth term in Congress. He's known as 'Good' Deeds, naturally, with a last name like his. Anyway, I was talking with him this morning on another matter and he agreed to meet with you. His scheduler, Mary, is expecting your call." She gave Amanda the phone number.

"My God, how did you arrange something so quickly?" Amanda asked.

"Like I said, I needed to talk with him anyway and I've become kind of a friend of the family over the years. And he's been around nine terms and most people outside Washington and Illinois still have never heard of him. That bothers him a little, although he'd never admit it. I told him you're fair and smart and including him in your story would help his profile on the West Coast." She paused before continuing. "He's a good man, Amanda. All I want from you is to treat him fairly."

"You can count on it, Sarah. How can I thank you?"

"No need. Thanks for the background on CFRG. Stay in touch."

Amanda replaced the receiver, realizing that despite their very friendly dinner the night before, she was still surprised that someone who was a player in this town could be so thoughtful, especially to a reporter.

That afternoon, Sarah was at a window in the public lobby of the Internal Revenue Service gathering up what she had requested. She paid the copying fee and left, her briefcase holding the last three years' filings of IRS Form 990 – *Return of Organization Exempt from Income Tax* – that had been received by the IRS from Citizens for Responsible Growth. Since CFRG was a non-profit entity, these forms are required to be filed annually and are available to the press and public.

She drove straight home, planning to spend the evening studying them.

It did not take that long, though. It was immediately apparent on reading quickly through the filings that, once the funding from Heimer

Myerhoffer had stopped, CFRG had fallen into a downward spiral. Replacement funding was not there, at least in amounts even close to the Heimer Myerhoffer levels.

By Sarah's estimation, CFRG had enough cash on hand for another six months, but even that would be based on greatly curtailed activities. After that, unless more money was found, Boone Malory would have no recourse but to close the doors.

Even with, or maybe because of that fiscal reality, Sarah reflected that CFRG was a good choice for her. Curtailing oil exploration was the right cause and was high on CFRG's agenda. God only knew how much damage had already been done by willy-nilly drilling, especially in parts of Alaska and in the waters off the California and Gulf coasts. And CFRG needed money. Desperately. But that was something Sarah knew she could accomplish, and rather quickly. She was frankly amazed that Boone had been able to keep CFRG afloat without Heimer Myerhoffer's money as long as he had. It was down to Boone and an office manager who doubled as the secretary and as the receptionist. Two employees total, compared to how many thousands for Greenpeace, Friends of the Earth and the Sierra Club?

Boone must be desperate, Sarah thought again and again as she read through the 990s and various CFRG news releases, public statements and other literature she found via Google.

Finally, she got up and went to the kitchen for a glass of wine. As she sat sipping it, she thought that CFRG would be the perfect fit.

CHAPTER 7

JARED WELCH'S OFFICE
TWO WEEKS LATER

Sarah arrived at Jared Welch's office on the 16th at 1:35 p.m. She was determined not to be late. Dressed in her usual uniform, she looked as good as she could make herself. To her surprise, she was greeted in the waiting area by both Jared and Boone Malory. Boone had obviously been early, too.

Sarah extended her hand. "Thank you for agreeing to meet with me." She turned to their host and smiled. "Good afternoon, Jared." Jared led them to the conference room, and Sarah thought to herself, *Good handshake. Firm, but his palm is a little damp. He's not afraid of germs, but something tells me he's afraid of me.*

They sat in comfortable, high-backed burgundy leather swivel chairs at one end of a table that would have comfortably held more than a dozen power players.

"Jared and I go way back, Ms. Cotton," Boone said. "He's done me several favors on The Hill, and I've learned that in this town, there's always payback."

Sarah laughed. It was a good, strong laugh Boone noted, and it carried a definite note of self-assuredness. "So I'm 'payback,' am I?" she said. "Well, hopefully this will turn out so well you'll owe Jared far into the future. And I would hope that we can all be on a first-name basis. Please call me Sarah. May I call you Boone?"

Self-assuredness is right, Boone thought to himself. *This woman is quite comfortable in her own skin.*

"By all means. Sarah it is. And I can assure you I have little interest in owing Jared any more than I do, but I'm here to listen to what you have to say."

Good response, Sarah thought. *This man is not an ass-kisser, however precarious his situation.*

Sarah decided that was the signal to take the floor, so for the next 30 minutes, she laid out what she had learned about CFRG, starting with what she learned at Boone's presentation at the Hyatt Regency, her research into CFRG's positions and finances and her conclusion that the organization, dedicated to a good and reasonable approach to environmental protection, was doomed if maintained on its present path.

She was prepared and her presentation was well-organized and thorough, though she referred not once to a note or a document. She had not even opened her briefcase. Boone noticed that, and so did Jared, who was impressed, as he had been so often and in so many ways, with Sarah Cotton.

She then spent ten minutes describing how she saw herself fitting into CFRG, summarizing her lobbying skills and experience, her fund-raising background and her willingness to risk working without pay for a time to prove herself. She paused, unsnapped her briefcase, extracted a freshly-updated resume and handed it to Boone, sliding a copy to Jared. She had made her play and skillfully landed the ball in Boone's court.

Boone looked at Sarah's resume without reading it, as a ploy to gather his thoughts. Finally, he cleared his throat. "Let me get this straight, Sarah." He was trying hard to maintain a firm voice and the tone of a professional skeptic. "You're telling me you want to leave your lobbying practice, especially the pharmaceuticals, which pay big bucks and can finance those Manolo Blahniks you have on your feet and the pearls and dress and blazer, none of which came off the rack at J.C. Penney. You want to trade all that in to wear jeans and Pendleton plaids and lobby for the tree huggers for no guarantee of a salary? You can call me a skeptic, but I don't get it."

As he said those words, Boone's voice had sounded harsh, even to him. Good, he thought. *Establish distance early. Easier to maintain later.*

Sarah was not put off by his words or his tone. "It's simple, Boone, at least to me. I've been at this for several years, and thankfully I've been able to put away enough money to last me some time. I'm good at what I do, but frankly I'm bored with corporate business. I've gotten very tired of trying to push for FDA testing of some damn drug that may not amount to anything anyway. I want to do something that has a chance of amounting to something." She smiled at Boone, then at Jared. It was a beaming, radiant smile, but not at all a flirtatious one. "And just so the record is clear, I like wearing jeans and tees, but I will still wear Blahniks and Prada when I'm on the Hill."

This sort of sparring – with occasional comments from Jared – went on for another half hour.

Finally, Boone raised his hand, as if in surrender. "Okay, I've heard enough. I get it, I think. And maybe your ideas would work for us. But it's not entirely up to me."

"Who is it up to?" Sarah asked evenly.

"The CFRG Board of Directors," Boone said. "Obviously, they're aware of our financial situation and they must approve any personnel changes, even when a prospective employee doesn't expect to be paid, at least on a guaranteed basis. The Board will be meeting in Monterey at the end of this month, I'm not certain of the date, but I'll put you on the agenda. Call my office tomorrow and Suzy will give you the date and confirm the time."

"Whenever it is, I'll be there," Sarah assured him, looking him in the eyes. "And it won't cost you a dime, if you're worried about that. I have enough frequent flyer miles on several airlines to fly around the world 20 times."

Boone stood, put out his hand to Sarah, who shook it firmly. "See you in California," he said.

And he was gone.

Jared looked at Sarah, who smiled again, this one the sly smile of a cat about to pounce on a bird. "Yes," she said as she pumped her fist in the air. "I'm in." She leaned over and kissed Jared on the cheek. "Thank you so much, Jared. You're a real friend."

The next day, at approximately the same time Sarah was replying to Boone's email confirming the date and time of CFRG's next Board meeting,

Jared Welch called Boone in his office in California.

"You were out of my office so fast I didn't have a chance to ask you what you thought," he said.

"I had a plane to catch," Malory replied. "I hadn't expected the meeting to take as long as it did."

"Well, what did you think of her? Do you think she can help you?"

Boone paused. "I think the honest answer is that I was quite impressed with her, and yes, I think it's possible she can help us." Another pause. "Of course, there's damn little she – or anyone – could do to cause us any more damage than losing Myerhoffer's money has already done."

"Do you think the Board will agree to give her plan a try?"

"I think the woman on the Board will look at her as an example of why women should run the country. And the men will be completely flipped out over her looks, especially when they realize her looks are connected to that brain."

"She is attractive, isn't she?"

"She's a goddamn goddess, is what she is. Who the hell could say 'no' to her? No wonder she's a good lobbyist."

Jared paused, said in a low voice, "Boone, if you don't hire her, you're a complete idiot." Malory was laughing as he hung up the phone, and Jared had the sinking feeling that he had helped the main love interest in his life slip away from him for good.

The day before the CFRG Board of Directors meeting, Sarah flew into Sacramento on Big Pharma's dime. She needed to talk to a recently-elected Senator from the Golden State, Harvey East, on AMHD-1, so she didn't have to use any of her frequent flier miles, after all. In fact, she picked up some more, especially flying first class, which she always did when on billable business.

She rented a car, to be dropped off at the Monterey Peninsula Airport and drove to her meeting.

Senator East was in his primary district office, he also had offices in several other cities around the sprawling state, so Sarah drove her rented Honda into the area around the State Capitol where the political commerce of California was conducted.

After Sarah had concluded her short briefing on AMHD-1, during which Senator East's eyes actually strayed from his fixation on her chest and crossed legs once or twice and met her eyes, the newly-minted power player told her that he had discussed the subject in some detail with "the gentleman from Illinois," as he referred to Homer "Good" Deeds. Sarah had no doubt that East had found it easier to meet Deeds' eyes than he had with her.

Sarah handed the Senator a "briefing book," a loose-leaf binder with all the latest information on AMHD-1, the FDA processes, contact names and numbers and talking points, all of which were favorable to the matter of expedited testing of the drug. East asked only a couple of questions, but they were enough to assure Sarah that he was at least vaguely aware of the issues and most likely a supporter of her client's position on this issue.

Unlike most lobbyists, who stuck to Washington and its familiar territory, Sarah liked to meet Senators and Congressmen in their states and districts, on their home turf, as it were. That showed effort and respect and gave the impression she was more a constituent than a lobbyist. She also kept her meetings brief and to the point.

After Sarah had thanked Senator East for his time – she also thanked the receptionist on her way out, a tactic that she'd also found to pay dividends – she headed for her rental car. It was then just 10:15 a.m., plenty of time for her drive to Monterey. The Board meeting was scheduled for 11:00 the next morning.

Sarah travelled down Interstate 5, then turned west around the south of San Jose to Santa Cruz, and from there followed the scenic coast highway to Monterey. Monterey is an old fishing village, now dominated by the tourism industry and the golf courses made famous, or more famous by Bing Crosby's legendary golf tournament, the Crosby Clambake. And its successor tournaments, which were not nearly as much fun to most golf fans.

She drove leisurely and arrived in Monterey mid-afternoon. After checking into her hotel, she set out on foot to locate the nondescript two-story office building which housed Citizens for Responsible Growth, as well as a few sole-practice accountants and lawyers, a bail bondsman, a tarot card reader/psychic and a State Farm insurance agency. The law offices had cardboard signs in the windows advertising such specialties as

$200 divorces and $300 bankruptcies.

Satisfied that she could easily find the place the next morning, Sarah set off to Cannery Row, a harbor side area which, like Fisherman's Wharf in San Francisco was home to a variety of bars, – upscale and otherwise, and restaurants specializing, naturally enough, in seafood.

She found a restaurant with seating on the deck overlooking the harbor and ordered a glass of "a good California chardonnay."
Pretending to study the menu, she barely glanced up when the waitress delivered her wine. She told her she would order after she had enjoyed the wine and the view for a few minutes. She lit one of her Turkish cigarettes. Even in California, the lifestyle Nazis had not yet managed to ban smoking outdoors.

After an excellent night's sleep on a very comfortable mattress, Sarah had breakfast in the hotel coffee shop, and at 10:50 a.m. walked in the front door of the CFRG office. She approached the receptionist/secretary – the only employee other than Boone Malory – and introduced herself, indicating she was there for the Board meeting in case the woman failed to remember.

"Hi, I'm Suzy Dillinger," the woman said, extending her hand. "I've heard a lot about you and I'm pleased to meet you in person. Can I get you some water or coffee?"

"No, thank you," Sarah responded. "I'm fine. And I hope whatever it was that you heard was positive."

"Very positive."

"I'm sure you get asked all the time about your name. You know, John Dillinger?" Sarah hoped she would not take offense to her question. It had just kind of popped out.

"Yes I do and yes, I am," Suzy responded.

"I'm sorry? Yes, I am, what?"

"Related to John Dillinger. It's a long story and if you move out here I'll tell you sometime. Meantime, let me tell them you're here."

Suzy Dillinger knocked once and entered the conference room. She returned shortly and told Sarah, "They said your inquisition starts in five minutes. They're going over minutes of the last meeting right now." She was smiling when she said "inquisition."

"No problem," Sarah replied. "I don't mind friendly inquisitions."

"This one should be mostly friendly." Another smile.

A little less than five minutes later, Boone Malory stuck his head out the door and invited Sarah to join them. There were five men at the table, all standing at their places to greet Sarah. Boone introduced her, in turn, to Cooper Courtney, William Tidey, Daniel Morawitz, Ralph Gard and Charles Buchino. Boone gestured to the speaker phone in the middle of the table and told Sarah, "And on the phone is Valerie Haught."

Cooper Courtney was the Chairman of the Board, but apparently Boone Malory ran the meetings. He introduced Sarah, recounting his meeting with her and referring to her resume, which he distributed around the table like a Las Vegas poker dealer. That was mostly for show, since he had briefed each director privately by telephone and had faxed them her resume a week before. He asked her to repeat to the Board what she had said to him in Jared Welch's office, and then he would open it up to questions from the members. Sarah stood at her place at the end of the table, farthest from Boone Malory.

"First," Sarah began in a firm and confident voice, "let me thank you for making the time on what I'm sure is a busy agenda to meet with me. Second, I want to assure you of my sincere desire to help CFRG successfully reach its financial and programmatic goals."

She then ran them through the main points she had made with Boone a couple of weeks previously; learning about CFRG at the Hyatt Regency meeting, her research into the organization and its financial struggles, its mission and goals and her desire to do something more meaningful than that which had made her financially independent.

Concluding, she told them, "I am considered by people I respect to be an accomplished lobbyist and fundraiser and want to help CFRG. I hope that does not sound like braggadocio, because it is not intended to be. But I came here determined to be honest with you and I think a review of my career will lead you to the same conclusion. I am happy to take any questions you have of me." She sat down, and her eyes met those of every Director in turn as she scanned around the table.

Ralph Gard, a retired Boeing engineer who lived in the Seattle area, spoke up first.

"I'll take the obvious question, Sarah. May we call you Sarah? We tend to be informal here."

"Informal is good," Sarah responded, smiling.

"Good. My question is why? I've done a little poking around and you're apparently one of the top lobbyists in Washington, and I assume by that and by what you've said that you get paid very well for what you do. All we could offer you is the chance to make a salary if you raise the money to pay it."

"Thank you for the compliments, Ralph, and I'll answer your question as I did when Boone asked me the same question. I have been representing clients, mostly in the pharmaceutical industry, and in all modesty representing them well, which means my work helps them financially. And they reward me financially.

"So as I look back on my career, I realize that all I have been doing has been for rather narrow – some might say selfish – goals, both those of my clients and of my own. I have recently come to the decision that it is time I channel my efforts toward a higher set of goals. When I heard Boone describe the mission and goals of CFRG, I decided that this organization is where I want to be. And since I'm financially secure I'm free to take the kind of chances I might not have been able to take a few years ago."

Valerie Haught's voice came through the speakerphone when Sarah concluded her answer.

"That's all well and good, and I appreciate your candor, but my question is how long you see yourself working for CFRG?"

"That's a fair question, but I can't give you a timetable, because I don't know. First, we've got to get this organization set financially so it can do its real work. I can't predict the future, but I can tell you I am committed to CFRG. If you agree to bring me aboard, I will not be taking a leave of absence or in any other way hedging my bets, as it were.

"I will resign from my firm and come to CFRG full-time, fully committed and determined to succeed. It's too important that we control oil exploration in sensitive areas like Alaska and off-shore, to come to this job half-way. Our own President has reversed himself and allowed expanded off-shore exploration, for God's sake."

Cooper Courtney asked what kind of wages she would require.

"As I told Boone, I'm prepared to enter into this with no salary for the first 60 days. By that time, we should have been able to get our fundraising going and I would like a wage that covers my living expenses in this area. After that, assuming I do the job in fundraising, a negotiated amount based on my worth to the organization, just as I'm sure you deal with Boone."

"Can we afford you?" Courtney pursued.

"I don't think there is much downside at all for CFRG," she responded. "Remember, I don't cost you a cent for 60 days. After that, you'll know that I either can or cannot raise the money to continue my association with CFRG. Where's your risk?"

Charles Buchino asked, "Three-part question, Sarah: first, how much can you raise, second, how long will it take to raise it and third, who do you see as the initial contributors?"

"Let me put it this way, Charles," she responded. "First, significant, second, 30 to 60 days and third, I will not reveal my financial leads at this time, but I will assure you they will be sources that will not embarrass CFRG in any way."

Gard asked, "When can you start?"

"Virtually immediately," she said. "But I must make it clear that I do have a few clients that I'm under long-term contract with that I will from time to time need to continue to provide with services. None will conflict with the goals of CFRG so that should not be a concern to this Board."

Bill Tidey asked Sarah what her first order of business would be if the Board agreed to hire her.

"All of my initial efforts would be directed toward raising the money required to allow CFRG to operate at the level required to be successful in advancing its environmental goals."

"Have you reviewed our current financial statements?" Tidey asked.

"No, I don't think current financial statements are to be shared with outsiders, so I have not asked for them. As I said earlier, I have reviewed the Form 990s and other public sources of information."

"Then you have a good idea of CFRG's current financial status," he said.

"I believe I do."

Boone's face reddened as the Board members glanced at him, nodding. He was suddenly very uncomfortable with the tones of voice he was hearing from his Board members. He was also more than a little intimidated at the way Sarah seemed to be controlling the meeting with her statements and answers.

The focus on the precarious financial condition of the organization further discomfited him.

The interview continued for most of another hour with more direct questions and equally direct answers. Boone Malory did not ask any questions or make any comments.

Courtney, joined by the other Directors, thanked Sarah for her time and interest and they took turns assuring her of their positive impressions of her. Courtney assured her they would get back with her shortly.

Sarah stood to make her closing comment. "Thank you for your time and the opportunity to meet with you. I told you earlier my first goal, if you agree, will be fundraising. I will leave you with my second goal, which will be to pressure the President to reverse his position on expanded oil exploration." She turned and strode purposefully out of the room.

After bidding Suzy Dillinger farewell, she walked out of the office, planning to return to her hotel to pack, check out and fly back to Washington. She literally bumped into Amanda Baines, who was walking up the steps of the building. It was hard to tell which was more startled.

"Amanda, hi! What are you doing here in Monterey?"
Amanda hugged her, which startled her somewhat because she was not used to hugs in Washington, especially in her line of business. "Good" Deeds was the exception to that, along with – on occasion and in private – Jared Welch. But Jared's tended to be a different kind of hug.

"My God, Sarah, I could ask you the same thing. I'm working on a story and just came by to see if Boone is available for dinner. Can you join us?"

"I'm on my way back to Washington, with a stopover in Galveston for a meeting, but thanks, Amanda. Can I have a rain check?"

"Sure, any time. And Sarah, thanks for arranging the interview with Congressman Deeds. I'm meeting him week after next." Amanda paused, then asked, "Say, were you here interviewing with the Board?" Sarah nodded and Amanda asked how it went.

"It felt that the Board was comfortable with me and will almost certainly want to hire me. But Boone didn't say much and seemed flustered or nervous through most of the meeting. I'm not interested in taking his job and I'm a little afraid that may be what he was thinking."

"I'll talk to him tonight," Amanda said. "You two would make a good team and I'll try to help make him more comfortable with you. Meanwhile, let's get together when I'm in Washington. I'll email you or call when my schedule is set."

"That sounds great, Amanda. I appreciate your help."

Amanda hugged Sarah again as they parted. As Sarah walked away, Amanda wondered why Sarah was dressed the same way she had been the night they had dinner in Washington. She didn't yet understand Sarah's working uniform rules.

Despite Boone Malory's reticence – or whatever it was – Sarah felt good when she got to the Monterey Peninsula Airport, where a ShareJet Gulfstream awaited her. She used ShareJet occasionally when her schedule dictated travel that could not be provided in a timely manner by the commercial airlines. She needed it today because she had a meeting in Galveston, Texas, that evening, then a late night flight to Washington. She had meetings the next day.

After Sarah left the meeting, Cooper Courtney called for a five-minute break so the members could use the restroom and consider their options. He also announced that he thought the Board should go into a short executive session when they reconvened, so Boone excused himself and announced he would take a 20-minute walk, which was his custom anyway, two or three times a day. Good thinking time, he always said.

When Courtney gaveled the executive session to order, he asked for comments from the members. Gord immediately recommended that the Board authorize Boone to offer Sarah the job, on the terms she had outlined. As he said, "If she's not able to raise the funds needed to pay her salary in the first 60 days, we're out nothing."

Valerie Haught's voice came over the speakerphone. "I'm going on her words and her tone of voice, because I could not see her face or body language, but she sounded like the real thing to me, gentlemen. And let's face it, CFRG is not long for this world as it stands now, with a few $1,000 and $5,000 pledges here and there, and not nearly enough of the latter.

This woman – from all that she said to us today - plays in the big leagues in D.C. and she sounds extremely comfortable that she can raise the money."

Around the table, heads nodded and murmurs of agreement were heard, but nobody had anything further to say, so Courtney summarized his feelings. "Boone is a visionary and a researcher, and given the resources he's invaluable to our cause because of those talents. But I know him as well as any of us, and I know he would be the first to admit that he is not a fund-raiser, and he's not comfortable as a lobbyist.

"I think Sarah is the perfect complement to him. Hopefully, she can raise the money and do the spade work with the elected officials and regulatory agencies." He paused. "Any objection to authorizing Boone to offer her the position?"

"If he agrees that she's a complement and not a threat," Gord said. "We should make it plain to him that he is being authorized to hire her on the terms she outlined, not ordered to." The others agreed.

Courtney threw the doors of the room open at the same moment Boone walked back into the building. "Great timing," he said. "We just concluded our discussion." He ushered Boone back into the room and closed the doors.

Courtney summarized the Board's position. He stressed to Boone that, as CEO, the decision was his. "But I assume the reason you brought her to us is that you wanted our take on her as well as our recommendation. And now you have them both."

Boone thanked the members and assured them he would have further conversations with Sarah to refine the shape of the employment agreement and conclude the matter as quickly as possible.

Courtney smiled and called the next item on the agenda.

CHAPTER 8

MONTEREY, CALIFORNIA
THAT EVENING

It was after 4:00 p.m. when the Board meeting adjourned. After thanking the members for coming to Monterey, Boone retreated to his office to sort his notes for follow-up and filing and just before 5:00 he headed for the door. He always needed a drink after a Board meeting. There were things about being a CEO that did not agree with his temperament, and listening to volunteers discuss and dissect his organization and his work for five hours was definitely one of them.

He started to say good-bye to Suzy when he noticed an attractive woman talking with her. It took a moment for his mind to register this, then Amanda turned to him and smiled.

"Amanda," he blurted, "what are you doing here?"

"I'm in town doing some background research for a story I'm working on, so I took the opportunity to stop and see your office. When Suzy told me a couple of hours ago that you had a Board meeting today, I came back hoping you'd jump at the chance to have dinner with the best old friend you're likely to meet tonight."

Boone, who was in as close to a playful mood as he ever got right after a Board meeting, said, "You don't know what I had planned tonight, so how can you assume you're the best old friend I'm likely to meet?" He looked at Suzy and winked. Suzy was laughing. Boone Malory was not known – to her or anyone else - as someone who joked around like this often, although his understated sense of humor – when he chose to use it

– could be delightful.

"Let's just say that I stand by my previous comment," Amanda said.

"You're right, too, Amanda," Suzy said. Boone stared at Suzy for a moment, then smiled and with a gesture toward the door said to Suzy, "See you in the morning." Boone led Amanda out of the office and toward a small restaurant that had sidewalk seating. It was a clear afternoon, without much wind and temperatures in the low 70s, so they sat at a sidewalk table in a corner where they could have a little privacy from the other customers, who were mostly drinking rather than dining at this hour.

Amanda ordered a spritzer and Boone ordered a Dos Equis. They gazed at the view of Monterey Bay, at the people passing on the sidewalk and glanced twice at each other before the waitress brought their drinks. Amanda started the conversation.

"Boone, my story is not about CFRG," she said, "but I'm hearing that you've got some serious financial issues."

"Fair assessment," he responded quietly. "As you know, we had a Board meeting today and the consensus was that we've got a year – maybe a little less – without an infusion of cash. I mean, there's no place else to cut. The staff is down to Suzy and me. And we're just not getting the contributions we need." Of course, when he said, "a year – maybe a little less…," he knew he was sugar-coating the situation.

"What are you going to do?" Amanda's eyes were intent on Boone's face as she sipped her spritzer.

"Well, today the Board interviewed a professional lobbyist who wants a career and lifestyle change and seems very interested in CFRG and our goals. And she claims she can raise a lot of money. The Board was impressed with her, as I am, and they authorized me to work out a deal with her."

"Are you talking about Sarah Cotton?" she asked innocently.

Boone stared, not sure what he just heard. "Sarah Cotton," he affirmed. "How in the world would you know that?"

"I know Sarah."

"How do you know her? I mean, she lives in Washington and you live in San Francisco."

"Our mutual college friend, Jared Welch, introduced us. I assume you remember he's a lobbyist in Washington, too."

"Go on." Boone found himself wondering if Jared Welch wasn't the puppet master, orchestrating this whole show. It seemed too much a coincidence that Amanda Baines shows up unannounced in Monterey for the first time on the same day he had Sarah Cotton out here for a Board meeting.

"Well, Sarah was interested in CFRG, and Jared knew that you and I go way back. She went to your presentation at the Hyatt Regency back there and liked the message. Jared also knew that Sarah was close to a couple of Congressmen I wanted to talk to about a story I've been working on."

"And what, pray tell, did you tell her?"

"Just what I know about you and about CFRG."

Boone was getting exasperated. "What you know about me and about CFRG?" Amanda nodded and Boone asked again what she told her.

"The truth," Amanda said simply. When Boone made motions with his hand indicating he wanted more, she said. "I told her how committed you are to CFRG and its mission, how sincere you are. I even lied and told her you're a nice guy." She smiled.

"And I told her that you would be the first to admit that fund-raising is not your strong suit, nor is lobbying." Another reflective pause. "And I told her that as nice and as honorable a person as you are, it would scare you to death to be working with her."

"You think she scares me, huh?"

"Maybe not yet, but when you see her really get going, she'll scare you. You're very different people, Boone. You're a persuader, most comfortable leading people to your point of view. She's a pusher, maybe not by natural instinct, but she's learned that's the way it's done in D.C."

Boone could not disagree.

He finished his beer, noticed that Amanda's spritzer was nearly empty and signaled the waitress, who was quite attentive, to bring them two more.

"So, Miss Fixer, what do you think of Sarah?" Boone asked.

"I like her. I liked her almost immediately after Jared introduced us. She's very successful but not full of herself. But she gets things done. I had been trying to get a private interview with Congressman Deeds of Illinois for a couple of weeks and was getting the run-around from his staff. She called him personally and got me an appointment with him within hours of my meeting her. She has powerful contacts and is well thought of." Of course, her story about trying to meet with Deeds was an exaggeration, if not a complete fabrication, but it effectively illustrated her point.

"And I think she's very sincere in wanting to do something more with her life and her skills. She likes what you and CFRG stand for and despite the differences in style between the two of you, I think you'd make a very good team."

"Why CFRG?" he asked. "Or do you know?"

"Yes, we talked about that, too. She's got a real interest in the environment, and she researched a lot of environmental organizations. She thinks most of them are controlled by crazies. That's why she was at the Hyatt. She wanted to hear about CFRG from the horse's mouth."

Boone sipped his beer, which had been delivered while Amanda was talking. He said nothing, just looked at Amanda, nodding for her to continue.

"Now I have to ask you a question, Boone, and I am being very serious when I ask it. I've known you for a lot of years, so think about the question before you give me a shoot-from-the-hip answer. Can you work closely with Sarah Cotton? With a really strong-willed woman?"

Boone stared out at the bay. Finally, he turned back to Amanda and said, "That's a good question. Sometimes, working with women has been a problem for me, and that might be especially difficult with one as powerful as Sarah."

"So what's next?" Amanda asked simply.

"I need to meet with her again in the next couple of weeks to get into what kind of deal she'd be happy with. And now that you've mentioned it, I need to satisfy myself that we can function as a team."

"When are you going to meet with her? Did you set up a meeting before she left?"

"No. I'll call her in a couple of days and set something up."

"I can call her right now. I have her cell phone number. She should be on the ground in Galveston by now."

"Galveston? What's she doing there? I thought she was going back to Washington."

"She had a meeting in Galveston on the way."

"How do you know that?"

"I told you we're friends. We stay in touch. Shall I call her?"

Boone looked stricken. "No, not yet," he said, "I need to check on my schedule and figure out how I'm going to approach this."

Amanda looked at Boone with the expression of a mother who has just heard her 16-year-old son explain to her why he still hasn't called a girl for the prom, when the prom was the next night. "Now, that's taking a real leadership position," she said. "I'm calling Sarah now and you can wing it when I hand you the phone."

Boone almost shouted, "Amanda, hold on. You're rushing me."

"Too late," Amanda announced. She had pushed a speed dial button. "Hello, Sarah, it's Amanda." She paused, listening. "I'm having dinner with Boone. Actually, so far it's drinks, but he wants to schedule a meeting as soon as he can, so I called because I have your number. Here he is." She thrust the phone to Boone, whose hand was suddenly so sweaty he could barely grasp the device.

"Sarah, I'm sorry for the interruption," he said, "but the Board authorized me to work something out with you and I'd like to meet with you in the next couple of weeks. The Board members were quite impressed, as I knew they would be."

"I've got meetings in Washington this week, but after that I can be flexible. Are you scheduled to be in the capital any time soon?"

"Not for another month, at least," Boone replied.

"Okay, pick a day in the next week and I'll come back to Monterey.

"How about next Friday?"

Sarah smiled to herself. *Hooked and landed.* "I'll be in your office at 10:00 a.m. next Friday. How would that be?"

"Thank you, Sarah, both for your interest and for your flexibility."

"Thanks very much, Boone. I'll look forward to seeing you again on Friday. May I speak with Amanda again before you hang up?"

When Amanda had the phone back, Sarah said, "Wow, Amanda, you're good. I owe you one. Thanks."

"Talk to you later, Sarah," Amanda said and closed the phone. She looked at Boone. "Well, that wasn't too painful, was it?"

Boone Malory nodded, but the look on his face was the befuddled look of someone for whom things had begun spinning out of control and could not understand why or how. He felt like his hand was shaking as he raised it to signal for more drinks from the waitress.

After the third beer, Boone had recovered some – but not all – of his composure and they ordered dinner, crab salad with oil and vinegar for Amanda and a cheeseburger for Boone. They caught up with each other and in the course of the conversation, Boone slipped in a few questions about Sarah that he hoped sounded sufficiently off-hand to Amanda.

They did not and Amanda suspected that Boone was finally in the process of concluding his grieving and might even be a bit smitten by Sarah. *Well,* she thought to herself, *my old friend could do a lot worse than Sarah Cotton.* She sometimes wondered why Boone had never made a pass at her and didn't know what she would do if he did. She loved the brilliant, enigmatic man, but he was too much like a brother for her to entertain any romantic thoughts.

In Washington the next morning, Sarah dashed off emails to Jared and Amanda thanking them for their assistance and reporting to Jared that she thought she was making progress on the CFRG front. To herself, she thought that maybe she was making progress with Boone as well. She had been attracted to him from the moment he stood up to talk at the Hyatt Regency. How that attraction would play out if they did, indeed, end up working together was another matter entirely. Office romances, she knew, could be decidedly bad news, and she had always avoided them.

While she was online, she went to the United Airlines web site and booked a flight late Thursday from Washington to San Francisco, with a connecting commuter flight to Monterey. She left the return flight open.

CHAPTER 9

As soon as he went into his office the morning of his meeting with Sarah, Boone Malory booted up his computer, checked emails – nothing important, meaning no new pledges – and went to Google and typed in "Sarah Cotton." He wanted to know as much as he could about this woman before seeing her in his office that morning.

There were several references on the site that related to Sarah Cotton. Most of them were newspaper stories on legislative battles in which she had taken part. Some contained photos and she was always dressed in her black dress, pearls, tan blazer and black pumps. He assumed her shoes, whether heels or pumps, were always black. That's all he'd ever seen her in.

There was also a reference to her employer's web site, which contained a glowing combination of biography and curriculum vitae on her. She had joined the firm eleven years ago, immediately after graduation (with honors) from Trinity College, where she had majored in communications with a minor in political science. It seemed she had focused her education on what was already her choice for a vocation.

Boone searched all references, making careful notes – sometimes printing out a page here and there – and after over an hour clicked out of Google. He sat for another hour reflecting on what he now knew about Sarah Cotton. She had apparently taken to lobbying immediately and naturally. Her rise in her firm had been meteoric by any standards. She handled clients, mostly blue-chip pharmaceuticals, usually reserved for the more senior and seasoned members of a firm, often former members of Congress or functionaries in one Presidential administration or another. The non-pharma clients for whom she had done work were generally prestigious and, from the stories he had read, appeared very pleased with her representation.

The Congressmen and Senators who were quoted seemed to consider her bright, forthright and honest – even those who did not agree with her client's position on a particular issue. She was unquestionably well-known and mostly well-respected by those who count for anything in the Federal government, it seemed.

And there was not one word tying her romantically to anybody, male or female. There was one reference, a piece from the Washington Post on the growing number of female lobbyists prowling The Hill, that made reference to her living by herself in her own "toney but unpretentious" condominium in the neighborhood around George Washington University.

Boone sat back in his chair, thinking. He felt he now knew a lot more about Sarah Cotton than he had before, and wondered why he had not bothered doing this research prior to the Board meeting. He would have been more prepared for the interview, perhaps thrown in a few questions of his own. But something was missing and at last it struck him what the missing piece was.

In all those references to her on Google, there was no reference that indicated Sarah had existed prior to her graduation from Trinity College. Nothing on where she had been born and raised, where she had attended high school or her family. He resolved to focus some of his interview today on filling in those blanks.

At 9:55 a.m., Sarah walked through the door of the CFRG office and greeted Suzy Dillinger.

"Good to see you again, Sarah," Suzy said. "I'll tell Boone you're here."

"No need," Boone said as he appeared in the lobby. He had leapt from his chair as soon as he heard Sarah's voice in the reception area. "Can I get you a cup of coffee or a bottle of water?"

"Black coffee would be great," Sarah said. Suzy jumped up and hurried toward the kitchen/break room to get the coffee and Boone escorted Sarah to his office. He gestured toward a well-used leather sofa and he sat in a leather wing-back chair, both gifts from a supporter, now dead, unfortunately.

When they were seated, Boone noted that despite the informality of this office, Sarah was again attired in her signature black dress, pearls, tan blazer and black pumps. He thanked Sarah again for her interest in CFRG and her flexibility. Suzy brought Sarah's coffee in and closed the door as she went out.

For her part, Sarah once again noted Boone's strong features and intent blue eyes. *He's a sturdy-looking man, and brilliant. That's quite a combination.* She knew this was Boone's interview and she waited for him to start it.

Sarah realized that she had basically taken over the interview with the Board and she was loath to do anything further to scare Boone, who began predictably by asking her again why she would want to leave her lucrative lobbying practice to take on a "project" like CFRG.

Sarah sat back and met Boone's eyes before she began.

"As I mentioned to the Board, I've done quite well, financially. I've been able to put away more than I'd ever dreamed I'd have, at least at my age. I want to do something more, and something that's not necessarily about money. As I also said, if I succeed, as I think I will, I expect to be paid commensurate to my value to CFRG.

"But there's another, more important, reason, and please bear with me, because it may be a difficult distinction to follow. I am tired of working for other people. I want to work for me. I know you are the boss, but I really want to work with you rather than for you. Does that make sense?"

Boone nodded, said, "Go on."

"You were inspiring at that event at the Hyatt in Washington, and you inspired me. I want to work with you to make CFRG as good and as effective as is possible. I've got a great interest in the environment, unlike most of my clients, who are generally interested in two things: getting their next medication approved by the FDA and getting their Federal tax liability decreased.

"My passion is petroleum. I want to see the world's use of petroleum products reduced. That includes oil and gasoline, but it also includes plastic products and other uses of petroleum. I'm interested to hear more of your views on this, but for now, my own opinion is that the best way to do that is to greatly curtail exploration for new petroleum sources, which will force a faster transition to alternate sources of energy."

"Certainly one of CFRG's primary goals," Boone agreed, and he was smiling.

Sarah nodded and continued. "After I heard you talk that day, I researched everything I could find on CFRG and concluded this organization is a perfect fit for me. With your brain and my skills and contacts, I think we can put this organization on the map." During her entire monologue, Sarah had been looking straight at Boone's eyes, and she liked what she saw – intelligence and character. Again. She thought she should stop now, and give Boone a chance to get a word in.

"How much do you think you can raise?" he asked. She had wondered how long it would be before that question came up.

"Let me start by saying that I already have some contacts, at quite a high level, actually, who have a strong interest in a moderate but firm approach to saving what's left of the environment, so my answer to your question may seem unduly bold to you, but I'm being very serious. I believe I can raise $500,000 within 30 days…." Involuntarily, Boone gasped and Sarah continued, "And raise the total to $1 million within three to six months and to $3 million within a year or so. And more as word of our good work spreads."

Boone could not have removed the smile from his face with a jackhammer. He was also, he admitted to himself, having a bit of a problem believing numbers like those. He knew there was a lot of money out there, but Good God!

"There's another thing," Sarah said evenly. "I know the limits of my abilities, and I have come to realize that, in the work I want to do, I need to partner with someone who has the conviction and intellectual integrity to do the right thing, even when the wind is blowing against us. Because it will. When I researched CFRG and you, Boone, here's what I heard from every source: you are a visionary, you are brilliant and you have the conviction and intellectual integrity I'm talking about.

"Your strengths do not include lobbying and fund-raising, but mine do. And your strengths compensate for my shortcomings. So, to summarize my position again, I concluded that you and I would make a terrific team. And not to put too fine a point on it, but there is one other thing. I tend to work better with men than with women."

Jeez, I wonder why, Boone thought to himself. *What man could say "no" to her?*

"When are you available?" he asked.

Sarah beamed. *Like I thought, hooked and landed.* She said, "Right away, but as I said at the Board meeting, I have a few long-term clients still under contract that I'll need to continue to work for on occasion. I'll wind those down as I need to and we can discuss that from time to time. They won't present a conflict with my work at CFRG."

"You were a little nebulous with the Board on compensation," Boone said. "You said nothing for first 60 days, but you're telling me you'll have a half million in hand in 30 days. Why don't we make it nothing for 30 days, California living expenses from then until we hit a million, then work on an ongoing package?"

"That suits me just fine," she said. "Thank you." *God, that smile,* Boone thought to himself.

"I have another question," Boone said. "This is the third time we've met and each time you've had basically the same outfit on. You don't strike me as a woman who does anything by happenstance, so I'd be interested in why."

Sarah smiled again. *He's more perceptive than most men.* "You're a brave man, Boone. Most men are afraid to question a woman about her dress. But to answer your question, I developed the habit of wearing what I refer to as my 'uniform' soon after I started lobbying. I've found that it makes me recognizable and that works to my advantage." She paused, a wry smile crossing her face. "Of course, I have several sets of my 'uniform.' You're not seeing me in the same clothes each time you've seen me."

Boone thought about that for a bit, then, realizing he'd skated onto dangerous ice and got away with it, so quickly changed the subject. "Before we go out and get some lunch, do you have any questions for me?" Sarah felt a small chill run up her spine as she thought of going out to lunch with Boone Malory. *What's that all about? It's just lunch!*

"I do, and thank you for the opportunity. Let's say I do what I'm telling you and the Board I will do, and I raise the money to put CFRG really in business, what would you do to reverse the President's policy to lift the restrictions on oil exploration in the U.S., both off-shore and in Alaska?"

Boone had thought about this often enough that he had little trouble reciting. "I'd develop a multi-phase approach and implement all phases simultaneously. I'd have to run the plan by the Board, of course. I haven't finalized it so far because we don't have the resources to do anything about it. But my initial thoughts are these:

"First, I'd develop a national advertising program discussing the risks and dangers of expanded oil exploration, especially off-shore and in sensitive areas like Alaska.

"Second, I'd develop information packages for the media, opinion leaders and other environmental organizations with the goal of getting them to support our position.

"Third, I'd turn you loose to lobby members of Congress and key state legislators and governors.

"Fourth, I'd develop and publicize a web site with information supporting our position and directed at the general public. And…what is this, five?

"Fifth, I'd promote alternative energy and try to get the alternative energy industry to join our coalition. Maybe even try to enlist T. Boone Pickens." The billionaire oilman out of Amarillo, Texas, had recently begun promoting wind farms as an energy source. Some skeptics felt his cause was driven more by the Federal subsidies and tax breaks that went along with alternative energy than a real desire to develop alternative sources, but deep pockets, Boone thought, were deep pockets.

"Sixth, I'd work with other organizations that are promoting energy efficiency to make those efforts more effective, and find ways to reward those individuals and businesses that conserve.

"Seventh, I'd work on the public to motivate voters to support clean energy sources and reduced petroleum use, and to make that support known to their elected officials at the state and Federal levels.

"And eighth, I'd propose raising taxes on petroleum products and dedicate those tax funds to the support of alternative fuel research and public transportation." He paused, took a deep breath. "Those are my initial thoughts."

Sarah was impressed. She said, "Good outline, Boone. I like them all, except the last one. I usually don't support new or increased taxes. Especially when they are intended for a specific purpose. Congress simply can't be trusted to maintain those tax earmarks in the future."

"I certainly can't argue with that," Boone said. "I'm born skeptic myself, and I'm open to rethinking any part of my plan. Now, how about lunch?" He stood, as did Sarah.

CHAPTER 10

MONTEREY, CALIFORNIA
THE SAME DAY

Boone was determined to be on his most gentlemanly behavior – he didn't know enough about Sarah at this point to know whether she was one of those feminists who were so baffling to him – so he held the door for her when she reappeared and they left the office. It was drizzling, not an uncommon occurrence in Monterey, and he held an umbrella over their heads. On the walk to the restaurant, the same one he had taken Amanda to a few days earlier, he was careful not to let his long strides outpace Sarah's. And he held her chair as he sat her at the table to which the hostess directed them.

Sarah noticed.

She liked that in a man and she was careful to convey sincerity when she thanked him for seating her. She also noticed that Boone seemed more relaxed with her now and their easy conversation during lunch reinforced that.

For his part, Boone, always a careful observer of people, noticed that Sarah attracted the attention of other women in the eating area, as well as many of those they had passed on the sidewalk. And the men seemed to have a hard time not being too obvious. He had not seen this – at least as clearly or as often – when he was here with Amanda, who was certainly attractive. But Sarah just seemed to draw eyes to her. Still, Boone was impressed that Sarah herself appeared totally oblivious to the stares.

Boone liked that.

The lunch passed quickly and on the wet and windy walk back to his office, Boone asked Sarah to tell him more about one of her answers during the Board interview, namely that she could not commit to how long she would stay at CFRG if the position were offered to her.

"I simply told you and the Board the truth," she said. "I said I tend to get bored and need to move on to something else, and that's the truth. One of the reasons I like lobbying, and I think why I've been successful at it, is that the issues are always changing and there are new problems to solve.

"But even at that, my practice has become so consumed by the pharma industry that I've started to get restless. That's why I started looking into CFRG and other organizations to begin with. So to further answer the question, as long as I'm being challenged, I expect that I'll be happy here, and I'll stay."

Boone considered her answer, and she went on, "But if your question is whether I'd ever leave you in the lurch, so to speak, the answer is no. If I ever get to that point, I'll work with you to plan a proper and orderly exit strategy for me. But with your agenda and strategy as you laid it out this morning – working to roll back the President's oil exploration plan and the other issues on your agenda – I think I'm in for the long haul."

"Thank you," Boone said. "That helps."

When they were back in Boone's office, he asked her, "Let me turn around a question you asked me this morning and ask you what the first thing you would do if I hire you."

Sarah let a pause pass before answering. "Boone, I need to say this again. I do not see myself being hired. Rather, I see myself being engaged to join you to stabilize and grow CFRG, to get our messages and goals in front of the American people and their elected leaders and to accomplish the environmental agenda you have developed."

Boone smiled. She liked his smile more every time he used it. "Okay, point taken and understood. And when you are engaged, what would be the first thing you'd do?"

Sarah liked the response. He's much less nervous with me now, she thought to herself. "The first thing I'd do, after you 'hire' me," she said with a sardonic smile, "would be to beat the bushes to secure both immediate and long-term contributors."

Boone's smile was broadening and he said, "And after being engaged as a partner and getting our financial house in order, what would you do next?"

"Well, Mr. Malory, with your policy guidance and approval, I'd go to every Congressman and Senator I know to push legislation to overturn the President's oil exploration decree, which I believe may be as illegal as it was ill-advised."

"Good answer, Ms. Cotton. Get the money, then start getting wins."

The lighthearted repartee continued and Sarah was becoming more convinced by the minute that she wanted to be part of CFRG. Likewise, Boone was becoming increasingly convinced he wanted to work with Sarah, to have her on the CFRG team.

Boone said, "You're very aware of my strengths and my weaknesses, and I yours." He paused before continuing, "although your only apparent weakness – at least in the sense that it scares me a bit, I admit – is that you are so independent. I know you don't need guidance in either fund-raising or in lobbying. But I will really insist on being kept in the loop on what you're doing. If I have that assurance, you will not need to worry about me looking over your shoulder or second-guessing you."

"Your analysis, and your concerns, are both valid and understandable. I have a reputation for working solo but I've also been in many situations where I had to coordinate my activities with those of other lobbyists who were fighting for the same things, or with a politician who was on our side. I know how the game is played, but the only way I can prove it to you is for you to take a chance on me."

"Let me think about it over the weekend and I'll call you Monday," he said. "Will that work for you?"

"Do you need the Board's approval to hire me?" she asked.

"Sarah, why don't we drop the use of the word, 'hire?' You're the one who raised that issue and it's valid. I've accepted it. And I already have the Board's approval to enter into an agreement with you if I so choose."

"Touché." Sarah stood up and Boone did likewise. He walked her to the front door, shook her hand – he fought the temptation to give her a hug – and she set off for the airport.

When the door had closed, Suzy asked Boone whether he was going to hire her, and Boone corrected her on the accepted use of the word, "hire." Then he said, "I think so." Suzy, who was aware of the situation with CFRG and had chatted enough with Sarah to get a sense of her, thought that Boone was making a very good move. She genuinely liked what she saw in the woman.

Boone then realized he had forgotten entirely about asking about her childhood – her life before Trinity College.

As she was waiting to board the small jet for the commuter flight to San Francisco, Sarah reflected again on how much she felt she would enjoy working with Boone, not just CFRG. She thought they would become good friends. She knew as she thought them that those thoughts were unusual for her.

Sarah called Amanda. Habits honed from her years of being the consummate lobbyist came easily to her. She filled Amanda in on the interview, and even spent several minutes telling her about Boone loosening up, the banter at lunch and the remaining feeling that a part of Boone was still a bit uneasy about her style.

"You'll overcome that, Sarah," Amanda said as a matter of fact and not of conjecture. "He's really a great guy when he settles down. You'll get along fine. When's he going to let you know?"

"He said he'd call Monday and I think he'll go for it."

"Great. I'll call him over the weekend a give him a push if he sounds like he needs it."

They said their good-byes and Sarah boarded the aircraft.

On Sunday, Amanda called Boone on his cell phone. "How did it go with Sarah?" she asked, getting directly to the point as good reporters are trained to do.

"It went fine," he said.

"Well, what's next?"

"I told her I'd call her tomorrow."

Jeez, she thought, *it's good old Boone. Getting anything out of him is like pulling teeth.* "And have you made a decision?"

"Yes."

"Well, are you going to hire her or not?"

"Amanda, you know I can't tell you until I talk to her."

"Oh, God, Boone, what's the problem?"

But she knew pushing further would get her nowhere, so she gave up and thanked him for talking with Sarah.

They hung up.

CHAPTER 11

MONTEREY, CALIFORNIA
THE NEXT DAY AND FORWARD

Even though Boone Malory knew in his heart, as well as in his head, that he had to get Sarah Cotton on the CFRG team – such as it was – it was a difficult decision for him to make. Quite simply, he liked his independence, and he had no doubt that she would be a hard charger. And at times, the odds were that sometimes Sarah would want to charge in a different direction than he, or with different timing than he envisioned.

She was also so damned attractive. Never a man adept at working with women, either on a personal or a professional level, she would be a challenge for him. He could feel the dampness under his arms whenever he thought of working with her on a daily basis. His nerves would be afire whenever she was around. He was at once threatened by, and attracted to, her.

Moreover, as silly as it seemed after three years, in a tiny corner of his mind he felt disloyal to his late wife when he acknowledged his attraction to Sarah.

But more to the point, he knew he had no choice about bringing her on. He was enough of a realist to understand that CFRG was done if he didn't bring her aboard. Or if, for whatever reason, she was not able to deliver the funding she was so confident of raising.

Boone called Sarah early that morning, as he told her he would and before he lost his nerve. She did not answer her cell phone and Boone left a message asking that she return his call.

When she checked her messages after leaving a meeting with a pharmaceutical client, she was pleased and a bit exhilarated that he had called Monday morning, as promised. She thought it a good sign and was confident when she returned the call. It was his cell phone number that he had left, and that increased her confidence. It meant he would not hide behind Suzy as a gate-keeper.

"Good morning, Boone," she said formally but in a casual and confident tone of voice. "It's Sarah, returning your call."

"Thanks for getting back to me so quickly, Sarah, and to get right to the point, I think CFRG needs your services," Boone said quickly. He was very nervous and referred to notes he'd made very early that morning on a legal pad. "I don't think this will come as a great surprise to you, but I know that your talents and abilities, along with your passion for protecting the environment, will be a great asset to the organization, to me personally and to the Board."

Even as he said it, he felt it sounded stilted, like he had just delivered a speech instead of carrying on a conversation. Sarah could tell he was reading from notes, but did not say anything about it.

"When would you like me to start?" she asked, sensing his nervousness and determined to make it as easy as possible for him. She knew she played her cards well, and she sensed that more good would be served by being easy on him than in playing him. Playing people, of course, was one of Sarah's over-arching strengths.

"As soon as possible," Boone answered.

"I'm very pleased, Boone, and I mean that. I think we'll make a great team and we'll put CFRG on the map. Can you give me ten days, or maybe two weeks? I have several projects that I need to push forward a bit and hand off to other associates in my firm before I make the move. Of course, I'll start mapping out my fundraising strategy as I'm winding things up here."

"That would be fine, Sarah. Is there anything I can do from this end?"

"I'd appreciate it if you could put me in contact with a realtor out there that you trust so I can start looking for a place to live." He assured her that he would have one call her right away.

"And I'd also appreciate your thoughts regarding CFRG near-term and long-term goals so I can use them in structuring my fundraising strategy. A simple email will be fine. It doesn't have to be anything fancy."

"No problem," Boone said. "I'll start on that right away and get you something within a day or two."

"Is there anything you need from me between now and when I get out there?" Sarah asked.

"Do you think you could prepare a letter or memo for me outlining our understanding – as you interpret it – of your joining CFRG? I think it would be best to have something in writing so I can send it to the Board, with my endorsement, of course."

"Of course," she said with cheer in her voice. "I'll start working on it as soon as I get back to my office. And Boone, not to sound too trite, but I have to tell you again that I really do look forward to working with you. We can do some great things together, I think. And rescinding the President's order opening up oil exploration will be a great place to start."

"And I look forward to working with you, Sarah. I promise I'll get to work on my memo to you right away as well. I'll talk with you soon."

After disconnecting the call, Sarah smiled and congratulated herself.

After flipping his phone shut, Boone let out a sigh of relief. It was not, he reflected, as bad as he had thought it would be. But, he knew he was going to have to learn, after all the years of being a "lone wolf," how to work with this woman who was both talented and disarmingly beautiful.

The next morning, Sarah Cotton called Caldwell Jones, the executive director of ERIN, a not-for-profit charity based in Houston. ERIN stood for Environmental Responsibility International. It was relatively little known, even in the environmental movement, but those who knew about the organization understood that it provided grants to a small and eclectic collection of other non-profits, mostly smaller groups which most needed the help. In other words, it was a funding organization, a provider of grants, rather than an organization that took action itself.

The Sierra Club, Friends of the Earth and Greenpeace were among those not on its grants list.

Those who bothered to wonder about such things assumed that ERIN had been endowed by one or more super-rich people with a soft spot for the environment and a few related causes. It did not publish a list of its contributors, but claimed its donor base was worldwide.

Jones knew Sarah, and not only because of her lobbying work. He picked up his phone immediately when his secretary announced the call. "Good morning, uh, Sarah," he said. "I've been looking forward to your call."

"Caldwell, I wanted you to be one of the first to know. I have been offered a position with Citizens for Responsible Growth."

"What is Citizens for Responsible Growth?" he asked, but there was no real surprise in his voice. Sarah filled him in on its history, direction and financial condition and told him she thought it was exactly the kind of organization ERIN had been set up to support. As she was talking, she clicked the mouse on her computer and shot an email to Jones.

"It's number one agenda item right now is to reverse the President's order opening up off-shore and Alaskan oil exploration," she told him to reinforce her last point. "And I just sent you an email with four attachments, a descriptive history of CFRG and it last three IRS filings."

"I assume you're calling to ask me to consider this CFRG for a grant," he said.

"That's exactly why I'm calling, Caldwell," she replied evenly. "And I need it quickly. When you look at those IRS filings, you'll see what I mean. Boone Malory is a good man, a visionary who approaches these issues reasonably. But he's living a hand-to-mouth existence. It's down to him and a secretary. I'm going to work for nothing for a while. That's how desperate it is."

"I understand," Jones assured her. "I'll look at this stuff you just sent me and talk with Mark and Paul right away. Call me back this afternoon." She knew Mark and Paul were the two key members of the ERIN Board of Directors and formed the Grants Committee.

"I really appreciate it, Caldwell. Talk with you later today."

Sarah hung up and turned her attention to wrapping up her business and briefing associates on clients, the status of work on their behalf and turning over files to those who would be taking over her duties. None of the associates she met with that morning could believe she was actually doing this – leaving her Big Pharma life behind and signing on with an impoverished little pimple on the butt of Big Environment.

But, truth be told, she knew that some of them envied her. She skipped lunch in favor of hurrying the wrap-up process as much as possible. She had told Boone she would need ten days to two weeks, but was increasingly anxious to make the move and was now shooting for one week.

In what seemed like the blink of an eye, it was 4:00 p.m. in Washington, 3:00 p.m. in Houston. She called Caldwell Jones again.

"Sarah," he said when he came on the line, "I have what I hope is good news for you."

"What 'you hope' is good news?" Sarah asked, a bit warily.

"Well, we didn't really get into specifically how much you were asking for this morning, so I don't know what you're expecting," Jones responded evenly. "But Mark, Paul and I talked on a conference call earlier, after I'd forwarded your info on CFRG. We agreed that CFRG seems like a perfect fit for ERIN money, especially with you going on staff there, so we agreed on an initial grant of two million dollars."

Sarah smiled to herself. It was all coming together.

"Is that okay, Sarah?" Jones asked.

Finding a neutral voice, Sarah said, "That's very nice, Caldwell. I very much appreciate it and will do my best to make ERIN proud of its investment. And thank Mark and Paul as well, would you, please?"

"I will indeed," Jones replied. "Now, as to the terms the three of us discussed, we're prepared to issue a check for $500,000 immediately and three more just like it 30, 60 and 90 days from now. Is that satisfactory?"

"That's great, Caldwell," she said. Please send the checks to the CFRG office in Monterey. The address is in the pdf file I sent you."

"Yes, I have it. And, Sarah, you can rest assured that there is more where that came from if you and Mr. Malory are as successful as I think you'll be."

"Thank you again, Caldwell. I'll keep you posted regularly on our progress."

They hung up. *Fund-raising is easy,* Sarah thought to herself, *when you know who to ask.*

Sarah punched the speed dial number for the CFRG office on her cell phone. Suzy Dillinger, as expected, answered and when she heard Sarah's voice, exclaimed, "Oh, Sarah, I'm sorry, but Boone's not in right now. He had a late lunch with an old friend and hasn't gotten back yet."

"Not a problem," Sarah said. "I just wanted to leave a message with you anyway. Can you let Boone know that he should expect a check from an organization called Environmental Responsibility International in two or three days. They're a granting organization out of Houston."

"Goodness!" Suzy exclaimed. "Already? You move fast, don't you?"

"I try. Can you just let Boone know it's coming and tell him I'm getting things wrapped up here more quickly than I thought and I'm planning to be in your office next Monday."

"That's great, Sarah. How much did you get from…what was it again?"

"Environmental Responsibility International. It's called ERIN, for short. And I'm not sure what they'll send, but they gave me the old 'check's in the mail' line and said it would go out today. And before I forget it, can you remind Boone that I need a furnished apartment for when I'm in Monterey and he said he'd refer a realtor to me."

"Will do, Sarah." Suzy hesitated a beat, then asked, "Do you think there will be any more checks besides from this ERIN group?"

"I hope so, Suzy. Take care and let me know when the check gets there."

"I'll do that. See you next Monday." Suzy hung up, vowing silently to strangle Boone Malory as soon as he walked through the door. He had not told her that he'd made an offer to Sarah, much less that she had accepted. It had been as if by accident that she'd learned that their little staff was going to expand by 50 percent.

Boone walked through the door 30 minutes later with a smile on his face. It faded when he saw Suzy glaring at him. "What's up?" he asked.

"You sneaky shit," she blurted. "You hired Sarah and didn't say anything to me? I thought you were still thinking about it because I can't imagine that adding someone to our small family would be a detail you'd forget."

"I thought you knew," he said, chagrined. "Or maybe assumed. And it was more like a merger than a hire." He ventured a weak smile.

"Well, just so you know, this phantom who's merged with us - and about whom you just thought I'd conjure up knowledge I could not have - has already raised some money. She called a while ago and said 'the check's in the mail,' or words to that effect."

"Jesus, Suzy, lighten up. I'm sorry. I thought I'd told you."

"And she also told me she was planning to be here next Monday, so you'd better get off your ass and either find her an apartment or find a realtor who can find one."

"I'll find her an apartment myself. We don't need a realtor." He paused. "Did she say how much?"

"No, she didn't say anything about what she expected to pay. Only that it needs to be furnished."

"I mean how much the goddamn contribution is," Boone replied.

"No, she said she did not know how much, only that it would be mailed today."

"Well she gets right on it, wouldn't you say?"

"Yes, and now, like I said, you'd better get right on it. She's going to be highly pissed if she gets here and has no place to hang up her clothes."

"Yes, ma'am, I will get right on it." Boone bowed in an exaggerated way, turned and walked back out the door.

Suzy grinned. She and Boone, it seemed, had always had this kind of easy level of familiarity between them. And both knew it never had and never would go any farther than verbal sparring. Suzy was happily engaged to a cop, a sergeant on the Monterey Police Department. In fact, they were living together in his house overlooking the Pacific and neither talked much about when they would tie the knot. Things were good now and neither wanted to risk damaging that.

When Boone returned just after 4:00 p.m., he was grinning again. As he told Suzy, "When I get off my ass, as you so tactfully put it, I get things done." He tossed a sheet of paper from his pocket notebook on her reception counter and asked her to email Sarah with both addresses. The managers of two apartment buildings – both within walking distance of CFRG's office building – had each agreed to hold a furnished apartment open through the following Monday so Sarah could look them over and choose the one she liked better. She should let Sarah know that, too, he told her.

"Nice to see you get something done for a change," Suzy said with a smile.

Boone was feeling better about himself – and about CFRG - than he had in a long while.

Two days later, Boone was in his office, on the phone with Cooper Courtney, the Board Chairman, filling him on the timeline with Sarah and her assurances that at least one check was on its way already. The mail was delivered to Suzy Dillinger as he was finishing up with Courtney, who was very pleased.

"Oh, my God!" Boone heard Suzy shout from her reception desk just after he had replaced his telephone receiver. He jumped to his feet and raced to the front of the suite, alarmed. There had been two instances when bums, the politically correct social engineers now called them "displaced persons", had come into the office demanding money, food or just a cup of coffee. One had gotten a bit too belligerent and threatened Suzy, who had quickly punched 9-1-1 into her phone.

Two officers, one of which was her fiancé, had arrived within minutes and over the course of the next 48 hours, the bum had been shown the error of his ways in the county lock-up.

But there was nobody around except for Suzy.

"What's wrong," he asked her.

Suzy wordlessly handed him an envelope, which had been slit open and on which was printed the name, address and logo of Environmental Responsibility International. He pulled the check out and his eyes seemed to have trouble focusing.

"Oh, my God!" he parroted. "That girl sure knows how to raise money. I wonder what she did."

"She probably asked," Suzy responded, dead-pan. "And she damn sure did it well."

Then Boone read the letter of transmittal.

Suzy had not even unfolded it, so he read it aloud. Neither could believe, even after hearing the words, that this enormous check would be followed in 30-day intervals by three more just like it. Suzy jumped up and hugged Boone as they virtually danced around the reception area. That was uncharacteristic on both their parts and both were momentarily embarrassed.

Then Boone said, "I guess Sarah wasn't bragging when she said she could raise money. Wow!"

"Yes, wow!" Suzy agreed. "Now, if I may be so bold as to suggest it, isn't it now time to get off your ass and start planning our attack? Now that we've got the money to attack with?" She smiled.

"I think that's a very good idea," he agreed. "And may I suggest that while I'm in my office working that you get off your ass and take that check across the street and put it in the bank before this bunch in Houston changes its mind."

Suzy thought that was a fine idea. She grabbed her purse, hit the back of the check with the deposit stamp and rushed out to the bank. As she left, she put the "Be Right Back" sign in the door's window and locked the door so Boone would not be disturbed.

When Boone went to his office, be called Sarah's cell phone and got the answering service. He decided to leave a message.

"Sarah, it's Boone." His voice, he knew, was over-excited but there was nothing he could do about it. He was excited. "We got the check from ERIN today. Great job! I can't believe you were able to do it so quickly. Suzy and I are looking forward to seeing you Monday. Suzy sent you an email on the apartments we've got on hold."

He paused, then added, "Oh, and if you'd like a rental car, we can set that up, too. Both apartments are walking distance from the office, so I didn't know what you'd prefer. Call if you can, but otherwise I'll see you Monday." He disconnected the call.

Boone sat, wondering how Sarah could raise two million dollars so quickly, and without a grant application detailing CFRG's programs and goals, how it planned to spend the money, the bona fides of the members of its Board of Directors and so forth. A thought crossed his mind, and as quickly flew away. He knew it probably didn't matter. What mattered was that CFRG was saved, at least for now. He started calling the Board members to give them the good news.

Sarah retrieved the message two hours later and decided it was not necessary to return the call. Boone was excited, which was no surprise whatsoever. She would spend the rest of the week wrapping things up with existing clients and packing the clothes she would need when she was in Monterey. She would only take two of her lobbying "uniforms" to the West Coast.

She was at home that evening when her phone rang and the caller ID read, "Amanda." She greeted her warmly.

"I understand that not only do you look like Wonder Woman, but you perform like her, too," Amanda said.

"What are you talking about?" Sarah asked.

"Boone told me about the money," Amanda replied simply.

"Oh, my." Sarah said. "That was quick. And I've never been compared to Wonder Woman before."

"Well, get used to it. That was the most excited I've heard Boone sound since his son was born. And he's really looking forward to working with you, even if he is still nervous. And shy."

"Well, thanks for the kind words, Amanda. And I appreciate your help with opening the door to Boone and with helping me understand him better."

"Any time," Amanda said. "And sorry to run, but I'm close to being late for an interview."

"Until next time, then," Sarah said pushed the "end" key. She felt very good about her budding friendship with Amanda, all the more because she was just not used to having a female friend.

She finished packing what she had already begun to think of as her "California clothes" into two large shipping boxes. She would drop them off at FedEx the next morning and have them sent to Suzy Dillinger at CFRG.

Sarah thought for several minutes about chartering a jet to Monterey, a part of her feeling it would make for a more dramatic entrance into Boone's world. In the end, she decided it would be too much and went online and booked on US Airways, connecting through Phoenix, arriving in Monterey Sunday afternoon. She emailed Boone and Suzy her itinerary and added that Suzy would be receiving a FedEx shipment that was actually her clothes. In the email, she mentioned that she did not think it was necessary to rent a car if the apartments were both in walking distance of the office.

Then she remembered to toss an umbrella into the box for rainy days.

CHAPTER 12

MONTEREY, CALIFORNIA
SUNDAY AFTERNOON

Boone was waiting that Sunday afternoon when Sarah walked off the commuter plane and into the terminal at Monterey Peninsula Airport.

She was not in her uniform today, he noted, instead looking quite "California cool" in designer jeans, an open-collar white shirt, a navy blazer, penny loafers and sunglasses. She was towing a small carry-on and had her Hartmann leather briefcase/purse slung over her shoulder.
If anything, Boone thought she looked better than she did in her power suit. In fact, she left him speechless as she strode up to him, her black hair billowing in her wake and her right hand extended. Sarah had always had a strong grip for a woman and she didn't disappoint him this time either.

"Hi, Boone," she said almost gaily. "Well, here I am. I've made the move and I'm all yours – and CFRG's, of course – for a while."

He greeted her, struck by the double entendre in her words, and held her hand for an extra second or so before relaxing his grip and withdrawing his hand. They were both quite aware of that extra second.

"Why don't we start by going to look at the apartments I found?" he asked. "Then, if either one of them works for you, we'll call Suzy. She wants to meet us at the office when you're ready to get the FedEx boxes."

"That sounds great," she said, "but I hate to make Suzy come to the office on a Sunday."

"Don't be silly." He grinned at her. "You couldn't keep her away. She's very excited about you joining us and she's got the office next to mine all set up for you. At least she hopes it's set up to your liking."

"I'm sure it will be fine, Boone," she said and walked with him to his Toyota Camry. When they were settled, Boone drove her into Monterey and went first to the closer of the two apartment buildings – closer to the CFRG office, in particular. The manager, a stout 50-something woman, led them to an elevator, pushed the button for the fourth – and top - floor, and escorted them into a spacious and airy two-bedroom, two-bath with a balcony and very nice furnishings. From the balcony, Sarah could look down and to the right a bit and see the building housing CFRG. The manager was filling them in on the monthly rent, deposit and lease requirements as they toured the place. Sarah liked the closet space.

After five minutes, Sarah sat down at the kitchen table and pulled out her checkbook. "I won't need to see the other one, Boone. This is perfect." The manager beamed. She extracted the paperwork from her large purse and put them in front of Sarah, pointing to the appropriate places for signatures and initials. She assured Sarah that an out-of-state check would not be a problem. "I now know where you live," she reminded Sarah with a mischievous grin.

Soon, keys in hand, Sarah and Boone were walking toward the CFRG office. Boone had called Suzy while Sarah was signing the 12-month lease. Suzy had raced to the office as soon as Boone had called her and fairly jumped into Sarah's arms as she and Boone walked in. She had already started coffee. She led Sarah down the short hall to her new office and Sarah entered to find a hand-painted banner on the far wall exclaiming, *"Welcome, Sarah, to CFRG."*

The boxes she had shipped by FedEx were in the center of the room and Suzy had scrounged a dolly to make them easier to move to her apartment.

In addition, Suzy had arranged a computer and printer, a supply of pens and pencils, note pads, paper clips and the like. She told Sarah to let her know if she needed anything else. "We've got a fax machine out front," she said pointing with her thumb toward the reception area. "But if you think you'll need one in your office, too, we can arrange that." She stopped herself from adding, *now that we've got some money.*

Boone told Sarah to go ahead and get comfortable, that he would roll the boxes back to her apartment. Sarah tossed him her key and he set off.

Sarah was seated at her desk, sipping the freshly-brewed coffee and organizing the supplies into the proper drawers. Suzy showed her how the computer and CFRG email system worked. "I've set up your email as 'sarah@cfrg.org,' but if you'd like something different, I know how to change it," Suzy said proudly.

"It sounds simple enough that I don't think it would be possible for me to forget it," Sarah said. "Thanks very much, Suzy."

They walked back into the reception area just as Boone returned with the now-empty dolly. He told Sarah that when she and Suzy were finished, he'd be happy to run her to a nearby supermarket to help her stock up on groceries. Suzy announced that she thought they had finished and said she needed to get home. She and "Sergeant Preston," as she usually referred to her fiancé, were going to dinner with another cop and his wife.

Boone was surprised at how grocery shopping with a woman injected an air of intimacy into the relationship. He could not remember grocery shopping with his wife. For her part, Sarah could not remember any man accompanying her to a market, not that she spent a lot of time in markets. Both could sense Boone's increasing comfort level around Sarah, and both were pleased with that.

Boone could not help noticing the treatment Sarah got from other shoppers and from the cashier, because of her looks and charming manner. Sarah liked the gentlemanly way Boone acted – with her and with perfect strangers – and was secretly pleased with his apparent protectiveness of her.

When Boone dropped her at the apartment, he had helped her carry her large haul of groceries and utensils up, he told her to take Monday to get herself settled. He would see her Tuesday. And if she needed his car to look around or shop for anything else she needed, all she had to do was ask.

Surprised at how tired she was as soon as Boone left her place, Sarah uncorked a bottle of Pinot Noir and ran a bath. She soaked, sipped her wine, thought about Boone and Suzy and CFRG and less than ten minutes after getting out of the bath was sound asleep. The beds had come with one set of new sheets. She had already made a note to pick up a spare set.

The next morning, with the French doors to the balcony open and a fresh ocean breeze blowing in gently, Sarah felt refreshed and invigorated.

She started unpacking the FedEx boxes, pleased at her efforts to fold her clothes in such a way that wrinkling from having the boxes heaved around by muscular FedEx crew members was held to a minimum. When she was finished, she walked over to the office and got Boone's car keys. She wanted to orient herself to this beautiful little city and pick up a few more things.

She found a Target and got what she needed.

When she had dropped her purchases off at the apartment, she drove Boone's car to the office to return the keys and decided to check emails from her other accounts.

"I knew you couldn't stay away today," Suzy said.

"You're a quick judge of people, Suzy. That's a compliment."

"Thank you."

"Where's Boone?"

"Getting organized, I think. He's developing a plan to spend some of the money you raised."

"He'd better. Those people are not in the charity business, even though they're incorporated as a charitable organization. If we don't show some activity and results, they can shut the tap off as fast as they turned it on." Suzy nodded knowingly, and Sarah went to Boone's office. The door was open and he waved her in when he saw her.

"Tell me the truth," Boone said when Sarah was seated in front of his desk. "Is that additional $1.5 million real?"

"Yes," she answered with conviction, "and there might very well be more than that if we show progress with this and can demonstrate the need."

"I'm impressed – maybe overwhelmed is a better word – with your having raised two million so quickly."

"I told you I have the contacts and know how to ask."

"Not to mention you're good at it," he said. "I just didn't realize how good."

"So what's the plan going to be?" she asked. The bullshit was over. It was time to get down to business.

"Well, the letter of transmittal made it clear that this grant is tied to our position on oil," Boone began. "Specifically oil exploration and the President's about-face on the issue." Sarah nodded, gestured with her hands for him to go on.

"Since we only have, and I use that word advisedly, two million to start, we need to be realistic about what we can do. I believe in staying inside the known budget for our immediate plans. We can propose what we'd like to do if we had the money as a secondary effort."

Sarah agreed. "Very prudent approach," she said dryly.

"So we can't think in terms of a national advertising campaign with that amount of money, but we can certainly develop a web site on the dangers of oil exploration off-shore and in sensitive areas like Alaska. Develop an electronic newsletter; build our list of emails of people interested in the subject. Maybe include a proposal to do some research into the possible consequences of the oil shale mining in the Rocky Mountain region. And Suzy has figured out all this social marketing stuff that I don't understand. Facebook, Twitter, that kind of thing?"

He looked at Sarah, who shrugged and smiled to acknowledge she didn't know that much about it either but had seen evidence of its potential. She said, "I've never been into that, but I've seen what it can do. The President had a whole social media operation in place during his election campaign. These people get on these sites and blog and chat and the word spreads like wild fire."

"So I'm thinking part of the plan would be to hand that off to Suzy and use some of the money to bring in a back-up secretary/receptionist when we need one. Just part-time, temporary."

"I think that's a great idea," Sarah said. "Suzy impresses me a lot, and more than just as a receptionist."

"And I think we monitor all news related to oil exploration and negative events, such as leaks and safety incidents, and take those opportunities to release statements, blogs and whatever calling public attention to the harm being done when those events occur."

Sarah smiled secretly to herself. That is exactly what she was waiting to hear. She nodded, gestured for Boone to continue. He was on a roll.
"I'm thinking that effort will require no more than two additional people, one to search the Internet daily for stories and one who would draft releases and be our media relations person. Both would do additional things, of course, but those would be their first responsibilities."

"And we should monitor issues involving oil production, refining and transportation as well as exploration. What's next?"

"I agree with that. And we also use our newsletter and releases to praise any Senator, Congressman or state legislator, for that matter, who opposes opening up exploration, and, based on what you just said, who supports tighter controls over production and transportation.

"Then there's our ace in the hole," he said, grinning at Sarah. "Her name is Sarah Cotton and she'll be lobbying on Capitol Hill, in the Energy Department and among the President's supporters." Sarah smiled and nodded. "Perhaps the first order of business for her would be to find some members who would introduce a bill to reverse the President's order." He referred to his notes, then continued.

"Our media relations specialist would also develop information packages for other environmental and conservation organizations and try to get as many of them as possible aboard our train.

"And the only other thing I have at this point is we need to prepare a budget. We haven't needed one in so long it's going to be a chore for me to build one from scratch, but the Board would certainly be more comfortable with one, and I suspect that our friends at ERIN would like to see a report showing how we propose to spend their money."

"That's good," Sarah said. "I'll work with you on the budget, and on that subject, we should plan an adequate budget for travel and expenses, not only for our trips to Washington – both of us – but when any oil-related environmental event occurs, I would like to be on the site, investigating and commenting. It will broaden our exposure and our perceived level of expertise."

"I hadn't thought of that," Boone admitted, "but it's an excellent idea. And I think you're the right one to be on site. God knows the media will pay more attention to you than to me."

"Good. I think we're completely agreed on the initial plan."

"And I think we should have the budget developed and agreed on by the end of the week," Boone said. "I can get the Board to act on it telephonically. Then we can get it to ERIN and see if they have any issues with it."

Sarah smiled again and congratulated herself on her choice of CFRG and Boone Malory as the next step in her life.

By the end of the week, Boone and Sarah had a budget, with the help and input of Suzy. Suzy loved the new direction her job was taking and Boone was continuously amazed at her multitude of talents that became apparent as they worked, at last, toward real goals.

He felt some significant embarrassment that he had not previously recognized her range of skills, her dedication and commitment. As they were working on the budget, the action plan was taking shape on a parallel course, but there was still work to do on the plan after the budget was finalized and Boone presented it to the Board. Approval from that body came quickly and Boone and Sarah co-signed a letter with a copy of the budget to Caldwell Jones at ERIN.

During these days, lunch was brought from a variety of restaurants, delis and sandwich shops in the area into the CFRG Board Room, where the three were doing their work. Sarah noticed that Boone was becoming more comfortable with her on a daily basis. She also noticed that Suzy was developing as a manager, as opposed to her previous role as support staff. When they broke for the day, Sarah would often retire to her office, close the door and work on the remaining business of her ongoing lobbying clients. She had her own personal computer in her office for this work, as well as a variety of devices such as cell phones and smart phones. She continued to dress casually, but could not dress down enough to escape her natural air of self-assurance.

Late one morning, Sarah announced that the working lunches were getting old and she would spring for lunch at a restaurant of Boone's choosing. Suzy, obviously relieved, said she had some errands to run for "Sergeant Preston" and that she would meet them back in the office in 90 minutes.

Boone picked a restaurant on Hartnell Street that he and Sarah could walk to. At the restaurant, the host walked them to a noisy table in the center of the large room when Sarah touched his elbow and pointed to a large open booth in the corner.

"That is reserved for groups of three or larger, madam," he said.

"That's okay," Sarah said with a sideways smile, and started toward the booth. "This will be perfect for us." She and Boone slid into it. The host gave up and walked back to his post at the restaurant's entrance.

"Do you always get your way?" Boone laughed.

"No," she replied quietly, "unless there's a corner booth involved."

"So," he said when the waitress had departed to get their water and iced tea, "how do you think we're doing?"

Realizing the possible double entendre implied in his question, Sarah asked cautiously, "You mean with the planning and all that?"

"Yeah. The planning, the budget, how this guy at ERIN is going to react when he sees it…and anything else that's important. Are we doing okay?"

"I think it's going great, Boone." She paused while the waitress set their drinks on the table and took their lunch orders, and when she departed continued. "In reality, I have to tell you it's going better than I was expecting. You're being very collaborative with Suzy and me. And I have to tell you I'm very pleased with the initiative Suzy is showing. I think she's a great asset."

"I've been surprised at that," Boone said.

Their lunches arrived.

Sarah said, "There's a conference of petroleum geologists in Galveston next month. I'm planning on attending. I want to listen in and see what I can learn. Maybe make a few contacts. And it will give me chance to run into Houston and pay a visit to Caldwell Jones."

"Should I plan on it, too?" Boone asked.

"I don't think it's necessary," Sarah said after a moment's thought. "It would probably be better, in fact, if we divided our time as much as possible. I can hear what they have to say and report that back to you and the Board. Meanwhile, you can stay here with Suzy and keep refining our plan of action. We need to make it portable – in a format we can get it out to other groups and decision-makers quickly – so we need more than just our internal plans."

"Good idea," Boone said. He changed the subject. "Are you getting settled in at the apartment, doing okay in Monterey?"

"Sure am. You didn't tell me about that gym two blocks away. I can walk – or run – to it, so it's been easy to keep up with my exercise program."

Boone assumed, from her toned shape and what she ordered to eat, that she was into healthy living, despite her occasional Turkish cigarette, so having an exercise program was not a surprise.

As they finished their lunch, the conversation turned to idle talk about world events, their dreams for CFRG going forward and how the Board members had reacted to the ERIN grant. When the waitress brought the check to the table, Sarah grabbed it, as she had said she would. Boone could not help his embarrassment at having a woman pick up the tab, but thought, *how often is it that a guy can have a beautiful woman buy your lunch?* On the walk back in the pleasant ocean air, Sarah asked Boone how he picked Monterey for the headquarters of CFRG. She was enjoying one of her Turkish cigarettes as they walked.

Boone turned toward the waterfront and they walked along the piers watching the fishermen, the fishmongers and the tourists. "We lived in the area. And maybe more to the point, the original benefactor of CFRG lived here. Not too complicated."

"We?" Sarah asked. "I was under the impression you're not married."

"Not now," he said quietly. "I'm a widower. My wife and son died in an accident three years ago."

"Oh, Boone, I'm so sorry," Sarah said. "I didn't know that." She could not have explained, even to herself, why she lied to him about that, but made a mental note to let Amanda and Jared know that she had feigned ignorance in case the subject ever came up between Boone and either of them.

"It's okay. That was the toughest thing I hope I ever have to go through, but like they say, time heals. I'm doing better now."

Sarah could see that Boone had grown solemn. "I'm sorry I asked," she said. "I didn't mean to bring up anything painful."

"It's okay, Sarah. Like I said, I'm doing fine now."

But she could see his eyes were watery. She chastised herself for bringing the subject up so soon. Of course, Amanda and Jared had told her about his wife and son and she wanted to get it out in the open between them, but she had done it too soon. In any case, it made her feel very tender toward Boone.

When they reached the CFRG office, she jumped ahead of Boone before he had a chance to open the door for her.

As she held open the door for him, she said, "After you, my leader."

She was smiling warmly.

Boone just smiled shyly and shook his head.

After a little over two weeks, the little group huddled in the CFRG Board room and felt they had their attack plan in shape. Then Boone and Suzy concentrated on finding the right people for the new hires CFRG would need to accomplish what was in the plan while Sarah kept Caldwell Jones of ERIN up to date on their work, all the while planting seeds regarding continued – and additional – funding for CFRG. She also stayed in touch with key senators, congressmen and committee staffers regarding reopened oil exploration and CFRG's concerns.

She also set up appointments with some of them for the days following the conference she planned to attend in Galveston. She would go to Washington from Galveston before returning to Monterey.

Boone, Sarah and Suzy had become more comfortable with each other each day they had worked together and Boone felt certain his new team had gelled. It still surprised him on many levels.

Amanda Baines had been in Santa Barbara doing a follow-up story on the spill from the oil barge *Wheeler* the previous spring. She had driven because she wanted to use a little of her accumulated vacation time to cruise the coast of Central California. She had always loved the scenic old coastal highway.

When she got to Monterey, she planned to stop at CFRG and get Boone's take on the *Wheeler* incident and its aftermath, which she viewed personally as a hell of a lot about nothing. At least nothing more than a near miss. But it would also give her a chance to see Boone and Sarah again.

It was late afternoon when Amanda got to the CFRG office. She could tell immediately that there was a different atmosphere in the office than the last time she'd been there. Suzy jumped up when she saw Amanda come through the door and greeted her with a hug.

"Boone drove up to San Jose earlier this afternoon to meet with some people from Apple," she said. "In addition to the grant, Mr. Jones at ERIN is also funding a new computer system for us. Boone is working it out with Apple to provide what we need this afternoon. Can you believe that?" It took Amanda a moment to remember what ERIN was, but when she had connected it to the cash windfall, she beamed and told Suzy she thought that was wonderful. Then she asked about Sarah.

"She's in and must be working on something confidential because she's got her door closed," Suzy said. "I'll buzz her."

When she replaced her telephone, Suzy said, "She's just finishing an email and will be right out, Amanda. Can I get you coffee or a bottle of water?"

Before Amanda could reply, Sarah burst from her office and walked to Amanda. "It's good to see you, Amanda," she said with genuine warmth.

"What brings you to Monterey?"

Amanda hugged Sarah and told her, "I was down in Santa Barbara doing a follow-up on that barge spill they had last spring."

"Well, how about an early dinner and you can fill me in about your story. I also want to hear how you got along with my friend, 'Good' Deeds," Sarah said. Sarah asked Suzy if she was available to join them, but Suzy demurred, saying that "her cop" would be home shortly after 5:00 p.m. and they had planned dinner.

"Maybe next time," Amanda said, then turned to Sarah and said, "Let's go, and you can tell me how you and Boone are getting along." Suzy rolled her eyes and smiled knowingly at Amanda.

"Let me run in and shut down my computer and we'll walk to the restaurant Boone and I usually go to." She hurried back into her office.

Amanda looked at Suzy and mouthed "Boone and Sarah" with a question in her eyes. Again, Suzy smiled and nodded. She would never say so, in the office or otherwise, but she secretly hoped that something developed between Boone and Sarah. She privately believed both used a dedication to their work to mask voids in their lives.

When the women arrived at the restaurant on Hartnell Street, Amanda asked, "So, you and Boone come here?"

"Yes. The food is very good."

"Breakfast, lunch or dinner?"

Sarah laughed. "Are you asking as a reporter or just being nosy?"

"Both. Does it matter?"

"I guess not. Just lunch."

Amanda nodded, her sly grin aimed squarely at Sarah.

The host, who by now had been well-trained by Sarah, immediately showed them to the large corner booth she favored, and left them with menus after announcing in a grand style the name of their server.

"Would you like a glass of wine?" Sarah asked her. "Since moving to Monterey, I must say that I have become even more of a fan of California wines." Amanda agreed.

"Now, what about the Santa Barbara story?" Sarah asked. "Is there anything more than what I heard at the time? Anything CFRG might be able to use to our advantage?"

"Santa Barbara was lucky," Amanda said. "It could have been far more serious than it turned out to be. It appears from everything I could find that the spill was between 5,000 and 6,000 barrels and could have been ten times that, literally. The barge – it was called the *Wheeler* – was carrying 60,000 barrels.

"But Clean Seas – do you know them, the oil clean-up operation? – got there quickly and cleaned up the majority of what leaked. Plus, Prime Oil had a tanker in the vicinity and was able to off-load the remaining oil from the barge. So Royal Energy got lucky in two ways."

"Did any of the mess make shore?" Sarah asked.

"Nothing that I could discover. And I asked around a lot. But like the report at the time said nothing seems to have reached shore. No wildlife damage, no vegetation, nothing except the hull of the barge."

"Hmmm," Sarah said as she reached for a sip of wine.

"Honestly, Sarah, I don't think there's anything there for CFRG except the potential of what might have been. A 60,000 barrel spill would have been another matter entirely. No way Clean Seas could have saved that much from reaching shore."

Amanda paused, considering what she wanted to say before saying it. "You could almost make the argument that this was a perfectly-planned incident to get lots of press coverage and call attention again to the dangers of offshore oil exploration. Almost like the President's enemies planned it. I don't think that's the case, but it was sure a thought I had as I was looking into all of it."

"What do the people in Santa Barbara think?" Sarah asked after refilling their wine glasses.

"I heard a lot of bitching about the use of barges to transport crude, especially in bad weather," Amanda said slowly, allowing her thoughts to form. "Beyond that, I think if most of them had their way, all of those offshore wells would be capped and closed down. Still, most are resigned to the ones that are there, but they sure don't want any more of them."

"So the bottom line, if I'm reading you right, is that Santa Barbara should be a hotbed of political support, and maybe financial support as well, for CFRG," Sarah said.

Amanda nodded. "Absolutely. But I don't think there's anything CFRG could say publicly at this point. Too much time has gone by, and the people in Santa Barbara were with you even before this spill. Now, tell me about your new life here."

"I'm very happy here, Amanda," Sarah said. "It's so peaceful, laid back, so different from Washington. Boone found me a very nice apartment just a couple of blocks from the office, so I haven't even needed a car to this point. And CFRG is headed in the right direction. We've made enormous progress developing our action plan and budget, both of which Boone really laid out very well, and Suzy and I have been working with him to refine them.

"I'm enjoying working with both of them and, frankly, finding myself dreading the need to go back to Washington. Boone isn't at all as resistant to working with me as I feared he might be. In fact, I think he's growing comfortable with our working together. He's also very passionate about our mission.

"With a rather limited budget – at least limited in the sense we can't yet get into any paid advertising program – we've developed a very credible campaign against the President's oil exploration program. I'll be going to Washington next week, after a conference in Galveston I'm going to, to start the lobbying part of it, and also to try to raise some more cash.

"God, that was more than you ever wanted to know and I've blabbered on enough," Sarah said. "Tell me about your session with Congressman Deeds."

"It went very well," Amanda said. "And thanks again for setting it up. He is a very nice man and was generous with his time. I was with him for over an hour and he answered all my questions about his position on the bill to help bail out California's budget deficit. That was the primary reason for the interview.

"Now, it's your turn again. Tell me about you and Boone – and not as related to CFRG."

"You are persistent, aren't you?"

"It's why I'm a good reporter. Now answer my question. 'No comment' does not look good in a story, remember."

Sarah convulsed into laughter, drank half her glass of water and took another sip of wine. She was starting to get just a bit tipsy and could feel it. "There really isn't much to tell," she said weakly. "Like I told you, he's less nervous and more himself than he was during our interviews. We're working as a team, and that includes Suzy, who's a real gem."

"And?" Amanda persisted.

"Well, since you're so obviously looking for something titillating, I'll admit that we are going to lunch together almost every day. We started by just ordering in and eating in the office. He's such a gentleman too, opening doors for me, holding my chair, things like that. He's even opened up about himself to me, about his wife and son, for instance. He's still hurting over that, and I did not let him know you or Jared had told me about it."

Sarah felt strange in the extreme, talking with someone else about her relationship with anyone, but somehow Amanda seemed different. For one thing, she was a childhood friend of Boone's.

"My goodness, Sarah," Amanda said. "He's going to lunch with you every day? You'll need to keep me posted on the progress of this affair." Sarah hotly denied that it was an affair, and Amanda could not help noticing that she was blushing as she did so.

The conversation returned to the things both of them liked best about Monterey as they ate their dinner and finished their wine.

Sarah walked Amanda back to her car before turning in the direction of her apartment.

CHAPTER 13

PANAMA CITY, PANAMA
MARCH, 2009

The dry season was almost over, and large, ugly, very black clouds swirled by as Akrum al-Kahtani and his daughter, Zara, who, as always, was dressed in her traditional Arab abaya, finished a very nice lunch in the restaurant which was situated on the top floor of the 5-star hotel in which they had adjoining suites.

After lunch, they rode the elevator down one floor and went into Zara's suite. Soon, the door chime indicated the arrival of the party who would be joining them for the afternoon. When Zara answered the door, a fairly non-descript man with black hair and an easy smile, entered. His name was Jet Jamieson, who was 37 years old and whose mother – unmarried at the time he was born – had named him Jet as soon as she laid eyes on the mop of shiny black hair he was born with.

He was a key member of the Akrum al-Kahtani organization his daughter had created in Jackson Hole, Wyoming, the previous month. None of the oil magnates who were part of the organization would have recognized Jet, but neither would they wish to. They were more than happy to have al-Kahtani do the "operational work," as they called it. It was called plausible deniability should the proverbial shit hit the fan.

Zara had called this meeting for only the three of them. She had developed an inventive plan to stage an oil spill near Galveston, Texas.

Today's meeting was to hear a status report from Jet on his plans to carry it out. Zara was the planner, methodical and thorough. She more or less trusted her father and Jet to implement her plans, but she always watched over and controlled the operations. It was her style, even when her father showed his exasperation with her. In fact, her father seldom questioned her. He knew she was brilliant in ways he could never hope to be. Had she been born a man, he knew, she would already have risen to the highest levels in the Saudi government, despite her American mother.

"Where are we?" Zara opened simply.

Akrum spoke first, telling them about the *El Gitano*, a Panamanian-registered single hull oil tanker of indeterminate age. Using one of his many documented identities, he had secured a one year "bare boat" charter. That meant they got the boat. Only the boat. No crew, no fuel, no cargo.

"Is it seaworthy, Akrum?" Zara asked. She never referred to him, in the presence of others, especially, as "father" or "Ab," always Akrum. In fact, she scarcely thought of the man as her father. He was a business associate, little more.

"Yes," he said. "It is old – the owners are not able to tell me just how old – but I was given a short cruise aboard her. She is functional and can easily be modified to suit our purposes."

"And the crew?" Zara asked, looking at Jet.

"I found a Venezuelan captain who is familiar with tankers and with the waters of the Gulf of Mexico," Jet responded immediately. Like Akrum, he had a variety of identities, fully documented, listing various names and nationalities.

"And the crew?" Zara repeated, impatience dripping from her words.

"The captain assures me he has an able Venezuelan crew, and that, if any of them becomes unavailable, he can easily recruit any others he needs."

"What about marine insurance?" she asked as if ticking off items on a checklist. She was doing just that, even though the checklist was in her head.

"Secured," Jet said as Akrum nodded.

"Yes," Akrum continued. "In fact, it is actually over-insured, by some three million dollars."

"And why the excess insurance?" Zara asked. "Or perhaps more to the point, what happens to the excess proceeds when something happens to the *El Gitano*?""In that eventuality," Akrum said flatly, "I'll file a claim for the full amount and use the normal proceeds to pay off the ship's owners. The excess coverage will provide us the funds to pay the owners a one million dollar bonus. The rest will be split between Mendoza, Captain Loumena and the crew bonuses. All will be paid, of course, through our offshore account."

"Wise," Zara muttered. "The status of the oil contracts?"

Akrum recounted his contact with Guillermo Mendoza, an old friend and associate in various business schemes – legal and otherwise - who was with Petroleos de Venezuela, S.A., more commonly known by the initials, PDVSA. Mendoza had contracted for the sale of 335,000 barrels.

"The *El Gitano* will be loaded with 350,000 barrels at the Jose Oil Port, "Akrum went on, "but as you know the sale documents will reflect only 335,000 barrels. The *El Gitano* will deliver 335,000 barrels to the Louisiana Offshore Oil Port." They were all aware that the oil port, known as LOOP, was located 18 miles south of Grand Isle, Louisiana. It was the tanker's only option as it was no longer allowed in U.S. ports since the *El Gitano* was a single-hull tanker.

Offshore oil ports were set up to accommodate those tankers so disallowed.

"And once it has offloaded the known quantity of crude at LOOP?" Zara asked, directing her gaze now at Jet, who would be in charge of the operation from that point on.

"When the *El Gitano* leaves LOOP," Jet said, "it will proceed west and when it crosses the underwater pipeline between the Great Mossy XX oil platform and the Galveston fuel terminal, it will begin dumping the remaining crude it has aboard, 15,000 barrels, give or take. About half of it – 7,500 barrels or so – will by that point be in those special plastic bags we've developed. If they work as advertised, they will first submerge, then begin dissolving on the sea floor and release the oil over the next 24 hours.

"We'll do this on a moonless night and the plan calls for the *El Gitano* to cross the pipeline at midnight, or close to it. The ship will then continue on a heading toward Panama after it has dumped the oil. I'll be aboard and confirm the spill with the Huff twins by 2:00 a.m."

"Sounds good, Jet," Zara said as she doodled on a pad. She never took notes or put anything to paper that she did not have too. She knew that anything that was on paper could be used as evidence if problems arose.

Jet nodded, continued. "The Huff twins will both have the identity badges of a special safety inspector by the name of Earl Bowfin. You know, like the World War II submarine?"

Zara looked at him like he was speaking Swahili, and Akrum just shrugged, indicating he had also missed the point. "It's not important," Jet went on. "One of our Earl Bowfins will call in an emergency rupture in the pipeline. At this point, the pressure gauges – both on the Great Mossy XX platform and at the onshore fuel terminal – will have 'malfunctioned.' Those malfunctions will cause both oil pressure gauges to indicate that a rupture has occurred, which, of course, will automatically shut down the platform pumps. One of the Earls will alert the platform superintendent and the fuel terminal manager of the rupture and resultant leak."

"I assume from what you are saying that you'll have one each of the Huff twins – as this man Bowfin – on the platform and at the fuel terminal simultaneously," Zara said.

"Bingo," Jet said in his usual casual but efficient manner. "We'll have a helicopter on the platform that will be there appearing to be making routine deliveries. It will take the 'platform Earl' back to Galveston."

"And the 'terminal Earl'?" Zara asked. She easily tired of Jet's word games but put up with them because she knew he was very good at planning and carrying out operations like this.

"He'll stay at the fuel terminal that morning, doing his best to add to the confusion of the situation. He'll act panicky, shout questions, demand answers, that kind of crap. After he's stirred things up as much as he thinks he can, he'll just slip away and get out of the terminal before he's discovered."

"Is there a real Earl Bowfin?" Akrum asked. He loved the intricate twists and turns of the operations his daughter conceived and Jet refined into operational plans.

"There is," Jet responded with a smile. "However, he's assigned to the refinery at Cherry Point, Washington. The reason we selected him is that we know he'll be on a vacation cruise with his wife at the time we're doing this.

"After the Huff twins have departed their respective scenes, they will both call in anonymous tips to key media outlets, the Coast Guard and the office of the Texas Oil Spill Prevention and Response Program. They'll make it sound like they're Mossy employees and, for obvious reasons, don't want their names used. They'll be on throw-away cell phones when they make those calls."

"And I assume the phones will be disposed of as soon as they have made the calls?" Zara asked.

"At the bottom of Galveston Bay," Jet confirmed.

Akrum looked a little troubled and Zara, picking up on it as usual, asked what was on his mind.

"Are we not running a risk having two men with the same identity in two different places at the same time?" he asked. "Will that not come out in the investigation?"

"It's possible, but not likely," Jet said, now quite serious. "Zara and I talked about it and weighed the possibility of it coming out against the problem of trying to find two separate identities that would hold up. And in the end, we decided it really doesn't matter anyway. Both the twins will be long gone. And once it's discovered that there really wasn't a leak from the pipeline, Mossy Oil's investigation will shift to looking into faulty gauges and monitoring equipment, while the Coast Guard and Texas authorities will focus on finding out about ships in that area that may have been leaking.

"Since we'll have to modify the *El Gitano* to allow it to dump that much oil that quickly, it cannot be allowed to be found and inspected. Therefore, when it reaches the Sigsbee Deep – the deepest spot in the Gulf of Mexico at over 12,000 feet - it will have a massive inert gas explosion that will cause her to buckle in the middle and sink quickly."

Akrum nodded, his face grave. "And the crew?" he asked.

"Will be rescued," Zara jumped in. "It will happen that the tanker PDVSA Goliat will be within 30 miles of the *El Gitano* when it explodes. Jet will be still be aboard and will see to the readiness of the lifeboats before he triggers the explosion. Captain Loumena will not list Jet on his crew manifest, of course, and will arrange for the captain of the Goliat to absorb him into his crew until he can slip ashore in Venezuela."

Akrum continued playing the devil's advocate. "Since the satellites will clearly show the *El Gitano* had crossed the underwater pipeline, will there not be a risk with the captain and crew?"

"They are being paid well to keep their mouths shut," Zara said. "That is why Loumena has handpicked each man. And, in addition to the fact that we are paying nearly double the wage they would earn on any other tanker, thanks to your over-insuring the ship, each will receive an annual bonus – without it coming out of your pockets - for the next three years if nobody opens their mouth about dumping the oil. Therefore, we add peer pressure to greed and I think the two motivations will serve to keep the men quiet. Mendoza and his men are also quite aware of the possibility of future work with us."

"And the news media?" Akrum asked.

"The Goliat and the crew are all Venezuelan and they are returning to Venezuela," she said. "There is no chance of the Venezuelan media covering the story or of any outside media – or maritime authorities, for that matter – getting to them down there."

"Will we also notify the media of the sinking of the *El Gitano*?" Akrum asked. "There will surely be some oil leaking from it as it goes down."

"No," Zara said. "All media contacts about additional oil sightings will be related to the Galveston pipeline leak. Hopefully, the *El Gitano* will be overshadowed by the pipeline leak and thus will get little notice. We certainly do not want any attempts to inspect it because of our modifications to it."

"And let me remind you both that I do not want any loss of life, hopefully not even any injuries, in this facilitation," Zara concluded and stared at both men. Both nodded in understanding. Zara had forcefully made the point that these operations, or "facilitations," as she liked to call them, would only be effective as long as nobody died.

"And the timing?" Akrum asked. "Are we still thinking August?"

"The second week of August," Zara said. "It must be the second week of August, when that convention of petroleum geologists is meeting in Galveston. That will add immeasurable drama to the event." She looked at Jet. "Do you see any problem with that?"

"None whatsoever," Jet said immediately.

"Very good. Let us make it happen, both of you. I must return to the States tonight. Jet, make sure Akrum is completely familiar with the plan." Jet and Akrum nodded and the meeting was over.

CHAPTER 14

Sarah Cotton never appeared visibly frazzled or rattled, but Suzy Dillinger could tell she was close to being overwhelmed with all the things she was trying to do at once. She stuck her head in Sarah's office and asked if she could do anything to help.

Sarah was reading the agenda for the upcoming meeting of the U.S. Association of Petroleum Geologists in Galveston. She had registered for it but suddenly realized what she had missed.

"Good grief!" Sarah exclaimed. "I haven't made travel arrangements." She handed a sheet from the registration packet she was reviewing to Suzy and asked her, "Can you get me reservations in the headquarters hotel and airline tickets, Suzy?"

"No problem," Suzy responded quickly. "Are the dates on there?"

"Yes, and I'd like to arrive the day before the conference starts and stay over two days after it adjourns. I want to meet with Caldwell Jones and I'd like to see some of that famous South Texas coastline while I'm there."

"And how about Boone?" Suzy asked.

"He won't be going," Sarah said. "We talked about it and agree it's better that we spread ourselves out rather than being in all the same places. And Boone's got so much to do working with the new web page designer. That web page is absolutely critical to us."

Boone was walking by just then and stuck his head in. "I won't be going where?"

"That conference of petroleum geologists in Galveston," Sarah said. "We talked about it right after I started here, remember?"

"Yeah, I do, but I don't remember why you want to go," Boone said.

"Just hoping to circulate and see what I can pick up from all those geologists that we can use to support our positions." She paused, looking mischievously from one to the other. "And...I've always wanted to have an affair with a petroleum geologist. I hear they're wild men. And either of you would just get in my way."

Boone grinned. "Well, good luck on both counts, then," he said. "Send us a postcard from your beachfront villa on South Padre Island."

Suzy piped up. "What about me? Maybe I could find a petroleum geologist, too."

"Oh, sure," Sarah retorted. "And what would you tell Sergeant Preston?"

They all laughed. The bond between the three of them was now secure, and Sarah loved it. She realized that, increasingly, she loved Monterey, too, and did not relish the idea of leaving it, even for a week.

The three of them were, without question, making progress on getting the CFRG messages out. Three new staff members were all showing great promise. The website was up and getting its share of hits, even though it was still being refined, and the first of the monthly Internet newsletters had just gone out.

CHAPTER 15

GALVESTON, TEXAS
AUGUST, 2009

On a Sunday, Sarah flew into George Bush Intercontinental Airport and rented an SUV for the hour-plus drive – depending on traffic – to Galveston. She found the Galvez Hotel and Spa without too much trouble and checked in. It was the headquarters hotel, so all the convention events would be in it.

Her room had a nice view of the Gulf, where she intended to spend some time on the beach. After hanging up her clothes, she rode the elevator back down to the lobby and located the registration and hospitality room where the geologists were signing in. She reported in and was handed a packet, which included a name tag with her first name in enormous letters, another program of events and the usual Convention and Tourist Bureau propaganda which supposedly listed the main attractions around downtown Galveston, but was actually a listing of those attractions that paid the most in annual dues and advertising to the Bureau.

She was greeted by one of the convention hosts, a pot-bellied, middle-aged Texan who introduced himself, between faintly leering glances, as Bobbie Ray Roberts. Why, she wondered, did Texans seem so damned attracted to two first names? Male or female, it didn't matter.

Bobbie Ray peered at her name tag and asked, "Are you traveling alone, Miss Sarah?"

"Yes," Sarah said, "I am."

"Well, if you need any help finding your way around or need any introductions, you just let me know, little lady. I've lived in Galveston all my life. Know every nook and cranny." Sarah thanked him but would rather have spent an hour beating on her thumb with a hammer than to spend ten minutes walking around Galveston with Bobbie Ray Roberts. She masked that feeling, however, knowing full well that it was entirely possible that Bobbie Ray could be of some help to her as the week went on.

She smiled one of those smiles calculated to accelerate the heartbeat of a man like Bobbie Ray and told him she had been following the story about the President's order opening up offshore drilling and the reaction to that. She said she had conflicting feelings on it and would really like to know what some of the experts at the conference felt.

"Do you know any geologists that are opposed to the President's position?" she asked.

"I do indeed, little lady," he said, "and I'd be happy to make the introductions, but first let me buy you lunch and show you a little Texas hospitality."

"You can just leave the registration area?" she asked, at least somewhat surprised.

"Little lady, it really isn't much of a difficult choice. Having lunch with a beautiful lady like you or registering a bunch of old geologists." He motioned to the ladies at the registration table. "They can handle it better'n I can, anyhow." He grabbed Sarah's arm and steered her toward the dining room next door.

My God, Sarah thought to herself, *I'm being hit on by an overweight Texas shit-kicker, but he is a petroleum geologist, a host of the conference, and will be good for introductions.* Her smile had never failed her, and it hadn't this time either.

When they were seated, he said, "I've never heard of the company you work for, Miss Sarah. What do you do?" She spent several minutes explaining CFRG, its moderate approach to environmental issues and what she did. She told him she hoped to make CFRG a temperate voice with which the oil industry could live, especially as compared with the alternatives. Sierra Club. Friends of the Earth. Greenpeace. Pure Earth International. He recoiled at the mention of each name.

Then he startled her by asking if she wanted to see a couple of pictures of his wife and kids. When she indicated she would like that very much, he snapped out a long plastic folder containing perhaps a dozen shots of a heavy but attractive woman, three kids who looked spaced between about 12 and 16 and a collection of pets.

"Greatest wife and kids in the world," he said, surprising her again. "And most of the animals are not bad either, except for those two cats." He thrust a thick finger at one photo. "Ying and Yang. Dumb as a box of rocks. Can you imagine two cats in Texas with names like that. I'd prefer Dead and Buried." He laughed heartily at his humor, which he obviously liked to practice with a new audience.

Sarah smiled, surprised at how inaccurate she had been in her original assessment of Bobbie Ray.

As they ate their lunch, Bobbie Ray assured her he thought there were those in the "bidness" who would welcome a group like CFRG as a moderate voice for environmental concern, and that there were geologists who had serious reservations about exploring in some of the "sensitive" areas. He promised to introduce her to as many as he could ferret out as holding either view.

"Just keep me posted on your whereabouts and availability to meet with some of them," he directed her.

Sarah gave him another of her big smiles, thanked him and grabbed the lunch check when the waitress delivered it. She got Bobbie Ray's business card and told him she would put him on CFRG's contact list.

She spent the rest of the afternoon relaxing on the beach and taking advantage of the very nice spa in the hotel. When she returned to her room, of course, she had the usual jumble of emails and phone messages, CFRG business and otherwise.

Late Monday afternoon, Sarah was coming out of a panel discussion on the most active fault lines in the earth's crust when she literally bumped into Bobbie Ray Roberts. He excused himself profusely and asked Sarah if she would be able to join him and a group of his friends – all conference attendees – for dinner. He told her that, because they were just geologists and not CEOs, the dinner would be Dutch treat.

It would be at a nice restaurant a block from the hotel, and he pointed in its direction.

"Are you sure a group of petroleum geologists would want someone like me intruding on their dinner," she asked.

"Little lady, I can tell you one thing for sure," he responded. "If there's anything a bunch of geologists would enjoy; it would be having someone from the real world at the table." She agreed and they set 6:30 p.m. as the time to gather in the bar at the restaurant.

Sarah walked into the bar at precisely 6:30 to find Bobbie Ray and his friends huddled at one end of the bar, each holding a bottle of beer in his hand. Sarah had noticed immediately in the morning's opening session that there were virtually no women in the ranks of petroleum geologists. She had no problem with that.

Bobbie Ray introduced Sarah to each of the other six men. When they were seated for dinner, he introduced her again and told them she was with a group called Citizens for Responsible Growth. He told them he'd only heard about the group the day before, when he'd met Sarah as she registered, but he assured them that he liked what he'd heard about the tonality of the organization, compared especially to "the crazies."

After dinner was ordered and the salads served, Sarah asked the men what they thought of the President's order opening exploration and drilling virtually anywhere, including in sensitive areas. She quickly learned there were three kinds of people at the table: geologists employed directly by oil or natural gas companies, consultant geologists who worked for one or more of those companies, and academics, university professors who taught geology or subjects related to it.

She also quickly learned that the five, including Bobbie Ray who worked directly for the oil and gas industry, either as employees or consultants, tended to be quite non-committal, even guarded, in their responses. The two academics, however, were of a different stripe altogether.

Dr. Steven Summer was a professor at Tulane University in New Orleans and Dr. Parker Firth was with Rice University in Houston. Both expressed strong opposition to the President's action. Sarah asked if either, or both, would be willing to write an article or white paper for CFRG's newsletter on the risks inherent in the program.

"Is there a fee involved?" Summer asked.

"That can be arranged," Sarah said and flashed her smile, "but remember that we're just a small non-profit."

"I wrote a paper on this exact subject four or five years ago," Firth said. "Of course, that was long before this President was in office, before most of us had ever heard of him. I presented the paper at this convention, as a matter of fact. I think it was in Kansas City that year, if I remember right."

"I remember that," Bobbie Ray said. "Caused a bit of a stir among some of the members."

"In any case," Firth went on, "I'd be happy to make that available to you. I'd like to review it first, to see if any updates are called for."

"Might be interesting," Summer said, looking across the table at Firth, "to have me write my paper without reviewing yours, then compare my concerns today with those you articulated a few years ago."

Firth nodded, and Sarah exclaimed, "That would just be terrific. Exactly the kind of dialogue CFRG is trying to encourage." She noticed that the others at the table were growing a bit uncomfortable with this three-way conversation, and suggested to Summer and Firth that they meet the next morning to discuss the details. They both agreed, knowing that the details would include their fees. They would meet in the hotel coffee shop at 9:30 a.m.

When the checks were delivered to the table and the tabs were settled, the group walked back to the hotel. Sarah quietly thanked Bobbie Ray for including her. She told him that meeting Summer and Firth made her trip to Galveston worthwhile to CFRG if she learned nothing else during the conference.

Bobbie Ray bowed and mimed doffing a hat and told her to think nothing of it, that he might have reason to seek her help in the future. She told him, "Any time. You have my card."

The next morning, Sarah was sitting in front of her laptop composing an email to one of the associates in her old firm in Washington. The man had asked for her take on a recent turn of events affecting the status of FDA trials for a new product developed by one of her former clients.

She was concentrating hard, quite conscious of her moral, if not legal obligation to help the firm and her old clients make the smoothest transition possible. After all, she had not given them a whole lot of notice. She had switched on the television to catch the early news, as was her normal routine, and she was paying close attention to it. The client work was pushed away and she was focusing on a breaking story on a Houston station.

Her focus was interrupted by the ringing of the room's telephone.

She answered it to hear the baritone voice of Dr. Steven Summer. "Have you been watching the news?" he asked.

"Yes," she responded warily, "I've been watching. I assume you're talking about the oil pipeline leak."

"Yes," Summer said gravely. "Dr. Firth and I both want to follow this story for a while, so I'm calling to ask if we can postpone our meeting this morning. Perhaps later this afternoon or tomorrow the picture will be a bit clearer." Sarah readily agreed, of course, and they hung up.

She snapped up her remote and turned up the volume on the television. She had selected one of the Houston stations rather than CNN or Fox because she thought that she would get more reliable reports from local reporters who knew the subject with which they were dealing.

Sure enough, the Houston channel had gone to exclusive coverage of a reported oil spill in the Gulf southeast of Galveston. Just as she turned her attention back to the TV, the channel broke away for "a word from our sponsors." Knowing that meant a string of at least six commercials, Sarah finished her email and fired it off into cyberspace, then put her laptop into sleep mode and focused her attention back on the television.

It seemed that there was an oil spill of undetermined size that was reported to be coming from an underwater pipeline owned by Mossy Oil, Limited. Details, the somber-faced but perfectly-coiffured young woman said, were sketchy. Her partner, a somber-faced black man with a shiny shaved head, agreed but assured the audience that they would "stay on top of this breaking story" until all the details came out.

Sarah picked up her cell phone and hit her speed-dial button for Boone's cell. It was two hours earlier in California and Boone would probably not yet be in the office, but she was sure he would be awake, probably having coffee while he read the morning paper in his kitchen.

He saw her name on the face of his phone as he was flipping it open. "Hi, Sarah," he said cheerily. "How's Galveston?"

"The conference is great, and I've met some people who may be very helpful to us, I think," she said. "But I'll fill you in on that later. The reason I called so early is that the local news is reporting a major – their word – oil spill that's coming from a Mossy Oil underwater pipeline southeast of here."

"How big a spill?" he asked, feeling a sense of excitement grow in his gut.

"Not sure. They apparently don't have that much detail yet. But Mossy is headquartered in Houston and has an office in Galveston, so I'm going to drive over there as soon as we hang up and see what I can find out. They may have statements or releases they're handing out, but there will for sure be a lot of media there and I'll listen to their gossip.

"Then, if I can, I'd like to rent a helicopter to fly me out to the rig where it started and try to follow the spill toward shore. And I'll take pictures."

"Can you get a chopper on short notice like this?"

"I think so. There are a lot of them around because they service all the drilling platforms. But I'm probably not the only one who thought about it so before I go to Mossy I'll try to get that lined up. It will cost a lot of money, Boone, but that's why I wanted a contingency fund in the budget. It allows us to look into incidents like this and not depend on the media or others for our information."

"I agree," Boone said without hesitation. "And it will look good on our activity report to ERIN, so good luck finding a chopper. And let me know whatever you get. I'd like to get a statement out to the media and our supporters pointing out that this is exactly the kind of problem that will get worse because of the President's about-face."

"That was my plan," she said.

"Do you need anything more in the way of assistance?

"Not right now, Boone. I'll let you know if I do."

They disconnected and Sarah awoke her computer and got on Google, looking for the helicopter rental service in Galveston that had been referred to her. She found what she wanted and made another call. A chopper had been reserved for her.

The Mossy Oil office in Galveston was small and served mainly to support the oil terminals and storage facilities in the area. Sarah didn't expect them to have much information, but she thought she could at least get inside the building. At the Houston headquarters, guards would keep people like her out of the building. She did not, after all, even have media credentials.

The Galveston office, it turned out, could not, or would not, provide any information at all and referred her to the home office. She knew going to Houston would be a waste of time so she went back to the hotel, opened her laptop and accessed her contacts directory. There she found what she was looking for.

Gabe Wenzel was Mossy Oil's Public Affairs Director, which was a fancy title for chief lobbyist. She had met him several times in Washington, but knew he spent almost all his time in Houston, using hired guns like her for their day-to-day work in Washington. In fact, one of her former associates did a lot of the Mossy work in D.C.

She called him from her cell phone, hoping his caller ID would get her through to him. He was sure to be frazzled with all the bad news breaking.

But luck was with her. Wenzel was just concluding a call with his boss, Dan Mirza, when his cell buzzed and he saw "Sarah Cotton" appear on its screen.

"Sarah, what a surprise," he said by way of greeting.

"Hi, Gabe. I just heard about the accident. I'm in Galveston for a meeting and it just came over the news. How bad is it?"

"The only thing we know for sure is that the leak is apparently coming from an underwater pipeline running from one of our platforms, Great Mossy XX, to the onshore fuel terminal. Why? I thought your clients were mostly pharmaceuticals."

"It's more in the way of a personal interest, Gabe, and it will stay between us. Again, any idea of how bad the spill is?"

"No idea at this point and I don't think anyone else does, either. We're busting our butts looking into it, though. You can bet on that."

"Thanks, Gabe. I know you're busy, so I'll let you go. I appreciate your time."

Sarah went downstairs, retrieved her SUV, and drove to Scholes International Airport, where Oil Services Helicopters operated a large charter operation, obviously mostly in the service of the companies operating and supplying the offshore oil platforms that formed, in essence, a sprawling offshore city along the Texas and Louisiana coastline.

Sarah checked in at the counter and was introduced to the pilot who would be assigned to her. When she told the pilot, a weathered man named Tim Bannister, that she wanted to fly out to the Great Mossy XX platform, then along the route of the underwater pipeline, she was assured he knew exactly where to go, that he had been out there earlier that morning to fly a Mossy Oil safety inspector off the platform.

"That's curious," Sarah said. "I'd have thought you'd be flying safety inspectors to, not from, the platform."

"He said he thought the problem was in the pipeline itself, and when he got the platform shut down there was nothing else he could do there."

"Oh," Sarah mused. "That makes sense, I guess."

Bannister was soon pointing ahead to indicate he had Great Mossy XX in sight. As they approached, Sarah, sitting in the left seat, asked Bannister to circle the platform so she could take some pictures. She had told him she just wanted to see it, not land on it. When she had snapped 20 or more pictures of Great Mossy XX from various angles, she asked Bannister to fly along the route of the underwater pipeline heading toward the fuel terminal. Two news helicopters were also circling Great Mossy XX and more were certain to be on the way.

Halfway to shore, Bannister spotted the oil slick and pointed to it. Again, she asked him to circle while she took more shots from all angles. She could clearly see oil bubbling to the surface and Bannister told her over the headphones that the bubbling oil meant the pipeline was still leaking. Sarah gestured with her thumb for him to take it down lower so she could get a closer look.

When they were flying at just 500 feet above the surface, Bannister said, "Looks like it's drifting outward, into the Gulf, not toward the shore. That's a lucky break."

Coast Guard vessels, with their distinctive orange stripes on gleaming white ships, were easy to spot, and there were several of them in the area. Then Sarah spotted the clean-up ships of the Texas Oil Prevention and Response Program. The Texas flags painted on their funnels made them almost as easy to spot as was the Coast Guard.

After circling for a few minutes, the air became more congested with news helicopters and Sarah told Bannister he could head back to the airport. She had seen what she had come to see, and, she thought privately, what she'd hoped to see. The leak was not likely to do much, if any, damage to the coastline, but it would still make great press for CFRG.

Back in her SUV, Sarah turned on her cell phone and called the CFRG number. She had turned the phone off while she was in the helicopter, at Bannister's request. Something about interfering with the instruments.

Suzy answered the phone and Sarah asked her if Boone was available. "He is," Suzy said. "Hey, I heard about that oil spill. Great timing, with you already in Galveston and all."

"Unbelievable," Sarah agreed.

"Let me get Boone for you. He just hung up. Been on the phone all morning. This is big."

Boone came on the line and Sarah began her report. "I just got off the chopper. We flew over the platform and circled the leak. I have a lot of photos and some of them will be damaging. I don't think any of the oil will reach Texas waters, let alone the shoreline, but it will still be enough to make our point about offshore drilling…"

"Did you get anything from Mossy?" Boone interrupted.

"No, when I talked with them, all they had was the name of the platform. Nothing on the size of the leak or possible causes. I still haven't heard anything about those numbers, not even speculation to this point. Why don't I draft a release and after you've reviewed it I can release it from right here in Galveston. It should get a lot of attention. You can cover the national media from your end, although some of them will be descending on Galveston soon."

"Good idea," Boone said. "Anything else?"

"I'm sure Mossy will have a news conference soon, and I'll be there. If I can, I'll ask any questions the media misses, but my guess is they won't miss much. I'll also list my cell number on the release and make myself available for comment here."

"Great timing," Boone said, "with you being in Galveston already."

"Isn't it?" she said. "If we play this right, it will be great for us. As it turns out, I couldn't have planned it any better."

She smiled wickedly to herself.

Instead of a news conference, Mossy Oil released a statement mid-afternoon on that same day. Copies were flying around the Galvez, where it was big news, especially among those gathered for the conference of petroleum geologists. Sarah ran into Bobbie Ray, who handed her a copy. Sarah took it to her room and read it carefully.

Early this morning, the monitoring equipment on the underwater pipeline between the Mossy Oil platform, Great Mossy XX, and the Mossy fuel terminal in Galveston reported a significant drop in pressure.

As soon as the drop in pressure was recorded, the system automatically shut down and all pumping ceased. An oil slick has been observed above the route of the pipeline, approximately 18 miles offshore.

Both the United States Coast Guard and the Texas Oil Prevention and Response Program were immediately alerted and the oil clean-up has already begun. Mossy Oil engineering and safety personnel have also begun an investigation, and internal testing of the pipeline is in process at this time, using robotic testing devices.

As the investigation and the clean-up progress, we will provide further information. It is Mossy Oil's policy, in instances of this sort, to provide full disclosure of all relevant information obtained through our internal investigation to Federal and State authorities, to the media and to the public.

Until further information is developed, Mossy Oil will direct all of its efforts to the clean-up of the oil and to determining the cause of this unfortunate incident.

Sarah sighed. She would like to have asked questions. In public. In a news conference. But Mossy was too smart for that. She couldn't blame them. They were doing exactly what she would do in the same circumstances.

Wednesday morning, the Houston Chronicle carried a story on the bottom left side of its front page. The headline read,

OIL LEAK REPORTED ON OFFSHORE MOSSY PIPELINE

Thought to be Small Leak, Now Contained

The story calmly recited the facts and did not differ very much from the Mossy Oil statement. The story included a few quotes from Mossy CEO Daniel Mirza, who expressed his pride and thanks for the quick work of Mossy personnel, the Coast Guard and the Texas authorities.

That same morning, a large banner headline and story at the top of the front page of the Washington Post read,

RUPTURED UNDERWATER OIL PIPELINE LEAKING; THOUSANDS OF BARRELS OF OIL IN GALVESTON BAY; BEACHES, McFADDEN NATIONAL WILDLIFE RANGE THREATENED

Galveston, TX - A major oil pipeline connecting a large offshore drilling platform and the Galveston refinery owned by Mossy Oil, Ltd. has ruptured.

The pipeline was shut down when monitoring equipment reported a sharp drop in pressure, but not before a huge oil slick was created. The U.S. Coast Guard and clean-up crews from the Texas General Land Office are at the site and are attempting to stem the tide of the slick and minimize damage, as much as possible.

Sarah Cotton, spokesperson for the conservation group, Citizens for Responsible Growth, who was in Galveston attending a meeting and saw the huge slick first-hand, said, "This is another major disaster that threatens our wildlife, beaches and oceans. Such disasters are the inevitable consequences of unrestrained and reckless oil exploration and drilling in environmental-

ly-sensitive areas."

Ms. Cotton said that she and CFRG have pledged to "continue to fight the President's ill-advised lifting of the ban on expanded exploration in such areas." She questioned how many of this kind of environmental disasters it would take for the Congress to override the President and re-institute drilling restrictions.

The story, which jumped to page eight and continued for two full pages, was more a stinging indictment of the oil industry in particular, and big business in general, than it was a news story about a single incident. In other words, it was a prototypical *Washington Post story.*

But it served to thrust Sarah Cotton and CFRG a step closer to the major leagues of environmental activism.

After talking to the *Post* reporter Tuesday afternoon, Sarah had turned on her laptop and begun drafting a CFRG news release. It had taken on added urgency, given the possibility she would be quoted the next morning in the single newspaper read by every one of the people who count in Washington. She used many of the same words and phrases she had used with the Post reporter.

When she had fussed over it for more than an hour and it finally felt right to her, she had emailed it to Boone. Less than 20 minutes later, Boone had called Sarah.

"This looks great, Sarah," he had said without preamble when she had answered the phone. "I think it gets our point across. Is it ready to send, as far as you're concerned?"

"Yes," Sarah had responded and then had remembered who the boss was. "Boone, I'd suggest we get it out right away, to all the media on our list, plus you might have Suzy or one of the others get on the Internet and get the names of all the media outlets in the Texas Gulf region and include them. Radio, TV and newspapers, all of them.

"Also, I just talked with a reporter from the *Washington Post.*" She had given him the reporter's name. "Please send her a copy, and also send one to whoever else is on our list there. And last, I think we should send copies to Caldwell Jones at ERIN and to all the names on our supporter list."

"I'll get on it right away. Should I include in the cover email that you're in Galveston?"

"Oh, yes, great idea. And include my cell phone number with the notation that I plan to stay here for the next several days, at least."

"Sounds good. Let's plan to talk at least daily."

"Probably more like two or three times a day, Boone. This is going to be very big for us." They disconnected and Sarah, suddenly famished, had cleaned up a bit and gone down to the coffee shop. A large cheeseburger and fries had sounded extremely good right then, and to hell with the calories. She hadn't eaten all day.

When he had hung up the phone, Boone had realized with a start that he had felt no nervousness during the conversation with Sarah, that they seemed to be on the same wavelength, where she seemed to think his thoughts and vice versa.

He was certain that they had become a team. In Galveston, Sarah had been thinking the same thing as she devoured a very large cheeseburger.

On Thursday morning, as Sarah was having coffee and reading the Chronicle in her room, her laptop pinged, indicating she had received an email. She looked and it was from Boone, so she opened it right away. The email's attachment was of a wire service story he had picked up from one of the Internet news services to which CFRG subscribed. As fate would have it, Sarah had just seen the same headline in *the Chronicle*. She opened the attachment and started reading.

OIL TANKER SINKS; CREW RESCUED

The El Gitano, a Venezuelan oil tanker, exploded and sunk in the middle of the Gulf of Mexico. It was returning to its home port after unloading a cargo of oil at the Louisiana Offshore Oil Port.

All the crew were reportedly safe after being rescued from their lifeboats by another Venezuelan oil tanker, the PDVSA Goliat, *which was approximately 25 miles away when it heard the El Gitano's distress call. The crew reported no injuries and could shed no light of the cause of a series of explosions in the mid-ship area that caused the ship to sink quickly. The ship was empty, except for seawater ballast, and no oil leakage was reported.*

The Goliat *is reportedly en route to the Jose Oil Port in Venezuela, which coincidentally is home port for both vessels.*

In Boone's email, he asked Sarah whether this incident should be commented on in CFRG's next newsletter, or even whether it called for another news release.

Sarah replied by email, *"I don't think so. The ship wasn't carrying anything but seawater and it sank in international waters. I think we're better off focusing on the oil spill here. If we jump on any incident involving a tanker, whether there is any environmental damage or not, I'm afraid we run the risk of being seen as hollering 'fire' too much. Call me if you want to discuss further."*

Boone read her response, decided she was right and replied to that effect. There was no reason to talk about it further.

That morning, the media along the Gulf Coast were reporting that the leak in the Mossy Oil underwater pipeline seemed to have stopped, and that Mossy Oil, Ltd. was still investigating, trying to determine the source of the leak, as well as its cause.

Various pundits – mostly paid "experts" who had business cards that said they were oil pipeline experts of one stripe or another – were estimating the size of the leak to be 10,000 barrels at the low end – to 30,000 barrels at the high end. All estimates were based on the size of the oil slick.

Some wondered if the slick was expanding and contracting, or if some of the pundits simply did not know what they were talking about.

The media, which had dozens of helicopters circling the slick like a flock of seagulls circling a fishing boat, was generally reporting that the oil was being effectively skimmed by the clean-up crews, with small amounts simply dissipating farther out into the Gulf. There was not a single report of wildlife obscenely fouled in oil, not a single sighting of crude oil on shore.

Sarah, wearing her lobbying "uniform," was quite the media darling that day. When her comments were reported in the *Washington Post,* most other newspapers and many in the broadcast media repeated them. Her skills were on full display. Whether talking with a stringer for a South Texas weekly or appearing with Anderson Cooper on CNN, she treated the reporter with the same respect and she repeated the same message.

Consistency, she knew, was the key. Play the same song over and over again, and soon everybody would be humming it. She blasted the opening up of expanded oil exploration, especially in coastal areas and in Alaska. She stopped short of blasting the President by name, but referred often to "the Administration."

She referred to past statements by Boone Malory, called him "the visionary Executive Director of CFRG." She called on the Congress to listen to the wishes of the American people and reverse this ill-advised policy reversal of the Administration.

Boone and Suzy, monitoring much of Sarah's activities via the Internet and the television in their office, were emailing recordings of interviews to CFRG supporters and other opinion leaders on their mailing list. And especially to Caldwell Jones at ERIN.

The CFRG brand had been transformed overnight into a major national player, if not yet a powerhouse.

That afternoon, the Mossy Oil investigation team gathered in the Galveston office. Ryan Cresta, the refinery manager for the Mossy facility in Galveston, was listening to Chuck Hughes, a superintendent who had been tasked with locating and repairing the leak.

"We found no leaks," Hughes said. "None. Zero. Nada. We've run the robots back and forth the entire line from Great Mossy XX to here and back. Several times. There's nothing." He saw the look on Cresta's face, the man clearly wondering how the oil could have appeared if there were no leaks.

"We've just now pressure tested the line," he continued. "It holds a steady pressure. We also examined and tested the pressure gauges and monitoring equipment and they're all functioning correctly."

"How can that be, Chuck?" Cresta asked.

"Damned if I know," Hughes said, then referred to his notes. "We've checked everything we can check. But there's one anomaly we've discovered.

We had a temporary safety inspector, name of Earl Bowfin, on *Great Mossy XX*, and he's the one who called in the emergency in the line. What doesn't make sense is that it also appears that a temporary safety inspector, also by the name of Earl Bowfin, was in our fuel terminal facility at the same time.

"Witnesses confirm both men in both places at approximately the same time, the time of the reported drop in pipeline pressure."

Cresta paused a beat before asking incredulously, "Are you telling us, Chuck, that we don't have a leak, never had a leak, all of our equipment is functioning correctly but we still had a false report of an oil pressure drop, that we've had a significant amount of oil bubbling up from a line that had no problems, and at that same time we had two temporary inspectors, both named Earl Bowfin? Am I misunderstanding anything?"

"I know it sounds incredible, Ryan, but I believe that's exactly what we have."

"Are you sure? Are you absolutely sure of all this?"

"I'm absolutely sure. I've been over and over the data. There's no mistake. Our system never leaked."

Cresta sighed, pushed the speaker feature on his phone and punched in Daniel Mirza's direct line, as he had been asked to do as soon as he had anything.

After listening to Hughes' report, Mirza asked, "How long has the pipeline been pressure tested?"

"It's been over eight hours now, Mr. Mirza," Hughes answered. "It's held a stable pressure level, no fluctuations."

"What about visual inspection?" Mirza asked.

"We've examined it inside and out. We've run the robots inside and the submersible the full length of the pipe to look at its exterior. No leaks, sir."

"Would it be your opinion, gentlemen, based on these data, that it was not our pipeline that caused the oil that was seen on the water?" Mirza asked. It was not a surprising question. He was known for his loyalty to his subordinates.

Hughes answered first. "I absolutely do not believe it was our pipeline." Cresta quickly agreed. Mirza asked Cresta what he planned to do next.

"Unless you tell me not to," Cresta answered without equivocation, "I plan to restart the pumping of oil, at a reduced rate of flow, with the submersible moving along the pipeline in the area of the oil slick photographing it."

Mirza was quiet as he sat, considering the implications of that action. Then he said, "Ryan, just to be sure we've done everything we can to be on the safe side, do me a favor and run your internal and external inspections one more time. Then, if they come back negative – as I have full faith they will – go ahead and start your test pumping program. I'm not second-guessing you on this, guys, but this is more a media event than an oil event and I want to be able to tell those jackals we were as prudent as possible throughout the process."

"Understood," Cresta answered.

"A couple of other things, Ryan," Mirza added. "Let's hold off any more press bulletins until your last test is run, and when you get to your report, lose the reference to Earl Bowfin, especially two Earl Bowfins. That will be red meat to the conspiracy theorists and confuse the issue. Especially when we need for the stories to state that our pipeline didn't really leak. Do you understand?"

"Perfectly, Mr. Mirza," Cresta answered. "In that case, Bowfin, either singular or plural, is irrelevant anyway."

"Exactly," Mirza said. "It's a subject for another time, a security check-up, if you will. But for now, keep me posted on the additional tests." He hung up without waiting for a response.

"Where the hell did the oil come from?" Cresta asked Hughes after he had pushed the disconnect button on his phone.

"Only thing I can think of is it was from a ship, probably a tanker that had some sort of malfunction and leaked as it was passing over our pipeline," Hughes said, his tone indicating he was far from certain. "I just can't figure, for the life of me, how that connects to the false readings we got on our gauges."

"I haven't heard any reports of ships of any kind leaking oil in the area," Cresta said.

"I know. Maybe it was a malfunction that the crew fixed and they didn't want to report it. They fine leakers pretty good."

"Don't I know it? And you're probably right, Chuck. I can't think of anything else that would explain it."

"Okay, meanwhile I'll start the test again right away and maybe we can start testing the line with oil tomorrow morning."

On Saturday morning, Mossy Oil issued its second statement to the media.

STATEMENT FROM MOSSY OIL, LTD.

Mossy Oil, Ltd. continues to inspect and test its pipeline from Great Mossy XX to the company's fuel terminal in Galveston.

The inspection and testing to date have not revealed any malfunction or leaks in its equipment or in its pipeline. The multiple pipeline tests have included internal tests, using robotic devices inside the pipeline, and external tests using a submersible with onboard cameras. The source of the oil that surfaced remains a complete mystery.

The results of future tests will be made known as those processes continue.

By Tuesday, a week after the oil spill, the national media had mostly lost interest in it. After the first, damning story in the Washington Post, that august journal had run scarcely a word about it, and when it did, it was in the form of a short, wire service bulletin in the "Notes" column in the business section. Some of those wire service reports included a caustic but thoughtful comment from Sarah Cotton of CFRG. The reporters liked her. She was available and she always had a good, quotable comment.

That same day, however, the Houston Chronicle carried its own follow-up story, which ran at the top of the local section.

GALVESTON'S OIL SPILL REMAINS MYSTERY

Mossy Oil, Ltd. announced late yesterday that it has restarted the underwater pipeline connecting the drilling platform, Great Mossy XX, and its Galveston fuel terminal. The same pipeline was suspected of a major leak last Tuesday.

Ryan Cresta, the manager of the Mossy Galveston refinery, reported in an interview with The Chronicle that no leaks were found in an exhaustive and repetitive series of tests on the pipeline and on the company's pumping equipment.

"The oil spill that occurred last week simply did not come from our pipeline," Cresta said. He acknowledged that the pipeline's monitoring equipment indicated a drop in pipeline pressure, which he attributed to over-sensitive or defective sensors. All sensors, gauges and related equipment have been replaced, he said.

Cresta could offer no explanation for the origin of the spill, but suggested it might have come from an oil tanker in the area. There have been no reports of tankers in the area which reported a problem.

The United States Coast Guard, working with Texas state authorities, is reviewing its satellite tracking data to pinpoint tankers in the area late last Monday or early Tuesday. The Coast Guard review of satellite imaging has been hampered by the fact that there was a heavy cloud cover and no moon last Monday night, so the review is dependent largely on thermal imaging.

The Venezuela-registered oil tanker, El Gitano, which sunk Thursday, was reported to be in the vicinity Monday night, but it had been bound for its home port after offloading its full cargo at the Louisiana Offshore Oil Port east of the Great Mossy XX platform. It sunk en route to Venezuela after several onboard explosions believed to have been caused by the build-up of inert gasses on the ship.

All crew members were rescued with no injuries reported. The captain of the El Gitano reported from Venezuela that the tanker had unloaded its entire cargo of 335,000 barrels at LOOP and was carrying only sea water as ballast en route back to its home port. He reported no issues with the vessel until the explosions, which happened in rapid sequence, consistent with those caused by inert gasses.

The captain also praised his crew for their quick response to his order to abandon ship, and saluted the crew of the PDVSA Goliat, another Venezuelan tanker, which rushed to the scene in response to the El Gitano's distress calls and picked up the crew.

The Coast Guard and the Texas Oil Prevention and Response Program quickly cleaned up the oil slick, and there have been no reports of damaged wildlife or of any oil reaching shore.

Although the investigation continues, at this point, neither Federal or state officials, nor Mossy Oil's investigators know where the oil came from.

The Galveston oil spill remains a mystery.

Sarah Cotton stayed in Galveston the entire week after the oil spill and the petroleum engineers conference. She was determined to fully exploit the opportunity that had been thrust in her lap. She called Boone after emailing him the Chronicle's follow-up story on the mystery oil spill.

"I got your email," Boone said. "Interesting story. Any idea where the oil came from?"

"None at all," Sarah said. "Obviously, it had to come from a pipeline or an oil tanker. It was too much oil to come from normal seepage." She paused for a beat before continuing. "But the brutal truth is that it doesn't matter, at least to us. We got great coverage, and if we keep this momentum we'll have put CFRG on the map."

"It actually helps our position that nobody knows where it came from," Boone said.

"How so?" Sarah asked. She was a master of the world of manipulation, but she was dealing with a subject now in which she had little background.

"The point is, nobody knows where the oil came from, but it came from somewhere. The fact that its source is unknown plays into the CFRG position about the unknown dangers of uncontrolled oil exploration. We can make the case that, in addition to all the known dangers, those that are unknown may be the worst."

Sarah paused. She was almost in awe of Boone's intellect. "You're absolutely right, Boone. I'm embarrassed I hadn't seen it that way."

"I've been in this war a lot longer than you have," Boone said reassuringly. "You'll pick up the angles quickly enough. And you really are a genius at playing the media. You were part of damn near every story I saw."

"Thanks. It was fun, in a perverse sort of way," Sarah said, then added, "Boone, why don't you write something up on that business about the unknown? We can use that in our newsletter and I'll work it into any interviews I can while I'm here."

"I'll get right on it," he replied. "How long are you planning to stay down there?"

"At least through the end of the week," she said. "I want to stay a few more days to see if anything more comes out of the investigations and try to milk the 'unknown factor' a little. I really like that. And I'll drive over to Houston and report in to Caldwell Jones on what I've been doing, although I'm sure he's aware I'm here. It would be kind of inconsiderate not to give him a personal report.

"And if he reacts as I expect him to, maybe I can shake loose some additional cash, too."

"God, I'd forgotten that ERIN was right there in Houston. Of course you should see him." Boone paused, unsure whether to continue, then did so. "I'm pretty good at spending money, and you're awfully good at raising it. So I think we're making a great team, don't you?".

Sarah felt an unexpected rush of warmth deep inside her when Boone said that. "Yes, we are, and thank you for saying so. Incidentally, I also need to follow up with Parker Firth and get the paper he promised me on the environmental risks of oil exploration."

"Can't he just email it?"

"Sure he could. But he is someone who can be helpful to us far into the future and I want to get the face time with him when I can. That kind of thing pays dividends, believe me when I tell you, Boone."

After hanging up, Boone sat at his desk reflectively. He marveled at Sarah's people skills. He marveled at the way she appeared on television. And he reflected that he was very happy that she would mention that this the guy Firth could "be helpful to us far into the future."

That meant she was planning for more than a temporary stint with CFRG. At least he hoped that's what she meant.

After calling Dr. Firth's office to make an appointment with him, Sarah drove to Rice University and found the building housing the Earth Sciences Department.

Seated in his small and nicely furnished but cluttered office, Sarah told him she appreciated his offer to allow CFRG to reprint the paper he had presented to the United States Association of Petroleum Geologists five years earlier.

Dr. Firth was in his early 50s, slight but vigorous-looking and he seemed fit and active. He was clearly smitten with Sarah Cotton, but he managed to keep his eyes above her neck most of the time. Her signature black skirt rode several inches above her knee as she crossed her legs.

"Ah, Sarah," he said. "Those of us who toil in the vineyards of academe appreciate the interest in what we have written of anyone in the 'real world,' except of course the IRS." He allowed himself a small smile at his witticism, which he had clearly used many times in the past. He handed her a copy of the paper, which was still warm from the printer. He had obviously printed her a fresh copy just before she had arrived. He also slid a disk across the desk top. He knew the electronic copy of the paper would be easier to insert in their newsletter.

"When you have had a chance to read this, I think you'll find that I address numerous environmental risks inherent in exploring and drilling for oil in sensitive areas, such as offshore, in the Arctic National Wildlife Refuge and so forth. Even though this paper is a few years old now, I've reviewed it in detail and believe it is still quite relevant."

Sarah nodded while flipping through the paper, taking in the major points quickly, as she had learned to do with the voluminous legislative proposals and bills she dealt with in Washington. "Again, we appreciate your willingness to let us reprint this – or parts of it – with credit, of course. Have you given any thought to how much effort and time it would take you to update the paper, Dr. Firth? And your fee for doing so?"

"First, why don't you and your associates take a good look at it," he responded. "You may find it adequate for your purposes as it is. And now, regrettably, I have a small but very bright and inquisitive class of graduate students who are expecting me in the classroom in 15 minutes."

Sarah stood, thanked Firth again and headed back to her SUV. The ERIN office was not far from Rice and she had decided to kill two birds with one stone. Caldwell Jones was waiting for her when she arrived. He had a large office, obviously expensively furnished, with a small conference table in the center, a couch with opposing chairs at one end and a large mahogany desk at the other. The only two other spaces in the ERIN suite were a large, well-appointed board room and the reception area. The ERIN staff consisted of Caldwell Jones and a secretary-receptionist.

Jones motioned Sarah toward the conference table in the center of his office. When they were seated and the secretary had brought Jones coffee and Sarah a bottle of imported mineral water, Jones said, "I appreciate that you have been copying me with CFRG's newsletter, releases and the coverage you've been getting over that unfortunate incident in Galveston. I've forwarded most of them to the members of the ERIN board, and we're all quite impressed." Jones had the superior and faintly condescending manner of a college professor and even in one-on-one conversations like this, he seemed to giving a speech.

"You have been consistently on message with comments about the damaging implications of the President's program on oil exploration," he continued. "Yet you've stopped short of attacking him personally or even directly. I think that's brilliant. And I think the result is that CFRG, literally overnight, has become one of the pre-eminent voices in this debate. That should bode well for future issues you take on. I think we made a very wise investment with our grant to you, and I can tell you that the board members agree. All of them."

"Thank you very much, Caldwell," she said. "It was a very fortuitous coincidence that I was in Galveston for that conference when the spill occurred. Especially given the revelation that the suspected pipeline actually does not appear to be the source of the oil." Jones grunted his agreement and Sarah continued. "Boone Malory made an interesting observation about that. He feels 'the unknown factor,' as he calls it, works in our favor, because it represents the unknown dangers. We can tick off a long list of known dangers, and the oil industry can take them one at a time and try to refute them. But they can't refute the unknown."

Jones chuckled. "I hadn't thought of it that way, Sarah, but Boone is absolutely correct on that. It's a brilliant observation." Sarah knew that brilliant was one of Caldwell Jones' favorite words.

She shifted in her chair, ready to get to the main goal of this meeting, at least to her. "Caldwell, I know things have been hectic in the last week or two, but I wonder if you've had a chance to review our request for supplemental funding. I think that request is even more appropriate now, in fact, after the exposure CFRG has had as a result of Galveston. Our message is sticking and I believe we're having an impact in the public debate over the President's oil program. We would like to be able to do some paid advertising to better reach the public, and we'd like to be able to track public attitudes through polling."

"You don't need to keep selling, Sarah," Jones interrupted, holding up his hands as if in surrender. "You've made the sale. I told you that I and the directors are convinced we picked the right horse in this race, as it were. CFRG is now perfectly positioned. We agree that you need to do some regular polling so you can track movements in public sentiment and we think the judicious use of advertising is a logical extension of the organization's public persona." He opened a file and slid a three-page document across the table to her.

"What's this?" she asked, although she was fairly certain of the answer.

"It's a revised ERIN commitment contract. The CFRG Board will need to approve it, formally, and based on that Boone will need to sign it and return it to me."

"That's very generous of you, Caldwell," Sarah said without glancing at the document.

"It pledges funding in the amount of $400,000 per month for the next two years. It is automatically renewed annually unless cancelled in writing by either party before the anniversary date."

Sarah had not expected the automatic renewal provision this early in the process, but was gratified by it. And by $400,000 per month. "We just asked for $200,000 per month," she said in a neutral tone of voice.

"I understand," Jones said. "But like I also said, you sold us on what you would do with additional funding. We just want you to do more of it." At that moment, the voice of Jones' secretary came over the intercom on his desk, announcing that his conference call was convening and asking if she should call him into it.

Sarah stood, lightly touching Jones' hand and flashing him her best smile. "I can't tell you how gratifying this is, Caldwell. We've worked hard and we'll work even harder to justify your faith in us. And I'll get this agreement approved, signed and back to you as soon as possible. I'm flying back to Monterey tomorrow morning."

Jones shook Sarah's hand formally and thanked her again for keeping him up to date on their activities.

Sarah returned to the Galvez Hotel and Spa, packed, and called Continental Airlines to confirm her flight to San Francisco the next morning. Then, she checked out of the Galvez, drove to George Bush Intercontinental, dropped her SUV off at Avis and took an airport courtesy bus to the Airport Marriott, where she checked in to spend the night. That way, it was just a short bus ride in the morning. She probably could have made a late flight that night, but she knew she was wound too tight to be able to sit still on an airplane. She was going to go to the Marriott's bar and get loaded. That, for her, meant three, maybe four glasses of wine.

She took the agreement with her to the bar, had a couple of sips of wine and decided to treat herself to one of her Turkish cigarettes. There was no smoking in the bar, which indicated that the social engineers had successfully invaded South Texas, so she took the agreement outside and read it while she smoked her cigarette. The automatic renewal clause then hit her, as did its significance. They would have a steady income stream as long as they did nothing to make ERIN want to cancel the agreement.

She went back into the bar and thought about the past two weeks as she sipped her wine. She thought about all the coverage she and CFRG had received since the oil slick had appeared a week ago last Tuesday. She thought about how well Boone, Suzy and the newbies in the CFRG office had done getting news releases and newsletters put together and distributed. And she thought about having asked ERIN for $200,000 per month and getting double that, indefinitely. She thought about how the functionaries in the White House must be crapping their pants over the collapse of public support for the President's oil exploration program, which she was sure was happening even as she sat there.

The next morning, she slept the entire trip from Houston to San Francisco, and even dozed some on the short flight to Monterey. With the two-hour time difference, she walked into the CFRG office a little before 11:00 a.m.

Suzy Dillinger jumped up and rushed to greet Sarah when she saw her, and Boone, hearing the commotion, came quickly out of his office. He almost hugged Sarah himself, but was not quite able to bring himself to do so. Suzy looked at him like she thought he was crazy. Like most women, she prided herself on being able to spot romantic possibilities before they happened. The three of them went into Boone's office, leaving the new associates in the outer office.

Sarah started by telling them she wanted to get back to Washington as soon as possible and strike while the iron was hot, so she probably wouldn't be in Monterey long.

In fact, she told them, she planned to spend the afternoon setting up appointments, and she wanted to talk first to the Honorable Homer "Good" Deeds. She made a mental note to include a dinner with Jared Welch while she was in the capital.

Then she briefed them on the investigation into the oil spill, the mystery of it all still hanging like the perpetual humidity over the Texas Gulf Coast. Boone asked a number of questions, some of which required explanation before Suzy understood them. She was still learning, but learning fast, Sarah noted.

Boone told her he had just about finished his paper on "the unknown factor." He was thinking of using that name for the title of the paper, as Suzy had suggested, and Sarah agreed. He said he would have a draft for Sarah's review by the end of the day or early the next morning.

Sarah gave Boone the paper by Dr. Parker Firth and slid the CD containing the electronic copy over to Suzy, explaining what it was. Boone assured her he would read it right away. Sarah gave Boone one of Firth's business cards – she had picked up several when she was in his office – and told him the good doctor would be willing to talk with him directly if he had any questions or comments on the paper, or if Boone thought the paper could use updating. She told him that Firth appeared to be an admirer of CFRG and its mission.

Then she got to the point she had been relishing since leaving the ERIN office the afternoon before.

"Finally, I have a new funding commitment from ERIN that you need to review, get Board approval for, sign and return to Caldwell Jones as soon as possible," she said almost matter-of-factly, sliding the agreement casually across his desk. "That is, if it's acceptable to you," she added mischievously.

"For more money?" Suzy asked. "How much?" Suzy was always impatient and wanted to get to the bottom line immediately. But Sarah didn't answer her, just sat and watched Boone scan the agreement. She knew when he got to the good part. His eyes stopped skimming and got wide. She thought she could even see tears welling up.

"Is this for real?" he asked, looking intently at Sarah.

"Caldwell Jones handed it to me yesterday afternoon," Sarah said with a shrug of her shoulders.

"They're going to give us $400,000 a month?" he asked, incredulous. "For two years?"

"I believe that's exactly what Caldwell told me," she said, having an increasingly difficult time keeping a straight face.

"We asked them for $200,000 and they give us $400,000?" Boone asked. "What the hell did you have to do to get this?" *Was that jealousy in his tone?*

"I didn't have to do a damn thing, Boone. You, Suzy and our new worker bees did it with our messaging and communications. Keeping Caldwell in the loop definitely paid dividends. He already had this agreement drawn up when I got to his office and I had the same first reaction you did."

Boone stared at the agreement for a full minute, then jumped up, raced around the desk and hugged Sarah.

Suzy smiled at them and when he released the hug, Suzy asked, "Don't I get a hug, too?" He hugged her too.

Then Boone said, "We're going to go out to lunch. The three of us. I'll even buy. This definitely calls for a celebration."

Then Sarah pointed out the automatic renewal clause in the agreement and explained what it meant.

Suzy gasped when the significance hit her and asked, "Sarah, you didn't have to do anything immoral, did you?"

Sarah looked thoughtful for two or three seconds, then said quietly, "No, not by my standards." She winked at Suzy.

Sarah thought about the hug from Boone as they walked to the restaurant. She had enjoyed it.

It was a nice lunch, with a nice bottle of wine, in the big booth Sarah always got. Happy talk. No business.

Later that afternoon, identical emails landed in the secure inboxes of Akrum al-Kahtani, Jet Jamieson and the two "Earl Bowfins," the Huff twins. It read:

Congratulations on the success of your operation.
ZaK

CHAPTER 16

Sarah Cotton had just concluded a promising meeting with Carl Benchley, a third-term Congressman from Portland, Oregon. The subject, of course, had been the President's expanded oil exploration program. He had seemed receptive to her arguments about the dangers – many of them unknown – associated with opening up exploration and drilling in sensitive areas. The "unknown factor" seemed to be gaining the response she had hoped for.

He had been preoccupied, however, with the reelection campaign he was facing. It promised to be a struggle, perhaps even an uphill fight. He had won his first three elections by fairly handy margins, but this would be different. His opponent was almost certain to be a retired major league baseball player who was well-known, well-liked, financially successful and a home-town boy.

Benchley had told Sarah he was afraid his record alone would not be enough to overcome the name ID and the charisma of his likely challenger. His district, like almost all of Oregon, was decidedly green, meaning an environmental agenda was a must, but the challenger would have one of his own, too. He wasn't stupid.

Sarah had given him a copy of her outline for a "Conserve Our Environment" campaign, based on Boone's exhaustive research, and had offered to work with him to implement it. It was full of hard-hitting stuff – current facts, projections and statistics. It was powerful,

Benchley had admitted, but he was going to need a boatload of cash to get his message out.

So there it was, Sarah had thought.
The quid pro quo, laid out on the desk in front of her like a rainbow trout ready for filleting. Some politicians were more subtle than others, she had thought to herself, but in the end most got around to the bottom line. Benchley was not among the most subtle.

Sarah had hinted broadly at the availability of campaign funding – directly and through independent expenditure campaigns – now and in the future, if he became visible as one of CFRG's most ardent supporters. She had known immediately that he was hers for the taking. He would be a poster boy for CFRG and its programs as soon as the campaign cash started rolling in.

Sarah knew the trick was to provide enough support to get his attention and to motivate him to action, but never all of it up front. Political contributions need to be treated like drugs. You gave them enough to satisfy the addiction but not so much that they burn out. So you keep the cash flowing, slowly but steadily, until one day the recipient was truly addicted and had no way out.

Sarah was happy to be on her way to dinner with Jared Welch. When she arrived at the Occidental Grill, less than two blocks from the White House, Jared was already at a nice table in a dark corner, a bottle of one of their favorite red wines sitting on the table decanting.

Jared stood and they shook hands, then hugged and kissed each other on the cheek. As always, Sarah looked stunning in her uniform, and she was wearing black high heels rather than pumps. Her pearls looked like they had been shined. He held her chair for her as she sat, then poured their wine, much to the consternation of the very alert waiter who had been hovering nearby. Jared waved him off with a smile.

"It's good to see you, Jared," she said brightly.

"You too, Sarah, and beautiful as always."

"You're such a charmer," she said as she raised her wine glass to her lips.

He raised his glass in a toast and said, "To friendship and to the evening." Sarah smiled, but it was not the provocative smile Jared had seen so many times in the past. They touched glasses and sipped.

After several minutes of small talk catching each other up on what had been happening in their work, the waiter reappeared and they ordered dinner. Jared asked for more on her new career with CFRG. She suddenly remembered something and said, "Boone said to say 'hi' for him and to thank you for setting up our interview."

"I talked to him last week," Jared said. "He told me how amazed he is with the amount of money you've been able to shake loose for him."

"I've been very fortunate so far" she said. "I got a start-up grant, and then another operating grant for two years that gets us on solid footing going forward."

"I never had a doubt, Sarah," Jared said with a kind of rueful smile. "Where did you get it?"

Sarah gave him a stare that was at once friendly and hard. "You know I can't and won't talk about that, Jared. There are a lot of organizations chasing environmental dollars and I always promise my benefactors that I won't release their names unless they want them released. There would be a pack of hungry wolves at their door by tomorrow."

"I see you haven't forgotten Fundraising 101," he said, a hint of sadness in his voice, realizing he was no longer really in Sarah's world. Not like he had been.

"But won't you have to list them on your 990?" he continued, referring to the IRS form non-profits were required to file annually.

"Yes, but chasing those down is more work than most people want to go to," she said. Their meals were served.

"Are you bored yet being a respectable citizen after all those years of being a shark swimming in the waters of Washington?" he asked.

"No, I'm enjoying what I'm doing. A lot. And I'm still lobbying, just not getting paid as well for it." She smiled again at Jared. She knew he badly wanted her to be bored and to move back from California.

After dinner, when they had emptied the wine bottle, Jared reached across the table and held Sarah's hand. He could feel the slightest pull-back. "I've missed seeing you," he said gamely. "You've always been fascinating to me, even when you've been a challenge and being around you is often very rewarding."

"Jared, you're a dear, but I'm afraid you're going to have to be satisfied with fascinating and challenging tonight."

He did his best to keep his face passive but his mind was racing and he fired questions so rapidly Sarah had no time to answer them. "Is this a new Sarah? Is there someone else? It isn't Boone, is it? Were you bored with me?" He finally paused, and Sarah recited his questions in her mind. "I don't know. Maybe. I don't think so. And no, I've never been bored with you, Jared."

He puzzled through that, then said, "Well, I guess another bottle of wine is probably not a good idea."

"Why don't we just have coffee and share a dessert?" Sarah replied. "You pick the dessert."

"Oh, brother," he said. "Times, they are a-changing." He signaled the waiter and ordered two coffees and one bread pudding. Sarah reached across, held his hand, smiled, and complimented him on his choice of dessert.

Jared told her he had thought of a couple of Senators he was close to who might be sympathetic to the CFRG goals and approach, and told her he would check with their chiefs of staff and see if he could get her appointments.

"Thanks so much for your help, Jared," she said. "You really are a good friend."

As they walked out of the restaurant, Jared asked if he could give her a ride to her condo. She smiled as she hugged him and kissed his cheek.

"Probably not a good idea tonight, Jared," she said. "I'll take a cab."

Jared nodded knowingly and walked away toward his car. As he walked, he thought, not for the first time, that he would never really understand women in general and this woman in particular.

In the back of the cab, Sarah wondered to herself why she had turned down an action-filled night with Jared. Was what she thought of as doing good things for her country affecting how she lived her life?

The next afternoon, Sarah had an appointment with her friend, the Honorable Homer Deeds. His office was in the Rayburn House Office Building on Independence Avenue. When she arrived, she was told by an apologetic receptionist that the Congressman was running late from a committee meeting.

When he arrived, he greeted Sarah in the reception area and apologized for being late but asked her indulgence while he made some important phone calls. Thirty minutes later, Deeds reappeared and ushered Sarah into his office. Only after he had closed the door did Sarah give him a hug and ask how he and Martha were.

"We're doing great, Sarah," the Congressman told her. "Martha is back in Illinois and won't return until after this weekend. I know she'll be sorry she missed you."

Sarah picked up a cardboard carrying case she had brought with her and set it on Deeds' desk. "Well, I'll miss seeing her, too, but here are three bottles of her favorite California wine."

"Sarah, Sarah," Deeds said in mock seriousness. "Are you trying to bribe a United States Congressman?"

"No," Sarah answered, also in mock seriousness, "it is a gift for Martha, and I'm quite sure she wouldn't think of sharing this wine with you or any other Member of Congress."

Deeds laughed. "I think you're absolutely right. She loves that wine and I don't think I'll be getting any of it."

Sarah got down to business. "As you know, I left the firm and am now working with Citizens for Responsible Growth."

"You were all over the news during that curious mess down in Galveston," Deeds said, "but I had never before heard of this, ah, Committee for...?"

"Citizens for Responsible Growth, Congressman, or CFRG. It's a small non-profit, headquartered in California, in Monterey."

"Why haven't I heard of it before?"

"It's small, it hasn't had much of a Washington presence and its resources have been quite limited. That's what I signed on for – to raise its Washington presence and to help raise money for it."

"Tell me about it," Deeds said, leaning back in his chair.

"It's an environmental organization, but it's quite different in its approach from most of the others that you have to deal with." Deeds was not considered one of the Congressmen who were "out front" on the environment. "Our style is less strident than most of them. We are not no-growth, but as our name implies, we're for 'responsible growth.' Our core belief is that growth is inevitable, but growth policies must be tempered by environmental realities."

Deeds steepled his fingers and sat thoughtfully for a moment. "Go on," he said.

"One of the environmental realities we see are the dangers – some unknown to anybody, as the Galveston mystery revealed – of uncontrolled oil exploration and drilling in environmentally sensitive areas, such as offshore and in the Arctic National Wildlife Refuge. We are very concerned about the President's about-face on this issue and we are calling on the Congress to overturn his order."

"Ah, so now we get down to the reason I am being blessed with your presence today," Deeds said quietly, smiling. He loved the give-and-take of political discourse.

"That's the main reason I'm here, Congressman," she said with a nod of the head. "That and to deliver Martha's wine."

"You know I'd do anything I can for you, barring any big conflict in my district. What would you like from me, specifically?"

"Thank you, Congressman," she said with great sincerity in her voice. "Of course, I'd like your support in overturning the President's order, and it would be great if you could think about others among your colleagues who might be good potential supporters, especially public supporters, of our position."

"Do you have a plan for how to go about reversing the President?" he asked.

"Congressman, you know me well enough to know that I would never ask you or any of your colleagues to take on the President of the United States in a vacuum. We realize this is a huge issue with many angles to it and nobody in your position would relish standing in front of a train carrying both the President and the oil industry. Our plan is to give you – all of you on the Hill - plenty of cover."

"What kind of cover?" he asked, a bit dubiously. He was thinking about a heavily-loaded train bearing down on him.

"We are developing a public information campaign that will include a call to action. Letters, emails and phone calls to the White House and

Members of Congress, letters to the editor in newspapers all over the country, calls to talk radio shows, that sort of thing."

"That kind of stuff costs money, Sarah," he cautioned. "You just told me your group doesn't have a lot of it."

Sarah smiled. "Congressman, I told we didn't have much in the way of resources. Fortunately, we've found some people with deep pockets and sympathy for our position and approach, and we've secured the funding necessary for the next two years."

"With you involved, I should have known," Deeds chuckled. "Okay, you know you can count on me, but you're going to have to help me. I've always believed that as a Congressman, I have an obligation to do what I can to leave this country to the next generation in as good a condition as I found it. Or better. Protection of the environment is important, but hasn't been one of my front-and-center issues. I'm counting on you to help me get up to speed on it."

Sarah extracted a binder from her briefcase and passed it to him. "Here's a briefing book that shouldn't take you too long to go through, but should give you a good grounding in the immediate issue, as well as material you should be able to use in your next reelection campaign. The Cliff Notes version is that if the President's order is allowed to stand and uncontrolled exploration along our coastlines is allowed to continue, the damage may never be able to be reversed. We saw that in Santa Barbara, where a barge carrying oil from a long-established well had an accident. We saw it again in Galveston. Oil started leaking, but nobody can find the source of the leak. It's the unknown that should scare everyone most."

Deeds promised to review the contents of the binder right away.

"And the other thing I'd ask you, Congressman," she said. "If there is anything in there that is confusing or not really clear to you, please let me know. I want to make sure we're communicating as clearly as possible. That's critical to both of us."

Deeds nodded his agreement.

"I've been increasingly uneasy about offshore drilling," Deeds said, "especially after the incidents we've had off Galveston and Santa Barbara. As you say, there were just too many unanswered questions, too many mysteries. That barge in Santa Barbara coming loose mysteriously is as troubling as the questions in Galveston."

"No question about it," she said. She knew she had "Good" Deeds firmly on her side.

"I'll look this over carefully and think about colleagues you should target next," Deeds said, effectively concluding the meeting, since the time allotted for it had elapsed ten minutes before. "When will you be back here?"

"Probably in about two weeks," she said.

"Good. Let's plan to get together then. Let me know when your schedule is firmed up and we'll schedule a little private gathering in one of the hearing rooms and I'll have some of my colleagues there."

Sarah gathered her briefcase and got to her feet. "Thank you so much," she said. "There's a reason you're known as 'Good Deeds.' Give my best to Martha, and tell her it's okay with me if she gives you at least a sip of her wine."

He laughed as he walked her to the door. "I knew you were trying to influence me with Martha's wine." They hugged and he opened the door for her.

As Sarah left the Rayburn building, her mind was focused on several things. Among them were arranging additional campaign contributions for Deeds. She also needed to call Boone Malory when she got back to her condo. She would report on her just-concluded meeting and ask him whether he would be able to pick her up from the airport the next day.

In her condo, she consulted her calendar and decided on her next D.C. trip.

She logged onto the Internet and booked her flights, then emailed the dates to Congressman Deeds. Afterward, she called Boone and told him she would need his help preparing sample environmental policy speeches for each of congressman Deeds' invitees, in addition to briefing books and sample campaign materials.

Boone was waiting when Sarah deplaned the next day just before noon.

She had sounded so enthused when she had called him the afternoon before and there was never a question in his mind that he would pick her up. To his surprise, he had found he missed her when she wasn't there. Her energy and enthusiasm were contagious. Of course, her looks didn't hurt a bit.

Boone had no trouble spotting her as she hurried from her plane, dragging her carry-on behind her, her briefcase and purse slung over her shoulder, her black hair streaming behind her. And she was wearing her lobbying uniform. He greeted her warmly, gave her a tentative hug around the shoulders.

"How was the flight?" he asked.

"I guess I got spoiled by all those years of working with big companies," she responded. "I miss flying first class or on a private jet."

"It's good to get out among the proletariat," he said with a chuckle. "Keeps you humble."

"Humble is over-rated," she came back. "I'll take the private jets."

"Well, as long as you're toiling away for CFRG, those days are over." He wrapped his arm around her shoulders and gave her another hug. "And just so you know that all of us slaves to the public good are working to make things better, I've got a good start on my first draft of the campaign packages you asked me for your meeting with Deeds and his pals."

"We need to try to make each one a little different in the details," she said. None of them will like it if they think it makes them sound like their strings are being pulled by the same puppet-master."

"That's what I'm trying to do," he replied quickly, "but it isn't always easy."

"How so?"

"I've lived with these issues so long it's hard for me not to cover all the points in every presentation," he said. "We'll have to work on it. And when we get names we can modify them to fit each Congressman, assuming you know enough about each of them to know their speaking style."

"Good. And once we get the names, I'll have to get busy trying to shake loose some campaign contributions for them."

"You can do that?" he asked, almost in wonder.

"Of course," she laughed. "What do you think lobbyists do?"

"Lobby for their clients."

"AND raise political contributions."

By that time, they were in Boone's car headed into Monterey. "Office or apartment?" he asked her.

"Drop me at the apartment, if that's okay with you," she said. "I'd like to put my stuff away and get out of these clothes and dress for Monterey."

"Do you want me to wait?" he asked.

"No need," she said, then changed her mind. "No, wait, why don't you come on up. It'll only take me a minute, then we can grab some lunch before we go to the office."

When Sarah unlocked the door, Boone carried her suitcase, as directed, into her bedroom and put it on the bed, then retreated hurriedly to the living room while Sarah closed the door and began her transformation. Boone noticed that her apartment seemed as neat and organized as she was in her work.

Her coffee table had periodicals from all over the world on it. Soon, she emerged, wearing jeans, a white pullover shirt and navy blazer.

"I'm much more comfortable now," she said. "Should we call Suzy and see if she can join us for lunch?"

"Good idea," he responded, "and you do look more like Monterey now."

Two days after Sarah's return to Monterey, Congressman Deeds' scheduler in Washington called her to confirm a meeting during her next trip with the Congressman and five of his colleagues. The names were given and Sarah carefully wrote them down. The meeting would be in his office. It could comfortably accommodate seven people.

Sarah went into Boone's office and gave him the names and what she knew about each of them, including speaking styles and pet issues.

CHAPTER 17

The *Royal Bearing II* was an 800-foot-long, double-hulled tanker belonging to San Francisco-based Royal Energy, Inc. Its six pairs of coated cargo tanks held a combined 500,000 barrels – or 42 million gallons – of Alaska North Slope crude oil. Each of its 12 cargo tanks was equipped with a centrifugal pump, driven by a hydraulic system, which could pump 1,000 cubic meters, or 6,290 barrels, per hour.

The giant ship had docked at the unloading facility at Royal Energy's March Point Refinery in Puget Sound mid-afternoon on New Year's Eve and unloading was scheduled to be completed by 8:00 p.m. It was scheduled to remain in port on January 1 and begin its return journey to Alaska on January 2. Most of the crew were already ashore, having been given the night off to party in Anacortes.

As it sat moored to the unloading dock, it was held stationary by big drum brakes and mooring cables while it unloaded its valuable cargo. A heavy containment boom surrounded the ship, floating in the ice-cold water.

The containment boom was required by the State of Washington when any tanker was unloading oil. The winter weather was typical for the Puget Sound: breezy and cold, with a thick evening fog moving in after a rainy, icy day.

A few minutes after seven, the unloading was nearing completion when suddenly, three of the mooring brakes loosened, detaching with them the safety cables, and imperceptibly at first, the bow of the huge vessel, now at the mercy of the wind and tides, backed slightly away from the dock.

This action caused the breaking and disconnecting of the marine loading arms' couplings from the cargo manifold flanges. Meanwhile, the tanker's hydraulic pumps continued operating, relentlessly pumping crude from the ship's tanks onto the deck, and because all of the deck scuppers were unplugged, the oil was free to spill through them and into the waters of Fidalgo Bay.

Captain Bernard Stevens and the skeleton crew he had to keep aboard until the unloading was completed were in the mess having a dinner of cold cuts. They were not allowed to use the stoves or ovens during loading or unloading.

Suddenly, the wind shifted and combined with wave action to slam the bow of the *Royal Bearing II* back into the huge, reinforced steel dock. Stevens and his small band of men jumped from their dinner table in alarm and bolted out to the bridge wing. Stevens immediately saw the mooring lines hanging limply over the side, then his eyes moved with horror to the uncoupled unloading arm.

With the ship bathed in bright halogen lights – as is standard in any nighttime loading or unloading operation – is was easy to spot the shiny crude gushing out of the unloading arm and pouring through the scuppers into the bay. The Captain immediately shouted for First Officer Forest Acton to get to the cargo control room and shut the pumps down and to find out why the hell the Deck Officer had not already done so.

Then he pointed at Second Officer Roscoe Harris and told him to take everyone else and re-secure the mooring, relocking the brakes to keep the tanker connected to the dock.

As they scampered forward, the crew soon discovered both the tankerman PIC – or person in charge – and the loading master PIC lying unconscious on the deck. When Acton, the first officer, arrived at the cargo control room, he found the deck officer slumped over his control panel, also unconscious. He quickly shut down all the pumps.

Captain Stevens, meanwhile, ran into the bridge and called the Coast

Guard to report the spill. He then called Oil Clean-Up Corporation, which immediately dispatched its clean-up boats to the March Point Refinery. The clean-up boats were always manned and ready whenever there was a loading or unloading in process in the area.

Stevens reported that he did not know how much oil had been pumped into the bay, but that the two pumps operating at that time had possibly been pumping while detached for as much as half and hour. He made a quick calculation and reported that it was possible that as much as 6,400 barrels of crude oil had been spilled, but that as far as he could tell, the oil containment boom was still intact, which – thank God – meant that most of the crude remained contained.

That relief proved to be short-lived, however. Almost as soon as he got off the phone with the clean-up company, the first officer reported via the Motorola hand-held radio each of the men carried that the oil containment boom was breached forward of the bow, had probably been torn loose when the *Royal Bearing II* had suffered the broken mooring lines. "The spill is not contained," Acton reported in a businesslike tone. "Repeat, not contained. I can see oil flowing out of Fidalgo Bay in the direction of Padilla Bay. Do you copy, Captain?"

"Copy," Stevens snapped, furious at all the things that had apparently gone wrong at once. What the hell happened to the leak monitoring system? He wondered. What about the surveillance camera systems? What caused the mooring lines to fail? And the coupling mechanism?

"Captain," Acton continued after catching his breath. He was running all over the forward deck, checking all the critical points in the unfolding drama.

"Go ahead, Forest," Stevens responded.

"We've got all three crewmen who were on duty up here, including the deck officer who was manning the control room, unconscious, Captain."

"Say again, Forest."

"I said that all three men are unconscious, the loading master on the dock, the tankerman on the deck and the deck officer collapsed over his panel. The tankerman and loading master seem to be coming out of it, but are in a stupor and can't stand up. They're incoherent and you'd better come see for yourself."

"I'll be right there," Stevens said and clicked off. He knew that standard operating procedure called for him to remain on the bridge in an emergency, but what he had heard superseded that protocol.

He got to Acton, who was standing near one of the men down on the deck, very quickly.

"It looks like they pissed themselves, Bernie," Acton said. He was always carefully formal on the radio, but he and Stevens had sailed together for many years and they were good friends. "Neither of them seems to have any idea what happened, but they reek of booze and I found a nearly-empty bourbon bottle over there and several paper coffee cups from one of the Anacortes coffeehouses."

Stevens gestured for Acton to follow and headed for the cargo control room, where they found the deck officer in much the same shape as the two outside; groggy, slurring his words, incoherent and unable to stand up. The smell of alcohol surrounded him like a cloak. A glance in the garbage can next to the control panel told Stevens that the circumstances were the same.

There was another paper coffee cup, from the same coffeehouse, and an empty pint bottle that had once held Wild Turkey. For some reason, the paper coffee cups stuck most in Stevens' mind. Like most ships, the *Royal Bearing II* was well-stocked with heavy china cups, made to hold the coffee's heat when outside in the cold and to take the punishment if dropped because of heavy seas. *Why the hell were these guys all using these flimsy paper cups?* he wondered, even though the answer to that question was among the least of his worries.

Acton, meanwhile, had set about organizing the crew that remained aboard – the skeleton crew and a few who had chosen sack time in their berths over New Year's Eve revelry in some tavern. Soon, Acton had four men cleaning up the oil on deck and he and Harris were evaluating the damage to the marine loading arm and the tanker's cargo manifold flange. In addition, emergency response personnel from the refinery were arriving and were put to work on the damage evaluation and clean-up parties. The captain headed back to the bridge to call the Royal Energy office in San Francisco, which was open 24/7 precisely because of the kind of incident the *Royal Bearing II* was experiencing.

At the same time Captain Stevens was making his way back to the bridge, six uniformed Royal Energy security personnel left the unloading dock and walked to a waiting van, which also bore the markings of Royal Energy Security. Nobody noticed the men, nor their departure.

Stevens' report to Royal Energy was short, to the point and devoid of references to unconscious men and empty booze bottles. Almost as soon as he was off the telephone, he had a call from Oil Clean-Up Corporation confirming they would be on scene shortly and that they had secured two empty barges which had been in the area and into which they would pump as much of the oil as they could. He told Oil Clean-Up that the Royal Energy emergency response crew had re-connected pumps to start removing the oil that was still inside the containment boom and had re-tethered the ship's bow to the dock.

Happy New Year, Stevens thought to himself. *The only way the year could have started any worst is if this goddamn ship had sunk.*

The three semi-conscious men were becoming more alert, even if maddeningly slowly. None had any idea what had happened, and they were all still acting confused and incoherent. Stevens asked Acton on the radio to find someone from the emergency response team that could break away and get the three men to the infirmary in the refinery. He wanted them to be observed, evaluated, sobered up and questioned by Royal Energy Security, in that order.

"And make sure they get a blood sample from those bastards," he growled. He knew their blood alcohol levels would be important evidence if the incident ever made it into court.

And he was very afraid it would.

The Royal Energy Security van, with its six passengers, drove past the refinery on March Point Road, then turned onto Route 20, heading for Anacortes.

Almost as quickly as the emergency crews arrived, Royal Energy's public relations action team would be departing San Francisco

International on a company plane, bound for Anacortes. They would work throughout the flight to develop the best possible spin on a very unfortunate incident.

Stevens, knowing his sleep during the next several days would be measured in minutes rather than hours, was nevertheless thinking about damage control as well, and not the type that involved repairing his ship. He had brought the bottles and paper cups with him to the bridge, and took them to his cabin, where he locked them in a heavy file cabinet.

At about that same time, the Royal Energy Security van pulled into the circular driveway of the Anacortes Inn and discharged its passengers. After they changed clothes and stripped the company insignia from the van, they headed for their rooms, knowing they still had time to enjoy one or more of the New Year's celebrations going on in restaurants and bars all over the town.

Just after Captain Stevens had called the Royal Energy office, a tall, trim and curvy woman who was considered hopelessly sexy by most of the men into whose sight she came, was dressing for a New Year's Eve bash at San Francisco's famed Mark Hopkins Hotel. Her date was to be the male anchor of the nightly news on the Bay Area's NBC affiliate, who, despite being three inches shorter than she, was considered the city's top straight catch. Of course, in San Francisco catches of the other variety were a dime a dozen, so she was looking forward to the evening with him.

She had been given the unfortunate name of Lulu LaFlint by her parents, and she had spent her life trying to disabuse employers, and men, of the idea that she was some kind of airhead or hooker. In fact, Lulu was a woman of prodigious talents, specializing in spin and damage control.

She had been chief of Royal's unofficial but very real spin team since shortly after Robert Beck, the company's CEO, had assumed command. Just as she had finished dressing and touching up her face, her company cell phone chirped.

"Bob Beck, Lulu," Beck said without preamble. "I know the timing is probably very bad, but we have a situation that I need you and your team on right now." She knew Beck was even-keeled and when he said right now, there was a reason for it. She groaned.

"Talk to me," she said. They had an easy relationship, which was all business but at the same time quite informal.

"There's been an oil spill up at Anacortes involving one of our tankers and our offloading facility. You know the area, and how the media and environmental groups will be on our asses like ugly on ape. I've got one of our jets waiting for you at SFO and the pilots are on their way. By the time you get there, I'll have a file delivered that's got all the details as we know them. And I'll keep you posted in flight on anything new."

"Jim and Jane are down in LaJolla on a little vacation," she said. Jim Fugit and Jane Kirk were her assistants, and had become a couple in contravention of company policy. She had told Beck months before that they were so good at what they did that she did not want any human resources weenies to try to do anything about it. Beck had passed along that word. "Can you have someone let the pilots know that we'll need a flight plan down to Palomar Airport in Carlsbad before heading up to Anacortes?"

"Already taken care of," Beck said.

Lulu asked, "How the hell did you know Jim and Jane are down there?"

"Knowing crap like that is why I'm paid the big bucks," he chuckled, then turned serious. "Lulu, I'm really sorry about this, for all of you. The timing sucks, but it has to be dealt with."

"Let the pilots know I'll be there within an hour," she said and they hung up. She then called Jim Fugit's number and caught them as they were heading out to dinner. Fugit put the call on speaker and she broke the news, told them how sorry she was that they'd have to spend New Year's Eve on a plane with her instead of at a nice dinner and, later, in a nice room.

"Plan to be at the Palomar Airport in about 90 minutes," she told them. "I've got to make a very sad phone call, then head for SFO. It may be a little longer than 90 minutes, but let's shoot for that.

"Oh, and incidentally, did you know that Bob Beck knew you two were in LaJolla before I told him?" she asked, a mischievous tone to her voice.

Jane gasped and Jim asked, "How the hell did he know that?" Lulu told them she'd asked him that very question, and what his answer had been.

After taking off her evening dress, stowing the jewelry and changing into traveling clothes, Lulu grabbed her gear – she and her team members always kept a bag packed for immediate departure – and headed for the airport, calling the TV anchor en route. By the time she hung up, she was quite upset, not because she'd had to break the date but because he hadn't sounded that pissed off about it.

Shortly after her call to the TV anchor and still fuming over his response, Lulu's cell chirped again. It was Beck.

"You'll be flying into Bellingham, Lulu," he said.

"I hope the pilots know that," she snapped, immediately regretting her tone.

Beck sensed the heat and ascribed it to being torn from her plans on New Year's Eve. "Yes, they are well aware of that," he said, a soothing tone in his voice. "I just wanted to fill you in on ground arrangements. Our people are working hard to make this as easy for you as possible."

She was by then thoroughly chagrined. "I appreciate that, Bob. Go ahead."

"You'll be met by a driver with a black Chevy Suburban, no company markings. He'll drive you to Anacortes, which is south of Bellingham. Winter jackets and gloves will be in the Suburban. You'll need them. And we've reserved three rooms for you and the others at the Anacortes Inn. If Jim and Jane decide they can't bear to be apart, make sure they get rooms with a connecting door. I don't want some snoopy reporter writing a sidebar that Royal Energy people are shacking up on the company dime."
"I'll take care of it, Bob," Lulu assured him. "I understand the concern. Most of the reporters will be looking for anything crappy about Royal they can find."

"One other thing," he said, his voice taking on an edge. "You remember that pain in the ass mouthpiece for Citizens for Responsible Growth, the one who was all over the news down in Galveston?"

"Sarah Cotton," she said quietly. "I'll never forget the performance she put on. Not a goddamn shred of evidence indicating where that oil came from, but she made hay for weeks with it."

"Well, stand by," Beck said. "She was spotted outside our refinery by security, and one of them checked the charter boat operators in the area and the captain of the *Whale Watcher II* tells us she's booked him to take her out to the site tonight. Paying a pretty penny for it, he told our guy, since it's a holiday."

"I'm almost looking forward to locking horns with her," Lulu said.

"Well, stay in touch and let me know if you need anything. Send drafts of statements or releases to me directly. Puget Sound is a lot more environmentally sensitive than the Galveston coast, so the enviro-crazies will be going nuts."

They concluded the call just as Lulu was pulling up to the corporate hangar at San Francisco International. She parked in a marked space on the side of the hangar around the corner from the doors and walked directly to the plane, which was sitting just outside the hangar. The co-pilot took her bag when she approached the stairway, they went into the plane and in a remarkably short time, they were in the air and headed south to Carlsbad. An hour later, they were on the ground at Palomar Airport, where Jim Fugit and Jane Kirk scrambled aboard. Soon, the Gulfstream III was climbing to the north, bound for Bellingham.

On the flight south, Lulu had talked with the refinery manager, who had scanned and emailed all the preliminary reports. As they were climbing to their cruise altitude, she emailed the reports to the others and they began reading them from their laptops at the same time. When they were finished, they talked generally about their order of battle once they were on the scene.

"You remember that bunch, Citizens for Responsible Growth, that was all over the Galveston deal?" Lulu asked them.

"Yeah, that bitch Sarah what's-her-name," Jim said.

"Sarah Cotton," Lulu nodded.

"Real bitch," he said.

"You can call her a bitch all you want, but she did a hell of a job in Galveston and she's used that incident to raise more hell in Washington over the whole issue of offshore and Alaska drilling. Before Galveston, nobody'd ever heard much of CFRG, but since then it seems to have become one of the power players in the field. Anyway, Beck told me she's been spotted already in Anacortes and that she's going out to the site tonight on a charter boat."

"Any statements or news releases yet from CFRG?" he asked.

"Not so far," Lulu responded. "If there had been, Beck would have emailed or faxed them to me."

"How in the world did she get there so fast?" Jane asked. "We hadn't heard about it until you called, and we have all the key word references in our laptops that would have alerted us to any news of that kind, whether it's ours or somebody else's."

"No idea," Lulu said, "but she's there and we'll undoubtedly have to deal with her. And like Beck told me, a spill in Puget Sound is going to be far more emotional to these people than one in Galveston, Texas."

The three quickly decided that their first response to the incident on behalf of the company should focus on the quick action of the Royal Energy first responders, the containment of the spill, and the clean-up efforts of Oil Clean-Up Corporation. "We'll want to make it sound like OCC is almost part of Royal, stress our role in training their people, and so forth," Lulu said.

Then she told them about the one report she had not shared with them. In it, Donald Pabst, the refinery manager, reported that when the bow of the *Royal Bearing II* had broken away from its moorings, it had dislodged the containment boom, allowing some unknown amount of oil to escape into the bay.

Even more potentially damaging to the company, Pabst had reported that three key employees involved in the monitoring of the unloading were found in what Pabst described as "a drunken stupor" and completely unable to function.

"Where are they now?" Jane asked.

"Apparently, Captain Stevens had them taken to the infirmary in the refinery," Lulu said, then a thought hit her. "I'd better call up there and make sure they're kept on ice until we can put this together." She consulted the list of phone numbers Beck had emailed to her and she soon reached Captain Stevens on the bridge.

He assured her that he had already taken that step, and that he had asked the doctor to take blood samples and to stay with them. That way, if any state inspectors or media showed up looking for them, it could truthfully be said that they were under a doctor's care at the moment and would be made available as soon as their conditions were stabilized. Lulu made a note to let Beck know that Captain Stevens was a thinking man and someone Royal should find a way of rewarding for his fast thinking.

Even if that reward were nothing more than a personal phone call from Beck expressing his gratitude.

The three dozed briefly but soon they came awake with the sensation of the plane descending. Lulu told them that as soon as they arrived on the scene, Jim should go to the ship and interview Captain Stevens and other members of the crew and develop a timeline they could use as evidence of the fast response. Meanwhile, she and Jane would go to the refinery and talk with Pabst, the doctor and the three drunken crewmen.

The Suburban's driver had the tailgate down and was awaiting their luggage when they stepped down from the plane. They settled into the comfortable seats for the hour drive to Anacortes. Beck had been right. They would need the heavy jackets and gloves.

In Anacortes, they quickly cleared refinery security and the driver steered for the administration building, where a pick-up truck was waiting to take Jim to the ship.

Captain Stevens was waiting for him and in a businesslike way took him through the unusual events of earlier that evening. He paused, realizing it was now approaching 3:30 a.m. He covered everything, from the broken mooring lines to the start of the clean-up effort. Captain Stevens recalled times with more precision than Jim could believe, and he noted them all. The timeline the spin team put together was going to be critical.

The captain told Jim that, based on his estimates and calculations, he believed the lines were pumping oil overboard for between 30 and 60 minutes, which would have resulted in between 6,400 and about 13,000 barrels in the spill.

He told him that he had sent the three men of the unloading crew to the infirmary and ordered them under the personal care of the doctor, who had been summoned immediately and was at the infirmary before the three arrived, according to what he had heard back from the men who had been dispatched to take them to the refinery compound. He added that their clothes smelled of whisky and he had locked the bottles and paper cups in the file cabinet in his stateroom.

Jim went with Captain Stevens to his stateroom and examined

the bottles and cups, then asked the captain to keep them there, under lock and key, until he knew what Lulu LaFlint and Jane Kirk learned at the infirmary.

Jim asked Captain Stevens whether he personally knew the three men in question, and the captain indicated that he did, at least in the sense that he had seen them before and they had unloaded his ship on several occasions. "When I talked with them, it was always small talk," he said. "You know, 'how's it going,' 'everything working okay?' and that kind of thing. They always seemed very professional and businesslike to me."

Captain Stevens ushered Jim to the forward area of the main deck so he could see for himself what had happened, pointing out the broken coupling that, when it had become disconnected from the tanker's manifold, had started the chain of events. As Stevens showed him around, he pointed out that nothing appeared broken or even slightly damaged except for the coupling.

"The two obvious questions, Captain," Jim said, "are how did the coupling break and why didn't all the built-in fail-safe systems we have shut down the pumps immediately?"

As they walked back to the superstructure to ride up to his cabin, the captain told Jim he had no idea how to answer either question. He went over the procedures for testing and visual examination of all the equipment used in a loading or unloading operation.

"Another question I have no answer for," Captain Stevens said, "is why the mooring drum brakes released the lines, which is what allowed the bow to pull away from the dock. I'm sure that's what broke the containment boom and allowed the oil to escape into the bay." He led Jim through the inspection and testing procedures of the mooring lines and drum brakes too.

"And to top it all off," Jim said, "we have the 'coincidence' of the three key crewmen all appearing to be drunk." He paused, considering, then added, "I'm thinking the company is going to want to get the ship out of here as soon as you finish unloading, so maybe I'd better take those bottles and cups now." The captain unlocked the file cabinet, put the bottles and paper cups in a heavy canvas duffel bag embroidered with the company logo and handed it to Jim.

Admonishing Captain Stevens again not to respond to any media inquiries without specific authorization of Bob Beck or Lulu LaFlint, he took the duffel bag and thanked the captain for his time and his insights. Then he added, "Captain, how soon can you be underway?"

"We normally take at least 24 hours after unloading is finished, but in this case we have to make sure the containment boom stays in place until all the oil is pumped out of the water. Then we have to clean up the ship and repair any damage done during the unloading. Even on a normal unloading, we get oil leakage on the deck and usually some minor damage to the equipment. I've already put out a recall of the crew so we can move that process along, assuming any of them are sober enough to get right to work." Jim thanked him and asked him to keep him posted on progress – or problems.

Soon, he was in the pick-up truck and moving in the direction of the refinery to rendezvous with Lulu and Jane.

In the infirmary, Jane Kirk and Lulu LaFlint had been talking with the doctor, who, as requested by phone, had with him the medical files of the three men, and Donald Pabst, the refinery manager, who had with him the men's personnel files. The doctor, a young-looking man named Dave Daugherty, told them that he had drawn blood from each and sent it to a lab whose chief technician he had called and explained the urgency. The tech had not been at a party and had agreed quickly to get out of bed and head for the lab. "He should be finished with the blood work in an hour or so," Dr. Daugherty said. "He'll call me when he has the results."

"Good job," Lulu said and made a note about that so she could give Bob Beck a complete rundown, including pointing out to him those who had shown exceptional initiative.

"Tell us about the men," Lulu said, "what you know about them."

"They've all been with us at least five years," Pabst said. "The thing about this whole mess that doesn't make sense is that all of them are very stable, very dependable. They are at work on time and they do their jobs well. And I've never known any of them to be drinkers."

He paused. "I assume you've heard about the booze smell and the whisky bottles?"

Lulu nodded. "I understand the captain has them locked up, and that's good, at least for the time being. What about the incident itself, the mooring lines and all? Has anything similar every occurred here?"

"Never," Pabst said immediately. "All the lines, the couplers, the containment boom, all of them are checked and rechecked as standard procedure. We inspect them before and after every unloading operation. This refinery has a 100 percent safety record." He suddenly looked down, disheartened. "At least it did until tonight, uh, last night."

Dr. Daugherty had been consulting the medical files while Pabst was talking. "There's no indication in the medical files that any of the men has ever had a substance abuse issue of any kind." Lulu noted that and asked the doctor for his contact information and told him he might be called on to address the media at some point.

"How about your current best guess on damage done as a result of this incident?" Lulu asked, turning back to Pabst.

"I've been in touch all night with Captain Stevens and we are on the same page here." He told her their estimate of the volume of the spill, and Lulu noted the range of minutes and of barrels, although she was sure Jim Fugit was getting the same data from the captain.

"The folks from OCC – the Oil Clean-up Corporation – have told us they're working on oil in both Fidalgo and Padilla Bays," Pabst continued. "The good news is they have two empty oil barges on site and the containment boom has been reconnected. That means we're pumping from within the containment boom directly to the refinery and OCC is pumping the oil that escaped onto the barges."

After another fifteen minutes, Lulu felt that they had enough for an initial statement, given what they would no doubt learn from Fugit's conversation with Stevens. She told Pabst that he should concentrate his efforts on the clean-up, finishing the unloading of the *Royal Bearing II* and keeping the refinery operating, and let her and her team handle the statement and deal with the media. At some point, she told him, they would probably ask him to address the media, too.

She gave both men her cell phone number and asked Dr. Daugherty to call her as soon as he had any results on the men, then asked Pabst to call with anything new, good news or bad. She told him that Jim was passing along to Captain Stevens Beck's desire that the *Royal Bearing II* depart as soon as possible after it was completely unloaded and the oil inside the containment boom had been collected, whether it needed to go to the Royal repair facility or was able to resume its regular run to Valdez, Alaska. Just then, Jim appeared and confirmed that he had passed that message to the captain. He was introduced to Dr. Daugherty and Pabst, then the spin team left them to their work.

The team used a conference room and after comparing notes, quickly drafted a statement for release to the media. They used the conference room telephone, which of course had a speaker feature, to call Beck, read him the statement and get his okay to release it. Beck asked about the whisky bottles and Jim told him he had them in a duffel bag. They had been put into individual plastic bags by Stevens and nobody but Stevens had touched them since they were discovered.

Beck told them that he wanted the statement released as soon as possible, and by whichever of the team would look the most tired and haggard. He wanted it to appear Royal was busting its butt to get to the bottom of the incident. When Jim told him Captain Stevens had already recalled his crew and hoped to be finished unloading by 6:00 a.m., Lulu set the news conference for 8:00 a.m. They hung up, then Jim called Captain Stevens and told him the news conference would be on the dock in front of the ship. No use hiding it, he told him, and it would give the reporters a front-row seat for the clean-up effort. He asked the captain to have as many of his men visible as possible, and working their asses off. And, he added, the captain himself should be visible on deck, supervising the work.

Royal would be seen as working around the clock.

Because of her girl-next-door wholesome look, Jane was tapped to make the first statement. Lulu asked her to lose her make-up and muss her hair beforehand.

The tired and frazzled look, but with an in-control-of-everything delivery, was the image Lulu LaFlint and Bob Beck were after. Jane had done it before and was quite good at it. Jim put the duffel bag in the back of the Suburban where it would remain hidden until they had learned from Dr. Daugherty about the blood test results.

STATEMENT OF ROYAL ENERGY CORPORATION

Anacortes, Washington, 8:00 a.m.,
January 1, 2010

Last evening at about 7:00 p.m., our tanker, the Royal Bearing II, was unloading its cargo of Alaska North Shore crude oil at the company's March Point, Washington refinery when an unloading arm somehow disconnected and between 6,400 and 13,000 barrels of oil were pumped overboard and into the water.

When any tanker is loading or unloading oil, it is surrounded by an oil containment boom designed to contain any spillage. Unfortunately, one end of this boom also became disengaged and an undetermined amount of oil escaped into the bay.

Our emergency pumps were quickly deployed and are in place as we speak, pumping the oil still within the containment area to the refinery. Oil Clean-Up Corporation immediately responded to our call last night and moved with great dispatch with two clean-up boats and two empty barges and is pumping the oil outside the containment area onto those barges. A third OCC boat is on its way to assist.

The clean-up operation will continue on a 24-hour basis and it is anticipated that virtually all the spilled oil will be recaptured and very little will reach any shore.

Royal Energy pledges its total efforts to containment and clean-up. A detailed examination of the surrounding shorelines will be undertaken and any effort necessary will be directed at cleaning those areas as well.

Finally, we pledge a full and detailed examination of all that happened to cause this incident and we further pledge our full and complete cooperation with Federal and state authorities in their investigations. Our company will be focusing its efforts on modifications or improvements in equipment and procedures that will keep such an incident from happening again, here or anywhere else.

We take very seriously our duty to continue to deliver the energy this country requires with as little impact on our surroundings as possible.

Royal Energy will continue to keep the public and the authorities informed of our progress.

Jane Kirk

Asst. Information Officer

As soon as the reporters started to gather around for the news conference, Jim Fugit broke away and went to talk with the refinery's clean-up crew, which was busily pumping the oil from inside the containment boom. He saw skimmers and pumps that were herding and pumping when he walked up to the foreman of the clean-up crew, Herb Smith, a small, wiry man whose weathered features made it difficult to estimate his age. Jim guessed he was in his mid-fifties.

He knew the man's name from the personnel roster Pabst had prepared for them. "Quite a mess, huh, Herb?" he said while extending his hand. "Jim Fugit. I'm with the P.R. department in San Francisco."

"Oh, one of the – what the hell did Pabst call you guys– the spin team?" Smith asked with a grin. Jim nodded and shrugged his shoulders, as if to say, "Somebody's got to do it."

"I guess that's what we're called," he said. "How bad is it? Not for publication."

"I'll tell you this for sure," Smith said. "It could've been a hell of a lot worse. A majority – a big majority – of the spill got trapped inside the containment boom, even though that failed for a while. And we're being helped by a lack of wind, as far as the stuff that escaped when the boom was loose is concerned. It's not moving as fast as it would have if we had a lot of wind. We've been damn lucky so far."

"How long do you think it'll take to get the contained oil sucked up?" Jim asked. Smith smiled at the terminology. He knew it was a bit more complicated than just sucking it up.

"I'd estimate 24 to 48 hours, and the way things are going right now, I'm betting on the low end of that range."

"Any reason the *Royal Bearing II* can't get underway as soon as you're finished with the contained oil?"

"Not as far as I'm concerned. I haven't heard about any damage to the ship except that goddamn coupling that started this mess. And I can see the captain has his crew humping at getting the ship cleaned up." He looked toward the center of the dock, where the reporters were crowded around Jane Kirk.

"And I see we've got a nice audience watching us today."

"Yes," Jim confirmed, grinning. "We staged that just so the reporters can see all you guys busting your asses to get everything cleaned up. So look sharp." He smiled at Smith, slapped him on the back, and walked back toward where the news conference had just broken up.

Jim Fugit, Jane Kirk and Lulu LaFlint packed up their gear and walked down the dock toward the refinery's infirmary.

Sarah Cotton had told Boone Malory and Suzy Dillinger in November that she was going to take a week off over the holidays to do some sightseeing in the Puget Sound area. When both had expressed shock that anyone would choose that area during the winter, she had told them that, aside from the weather, it was a perfect time to visit because the normal tourist hoards would be missing. A friend from her college days had convinced her, she had told them, that as long as she dressed for it, it was the perfect time of year to see the beautiful area.

She had shown them brochures of the inter-island ferries that shuttled people back and forth to the numerous small islands in the Sound and the Strait of Juan de Fuca of kayaking adventures for the very hearty, whale research centers, small inns and restaurants, local entertainment and of course, the wonders of winter wildlife.

She would not be able to do any whale-watching, she had told Suzy in response to her question, because the Orcas that made the area their home normally leave in October and return in early Spring.

Sarah had arrived at Seattle-Tacoma Airport on December 27. As she had told Boone and Suzy she would, she had island-hopped and stayed at a variety of small inns and bed and breakfasts and had arrived in Anacortes on the 30th. The morning of the 31st, she had driven to Whidbey Island for the day and was on the Deception Pass Bridge returning to Anacortes early that evening listening to a local radio station.

Its call letters were KWLE and billed itself as "The Whale." A few minutes before seven, a news bulletin interrupted regular programming. The news reader spoke in very somber tones of a reported oil spill at the March Point Refinery, owned by the Royal Energy Corporation. The spill, he said, was reported to have occurred at the refinery's unloading dock. More details as they become available, he said, and back to regular programming.

When Sarah reached the end of the bridge, she pulled her rental car over into a turn-out where she could safely use her phone to call Boone. She doubted he was out at any kind of New Year's Eve party.

Sure enough, Boone answered his cell on the second ring. "Boone, you're not going to believe this," she said, "but I'm about 15 miles away from another oil spill."

"You've got to be kidding me," he responded. "Where?"

"There's a refinery at March Point, right next to Anacortes, where I'm staying. The Puget Sound area is as pristine as it gets. It was apparently a spill that happened while a tanker was unloading Alaska crude."

Boone laughed, feeling just a bit guilty about it. "I'll be damned. You do have perfect timing, don't you? You go to Galveston for a conference and stumble into a spill, and now you're on vacation and have another one dropped in your lap. You should never be allowed to travel. You cause oil spills; it seems to me."

Sarah was impatient to get to the site. "I'll call you as soon as I know more, but we should plan on making our presence known as long as I'm here. It sure worked well for us in Texas."

"Damn sure did," he agreed and they disconnected. She started her car and drove as fast as she dared in the direction of March Point. Her cell chirped again.

"Sarah, it's Win Mifflin," the voice said. She smiled.

"Win, where are you?"

"I'm near enough to Anacortes to call and see if we can have dinner tomorrow," he said. Win was a sometime business associate.

"That would be great, Win. Call me tomorrow and we can work out the details. I'm driving right now and couldn't write anything down if I needed to."

"Be happy to, Sarah. It will be great to catch up. I've got a new project going and I want to hear about your latest adventures." She laughed and they disconnected.

She continued on Route 20 until she reached March Point Road and turned north toward the Royal Energy unloading dock. News crews were already on site, but were being kept outside the fence and away from the dock by security people. She could see a lot of what she assumed were refinery personnel scurrying about inside the compound.

Sarah parked, locked her car and walked across the street to the small knot of reporters outside the gate. The buzz among them seemed to be that this could be a large spill, but nobody was talking yet. She could see two Coast Guard vessels in the bay and what appeared to be a couple of Coast Guard officers in uniform on the dock. The Oil Clean-up Corporation boats were also visible in the bay.

A reporter from one of the local radio stations, an oily little squirt with a pockmarked face and an impossibly deep voice, saw Sarah and moved as close to her as he could get in the crowd. He asked her who she represented. Rather than answering him directly, she asked him how his station heard about the spill.

"We got a tip at about 6:15," he boomed in his important-sounding voice. "Anonymous caller. I got here about 7:00. Assholes haven't said anything yet." His breath was rancid and she backed away from him quickly, nodding her thanks.

Sarah decided to drive back to Anacortes, where she knew it would be easier to find a charter boat for rent. She wanted to see the mess first-hand, and try to get some photos. Maybe she would charter an airplane tomorrow, too.

On the waterfront in Anacortes, she spotted several boat charter operations, both for fishing and for sightseeing. All appeared closed, but at the office of Capt. Eddie's Whale Watching & Excursions, she saw lights in the windows of whatever was on the second floor of the building. Maybe Captain Eddie lived there. She called the number that was painted below the lighted sign.

"Captain Eddie's," a gruff voice said.

"Hello," Sarah said. "I'd like to charter a boat."

"Really?" Capt. Eddie said. "When did you have in mind?" He did not get asked for charters much during the winter, and he could use the money.

"Tonight. As soon as you can. I'm in front of your building now." She saw a curtain pulled aside as he looked out.

"How long a trip are we talking about?"

"Probably three or four hours."

"When?"

"Tonight. I just told you that. As soon as we can." She would need to go back to the Anacortes Inn and get her heaviest coat and her camera. She wondered if Captain Eddie had already started his New Year's eve festivities.

"Where would you like to go?"

"To the March Point refinery and around Fidalgo and Padilla bays."

Captain Eddie had heard about the spill and his antennae went up. She must be a reporter, and probably a big-time reporter. Someone on a fat expense account. "It's a holiday, miss," he said, "so it'll be double the posted prices you see down there."

"That won't be a problem," she assured him, not even looking for the price list painted on the side of the building.

"I'll be down in 20 minutes," he said. "Give me time to take a shower and call my first mate."

"I need to run back to my motel and get my heavy coat anyway. I'll be back in 30 minutes." They disconnected.

When she returned and parked, she saw two men standing on the dock next to *Whale Watcher II*. Captain Eddie stepped forward and introduced himself and his first mate. As he helped her aboard he said, "No guarantees on how close to the spill we'll be allowed. Price will be the same either way. Three hour minimum."

"Just cast off as soon as possible, please," she snapped. "I know the Coast Guard is already there, so I realize you can't give any guarantees."

He wondered why the refinery guy had asked him about her when he called earlier. But he liked this spunky chick.

And he liked the way she looked, even wearing that bulky coat. Some kind of ski parka, he thought, although he'd never been skiing himself. Got enough of the fucking cold on the boats.

When they were underway, Sarah asked Captain Eddie to get as close to the spill as possible. "Naturally," he growled. She assured him that if he got too close and some of the oil got on his boat, she would pay for the cleaning.

Captain Eddie proved to be quite adept at dodging the Coast Guard vessels that were cruising in the vicinity of the *Royal Bearing II*, Sarah got some excellent – and revealing – shots of the slick from a number of angles, and the *Whale Watcher II* did, indeed get a light coating of Alaska North Shore crude on its hull.

Sarah was able to get shots – from a distance - of the crew cleaning the deck of the tanker.

She also got some photos from fairly close range of the area where the containment boom had failed before a Coast Guard patrol boat hailed them on a loud speaker and told Captain Eddie in no uncertain terms to vacate the area at once. As they were departing the area to return to Anacortes, Sarah snapped a few final photos, these of the lead boat of the Oil Clean-up Corporation arriving on the scene.

"Captain Eddie, you're a darling," she exclaimed. "That's all I need. You can head for home, run my credit card and still make one of the New Year's Eve parties." It did not take any additional prodding. The *Whale Watcher II* turned and headed for Anacortes.

Sarah called Boone from her car as she drove toward the Anacortes Inn.

She told him she would email her photos as soon as she booted up her laptop. In turn, Boone confirmed that he had been able to book a private plane for first light so she could fly over the oil spill, too. He gave her the name of the air charter company and told her they had reported that first light this time of year was not until almost 8:00 a.m. She knew that, of course.

Sarah was at the Anacortes Airport at 7:30 a.m. so she could get the paperwork out of the way and be in the air at daybreak. She told the pilot she wanted to circle the oil spill at March Point at no higher than 1,500 feet, preferably lower. The pilot, who was also the owner of the air charter company, told her there would be no problem unless the Coast Guard issued a fly-over restriction. They hadn't yet, he told her, but that order could come down any time.

He was a short, wiry man of 40 or so, wearing worn khaki pants, a weathered leather A-2 jacket and a billed military-style pilot's crush cap.

In all, he was dressed in a style favored by many civilian pilots since World War II. It was as much their uniform as were her black dress, pearls, tan blazer and black pumps. He completed the paperwork quickly, swiped her credit card and walked quickly out the back door to the plane, which was parked on the ramp just behind his office. He got Sarah in the right seat, helped her strap in and commenced his walk-around inspection of the plane.

Then, satisfied that there were no leaks or other observable problems, he jumped into the left seat and ran down his pre-flight checklist. Soon, they were airborne and turned in the direction of the Royal Energy unloading dock. A light mist was hanging from low clouds and it was cold and just a bit breezy. Typical weather for this time of year in the Puget Sound area.

From the air, Sarah could see much that she had not seen – or could not see - the night before. The oil that had escaped when the containment boom was breached was clearly visible in the two bays. The OCC clean-up boats were scuttling around the outside of the floating oil, skimming and pumping it into the two barges. She took lots of photos.

God bless digital cameras, she thought to herself. No film to change, and you could take thousands of shots and then take your time deciding which ones you wanted to print or otherwise use.

Over the dock, she could see the lines that were pumping the oil that had been kept inside the containment area. She assumed they were pumping it straight to the refinery, where she expected it could be cleaned and refined. She could not see much oil at all that had reached a shoreline, and where there had been shore contact, clean-up crews were on site, likely had been so all night. Some of the portable halogen lights were still on. She was impressed by all the efforts being made.

She noticed a fairly large group of people clustered on the dock who appeared to be listening to someone who was in front of them and realized that Royal Energy was probably already starting its public relations damage control at the same time the damage control on the water was taking place.

She wished she had checked on that before jumping in the airplane.

Even so, Sarah felt sure she had gotten some fairly damaging photos and told the pilot he could return to Anacortes. The Coast Guard had never ordered them out of the area, even though they had been flying quite low.

Back in her room, Sarah called Boone and reported what she had seen. "I think some of the shots I got will be good, but not great," she told him. "From what I saw, they're doing everything they can to contain, remove and clean up the oil. But the fact still remains that there was a pretty good size spill in a very sensitive area."

"Good job, Sarah," he said. She smiled to herself. Like most people, she enjoyed compliments and liked that Boone was good at giving them.

"I have a statement drafted," she told him, "and it will have photos attached. But it's designed to be a response to the Royal Energy statement that was probably being delivered when I was flying over the dock. That's what it looked like, anyway. If that's what it was, we may need to adapt it a little if they said anything I'm not expecting, but I'll email you my draft as soon as we hang up. I'd like your take on it."

"I'll look at it right away and get back with you with any comments I have. When do you plan to be back here?"

"It depends on what happens here, but I'd guess two or three days."

"Good," he said, paused and went on in a quiet voice. "I miss you."

Sarah felt a tingle, and her face got warm. With a smile, she softly replied, "I miss you, too."

At 1:00 that afternoon, having been given the green light by Boone, Sarah released CFRG's first statement about what the media were now calling "The Anacortes Oil Spill."

PRISTINE PUGET SOUND ENDANGERED BY OIL SPIL

While unloading a cargo of over half a million barrels of Alaska crude oil at the March Point refinery in the pristine Puget Sound, the unloading mechanism on the tanker, Royal Bearing II, apparently experienced a catastrophic failure, pumping untold thousands of gallons of crude oil into Fidalgo Bay, Padilla Bay and the area around Anacortes, Washington.

This is just the latest in an appalling string of incidents attributable to the oil industry which have resulted in serious environmental damage, as the attached photos graphically demonstrate.

While the clean-up and recovery efforts of Royal Energy and the Coast Guard are to be commended, the fact of the damage cannot be swept away and should never be hidden from the American people.

The Administration's policy of essentially removing all restrictions on oil exploration and drilling in the pristine and sensitive areas of America must be overturned by the Congress. The alternative is a continuation of the kind of catastrophe we have witnessed here in Anacortes. In fact, we fear that with reduced oversight, these incidents will increase in frequency.

Citizens for Responsible Growth urges all Americans to contact their congressional representative and senators and demand that they vote to overturn the Administration's policy and establish an immediate embargo on all new oil exploration in America until an acceptable policy can be developed specifying areas in which oil exploration is inappropriate. Further, we encourage all Americans to demand that the Congress increase its support of the development of clean, renewable energy.

Several interviews took up most of the afternoon, including one with CNN.

After their news conference on the morning of January 1, Jim Fugit caught up with Lulu LaFlint and Jane Kirk in the small conference room in the infirmary. Jim brought the women up to date on what he had found out about the spill. It did not take long.

Consulting his notebook, he said, "Nobody knows how it could have happened, why it wasn't detected immediately, why the unloading arms' coupling and line brakes failed, why the key unloading personnel were all found passed out drunk or why the containment boom detached. As Captain Stevens described it to me, it was the perfect storm. Not an original statement, I know."

Lulu asked whether he had confirmed the volume of the spill and how much escaped the containment boom. "Stevens is still standing by the original estimate of between 6,400 and 13,000 barrels in the spill, and the clean-up folks estimate that ten to 30 percent of that escaped the boom. OCC is on site and may have a revised estimate for us by the time they finish."

"At least the weather's been calm," Jane noted, gazing through the conference room window at the soft fluttering of the flag on the flagpole.

"And that's really helped," Jim said. "Everybody's mentioned that, and everybody seems to feel that, as of now, the expectation is that this will all be able to be cleaned up with little to no damage to any coastline. The media damage is something else entirely. The environmentalists are already all over this, mainly that damn Sarah Cotton, who, of all people, just happened to be in the area when the spill occurred. How does that happen?"

Lulu's cell phone buzzed and she saw on its face that Bob Beck was on the line. When she pushed the button to answer it, she said, "Hi, Bob."

"I liked the statement and I liked Jane's delivery at the news conference. She had just the right look, I think. Where are you on your fact-finding and what's our next step?"

Lulu already had the outline of the next release in her laptop, pending new information from Jim Fugit or from others on the scene. "Here's what I'm thinking right now, Bob. Keep in mind that this may change if new information comes to light. But for now, the points are these: first, Royal will pay for all clean-up costs and damages related in any way to the spill.

"Second, virtually all the oil will be cleaned up within 48 hours from when it was first detected.

"Third, a complete investigation and analysis of the incident has already been undertaken by Royal, along with an evaluation of all procedures used in our unloading operations and the results of our investigation will be shared with the authorities so new rules or procedures, if called for, can be implemented.

"Fourth, an inspection and testing of all unloading equipment will be performed, including on the vessel in question, all of our other vessels, and at all of our refineries and unloading facilities. Again, any problems uncovered will be shared with the authorities and with all other companies using the same equipment.

'Fifth, we would like to thank and congratulate the people of Oil Clean-up Corporation for their very quick response and their effective work in cleaning up the oil that escaped the containment boom.

"And sixth, our thanks go out to the entire Royal Energy family who worked around the clock over the holiday to clean up this spill."

Beck let that sink in, and a moment later said, "I like it. That's good."

Lulu smiled and gave high fives to Jim and Jane. Then Beck continued.

"Lulu, I don't want any misunderstanding about this. I want to keep the three people who were found unconscious under wraps, as much as possible. If anybody asks where the people are that were working during the unloading, just tell them they all became ill and are being treated for food poisoning in the infirmary, or something like that. Tell them that they will be a central focus of our inquiry. Tell them that they will be made available to the authorities when requested. There's no reason they should be made available, under those circumstances, to the media."

Lulu knew better than to question Bob Beck's direct orders. "I understand," she said.

"When do you plan the next statement?" Beck asked.

"Jane told them we'd update them in 24 hours," she said, "so I was planning on 10:30 a.m. tomorrow, with Jane still doing the talking."

Beck agreed.

Not long after her call with Bob Beck had concluded, one of the doctors found the three members of the spin team in the conference room. He told them the men on duty the night before were now well enough to be interviewed, if the interview was brief. He said he would have them brought to the conference room.

Lulu told him she would prefer that they interview them individually, so the doctor showed them to the rooms where the men were being kept under observation. The spin team split up, each taking one of the men and armed with the same list of questions.

An hour later, when they were back in their conference room, they found they'd gotten remarkably similar stories, differing only in a few details, which led them to believe the stories had not been rehearsed. In fact, it would have been virtually impossible for the men to rehearse a story since they had been kept in separate rooms since they were found.

All three vehemently denied drinking on duty. They had no idea why liquor bottles had been found near their duty stations, nor why they smelled of alcohol. All reported that a security man had brought them a burger and coffee just after the unloading had begun. They all suspected the burger as the culprit in making them sick, although one thought there was something faintly "odd" about the taste of the coffee.

None remembered passing out, but all remembered coming out of the haze. However, the doctors had confirmed that the three had blood alcohol levels of .27, .29 and .29, over three times the limit for driving in most states. They may have gotten food poisoning, the doctors agreed, but they were still drunk.

The spin team agreed again that the best course of action was to avoid discussing the condition of the unloading personnel at all, but instead to stress the rapid response to the spill, the minimal damage caused, the testing and inspections that would uncover any equipment failure involved. They would mention that the crew, who had eaten together before starting work, all appeared to have gotten food poisoning from what they ate, but nothing beyond that.

Lulu LaFlint called Bob Beck to update him on the interviews and their spin plan. She took perverse pleasure in interrupting his New Year's Day dinner, which she saw as payback. She was still pissed at the TV anchor and had every intention of remaining so.

Beck agreed with everything she said and repeated that he wanted to soft-pedal the details concerning the men and wanted to avoid a liquor implication completely, at least for the time being.

Lulu, Jim and Jane went back to the Anacortes Inn for drinks, dinner and bed. Only one of them, of course, would sleep alone.

The following morning at 10:30, Jane read the latest statement without allowing questions, saying that the statement contained all that Royal Energy knew at this time. She added, however, that at that point, some 80 percent of the oil had been cleaned up and Royal was confident that number would be 95 percent or better by the next morning.

On January 3, Sarah Cotton picked up a rumor that was circulating among the reporters still on site that three key unloading employees had been found drunk and incapacitated.

Sarah spent most of the day talking to reporters and a couple of refinery employees she had charmed, then called Boone and, in an un-characteristically-excited voice, told him about the rumor. He asked where she'd learned about this, and whether anyone had any evidence to back up the rumors.

"I haven't talked with anyone who actually saw them," she said. "It's all hearsay, stuff I picked up from Royal Energy refinery workers and reporters. I have to admit that if it's true, Royal is keeping a real tight lid on it. Royal plans another news conference tomorrow morning at 10:30 – that seems to be their favorite time now - and I plan to be there. If none of the other reporters asks about the rumor, I'll ask about it. That should get Lulu LaFlint's heart going, and even spook Jane Kirk, who I assume will be their mouthpiece again. She won't answer the question, but it will still be out there publicly."

"Good job, Sarah," Boone said. "Then what are your plans?"

"I've heard that Lulu and the spin team are checking out of the hotel in the morning, so I assume they're heading home. In that case, I'll stick around for a day to milk the media and come back to Monterey on the 5th."

"Can we go ahead and refer to the rumors – call them improprieties by Royal personnel or something like that – in our statement?"

"I was going to ask you for the okay to do just that."

"You've got it."

"I'm booked on a flight out of SeaTac day after tomorrow." She gave him her flight information and he assured her he would pick her up.

Sarah drafted her statement for the next day and emailed it to Boone as a draft.

She added to her transmittal email the caveat that she may need to tweak it depending on what Royal said at news conference the next morning.

The spin team had breakfast at the Anacortes Inn on the morning of January 4, after packing and checking out. Lulu decided that she would take the point today, so to speak. She was skilled in front of the media and her stepping in at this point would perhaps keep the reporters a little off balance. Jane and Jim enthusiastically endorsed the idea.

They had spent much of the day before at the dock watching the clean-up work. They talked to all the key people involved in the effort, including Captain Stevens, who was busy getting the *Royal Bearing II* ready for departure on the 5th. Beck had backed off his demand to get the ship out of there earlier, deciding that it would have looked too much like Royal was trying to hide something.

The spin team got no new information on the cause of the mechanical failures.

While Jane had started drafting the statement for the following day, Lulu and Jim had gone to the infirmary where they again interviewed the three men who had become so central to this incident and ultimately to Royal's culpability. This time they had all three brought into the conference room and interviewed them together.

Once again, they had vehemently denied – offered to swear under oath or take lie detector tests – that they had not been drinking during the process. Company regulations prescribed that they refrain from drinking alcohol for 12 hours before a loading or unloading operation, and all stated emphatically that they had adhered to that regulation. None could explain their blood alcohol reading.

The spin team was frankly getting bored at that point. They were hearing the same thing over and over, and they were anxious to get on the company jet that would be awaiting them in Bellingham the next afternoon. They were looking forward to getting home and out of this cold and drizzle.

San Francisco could be cold and drizzly, but here it was constant, at least until it got cold enough that the drizzle turned into snow or a freezing rain.

They had called Bob Beck after Jane finished and got his approval for the statement. He had liked Jane's approach, stressing all the positives and making no reference to any of the mysteries. Lulu had told him it was her intention to read the statement and take no questions if she could help it.

At 10:30 a.m. on January 4, three and a half days after the problem started, the reporters, cameras and microphones that remained, most had long since left, were gathered once again on the dock and Lulu read the statement:

"*It is now estimated that over 95 percent of the oil has been removed from the water. The clean-up effort continues, with the crews scouring the waters around the site looking for any missed oil. Very little oil has reached any shoreline, and where it has, clean-up crews are on site. With the exception of two – two – waterfowl, no birds or animals have been found to have had contact with the oil.*

"*The Royal Bearing II has unloaded the last of its oil, repairs made, all equipment has been inspected and tested, and will cast off for Valdez tomorrow.*

"*Royal Energy will continue with its investigation, focusing on the inspection, testing and evaluation of all of its unloading equipment and procedures, in an attempt to determine the cause of this accident. Any problems discovered in this process will result in replacement or redesign of equipment and/or modification to procedures so that such an accident cannot be repeated. As we've said from the beginning, Royal Energy will pay for all costs of this clean-up effort, including compensating the Coast Guard and the State of Washington for all costs they have incurred.*

"*Again, we salute our own employees, Coast Guard personnel and the Oil Clean-up Corporation for their tireless work.*"

When Lulu finished it appeared the reporters, who, in fairness to them, were bored out of their minds at the lack of news, were going to go along with Lulu's admonition that there would be no questions.

However, Sarah jumped from her seat and asked in a loud and firm voice, "When you said you saluted your own employees, does that include the unloading personnel, who I'm told were found drunk and passed out when the leak was discovered?" Suddenly, the reporters were abuzz.

Lulu shot her a look of total surprise, one that she'd had the opportunity to practice on several occasions. She said, also in a loud and firm voice, "I have no idea what you're talking about. Now, if you'll excuse me, we have a plane to catch. My phone number is on the statement if any of you ladies and gentlemen have any questions as to our ongoing investigation."

She gathered her things and she followed Jim and Jane, who were hurrying to the waiting Suburban. She noticed that her knees were a little wobbly and she did not like that at all. She was used to being in control. *Where did that green bitch hear about that?* she wondered, and vowed to put a lid on this whole facility until she had all the answers. The plan to leave today was sounding better all the time.

On the way to Bellingham, Lulu called Bob Beck to report on the news conference and the fact that Sarah Cotton somehow knew about the situation with the unloading personnel. Beck told them he had anticipated a leak – you can't really expect there not to be a leak when so many people knew about the men, he had said – and he had talked with the refinery manager and the three men would be put on a paid medical leave of absence. They would be confined to their homes and only the doctor allowed to see them.

Beck thanked Lulu and her team – she had the speaker function activated – for interrupting their New Year's plans to respond to this crisis, and told them to take a week off when they got back. Lulu agreed, with the proviso that they all keep their cell phones with them in case of new developments or media inquiries. Beck thought that very wise.

The jet was waiting when they reached the Bellingham airport. They remembered to leave the jackets and gloves in the Suburban, Lulu thanked the refinery manager and they boarded the jet. The jet had not even started its takeoff roll when Lulu dozed off in her seat, wondering how the hell Sarah Cotton – *the too-clever bitch* – had found out about the unloading guys and the booze.

At about that same time, Sarah Cotton was issuing another statement on behalf of Citizens for Responsible Growth.

ANACORTES OIL SPILL – A LESSON FOR AMERICA

As much as 550,000 gallons of Alaska crude oil were released into the pristine waters surrounding the March Point refinery near Anacortes, Washington. While unloading its cargo, the tanker Royal Bearing II suffered a bewildering series of problems. Its unloading arm broke, the mooring system failed and the mandatory oil containment boom came loose in the area of the bow of the ship.

This is another in a long line of failures on the part of the oil industry.

The crew, both on the ship and on shore, failed in their duties, the monitoring safeguards failed, the mechanical equipment failed and the oil containment boom failed. Just as the current Administration in Washington, D.C. is failing in its responsibilities to our environment.

Perhaps most troubling, there are widespread rumors here at the scene, unsubstantiated at this point, that three key personnel of the unloading crew were extremely intoxicated during the unloading process. So intoxicated, according to the rumors, that all three were found passed out at their stations after the oil spill was discovered. We at CFRG call on Royal Energy to make these men and their medical files available to the authorities and to the media so that we can all separate fact from rumor and learn the truth.

The Puget Sound was very, very lucky this time around. A major oil spill has apparently been contained with minimal environmental damage, and for that we commend Royal Energy, the Coast Guard and Oil Clean-up Corporation. However, we must keep in mind the unpleasant fact that next time, America might not be so lucky.

Open oil exploration and refining in America must be stopped now! Then, future permits can be issued on a case-by-case basis, depending on the sensitivity of the area in question.

Citizens for Responsible Growth urges you to contact your congressman and senators and express your concerns with this administration's oil exploration policy.

CHAPTER 18

Win Mifflin was seated in the dining room of the Anacortes Inn when Sarah walked in. She smiled and waved, but was not really looking forward to a dinner with a business associate. It had been a long day, with the Royal Energy news conference, her news conference and the media interviews and tapings. A bottle of wine was waiting at the table when she sat down.

"Well, what brings you to beautiful downtown Anacortes this time of the year?" Win asked with a mischievous smile. "Or should I even ask?"

"Don't give me that," she shot back with a smile. "I was taking a few days' vacation, doing the winter tourist thing. It's not as crowded up here as it is in the summer." She stopped and smiled again. "But it was a hell of a coincidence, wasn't it? The oil spill has turned it into work."

"I'll bet," he said with a not-quite-sympathetic tone. "I don't think you're ever on vacation, never mind relaxing."

"What about you, Win?" She changed the subject. "What brings you up here in this corner of the world?"

"I just finished a major project for my biggest client," he said. "And I'm out of here tomorrow." He was a retained consultant for several firms, but she knew who his biggest client was.

"How did it go?"

"In terms of timing – getting everything done on time and so forth – it went exceedingly well," he said. "And all the technical aspects worked to perfection. I don't know about the quantifiable end result. I don't think the end result was quite what the client was looking for, so they probably won't be entirely happy."

Sarah sipped her wine, gave him a questioning look. He continued, "I'm known for results, and I just don't know if the results here are what they expected."

"Will it affect your relationship with them?" she asked coyly.

"I hope not," he said simply.

The salads were served then, and their conversation moved to current events, the oil spill, to the fact that nobody had been injured or killed in the accident, unless one counted the three crewmen who appeared drunk.

"Sarah!" The cry came from halfway across the room, which was almost full, given the number of reporters around for the spill and its aftermath. Sarah spun in her chair and was startled to see Amanda Baines heading her way. She jumped to her feet and rushed toward her without explaining the interruption to Win. They hugged and squealed, which baffled Win. He had never known Sarah to be that demonstrative, had never seen her hug another woman – or a man, for that matter - in all the time he had known her.

"What are you doing in Anacortes?" Sarah asked.

"*The Chronicle* finally made a decision on the oil spill – I think mainly because Royal Energy is a San Francisco firm - and decided to send me," Amanda said. "I called Boone and he told me you were up here and where you were staying, so I made reservations here, too." Sarah pulled her to the table.

"Please join us," Sarah said. "Amanda Baines, meet Win Mifflin. Win, Amanda Baines." Win was on his feet helping Amanda with her chair. He waved at the waitress, who appeared quickly with water, a menu and another place setting.

"We've just been served our salads," Win said. "We'll wait while you order."

"I hope I'm not interrupting anything," Amanda said, and without waiting for an answer asked, "How do you know each other?"

"I've used Win as a consultant many times over the years," Sarah said.

"Oh, you're a lobbyist, too?" Amanda asked, turning toward Win.

"No, no," he said, "but I do consulting with and for lobbyists for special projects."

"What kind of special projects?" she asked, curious and intrigued by the enigmatic-looking man. He was not especially tall, but his black hair gave him a mysterious look and he had the somewhat weathered complexion of a man who has spent much of his life outdoors, even though at first glance he would have seemed to most people to be an accountant or computer programmer rather than an outdoorsman.

"Amanda, back off," Sarah said, somewhat sharply. "You're sounding too much like a reporter."

"Oh, God, a reporter," Win said in a mock groan. Amanda nodded, smiled brightly. Her salad was delivered and they all started to eat.

They made small talk over salad and dinner. It was clear to Sarah after only a few minutes that Amanda was quite attracted to Win, and that Win, who seemed always on the hunt, was taken with Amanda as well. When they were almost finished, Amanda asked, "Sarah, how do I get from here to the March Point Refinery. I want to take a look at it before they've finished with everything out there."

Sarah started to answer, but Win interjected, "It's a dark country road, Amanda. Why don't you let me drive you?"

Again, Sarah started to speak but this time Amanda cut her off. "Perfect. Can we go now?"

"As soon as we get the check," Win responded quickly before Sarah could interrupt. The check came and Amanda let *The Chronicle* treat. As they stood, Sarah snapped, "Good night" and marched off toward her room. But not before she had given Win the stare of death. As she marched, she thought, not for the first time, that "men" and "common sense" frequently do not belong in the same sentence.

Win knew quite well that there would be no access for Amanda or anyone else not in possession of a Royal Energy security badge that night. It was under lockdown even then, four days after the spill. Soon they were back, walking into the lobby of the Anacortes Inn. On the drive they had talked about how they knew Sarah and why she had reacted as she had when Win offered to drive Amanda.

While Amanda seemed genuinely puzzled by Sarah's behavior, Win was quite sure why she had acted as she had.

In the lobby, Amanda asked if she could buy Win a thank you drink. He said that would be fine and they went into the bar, which was largely deserted. In time, Win reciprocated with a you're welcome drink and later still, Amanda bought another thank you drink.

Feeling just a bit tipsy, Amanda said, "It's getting late."

"May I escort you to your room?" Win asked in his best formal voice. He liked this lady and didn't want to blow things at the first available opportunity.

"That would be nice," Amanda replied, and she thought it might have been a bit too quickly. She stood, gathered her receipt and took Win's arm as he led her toward the elevators.

At her room, Amanda hugged him and thanked him for his courtesy, but she held on to his hand and her eyes made it clear to him that a kiss would not be unwelcome.

He kissed her, tentatively at first, but when she responded, it became much less tentative.

She backed off, slid her key card in the slot and pushed the door open. Win hesitated a beat and Amanda grabbed the front of his jacket and pulled him into the room. In very short order, they were on the bed, then under the covers.

The next morning, Sarah was just finishing her breakfast in the grill, had just asked for her check, when Win and Amanda walked in hand-in-hand and were shown to a table where they could not see her. She pointed to their table and asked the waitress to put their breakfast on her room and to tell them it was courtesy of Sarah.

She strongly suspected what had happened during the night and if she was right that it was probably the start of problems for her in the future. She left through a side door.

Win asked the waitress for the check when he and Amanda had finished their breakfast and were sipping coffee. She told him that Sarah had taken care of it already. He looked around and didn't see her, and Amanda said, "How nice of Sarah. Where is she?" The waitress said she'd left right after they arrived.

They got up to leave. He said, "I'm not sure she did it to be nice." He had a troubled look, then it vanished and he continued, "I suppose you need to work on your story."

Amanda said, "Yes, at some point. You said you were leaving today. What time?"

"My flight's at 5:30 p.m., so I probably need to leave for SeaTac by 2:00 p.m. at the latest."

"Anything until then?"

"Nothing I have to do."

"I was hoping you'd drive me out to the refinery for an hour or so."

"No problem. Be happy to."

She took his hand as they walked toward the elevators. "What did you mean when you said you don't think Sarah bought breakfast to be nice?" she asked.

"I've known her a long time, and we're good friends. I just saw a look on her face last night when we left to go to the refinery. Maybe it's nothing."

She pulled him off the elevator when it reached her floor and led him toward her room. When she'd opened the door, she put out the "Do Not Disturb" sign and closed and bolted the door.

"I thought you wanted to go to the refinery," he said, but offered only token resistance as she pulled him toward the bed.

"It's just 8:15 a.m., for God's sake," she scolded. "We've got time for some more time to ourselves before I deal with my responsibilities." She looked intently at him as she started unbuttoning his shirt. "It's been a long time for me. I could get real used to you and I want to take advantage of the time we have here."

"And I don't have any input in this?" he asked, but his tone was clear and he was smiling as he began unbuttoning Amanda's blouse.

In her most sultry voice, Amanda said, "Oh, on the contrary, I was hoping you'd have all the input in this." And she pulled him down to the bed and kissed him hard.

As they were shedding the remainder of their clothes between kisses and gropes, he said, "I could get real used to you, too, Amanda."

Later, as they were dressing again and gathering Amanda's camera and laptop in preparation for the trip to the refinery, she said, "When you said you could get used to me, I hope that means you would like to get together again."

She paused, and was surprised at herself for feeling embarrassed at the statement. She had, after all, dragged what amounted to a perfect stranger into her room last night and screwed his brains out, taken a little time for breakfast, and done it again.

Why the hell should anything embarrass me at this point? But she added, "This must sound strange to you, but I've never been this forward with a man. I don't know what got into me, but there's something about you that makes me that way." She was blushing and Win was charmed by it.

"Let's just say, in that case, that I'm even more flattered than I was before," he said. "And, for sure, I am just as attracted to you. The problem is that I travel a lot in my work, and I'm seldom in one place for more than a few days. But I'm through the Bay Area fairly frequently, and I'd love to take every opportunity I have to see you. That is, if that kind of arrangement works for you."

"I'm what you might say 'between commitments' at the moment," she said with a smile that was now more happy than embarrassed. "And a 'catch-as-catch-can' relationship sounds kind of exciting. Maybe even a little bit wicked for a nice girl like me. Actually, *The Chronicle* has had me on the road more and more in the last few months, so I'm in kind of the same situation you are."

"Then let's plan to stay in touch and see each other whenever we can," he said. "See how things work." He looked at his watch, a gold Ulysse Nardin Maxi Diver, and said, "We'd better haul ass if we want to get you to the refinery with enough time to do anything there before I have to get to the airport."

She said, "Why don't you just drop me at the refinery and then go about your business. There's really no reason for you to hang around while I interview people and all that. I'm sure Sarah will be out there later and if she's not, I'll get a cab back to the hotel." He nodded.

Amanda had noticed his watch, which was both large and distinctive. She asked him about it as they were driving to the refinery.

"It's an old watch that I've had since I was in the SEALs – you know, in the Navy?" he said.

"My God, do you mean to tell me I've just been serviced by a Navy SEAL?"

"You have," he answered with a smile and in mock seriousness. "And I hope the service has been satisfactory to the lady."

Amanda broke out laughing, then said theatrically, "Yes, sailor, the service was quite commendable. I applaud your dedication and your vigor." Win reached across the console and took her hand. She squeezed tightly, feeling very warm inside.

When they got to the refinery, Amanda stated her business and showed her press credentials at the security shack and they were waved through and directed to the visitor lot in front of the administration building. Amanda saw Sarah's car and said, "Sarah's already here. She'll give me a ride back."

She gave Win a kiss, grabbed her laptop case and handbag and hopped out. He turned back toward the gate.

Amanda was signing the visitor registry in the reception area when Sarah came out of a hallway, having tried – unsuccessfully – to learn anything from the refinery manager about the three men who had been reported to be drunk.

"Little bit of a late start today, huh, Amanda?" she remarked cattily when she walked up to her. They went into a corner of the reception area and Amanda thanked her for buying their breakfast that morning, then told her she was late getting to the refinery because she'd been working in her room earlier.

"Working alone?" Sarah asked, again a sharp tone to her voice.

"Not entirely," Amanda grinned. "Can we have dinner tonight?"

"That would be nice," Sarah said, her tone softer. "I've already delayed my flight home by a day. Will Win be joining us?"

"No, he's leaving this afternoon. He just dropped me off here. Which reminds me, can I catch a ride with you when you're ready to head back to Anacortes?"

"Sure. I'm going to nose around for awhile, hang out and see if I can pick up on anything. Why don't we figure on meeting here at, say 2:30 this afternoon? I've got some work to do this afternoon in my room. Alone."

She could see right away that her sarcasm was not lost on Amanda, and she suddenly felt bad for the way she was treating her. She would talk further with her at dinner.

That night at dinner, Amanda filled Sarah in on the events of the last 24 hours. "I don't know what got into me," she said. "I'm not like that, but that man turned me on like I haven't been turned on in a long time. And he seemed to feel the same about me?"

Sarah laughed. "With most men – Win most certainly included – being turned on is a constant and usually has only a tangential relationship to who the woman involved is." She paused a beat. "So, are you planning to see him again?"

"That's what we talked about this morning. He said he travels a lot, but gets to the Bay Area from time to time, so we'll get together as the opportunity presents itself. But we were both pretty clear that there are no strings attached to whatever relationship we have."

Sarah was quiet for a couple of minutes, which to Amanda seemed much longer. Finally, Sarah said, "Amanda, I haven't known you that long, but we seem to have gotten along very well, and I consider you a friend already. And I tell you this as a friend. I've known Win for a number of years and he can be, well, different. His clients expect what he does for them to be kept very close to the vest. He'll never be able to talk with you about his work, and you should not even try to ask him.

"He'll shut down on you. I know what he's done for me in the past, and it's all been very straightforward. But I don't know his other clients, and I think some of them hand him dangerous assignments. But I don't know that, really. He's a good guy but mysterious. The only thing I know for sure about him is his cell phone number. Just be careful."

"But he seems so sweet, so attentive," Amanda said, alarmed.

Sarah put her hand over Amanda's. "I don't mean to say you have anything to fear from him. He really does treat people he knows well, in my experience. But he lives a secretive life and I don't want to see you hurt emotionally. My advice is to be very careful to contain your emotions, and assume whatever you have with Win Mifflin will probably be temporary and only physical. Not that physical is bad. A little lust from time to time has worked wonders for me in the past."

Amanda digested all that Sarah had said, and at last smiled. "It's been so long since I've felt that turned on. I'm okay with just lust. I think."

CHAPTER 19

Randolph Aglee gazed, as always with a combination of awe and fondness, at the massive vessel that stretched before him from his perch on the port wing of the bridge, high above the deck and the dock to his left, where the last of the one million barrels of North Slope crude was being pumped into the massive tanks of his ship.

The Trans Alaska Pipeline Service – or TAPS - terminal at Valdez never ceased to amaze him. Mammoth and efficient, set against the backdrop of huge cliffs that rose from all sides, the port and the terminal always gave Aglee the incongruous impression of having sailed his ship into a harbor next to a Swiss alpine village. Absurd, he knew, but Valdez did, indeed, look much like such a village.

Master Mariner Randolph Aglee was a 35-year veteran of the sea, the last 25 as the captain of various oil tankers belonging to Petroleum Exploration and Refining, Ltd., more commonly known as PERL Oil. For the past eleven years, his charge, as it was this night, was the *Mar Ascensor,* a Very Large Crude Carrier, or VLCC. Tall, with a weathered face and a full head of salt-and-pepper hair, he had a bit of the look of a mature movie star to him and his bearing exuded the confidence of a command veteran. His men looked on him with a combination of awe, respect and fascination.

He loved the ship, as he had dutifully loved each one on which he had served, especially each one he had the honor of commanding. And unlike some of the captains he met and mingled with in the sailor bars that surrounded every port he visited, he truly considered it an honor to command a vessel. Especially one as magnificent as the *Mar Ascensor*.

He was also proud of his record as a captain. There had been no spills and no serious damage to any of the tankers he had commanded. He began each journey with a silent oath to himself to maintain that record.

Now, as the loading was completed and the tanks were being sealed, departure time was nearing and the usual knot in stomach began forming. A prudent and realistic man, Aglee was never able to ignore the anxiety he felt leaving the Valdez terminal.

The route from the terminal to the open sea was tricky, with rocks jutting out of the water and an impossibly narrow neck of water – Valdez Arm - through which to affect the passage from the harbor out into Prince William Sound. And once in the Sound, he must navigate through a gauntlet of small islands, some little more than protuberances, before passing through the Hinchinbrook Entry and out into the Gulf of Alaska. At this time of year, ice floes were an additional cause for concern.

The 1989 *Exxon Valdez* disaster had made Aglee, like all tanker captains, both vigilant and nervous about this part of the journey. This trip, he was even more nervous, for it was to be the *Mar Ascensor's* final voyage as a PERL Oil vessel, and his final voyage before his well-earned retirement. After unloading his precious cargo at the Long Beach refinery, this still-magnificent ship – at least in Aglee's eyes – was being transferred to a new owner, one based in Jakarta.

The *Mar Ascensor* was a double hull ship, designed and constructed in response to the Exxon Valdez disaster. That unfortunate vessel was single-hulled and when it ran aground on Bligh Reef, it dumped 240,000 barrels of crude into the waters of Prince William Sound. Even after all these years, the effects of that spill on land and water wildlife were still being felt. As were its effects on the public scrutiny over the transport of crude oil.

Promptly at 9:00 p.m., Captain George Hubbard, the harbor pilot, boarded the *Mar Ascensor* and, once on the bridge, met with Aglee to prepare for the tanker's departure through the hazardous channels on the way to Prince William Sound. The two men had done this many times over the years, and each liked and respected the other.

Aglee would not have wanted the harbor pilot's job, serving his ships only through the slow and nerve-wracking process of inching through to open sea, then turning them over to their masters for what Aglee loved most – the serene days of being on the sea, as one with his ship. He was a seaman because he loved being at sea. He did not love the slow-motion ballet of inching his ship into and out of difficult ports. And Valdez was as difficult as they came.

When the two captains had gone over the departure plan and agreed that all was in order, they sat down over coffee to catch up with each other until the scheduled departure time of 11:00 p.m. Because Valdez Narrows was a mere three-quarters of a mile wide, arriving and departing tankers were precisely scheduled, as if they were airliners sharing a single runway.

A little before 11:00, Captain Aglee surrendered command of the *Mar Ascensor* to Captain Hubbard, and the mooring lines were cast off. With the assistance of two tugboats, *Helping Hand and Helping Hand, Too*, both owned by TAPS, Hubbard began the slow process of pulling, more than steering, the massive ship away from its berth. As it inched farther from the berth, Hubbard commanded engagement of the ship's screws, making turns at the slowest possible speed.

With the tugs on either side of the bow, the *Mar Ascensor* was guided slowly through Valdez Narrows, slipping into Valdez Arm. This always caused a shiver to lance through Aglee's body. The Exxon Valdez was always on his mind in Alaskan waters.

Just as the ship passed from Valdez Arm into Prince William Sound, Captain Hubbard smiled as he turned the ship back to Captain Aglee. Hubbard went below and debarked to the *Helping Hand, Too*. The tugs blew their powerful whistles, one of Aglee's favorite sounds, and turned away in unison, sending the *Mar Ascensor* on its way to the Gulf of Alaska in the company of an ocean-going tug and a specially-equipped prevention and response vessel, designed to be immediate responders in case of any untoward exigencies that befell a ship in Prince William Sound. These boats had made the passage through Valdez Arm tethered to the two guidance tugs. They were untethered just before the *Helping Hand* and the *Helping Hand, Too* disengaged from the Mar Ascensor and turned back toward the Port of Valdez. It was almost 1:30 a.m.

There was no moon, a dark cloud cover stretching across the sky. The black water of the widening channel blended into the black horizon, giving the effect that there was no line where the sea ended and the sky began. Navigation, however, was not a problem. Like all VLCCs, the Mar Ascensor had a very sophisticated GPS navigational system, not to mention the best radar and depth-monitoring sonar this side of the United States Navy.

The problem, Aglee knew, was seeing anything in the water that could cause a problem if hit hard enough or at just the right angle. Aglee turned to his First Mate, Mike Reffitt, known to all since the first grade taunts about his name, as Rabbit. "Get two look-outs out to the bow," Aglee told the man.

The lookouts would be watching for any change in the color of the water that might mean shallows or floating ice, things they could not see from the bridge on a moonless night. In truth, the lookouts would do little good, Aglee and Rabbit both knew. If they spotted anything, it was highly unlikely the giant ship could be maneuvered away from it. But it was a precaution that Aglee always took, anyway.

Rabbit had been Aglee's first mate for eight of his years on the Mar Ascensor, and knew what his boss wanted almost before he said it. Short, round and nearly bald, Rabbit was the physical antithesis of Aglee, but their minds were as if linked.

He was already reaching for the bridge phone as Aglee began speaking. He knew that in this area, still close to Columbia Glacier to their starboard side, ice was possible, though not probable, especially in the busy sea lanes. Reports from inbound tankers were that the lanes were relatively clear, but Aglee never took anything for granted. Rabbit barked his orders and soon two seamen appeared far in front of them, near the tip of the bow where their view would be least obstructed.

At Aglee's nod, Rabbit was on the phone to the engine room ordering an increase in speed. They would not go to cruising speed yet, not while they were still in the relatively confined spaces of Prince William Sound.

For an hour, the ship inched toward the open sea with the forward lookouts reporting only a few sightings of ice. Fully loaded, the *Mar Ascensor* sat quite low in the water and moved with the grace and agility of a hog in mud. Aglee, satisfied that things were moving smoothly, turned the bridge over to Rabbit so he could go to the officer's galley, one deck below the bridge, to grab a cup of coffee. He knew Rabbit would want one, too.

Just after Aglee stepped back on the bridge, handing a mug of hot coffee to Rabbit, the ship was hit with an unexpected squall that sent sheets of freezing rain and sleet over the deck. The lookouts ran for shelter. Rabbit immediately ordered the engine room to cut the speed of the *Mar Ascensor* and prepared to sail on using the ship's own navigation system. In aviation terms, it would have been called IFR, or instrument flight rules.

Suddenly, all lights went out, those on the bridge, the so-called running lights that basically outlined the ship to give it visibility to other ships in the pitch black of an arctic night, even the lights on the command and control console on the bridge. Aglee was flying blind. He immediately ordered all available hands on deck with powerful, battery-operated lanterns, and called the trailing support ships to play their powerful spotlights on the *Mar Ascensor*. He was desperate to get the ship lit up in a busy channel like this, and, as if by divine providence, the squall abated as the crewmen appeared on deck.

Then, with deep dread, Aglee noticed something far more ominous: the absence of noise and of the faint vibration that was always there on a ship under power. Almost immediately, the voice of Elwood Quigley, the chief engineer, came through on the intercom from the engine room. "Captain," Quigley shouted in a panicked voice that was completely unlike him, "all systems have shut down. We have no power."

Rabbit added, more quietly, but with no less a sense of urgency, "Randy, it looks like we've lost everything." He was staring at the navigation console – the GPS system, the range and depth-finders and all the rest – but all gauges and displays were completely dark, no information displayed, no needles moving, nothing. They were dead in the water, drifting in a very busy shipping lane with one million barrels of crude oil aboard.

Without being told, Rabbit announced to Aglee that he was heading down to the engine room to see if he could help Quigley troubleshoot the problem and fix it before this turned into a real mess.

In the engine room, Rabbit expected to find Quigley as he usually was, even in emergencies, quietly and efficiently going down one of his mental checklists to isolate the problem. Instead, the man was slumped over his controls, not moving. As soon as he reached Quigley's control console, Rabbit knew the man was dead. His eyes were open, his tongue protruding slightly, flecks of blood circling his mouth.

Quigley had been with Aglee and Rabbit for many years and the men had formed the kind of comradeship that is bonded by weeks at sea, depending on each other, learning and respecting the special skills each possessed, and confiding in one another.

Rabbit was reaching for the phone to report the unthinkable to Aglee when he had a more urgent thought. He put down the phone, calling out to Carl Brown, Quigley's assistant engineer, who was running around the massive engine room looking for – what? He had no idea. Just something out of the ordinary that would cause a complete power outage.

When Brown hurried over to the console, he was taken aback by the sight of Quigley's body as much as by the scraping sound on the starboard hull. "What the fuck is going on, Mr. Reffitt?" Brown asked, his voice a shade beyond anxious, heading toward panic.

"I'm not sure, but it looks like Chief Quigley's had a heart attack," Rabbit told him, not sure even then whether he believed what he was saying.

At that moment, both men heard a loud pop, an explosive but distant noise, like a clap of thunder in the distance. Rabbit ran, desperate to get back to the bridge to report to Aglee and to help his boss and friend figure out what was happening. And to fix it. He told Brown to continue looking for the cause of the engine failure and call the bridge with anything he found.

Running for the ladder – or narrow stairway – that would take him up the equivalent of twelve stories to the bridge, for with no power the elevator obviously would not help him, Rabbit encountered a man whose name he did not know, but recognized as a new oiler who had come aboard in Valdez because Robbie Hanson had not shown up. Rabbit knew the new oiler came with the recommendation of another PERL Oil captain, so he hadn't thought much about it when Quigley had told him about the new man.

Ship hands were notoriously unreliable, susceptible to the urge to get drunk or laid – or more likely both - and Robbie was a young, good-looking kid who, he imagined, was at this moment sleeping off a drunk next to the lonely wife of another seaman who was in some distant part of the world.

The new man looked more like a businessman than a ship's oiler, his whole manner projecting something other than a man who worked in the hot, oily and smelly bowels of a ship.

The new man asked what was going on and how he could help. Rabbit pointed and told him to get to Carl Brown and do what he could to help him. Only later did it strike Rabbit that the man was far calmer than any of his shipmates. Certainly calmer than he felt himself.

Out of breath but back on the bridge, Rabbit saw the worry and confusion on Aglee's face. The helmsman stood at his station, helpless but prepared to resume his duties when – if? – power was restored and there was something to steer.

"What was that noise?" Rabbit asked his friend and boss.

"It seems like we've hit something, but I haven't got a clue what it was," Aglee answered, his teeth clenched so tightly it was hard to hear him. "I've ordered an inspection, but how the hell do we hit ice or anything else when we're almost dead in the water?" Rabbit could only shrug. He was as bewildered as Aglee.

The sky was still black. Dawn was not due this far north for another couple of hours, and Aglee said, "Well, let's get people with the big lanterns to see if they can figure out what we hit and what kind of damage we have. And signal the response ship to close in and see if we're leaking any oil. What's the situation in the engine room?"

"Woody Quigley's dead," Rabbit reported, and Aglee stared at him, bug-eyed. "I guess he had a heart attack or something. No sign of anything else. Carl's taking over and he and that new oiler are troubleshooting how we can get back under power."

Suddenly, the lights came back on as the first faint vibration signaled the engines restarting. Almost imperceptibly at first, the big ship began to move forward, its massive screws still making the slowest turns. Aglee was on the phone instantly, asking Carl Brown what they had found and how they had fixed it. Brown, totally befuddled, reported that he had found nothing, done nothing. Just all of a sudden, the engines restarted and electrical power was restored. No, he had not seen the new oiler recently, but would ask him what he'd found when he located him.

Two seamen were rigged to drop over the starboard side to check for damage. A third was stationed at the winch attached to the railing to lower them over the side and to retrieve them when they had completed their inspection. As the rigged seamen stepped over the rail and prepared for the descent, an enormous explosion detonated immediately below them, deafening all in earshot and engulfing the starboard side of the *Mar Ascensor* in flame.

The two men who had just stepped over the rail were blown back on deck and, along with the man at the winch, were quickly turned into human fireballs as a thick, oily smoke engulfed the ship's huge main deck.

The screaming of the three seamen was completely drowned out by the roar of the fire. From the bridge, Aglee, Rabbit and the helmsman could see nothing as the smoke surrounded them, blanketing the ship's superstructure as if it were in the thickest fog.

Aglee, acting on instinct, had personally issued the mayday distress call to the ocean-going tug and the prevention and response vessel that were now alongside the *Mar Ascensor.*

He trained his binoculars on the place on the forward deck where the three crewmen had stopped writhing and lay still amid the flames. It was obvious they were dead. Dear God, what a way to die, he thought. He knew who the young men were – did not know them well – and dreaded calling their families. His own unblemished safety record, now shot to hell, did not even occur to him as he thought of the agonizing suffering his three men had just endured before, blessedly, death came.

In what Aglee thought was quite a short time, it seemed the *Mar Ascensor* was flanked on its right by several additional boats - thanks, no doubt, to how little distance she had put between herself and Valdez Arm before her troubles began. Several of the vessels belonged to the United States Coast Guard, which maintained a normal and regular vigil in this area, and for good reason.

Besides the Coast Guard vessels, a variety of others were closing in. In addition to his own escort vessels, other TAPS emergency response boats and barges with skimmers responded quickly to the mayday call.

Soon, Aglee knew, an oil containment ship would hurry up from its station just aft of his ship and surround the *Mar Ascensor* with the containment booms designed to stem the spread of whatever oil was leaking from his ship. Aglee tried to piece together in his mind what had happened. Perhaps they had drifted into an obstruction, such as a small iceberg, while they were powerless. Perhaps that breached the outer hull and created a spark that ignited the oil that inevitably seeped into the space between the *Mar Ascensor*'s twin hulls. He could not clearly remember how long it was between the initial sounds and the explosion, and if he could he would not be able to explain it.

Still, the fire raged over the forward half of Aglee's ship, even as Coast Guard cutters shot streams of water onto and into the ship. Suddenly, something hit Randolph Aglee with a terrible clarity. This was not just the *Mar Ascensor*'s last voyage for PERL Oil. This was be the last voyage of Captain Randolph Aglee, master mariner, former holder of a perfect safety record in command of ocean-going vessels.

"It's a hell of a way to end a career, isn't it, Rabbit?" Aglee glanced over at his old friend, not the least bit self-conscious at making such a statement in front of his helmsman.

Rabbit felt sick, knowing Aglee was right and realizing again that they would never again set sail together. That, in fact, his – Rabbit's – career as a mariner might be over, too. But there was more on his mind. "Don't you think we ought to prepare to abandon ship, Captain?" Rabbit asked formally.

He knew the Coast Guard and the TAPS boats would continue to fight the fires and try to save as much of the ship and its oil as possible, but he also knew it could get worse at any time and the prudent course of action now was to get the rest of the men off the ship and let the Coast Guard and TAPS do what they were trained to do. The ship had already been slowed to a stop. Aglee ordered the engines and electrical system shut down. Another spark might be all it would take to turn this thing into the biggest bomb since Nagasaki.

At about that same time, the new oiler removed his glasses, work clothes and steel-toed boots – standard seaman's footwear – and revealed a thermal wetsuit. He found a life-preserver in the crew locker area one level above the engine room and headed a few feet farther aft to the open area used for tossing galley garbage overboard. Hidden behind some storage bins were some things he had secreted there before the *Mar Ascensor* left its berth at Valdez: an adequate length of Kevlar rope, a climbing harness, a headlamp, boots and Metolius gloves. He glanced at his Ulysse Nardin Maxi Diver watch and smiled. It was just after 5:00 a.m. First light was still several hours away.

Once he had donned all the accoutrements, he lashed the rope to a railing inside the garbage bay with a knot that would hold so long as there was tension on the line but would loosen easily when the line went slack. With all the cover he needed provided by the raging inferno forward on the ship, he slipped over the side of the massive, flat stern and easily rappelled down the side. The deadly churning of the screws that would have made his maneuver impossible had the engines been running was not an issue. Instead, in the relatively calm water behind the ship sat a small inflatable of the type used by the U.S. Navy SEALs and other commando units the world over.

With its incredible buoyancy and light weight, the 150 horsepower Mercury engine could make the boat almost fly over the water. And its flat black color made it almost impossible to see in the dark even if one was looking for it or at it. In the midst of all the chaos surrounding the *Mar Ascensor*, the oiler and the man at the helm of the inflatable were confident that, in the unlikely event anyone did spot them, it would be assumed they were just two more men trying to help avert an economic and biological disaster of monumental proportions.

On his second try, the oiler landed in the inflatable. The lightweight rubber boat simply refused to sit in one position. All the Coast Guard and other vessels in the area were, after all, churning up the water in their efforts to move closer to the stricken ship and making the little boat move around. But the man at the helm was experienced and on the second attempt positioned the boat to meet the oiler.

Once the oiler was aboard, he flipped at the rope expertly and ducked as it fell toward them and into sea, then pulled it into the inflatable. The other man fed the Mercury throttle, and disappeared around the port side of the ship. Soon it was racing in a straight line 90 degrees away from the *Mar Ascensor*. In minutes, it was out of sight of anyone on any of the ships in the area, even if anyone had happened to be looking for them. And as far as anyone could tell when they began to inspect the ship later, the oiler had never actually been on the *Mar Ascensor*. There was nothing left on the ship traceable or connectable in any way to him.

ANOTHER MAJOR ALASKA OIL SPILL

Anchorage, Alaska, Friday (AP). The crude oil tanker Mar Ascensor, a PERL Oil vessel carrying one million barrels of crude oil from Valdez, destined for Long Beach, California, struck an iceberg or some other submerged object this morning, causing an explosion and fire that killed three sailors who were trying to assess the damage to the ship.

The collision and fire occurred in the northern part of Prince William Sound, near the site of the Exxon Valdez tragedy in 1989.

Coast Guard and oil containment vessels from Valdez are on the scene, fighting the fire and running containment booms around the ship. No estimate is yet available on how much crude oil has leaked into the Sound. The Coast Guard estimates the fire will be contained sometime tomorrow, and the tanker's surviving crew members have been evacuated and are being treated for a variety of minor injuries and smoke inhalation in an Anchorage hospital.

In addition to the three crewmen killed in the fire, another died of an apparent heart attack and one is missing and presumed drowned.

CONSERVATIONISTS OUTRAGED; DEMAND ACTION

Washington, D.C., Saturday (Washington Post). Conservationists expressed outrage today over the Mar Ascensor oil spill in Prince William Sound, Alaska, Friday morning, and called on PERL Oil to pay for the massive clean-up effort that will be required.

The Sierra Club, Greenpeace and a host of other environmental organizations, joined together in a show of unity. Even the usually-moderate Citizens for Responsible Growth joined the chorus.

Sarah Cotton, Public Affairs Director and chief lobbyist for Citizens for Responsible Growth, also called for new and stronger government regulation of petroleum exploration and production, ultimately leading to a phase-out of all petroleum products, which, she said, endanger the current and future well-being of the planet.

The billionaire environmentalist and former Vice President added that it is imperative that the use of petroleum products be eliminated to reduce the hydrocarbon emissions that are causing global warming and destroying the earth's eco-systems. "While an oil spill of this magnitude attacks the econ-system of the Gulf of Alaska," the former Vice President pointed out, "if this ship had reached its destination, fully one million barrels of crude oil would have been made available for the destruction of all the earth's eco-systems."

PERL OIL STATEMENT

LONG BEACH, CA – Statement of Fleming D. Worthy,
Chairman and CEO of PERL Oil:

"The incident today aboard the Mar Ascensor is a tragedy on many levels. A spill of any amount of oil in the beautiful and delicate eco-system of Prince William Sound is certainly a tragedy, and one for which this company takes full responsibility and which PERL Oil pledges to clean up at the earliest possible time. We are grateful that the spill was no worse than it was, due to the heroic efforts of the United States Coast Guard and the oil containment teams of Trans Alaska Pipeline Service, which responded with incredible speed and efficiency.

"It is also a tragedy on a deeply personal level to the PERL Oil family. We lost at least four members of our family – Mar Ascensor crew members who perished while attempting to contain the damage on the ship.

"Finally, it is a tragedy for this company itself, being, as it is, the first and only incident of this kind in the long and proud history of the company. I guarantee that PERL Oil will not only provide the funding for cleaning up Prince William Sound, but will use every means at its disposal to determine the cause of this tragedy and take steps to assure that it cannot be repeated."

CHAPTER 20

Now that Akrum al-Kahtani had the attention of the chief executive officer and one trusted lieutenant from each of nine of the largest U.S. oil companies, he began.

"I've talked with each of you privately about the agenda today, so we all know why we're here," al-Kahtani began. "The man who recently was sworn in as President of the United States is one some of you publicly and financially supported. But he is now determined to open vast new areas of Federal land to oil exploration, and appears committed to reinstating offshore drilling, long-term.

"During the campaign, he said all the politically-safe things about freeing America from its dependence on foreign oil. But I don't think any of us thought about the true ramifications of such a policy. For my country, the ramifications are clear: we are the major foreign supplier, so success in freeing America, as he calls it, would seem a clear economic threat to us. What has not been clear until the past few weeks is what the effect of new exploration and offshore drilling will mean to everyone in this room."

The man paused for effect and took a sip of his now-cold coffee. Continuing, he said, "Who among us actually thought he would be any more successful than other Presidents before him? Not I, and I so advised my government. For each of you, the success of this President's new oil policy presents a threat as severe to you and your companies as it is to me and my country. The President has built such momentum in the Congress that even leaders of the opposition party are jumping aboard to make sure they can share in the credit.

"The continuing terrorist threats of the Islamic jihadists have made the goal of so-called 'energy independence' all the more appealing to the mainstream in this country, as well as in Western Europe, where the British Prime Minister and leaders of the European Union have not only endorsed the President's policy but vowed to follow his lead by opening new areas in the North Sea and other areas of Europe for similar exploration and drilling."

A few heads nodded in agreement, but others remained steady, eyes fixed on the diplomat.

"Some are even speculating that Russia may be convinced to join this 'energy independence' coalition, and European governments will make such a move more appealing by sanctioning vast new networks of pipelines to get oil from the Caspian region to European markets.

"And what does this mean? We have seen the price of crude drop from $140 per barrel just a year ago to closer to $60 today. The value of each of your companies has declined as the value of your known reserves has plummeted. In the past, our industry has always understated – by a significant degree – the amount of our unproven oil reserves, as have we understated the potential for new oil fields, which we all know exist. That understatement has kept the price of crude high and benefited us all.

"If the President is successful, crude prices will drop further and the value of your companies, as well as your profits, will follow. Please, ladies and gentlemen, let us make this a discussion. I do not feel the need to do all the talking, even though we all know that is all diplomats are qualified to do." Chuckles around the table helped relieve the tension which rose while al-Kahtani was talking, saying the things each of them had been thinking privately for weeks.

For a moment, no one spoke. Kristina Vandam broke the silence. "Akrum, we all know why we're here, at least in general terms, and we all agree with your premise, again at least in general terms. You've briefed us all and if we weren't in general agreement, we wouldn't be here. Why don't you give us the details of your plan?"

"Very well," al-Kahtani said. He picked up his cell phone, hit a speed dial number and a moment later the conference room door opened and a young woman clad in an abaya and niqab entered the room. Her eyes were dark and piercing but they were all about her face that was visible. The black garment reached the floor and other than her eyes, only her hands were visible, the nails carefully manicured and covered in a clear varnish.

Al-Kahtani introduced her as his daughter, Zara. She was American-educated, he told them, but deeply committed to her Arab roots, adding that she was also deeply committed to assuring that the terrorists who were destroying Islam's reputation in the Western world were discredited.

"My daughter is a very accomplished young woman," al-Kahtani told them. "I propose that we engage her as our facilitator. By that I mean we turn over to her the implementation of the strategies and actions to protect our interests that we as a group decide. She will organize the necessary manpower and materiel needs, and she and her associates will accept all risks. Our identities will be known only to Zara.

"I know you are wondering why I would suggest my own daughter for this task. Let me explain."

For most of an hour, al-Kahtani kept the men and women in the room spellbound as he recalled her background. He told them how she had infiltrated a radical Islamic cell at Georgetown University – even though that is not where she was enrolled - and worked with the radicals as they developed an elaborate and exceedingly clever plan to blow up the U.S. Capitol by implanting themselves over a period of months as cooks, janitors, maintenance workers and other menials who, once in place, became like the furniture, never again to be noticed.

The only flaw in the plan was that Zara was feeding data on the plan at every step of its development and initial implementation to the Federal Bureau of Investigation, which worked with the Secret Service and the Capitol Police to stage a coordinated and stealthy sweep which resulted in every member of the cell disappearing at virtually the same time. Zara, of course, had to disappear as well, and she had been whisked to London, where she became a member of the Saudi delegation to the United Kingdom under a different name. Because of her abayas and naqibs, the need to change her appearance was not germane.

He told them about how she had been engaged by another member of the Saudi royal family to research a British-American pharmaceutical company he wished to take over at a reasonable price. She had discovered with remarkably little effort the company's very promising developmental work on an antidote to the anthrax spore – a breakthrough that, once tested and certified, would be worth billions in contracts from governments and health care practitioners around the world.

Even better, she had discovered that the major stockholder and CEO of the company, a fat Brit, had two unfortunate appetites: very young women, usually in groups of two or more, and very fine cocaine. These appetites required more cash than was available from his salary, after paying mortgages on an elaborate townhouse in London's West End theatre district and on an enormous country home near Wimbledon, where his wife and four children resided unless they were in the city for a play or social event. Most of the time, his expensive, paid harems were able to share the townhouse with him and his vast stash of coke.

He balanced his personal books, as Zara discovered, by cooking the company's books and scraping substantial sums off the top each month. In the end, when confronted with the alternatives, such as divorce, jail time and public humiliation, the man accepted a reasonable offer from the Saudi prince.

After two additional examples of past exploits that only solidified the collective certainty in the room that this young woman not only knew what she was doing, but got it done right, al-Kahtani suggested that they break for two hours for lunch and enough time to check in with their offices if they needed to. They would hear and discuss the outlines of his plan after lunch.

There would be no specifics, al-Kahtani told them when they reconvened, because if they all agreed on the need for this little cartel, Zara would develop and carry out such specifics. This, he reminded them, meant all those in the room were insulated from any implication or legal fallout that might arise as a result of any action taken by the cartel. He motioned to Zara, who stood.

"I am pleased to be with you," she said in excellent English with a slight but noticeable Arabic accent. Her voice had something of a distant quality because she was speaking through heavy netting in the black cloth that covered her nose and mouth. "We have developed a simple plan that we believe will be effective enough that it will result very quickly in crude oil prices in the $150 to $170 per barrel range."

The electric jolt that passed quickly around the room told her they were sold on the idea, with or without further explanation.

"Basically, we will follow a rather simple two-pronged plan," she said in a firm voice that exuded confidence. "First, we will initiate a series of petroleum-related incidents that will be designed to provide sensational media coverage, to cause alarm among the people of the United States and to rally environmental groups to pressure the new President and the Congress to drop these plans for new exploration, and in fact to expand the restrictions on new exploration already in place."

Seeing the expressions of alarm on some of the faces at the table, Zara hurried to add, "These incidents will be carefully planned to control the financial and environmental costs. They will be designed, in other words, for maximum news and political impact and minimum damage.

"Inevitably, some - perhaps all - of these incidents will involve assets of some of your companies." Her eyes scanned both sides of the table. "The plan provides that if a particular incident causes material loss to one of your companies, all here will share proportionately in that cost. The incidents will be carefully planned to minimize any chance of harm coming to any of your employees, contractors or the general public. While there can be no guarantees on this point, for obvious reasons, I can assure you that I know how to plan such events and the people I employ are the very best. And the incidents will follow no pattern. I have not planned details, of course, but I would plan incidents that involve a range of assets – oil tankers, pipelines, refineries, that sort of thing – so that the authorities are less able to track my plans and activities.

"The second part of our plan," she went on quickly, "is to work with, and provide funding to, one of the major environmental groups. That group will lead the charge on further exploration restrictions. In essence, they will be our message-carriers."

Mark Mazurka raised his hand and Zara nodded toward him. "Miss al-Kahtani, if one of these incidents, as you call them, involves one of my ships or facilities, will I know about it in advance?"

"Of course," Zara replied coldly, "and please call me Zara. I do not think the sobriquet you used really fits me." Mazurka looked mystified and Zara was sure he had no idea what sobriquet meant. She continued, "Any incident will require some level of coordination with the company in question, so of course I will involve you in it before the fact. But it is also important, in my opinion, that each member of our group here be forewarned so each company's public reaction can be as timely as possible." She also knew doing so would ensure each of the CEOs at the table would never be able to back away or betray the plan.

It fell to Paul Diles, the accountant, to ask the question that was on all their minds. "What's this all going to cost us, Zara?"

Zara al-Kahtani, as usual, was prepared for the question. She pulled eighteen copies of a document out of her portfolio and passed them around the table. The document was short, simple and to the point. She would receive a monthly retainer for expenses, covering direct costs, such as manpower, materiel and transportation. Expenses would be documented and reconciled against the retainer each month.

In addition, Zara would receive a monthly fee of $1,000,000. The real payoff to her would come in a form of profit-sharing. That is, she would form a petroleum distribution company which would, once the plan had been successfully carried out and oil prices had moved above $120 per barrel receive an oil contract from each of the companies – apportioned according to the size of the individual companies – each year for the next 20 years, at today's price.

Zara's father would open a bank account in the Cayman Islands. Each company would sell oil at a discounted price to another offshore oil entity – again on a size-based formula – which would resell the oil at market prices and the profits transferred to the Cayman Islands account, against which Zara's fee and expenses would be drawn. In addition, the sharing of damages suffered by individual member companies from Zara's incidents would be handled through this method. An accounting of all activity in the Cayman Islands accounts and the offshore oil entities would be shared with all members at each future meeting of the group.

That was it in a nutshell. There was no written agreement to sign, nor was there any need for one. The fact that there were 20 people in the room – men and women who were sometimes friends, sometimes enemies and always competitors – ensured that, once agreement was reached, none of them would think to renege.

Zara asked for the documents to be passed forward and gathered them and pushed them into the shredder set against the wall to her right. Then she sat.

Akrum al-Kahtani looked up and down the table. "Comments, my friends? Questions?" he asked.

Gord Waters started it. "You alluded to it, Zara, but could you talk some more about whether, or how likely, we are to have injuries, or even fatalities, to our own employees, our customers and contractors, even the general public, as a result of these incidents?" he asked in his quiet and polite way.

"Nobody can completely rule out what the military people call collateral damage when we create an incident that will have the galvanizing effect on people and politicians that they must have," Zara replied, staring intensely at Waters. "All I can do is give you my word that I will make every effort to avoid deaths or injuries to anyone. My father can tell you that I am quite good at this. There was not a single injury, let alone death, in the operation against the Georgetown jihadists. Beyond that, I can give you nothing but my word." Waters thanked her and his nod indicated the answer was all he could reasonably ask for.

"Do you have any initial plans for the incidents?" Nick Mansourian asked.

"No," Zara replied curtly. "I have done no thinking or planning aside from the framework of the overall plan we are discussing today, other than, as I said earlier, that they should involve a range of assets, from tankers to pipelines."

Beck asked, "How long do you think this whole facilitation will last? How long, from now to when we accomplish the goal?"

"I'm thinking 18 months," Zara replied carefully. "But that depends on how the incidents appear to the public and the politicians. It may be longer. Hopefully, it will not be that long."

"How will we communicate with you?" Fleming Worthy asked. "And you with us? And, for that matter, how do we communicate among ourselves about the affairs of this group?"

Akrum al-Kahtani lifted his hand toward Zara, indicating the question was his to answer. "It would appear that the idea of this little group and its mission is agreed upon, and the questions are only in the details. In anticipation of that, I have taken the liberty of bringing along a supply of identical laptops and of international cell phones. There is one for each CEO. Communications between us must be by the CEO only, although I asked you to bring your most trusted advisor or associate to this meeting so there is a back-up in place at each company in the event, God forbid, of the incapacitation or death of any of us. Zara is my most trusted associate, so she will replace me and serve a dual role in case of my incapacitation or death.

"In each of the cell phones, I have programmed into the speed-dial numbers my number and the numbers of all the other CEOs. In each of the laptops, which have encryption and decryption programs and satellite internet connections, I have installed coded email addresses for each of us."

Al-Kahtani sat back. "If you have any further questions as time goes by, as you surely will, simply email them to all and I will respond to all. I will communicate with Zara to get answers only she possesses."

"Will we meet as a group again?" Mirza asked.

Al-Kahtani nodded. "I believe that is inevitable, although we should be judicious about such meetings. If the word got out to the press who was in this room, the speculation would be something none of us wish to contemplate." He looked at Mirza, a man he genuinely liked. "But when the need to meet arises, I will make the same arrangements I have made for this meeting. I will send anonymous jets for you, and it will be somewhere else, and again at a location where we are unlikely to be recognized or connected with each other."

All eyes stared at al-Kahtani, waiting for more. He said nothing. There were no more questions. He stood. "Ladies and gentlemen, I think today we embark on a path that will yield great riches for your companies and for my country. I think we have done the work we are paid to do for them. Let us adjourn for now and return to our homes. The laptops and cell phones I discussed have been placed in your rooms. Instructions for the laptop programs are on a sheet of paper which is inserted over the keyboard. I suggest you shred it once you have the machine up and running.

"I bid you all good day." They all stood, somewhat awkwardly, shook hands around the table and started to move to the door, awestruck and filled with a mixture of hope and trepidation at what they had set in motion this day.

CHAPTER 21

SAN DIEGO, CALIFORNIA
APRIL, 2010

Jet Jamieson was not looking forward to this meeting with Zara al-Kahtani. He knew his last assignment – or facilitation, as they both called them – had resulted in some unacceptable consequences. And Zara al-Kahtani did not quietly accept the unacceptable. There had been deaths – four of them – on that damned oil tanker in Prince William Sound.

But what could he do? He was supposed to make it look like an accident, a mechanical malfunction, and shit happens when a ship that size has a mechanical malfunction.

Jet was a former Navy SEAL, but for this meeting, wearing wire-rimmed glasses, chinos, Johnson and Murphy tasseled loafers and a blue oxford-cloth button-down shirt, he appeared as mild-mannered as an accountant, or maybe a college professor. In fact, he was far from mild-mannered.

He had decided to bring along the Huff twins. Slump and Tweeter – nobody knew their real first names or where they got those stupid nicknames – were truly identical twins. Their appearances, voice, mannerisms – even DNA and fingerprints – were remarkably identical. They had met Jet when they were all part of the same SEAL team. They could be – in fact, most of the time were - mild-mannered and friendly, but in the right situation they could be as deadly as Jet. They were six feet tall, blond, trim and very muscular. Most women found them quite appealing, but they had an indefinable air about them that made them seem unapproachable.

The SEAL team they had all been part of was like the famed SEAL Team Six, but far more secret. The jobs they had been assigned by two Presidents were more highly-classified than any other actions by any other unit of the United States military. In fact, it was said that there was no paper or electronic trail of their assignments anywhere, even in the most secret files and databases of the Pentagon, Langley – home of the Central Intelligence Agency - or Fort Meade – home of the National Security Agency.

Zara al-Kahtani walked into the suite at the Hotel Del Coronado wearing a black chador. Jet had swept the suite after checking in as a precaution against listening devices. He thought the possibility of such devices was so remote as to constitute complete fantasy, but he could not escape the precautionary ways of his days in the clandestine service of his country.

He always carried an electronic device in his briefcase for this purpose, and used it wherever he went. To the half-assed screeners at airport TSA checkpoints, it looked, felt and operated like a small Remington electric shaver, but it was much more than that. Zara had told him more than once that she did not feel his sweeping of their meeting places was foolish or unnecessary, that in fact she appreciated his attention to such details very much.

Zara was not surprised to see the Huff twins with Jet when she entered, and knowing the three men were fluent in Arabic, spoke in that language. It was a further precaution against unknown eavesdroppers, such as maids in the hallway or in adjacent rooms who might overhear them. Especially if the conversation got animated.

Zara was quite fond of the Huff twins, and truth be known, the twins' allegiance lay much more with Zara than with Jet.

They adored her because of the precise way she thought things through and for the respect she showed for them as individuals. She did not treat them as a circus act because of their identical appearance.

Jet, on the other hand, had been too much of a wild card during their SEAL days for their taste. Even among the hard-headed and hot-blooded men of SEAL Team Six, Jet had been too over the top too many times.

When the Huffs had joined SEAL Team Six, he had immediately given them the nickname, "the Bobbseys." That had pissed them off badly. They were proud that they were twins, but equally proud that they were individuals. Still, when Jet had approached them with the offer of SEAL-type work at a rate of pay neither of them had ever dreamed of, they had jumped at it.

"I am both pleased and dissatisfied with the results of the Prince William Sound incident," she said in her native language. The men sat expressionless, knowing that to interrupt Zara was out of the question, and she continued. "I am quite pleased that the oil spill itself was so minimal as to be of no consequence to the environment in the area. I am also pleased that the damage to the *Mar Ascensor* was not extensive and easily repairable.

"However" – and her voice got very grave – "the loss of four lives is not acceptable, either to me personally or to the members of the cartel who are paying us." She paused and stared intently into the eyes of each of the three men. It was always surprising to Jet and to both of the Huffs how this Arab woman could be so intimidating to them.

"Our clients do not operate in our world," she went on, "and they want no more damage than is necessary to make our point to the public and to the politicians. They will not tolerate the deaths of anyone in our operations, especially those of their own employees. I have already heard this from each one of them."

She sat down in an armchair across from them, now clearly waiting for a response. Jet looked at the Huffs and leaned forward.

"Zara," he said in a steady voice, "the operation in Prince William Sound was a success, and 'our clients,' as you call them, must realize that. No oil reached shore, at least none that's been reported. The surface oil was skimmed up and collected, and the ship is in port here in San Diego for repairs." He paused, thinking. "I hear the repairs will take several months, but she's being sold anyway, so that's not interfering with PERL Oil's operations, just delaying cash flow a while."

"I know what went well, Jet," Zara snapped. "How do you explain the four fatalities? How do I explain them to our clients?"

"They were, for the most part, accident-related," he responded quietly. He knew her temper and had no desire for it to become more edgy than it was already.

"I know that, Jet," she responded icily. Sometimes her icy responses were more dangerous than the temper flashes. "I know they were accident-related. But it was our accident. We staged it. We created it. And what do you mean by 'for the most part'?"

"I'm talking about the engineer – what's his name? – Quigley? When I went to his station to give him a sedative, he was already slumped over his control board. I think he'd had a heart attack, a seizure, something like that. I checked his pulse. There was one, but it was faint. I couldn't take the chance of him waking up at that point so I went ahead and gave him a shot of our sedative."

"So our sedative may have, in fact, killed him," she said. "If that's what the autopsy finds, that should be interesting to the investigators. And what about the other three?"

"Zara," he said in a weary tone. "That was the law of unintended consequences at work. Who could have predicted that with a total power outage aboard ship, the captain would send two seamen over the side to see if there was any hull damage from whatever he thought he'd struck? And as it turns out, the timing was bad, because at the same time they were over the side, the explosive detonated. The fireball got the third man, who was on deck working the manual winch." He sighed before continuing.

"It was a freak accident, Zara, nothing more. The captain made a bad – or at least an unexpected decision – and it resulted in three dead men.

"And let me remind you that this was a complex assignment that came with built-in risks that could not be avoided because there were so many unknowns. But we still accomplished our goals."

Zara nodded, acknowledging his point but responded evenly, "Let me be as clear – to all three of you – as possible. The cartel we are working for is composed of people who manage large companies. They are not street thugs or Mafia dons. Damage in the defense of profit is one thing. Dead employees are quite another. They will not tolerate this kind of collateral damage in future operations, if there are future operations. The whole facilitation is in danger. They may pull the plug before anything else happens.

"But if they don't, if they take my word that this was an

unfortunate aberration, I absolutely do not want any future fatalities."
She pointed a finger at Jet and said, "You must take whatever
precautions necessary to avoid any death – even serious injury – to
anybody. Do I make myself understood?"

"I understand," Jet said simply. "I'll design more caution, more
margins for error, into my future facilitations. You can tell them that. I'll
plan on erring on the side of failing in the mission if lives might become at
risk. Will that work for you?"

She did not rise to the gentle taunt in his last question. "No fatalities
is mandatory, Jet, as long as you understand that clearly."

"I got it, I got it," he said, throwing his hands up in a motion
of surrender.

Zara did not appreciate Jet's attempts at humor, nor did she appreciate
his referring to his assignments as "my…facilitations." She knew his type
very well and was aware that he had little regard for human life, except that
of his own, and perhaps a few close friends or associates, such as the twins.
And hers, but probably only because she sent so much money his way.

Despite her protestations to Jet and the Huffs, Zara was not
completely unhappy.

Deep inside, in a dark place, she knew that a few fatalities that could
possibly be traced back to the cartel could be of great bargaining value
sometime in the future. Hopefully, the time would never come when she
needed such a bargaining chip, but it is always nice to have the insurance.

The Huff twins had said nothing throughout the meeting, simply sat
and nodded at everything Zara said. They knew where the money was
coming from, even if it was Jet who actually handed them the envelopes
with the cash.

CHAPTER 22

SCOTTSDALE, ARIZONA
APRIL, 2010

Two days after Zara al-Kahtani's brief "meeting" with Jet Jamieson and the Huff twins in San Diego, nine private jets with no markings save their mandatory tail numbers delivered the members of the cartel to the Scottsdale Aviation Services Center, a fixed base operator at Scottsdale Municipal Airport, northeast of Phoenix. A tenth jet delivered Akrum and Zara al-Kahtani.

There was absolutely nothing about ten corporate jets flying into Scottsdale on a Thursday morning in April that was out of the ordinary. The airport was always alive with corporate and chartered aircraft, especially during the golf season. It was over a year from the meeting in Jackson Hole, and it was just the second meeting of the cartel, called by Akrum al-Kahtani to discuss actions to date.

Eager young hosts employed by the Scottsdale Aviation Services Center met each plane in turn and directed the occupants – two to a jet – to the Executive Conference Room at the Center.

The nine oil executives and their designated deputies mingled over coffee, juice, croissants and bagels. Once or twice, Zara caught one of them casting a glance at her, and not necessarily friendly ones.

Just before 10:00 a.m., Akrum al-Kahtani called the meeting to order, thanking them for their attendance and assuring them that he would have them on their way in time to make it home that night, or possibly early the next morning in the case of those from the east coast.

"It's been over a year since we began this effort," he began, "and Zara and I wanted to bring you up to date on our progress with respect to our, shall we say, structured events, and with respect to reversing the President's oil exploration and drilling plan. You all remember Zara from our first meeting. I'll ask her now to bring us all up to date on our activities."

He carefully used the first person, plural, to reinforce on those at the table that they were all in this together.

Zara, again wearing a black abaya with a niqab veil that covered her face except for her eyes, said in her slight Arabic accent, "Welcome to Scottsdale and like my father, I thank you for taking the time to be with us today.

"To date, as you know, we have successfully caused four incidents: the Santa Barbara oil barge incident, the alleged pipeline leak at Galveston, the Anacortes unloading malfunction and the Prince William Sound tanker explosion. The companies that bore the brunt of these incidents were Royal Energy, Mossy Oil and PERL Oil."

She nodded toward Robert Beck. "I want to apologize to Mr. Beck for having to subject him and his staff to two of the incidents, but I want to assure all of you that the location and the impact of the event on the public were my sole criteria for staging each incident. I was not in any way picking on Mr. Beck."

"And I hope, Ms. Al-Kahtani, that Royal Energy is not going be selected for another of your, ah, planned events," Beck said, not at all in jest.

Zara smiled at him, then realized he could not see it because of her veil. "No, Mr. Beck," she said, "Royal Energy will not be subjected to any further actions on our part. And, on that subject, I hope the three of you who have suffered damages from our actions have supplied Akrum with your costs, or if you haven't, that you will as soon as possible. As you will remember, Akrum will apportion the damage costs across all the member companies as soon as all your costs are in to him."

Kristina Vandam of Prime Oil spoke up. "Can you go over again how you're going to handle payments and receipts for damage costs?"

Akrum al-Kahtani got to his feet and said, "Kristina, let me answer that. We have established nine individual oil broker companies in four different tax haven locations. For instance, in Prime Oil's case, you will sell oil at a discount equal to your share of the damages incurred by the three companies. The broker will immediately sell the oil to one of our nine other brokers at the same price, and the second broker will sell the discounted oil to Royal, or Mossy or PERL. They will then sell the oil contracts on the open market and recoup their respective losses.

"With the use of offshore oil brokers in four different countries, the transactions will be next to impossible to trace and we avoid any direct transactions between any two of you."

"How long do you expect a transaction such as this to take?" asked Rodney O'Connor of American Energy.

"We could complete a transaction such as this within an hour," al-Kahtani said, "but our plan is to phase it over a three-day period to make it even more difficult to trace or detect." As he said the last, al-Kahtani surveyed the eighteen faces around the table. All heads were nodding and he could detect a slight smirk on some lips. He was proud of his plan and the reactions around the table only made him more so.

Zara got back to her feet. "I would like next to address the subject which is probably foremost in your minds at this time: the most recent incident, with PERL's *Mar Ascensor* in Prince William Sound." The now-grim faces staring back at her verified it was indeed on their minds.

"As you know, the reports from the scene indicated four fatalities and one crew member missing and presumed drowned. The missing crewman is not an issue. He was one of ours and he is neither dead nor missing. Further, we believe the death of the Chief Engineer was due to a heart attack, a stroke or another sort of seizure. He was found by our people slumped over his control panel." She paused, took a sip of water.

"The death of the other three crewmen, I'm afraid, was the result of a freak timing coincidence. The captain apparently feared his ship had struck something in the water, an iceberg for instance, that may have contributed to the power loss. He sent two men over the side to inspect the ship and determine the extent of damage, if any. At that same moment, the timed charge we had installed in the same area above the waterline detonated, starting the fire which resulted in the deaths of the crewmen. This was the charge which was designed to damage both the inner and the outer hull, but only enough to cause the modest oil leak."

She turned to Fleming Worthy of PERL Oil and said, "I offer my deepest apologies, and those of my father and the other members of our team, to PERL Oil for this tragic accident."

Worthy's scowl indicated he was not yet ready to accept Zara's apology. "I thought your procedures were going to be designed to cause no harm to any of our employees, contractors or customers." He thrust a finger at Akrum and asked, "Isn't that what you told us in Jackson Hole?"

Mark Mazurka of Mazurka Oil said, "That's what I heard, too, and I got to tell you, this pisses me off big time." Several heads nodded. Akrum jumped to his feet to address Worthy and Mazurka, but Zara cut in.

"I repeat my apologies to PERL and its employees. I told you in Jackson Hole that our incidents would be carefully planned to minimize any chance of personal injuries. However, as people in your positions must know better than most, there can be no guarantees. Our planned incidents are designed around risk.

"Think again about the probability of crewmen being lowered over the side of a tanker that size at exactly the same time, and at the same place, as our previously-installed and armed device detonates. If they had gone over the side a minute later, the explosion would already have occurred. Twenty yards farther forward, or farther aft, and it would not have been so bad."

"Can you guarantee there will be no further deaths or injuries in future operations?" Worthy demanded.

"No, sir, I cannot," Zara replied, perhaps a bit more sharply than she intended. "That is a guarantee that is impossible to meet. As I said before, the incidents we plan are high risk by design. They must be, to have the desired effect on public opinion. Every one of you has had workers killed in your own daily operations. All I can tell you is what you tell your shareholders and surviving employees: we will do our best to minimize risk, minimize danger. But minimize and guarantee are two different things entirely. We will do our best to minimize the danger. You have my word on that."

"Why don't we take a 15-minute break?" Akrum al Kahtani suggested, but it was more in the way of an order.

During the break, Worthy, Beck, Vandam and Gord Waters stood in a circle, sipping iced tea and discussing the risks they had agreed to take in pursuit of a sharp increase in oil prices – perhaps to as much as $170 per barrel. By the time Akrum summoned everyone back to the table, the brass ring of $170 oil had satisfied their risk and safety concerns. And to be sure, oil prices had already begun to climb.

When everyone was seated, Worthy spoke. "I obviously do not wish any harm to come to PERL Oil employees, or those of any of your companies, either, for that matter. But I understand there is risk to your plan, Akrum, a plan to which all of us in this room have agreed." He looked around the table, noting the nods. "I think I speak for all of us when I say we want to continue this effort, but we ask you to please use extreme caution when our people are involved."

The eight other CEOs seemed to be nodding affirmatively, but Mark Mazurka leaned over to Daniel Mirza and whispered, "I don't remember Fleming talking to me about continuing with this cartel."

Mirza whispered back, "Fleming is just being Fleming."

"Thank you, Mr. Worthy," Zara said, standing. "Now, to get to the rest of today's briefing. I am told by our political advisors that they have made good progress with some of their targeted Congressmen and Senators in putting together a coalition on Capitol Hill to reverse the President's order opening up oil exploration and drilling. Our advisors tell us that one more oil-related incident should be all that is required to tip the scales completely in our favor."

"In addition, we are working, through our advisors, providing funding to non-profit environmental organizations to help them rally public support for our cause."

Kristina Vandam asked, "Can you tell us which elected officials you're targeting and which environmental organizations you're working with?"

"I can, but I will not, for three reasons," Zara answered. "First, I believe that too much detailed information exposes all of you to risks that are unnecessary. Second, it exposes the people we are working with to unacceptable risk of exposure. And third, I consider this information to be proprietary."

"May I assume your answer is not negotiable?" Kristina asked sharply.

"You are correct; it is not," Zara answered, just as sharply.

Paul Diles, wanting to change the subject before Kristina and Zara came to blows, asked, "Can you tell us about the next incident, the one you referred to earlier?"

"We are in the very early planning stages," Zara responded evenly. "I anticipate it will be a larger oil spill, longer in duration. We must shake the public out of its lethargy. But we will be planning it so as to have no serious on-shore environmental impact. The goal will be to generate more intense media coverage over a longer period of time. We need for the public to get mad. If the public gets mad, the Congress will have to act to overturn the President's order, unless the President reverses himself again first."

"I assume that means the next one will cost us more in damages, then," Mazurka said.

"I just do not know at this time," she replied, "but I think we can assume it will."

"When will it happen?" Mazurka asked.

"We do not yet have a timetable, but I would – tentatively - put it between 60 and 120 days from today," Zara said.

"What will be the risk to our employees – whichever of us is chosen for the next action?" asked O'Connor.

"As I said before," Zara began patiently, "there will always be some level of risk, both to your employees and to the environment. There are also risks to my people. But again I assure you we will take extraordinary measures to minimize them."

Akrum al-Kahtani stood and raised his hand, commanding attention.

"I wish to repeat what has been said several times, my friends," he said. "The fewer details any of us have, the lower the risk to any of us personally, or to our companies' interests. Now, I believe we have covered our activities to date and our expectations for the near future quite thoroughly. We told you we would have you on your way back to your homes in an expeditious manner, so I will ask now whether there are any further questions."

He paused, almost imperceptibly, and when no hands were immediately raised, he went on, "Good, no further questions, so I will adjourn this meeting and thank you again for coming. We have arranged for a lunch to be served, so let us take another short break while the staff sets the table. Then, your jets will be awaiting you."

When the lunch was served and the servers had withdrawn, al-Kahtani tapped his glass to get everyone's attention and said, "One other thing, my friends. Before you depart, please leave the laptops and cell phones we provided you in Jackson Hole with Zara and she will issue you new ones." There were perplexed looks around the table.

"What's the point of changing them now?" Worthy asked. "And what happens to the ones we turn in?"

"It is a simple security precaution," al-Kahtani answered evenly. "Given our mission, I am certain you would all agree that every security precaution we can take, however minor, is worth taking. The old ones will be destroyed before we leave Scottsdale, the memories in each electronically and magnetically scrubbed to assure that no data – even a phone number or email address – remains."

Zara moved around the table, picking up a laptop and cell phone from each CEO and handing out replacements. After all the petroleum executives had boarded their jets and departed from Scottsdale Municipal Airport, Akrum and Zara al-Kahtani remained in the conference room.

Zara moved from device to device, downloading all data onto a thumb drive. When her thumb drive was loaded with every piece of information on every laptop and cell phone, she called a company she had put on standby several days earlier and a panel truck soon appeared and took possession of the devices. Within an hour, the devices would be in an industrial incinerator where they would all be turned into molten plastic and metal.

As Akrum and Zara settled back in the chairs at one end of the conference table, they felt quite satisfied with the meeting and the outcome. The thumb drive Zara now had on a lanyard around her neck under her abaya was the best kind of insurance there was. Both knew they now had the cartel members locked in for the duration of the project. There would be no deserters. Not without serious consequences.

CHAPTER 23

After the panel truck had departed with the laptops and cell phones that were destined for cremation, Zara hit a speed dial number on her cell phone and spoke quickly in Arabic. Two minutes later, Jet Jamieson knocked and entered the conference room.

Akrum al-Kahtani had reserved the conference room for the day and thought it was the best secure place available to begin planning for what they hoped was to be the last incident, or facilitation, as Zara and Jet usually referred to them. The Huff twins had come over from San Diego with Jet but they remained outside the conference room in a comfortable lounge area. They might be summoned, or they might not.

Zara got right to business. "We've discussed many different options for our next facilitation." She loved the word. "We have previously ruled out oil tankers and underwater pipelines, because we have already used those. For a variety of reasons, we have also ruled out storage facilities, refineries and on-shore oil wells.

"When we last discussed this, we have narrowed our choices to a pumping oil platform or a floating deep water drilling rig in the Gulf of Mexico."

"A floating drilling rig would be a better option than an oil platform," Akrum ventured. "We could very plausibly arrange a blowout with an explosion that would result in a significant event, a lot of oil spilled."

Jet immediately agreed. "If we pick the right drilling rig, it would be the incident that would force the President to rescind his order, rather than waiting for the Congress to force his hand. More bang for the buck."

"Yes," Akrum said, smiling, "I love that American expression. More bang for the buck." Jet grinned at him.

Zara had by now removed her niqab, and the fire in her eyes was unmistakable.

"More bang for the buck?" she asked incredulously. She looked at Akrum. "Did you not hear what the cartel members said in this room not two hours ago? They want no more fatalities, not even any more injuries. And they are concerned with the costs they incur with each of these facilitations. We need something that gets huge press coverage but without loss of life or huge costs to them."

Zara was excited and paused to catch her breath. "A floating drilling rig with a blowout is too risky. We can't control it. It is out of the question." Another pause as she stared from one man to the other. "I will not allow it."

"Zara," Akrum began in a conciliatory tone. He knew his daughter and her temper. He did not want to spark it further. "I think you need to keep an open mind until Jet and I can do some more research and planning for the right drilling rig on which to have our next incident."

"I agree," Jet jumped in, grateful for Akrum's intervention. "Just let us take a look at the best possibilities and see what we can come up with."

"Out of the question," Zara snapped, not mollified at all. "Completely unacceptable. You cannot plan something involving a blowout and explosion on any deep water rig and expect to be able to control the situation. It must be an offshore oil pumping platform. We can reasonably manage an incident on one of them. End of discussion. Please use your time to start planning for something on an offshore oil pumping platform. Must I make that in the form of an order?"

Akrum and Jet tried one more time to convince Zara to let them look at a floating drilling rig, but soon concluded that she was not going to back down.

"No, no and no," Zara said with force. "Drop it and start looking at offshore platforms. Let's meet in a month and see where you are in your planning. And don't forget, there are to be no injuries or fatalities. Are we clear on that?"

Akrum and Jet both nodded, then Akrum spoke. "Can we make the next meeting in six weeks instead of a month? We will need more than a month, I think, for Jet and me to investigate and plan it, and to make the preliminary arrangements."

Zara agreed, thankful that she had finally beaten them down.

The Scottsdale meeting was now over, and Akrum, Zara, Jet and the Huff twins walked out to the private jet. It would drop Jet and the Huffs in San Diego before taking Akrum and Zara to their destinations.

CHAPTER 24

GALVESTON, TEXAS
THE NEXT WEEK

Jet Jamieson walked through the solid oak door into the offices of Gulf & Gulf, PLLC, in a modern building in downtown Galveston. He thought a name like Gulf & Gulf might be the most perfect name ever contemplated for a law firm specializing in the oil *bidness* of the Texas gulf coast.

When he identified himself to the very attractive receptionist, she showed Jet immediately through another set of solid oak doors into a conference room that could only be described as opulent. Akrum al-Kahtani was sitting at the table, sipping on a cup of coffee.

Gulf & Gulf was not Akrum's principle law firm in the United States, but he had engaged it for several small tasks over the years, enough so that he had no problem using the firm's conference room and the firm had no problem claiming attorney-client privilege should the matters discussed in the conference room ever be subject to an inquiry by a law enforcement agency.

As it happened, in this case there was nobody in the room except Akrum and Jet. It had been six days since the Scottsdale planning meeting with the cartel and both Akrum and Jet were frustrated over Zara's intransigence regarding the next facilitation.

The frustration was compounded by the fact that the best that could be said of the relationship between Akrum and Jet was that they "sort of" trusted each other. And that trust – born of necessity – was singular in tense and extended only as far as each other's current needs.

The two men greeted each other and shook hands in much the same way two dogs from the same neighborhood would circle and sniff each other to make sure of the other's intentions.

"Where are we on our next – to use Zara's term – facilitation?" Akrum asked as he sat back down, gesturing for Jet to sit as well.

"I've found the perfect candidate," Jet said. "*The American PERL I,* a floating deep water drilling rig 35 miles off the coast of Louisiana. It's a joint venture between American Energy and PERL Oil."

"Are you absolutely sure?" Akrum asked quietly. Jet nodded. "Tell me about it, then," Akrum said and sat back in his chair to listen.

Jet gave him the full run-down. "It's doing exploratory drilling in a new field and they project they'll find oil in the range of 10-15,000 feet under the sea floor. The water at the site is about a mile deep. At this point, the information I'm getting is that they've drilled down to about 8,000 feet and all signs are still positive.

"There's a possibility that there will be a methane gas pocket above the oil, which as you know makes for perfect conditions for a blow-out, even if they do everything right – follow all the procedures."

Jet paused, his face twisting into a sinister smile. "And with the tweaking I can do, I have no doubt we'll have a major blow-out. I've got almost everything in place and should be ready to rock and roll in the next few days."

"Then what?" Akrum asked.

"Then we wait until the conditions are just right and I'll activate the blow-out plan. The rig is operating 24 hours a day. I would guess, based on what information I've got, we should get our blow-out within thirty days."

"What kind of damage are we anticipating?" Akrum could not shake the feeling of dread, knowing what Zara's reaction would be, and instead tried to focus on the riches that awaited complete success.

"Damage will be significant. I have our explosive devices fixed in place already. When the conditions are right, the blow-out will be ignited by our explosives. There will be a lot of loud noise and a lot of fire. We're going to have injuries – no way to avoid them – and a decent chance the whole rig will be destroyed and sink. But it would probably take 48 hours for it to sink, so rescue operations will have a good chance to work."

"How much of an oil spill are you anticipating?" Akrum asked.

"Hard to predict," Jet answered evasively. "All my analyses indicate the blow-out will cause oil to flow out for a while. The blow-out preventer will be disabled and the crew will be unable to shut off the oil flow completely."

"How much oil will be spilled, do you think?" Akrum persisted. He was weary of Jet's evasive answers and self-assured lectures.

"There's no way to tell for sure, but I think it will be the biggest one we've arranged," Jet answered, aware of Akrum's pique. "I would anticipate a significant spill that, given the volume and distances, will probably reach shore, and probably in what Zara refers to as 'environmentally-sensitive areas.' It will take them some time to stop the oil flow, from what I see of the geologic projections and the estimated pressure the crude is under down there."

"Will they be able to stop the flow with the usual methods?" Akrum asked, his anxiety increasing.

"I think they'll go through the usual menu, yes," Jet said. "They'll probably try to repair or cap the blow-out preventer, drill relief wells and plug this well with cement. Their only other option would be to just let the well flow itself out, which isn't in the cards. That will not be allowed to happen.

"This will be a very big and very costly spill that will get the world's attention, especially Washington's. If it comes off as planned, this should more than satisfy your clients. All of them."

"Yes, my clients will be quite satisfied," Akrum nodded. "Unfortunately, the cartel members will be quite displeased and Zara will be furious."

Jet nodded in understanding. "I've done some initial planning, as well, on an oil pumping platform that's about 100 miles off the Louisiana coast and sits in water that's about 350 feet deep. "I'll get the plans on that to Zara in the next couple of weeks, which should buy us some time with her?"

"Are you using the Huff twins?" Akrum wondered.

"I am, but only for the pumping platform," Jet answered, "even though they're not the best in planning and organizing, but involving them should help me satisfy Zara. But since they're obviously completely loyal to her,

I've excluded them from anything on the *American PERL I* facilitation."

"Good," Akrum nodded. "Zara will be putting pressure on us to perform flawlessly on the oil platform spill, so we'll need to be able to assure her on the issues of casualties, the volume of the spill and so forth."

"It won't be easy to slow-pitch her," Jet warned. "She and the cartel members will go ballistic when the *American PERL I* blows, and – if everything goes right – continues spilling oil."

"And when that one blows, I don't think there's any question that she and the cartel will call off the oil pumping platform spill," Akrum added.

"Nor do I," Jet agreed casually. "That's why I've got the Huff twins doing the planning. I don't want to waste my own time."

"We need to be very careful not to do anything that would cause Zara to be at all suspicious of any involvement on our part with the blow-out," Akrum warned unnecessarily. "She is, and always has been, a very dangerous woman when she thinks she has been wronged."

"I know that, Akrum," Jet said earnestly. "Believe me when I tell you I'm doing everything possible to make the *American PERL I* look like an accident."

Jet went through his plans another time, and he and Akrum were both satisfied with the facilitation as planned.

Both felt very satisfied as well with the rich payday that awaited them when this operation was concluded.

But they were both very fearful of Zara's wrath if she ever learned of their duplicitous involvement in what she would see as a calamity.

There are always risks when one double- or triple-dips, Akrum thought to himself as they prepared to leave Galveston.

Zara was concerned that Jet and Akrum seemed to be taking longer than normal to select and plan what she firmly believed would be their last facilitation. What was more troubling to her was that she was having difficulty in contacting Jet when she sought – or needed – reassurance that all was on target.

She acknowledged, however, that sometimes being out of touch was normal for Jet, given the nature of his line of work.

They had been scheduled for a status meeting in early May at George

Bush Intercontinental Airport north of Houston, but Jet had asked in an email whether they could take care of their business with a telephone call. He had encountered an unexpected scheduling conflict. Zara's sense of unease was not helped by Jet's request because it was unusual for the man, who was such a meticulous planner.

Still, Zara had agreed to Jet's suggested date and time and told him they would speak Arabic on the call.

When they were on the phone, Zara quickly got down to business. "What is the status of the next – and hopefully last – facilitation?"

"I've picked an offshore oil pumping platform and the Huff twins are working out the last details and arrangements as we speak," Jet said.

"Where is this platform?"

"Approximately 100 miles off the Louisiana coast in about 350 feet of water. It is pumping from several wells – five, I believe – plus it receives oil from two other platforms. It has an operating crew of fifteen men and is about 25 years old."

"When do you plan for the incident to occur?"

"Somewhere between five and eight weeks from now, Zara."

"Why so long, may I ask?"

"Because having a reasonable size of spill without any injuries to the crew requires more detailed and meticulous planning. And I would remind you that you are the one who specified no injuries, if you will recall."

"What are the details of the incident so far?"

"The twins and I have planned an explosion and fire, with oil pumping uninterrupted because the shut-off valves will fail to operate. Oil will continue to flow into the Gulf until the shut-off valves can be repaired and the flow shut off.

"We will have a helicopter on the pumping platform and another on each of the adjacent platforms. We will have the lifeboats inspected and fully operational, so all crew members should be easily rescued."

"What is the name of this platform and who owns it?"

"It is the *Monarch 51* and it is owned by Mazurka Oil."

"I wish another update one week from today – telephone is fine – and I expect you to be able to supply me with the planned date of the incident at that time."

Jet sighed audibly. "I will do my best," he said finally.

When they disconnected the call, Jet thought he had adequately – perhaps even masterfully – pacified Zara.

Zara's intuition told her she was being pacified, which she thought of as a nice way to say, bullshitted.

The Huff twins – Tweeter and Slump – thought they had completed all the planning for the *Monarch 51* oil pumping platform spill. It should be relatively easy, they thought.

They would gain access to the *Monarch 51* via a supply helicopter, drug the small crew, install their explosives, override the safety switches on the pumps and valves, open them up, depart the platform on the same supply helicopter and set off the explosives as they leave.

Tweeter commented to Slump – or maybe it was the other way around – that he could not understand why Jet's making them go back over the plan for the umpteenth time rather than just approving the goddamn plan we've got.

Slump – or maybe it was Tweeter – responded, "I don't have a clue. He seems preoccupied with something else he's working on that doesn't involve us or Zara. I think he needs to concentrate on one client at a time instead of spreading himself all over the map."

"He knows Zara demanded his full attention until these facilitations are completed, however long that takes."

"Well, Sandy Agria told me that she saw Jet and some Arabian man she didn't know meeting with Kirk Klenner, her boss at Pure Earth. She couldn't find out what they were talking about except that it seemed to be a big fucking secret and has to do with one of Pure Earth's major goals."

Pure Earth was a well-funded and radical environmental organization that was headquartered in Houston and considered the Gulf Coast its home territory. Sandy Agria, who had worked with Zara and the Huff twins on projects in the past was now working for Pure Earth. Zara had wanted eyes and ears inside Pure Earth for a variety of reasons, which the Huffs suspected had a lot to do with this business of the President's order on offshore oil exploration. When they had first met Sandy Agria, the Huff twins had almost immediately adopted a little sister relationship with her.

"She also told me that over the last few months, she's seen several big wire fund transfers from Pure Earth to offshore tax havens and charged to pollution research on Pure Earth's books, with no more detail in their accounting system."

"How the hell does Sandy know Jet, and for that matter, why we would give a shit about what he's doing?"

"Don't you remember that we worked with Sandy on that pharmaceutical operation that Zara and Jet ran a couple of years ago?"

"Shit! I forgot all about that. Should we give Zara a heads-up?"

"No, we better not. She told us to deal directly with Jet, so let's hold off for a while and see what happens. For all we know, Pure Earth may be involved in this facilitation."

Instead of calling Zara, the Huff twins, Tweeter and Slump decided to go have dinner and a few beers while they played pool.

CHAPTER 25

GULF OF MEXICO OFF LOUISIANA
JUNE, 2010

The *New Orleans Times-Picayune's* front-page was entirely taken up by one story, along with several photographs. The banner headline drew the reader's immediate attention.

KILLER DRILLING RIG EXPLOSION

A massive explosion and fire rocked a floating deep-water drilling rig last night. The rig, the American PERL I, is located about 35 miles south of the Louisiana coast in an area known as the Mississippi Canyon.

Early reports indicate that 110 of a crew of 125 have been rescued, although at least twenty of the rescued crew members are suffering from various injuries and burns. The remaining fifteen are missing at this time and it is presumed that they were killed in the violent explosion and fire.

The rig is reported to be still burning and listing badly. Support boats are on the scene looking for survivors and spraying the rig with water. Knowledgeable observers on the scene have told our reporters that they expect the American PERL I to sink.

Oil is still gushing from the well, which is approximately one mile below the surface. American Energy, Inc., issued a statement early this morning praising the firefighting efforts and pledging all possible efforts to locate the missing crew members and to stop the flow of oil. It has already launched a comprehensive investigation of the incident and pledges its cooperation with state and federal authorities, who are conducting their own investigations.

An American Energy spokesperson indicated the explosion and fire was most likely the result of a blow-out caused by a huge burst of gaseous hydrocarbons and oil from the well. The company had just completed the exploratory drilling on the well and was in the process of analyzing and processing the results.

The White House issued a statement from the President saying his thoughts and prayers were with the missing and injured crew members and their families. He has also directed the Department of Energy and the Environmental Protection Agency to conduct a complete investigation of this terrible accident.

In addition, the White House statement indicates that the President has directed his policy staff to reevaluate the government's current position regarding the opening up of oil exploration and drilling in environmentally-sensitive areas.

STATEMENT ISSUED BY CITIZENS FOR RESPONSIBLE GROWTH

Contact: Sarah Cotton, Public Affairs Director 202-555-1122

Citizens for Responsible Growth (CFRG) is appalled with yet another tragic and catastrophic oil disaster. Last night, an explosion and fire on the American PERL I, a deep water drilling rig just 35 miles from the coast of Louisiana, left fifteen crew members missing and presumed dead, and another twenty injured, some seriously.

A large oil slick has already appeared over the site and at this time we have been offered no estimate of the amount of oil gushing from the well. Neither have we been offered any idea how the flow will be stopped, how long that process will take, nor how much oil will have escaped by that time.

This is clearly a human and ecological disaster.

The President must seize the initiative and reverse his ill-advised order opening oil exploration and drilling in environmentally sensitive areas.

In addition, a thorough investigation and review of current safety procedures and requirements must be undertaken by the government. This terrible accident clearly points to faulty procedures and/or requirements.

We cannot allow the rash of oil-related accidents that have plagued us over the last year or so to continue.

STATEMENT ISSUED BY PURE EARTH INTERNATIONAL

Contact: Kirk Klenner 713-555-7733

Pure Earth International is horrified with the explosion, fire and oil spill that occurred last night just off the environmentally-sensitive Louisiana coast. This inexcusable incident is a tragedy that affects humans, wildlife and an already-fragile ecosystem.

Wildlife threatened by this disaster include:

<u>Ocean Surface:</u>
  Brown pelican
  Sea turtles
  Reddish egret
<u>Ocean Sub-surface:</u>
  Shrimp
  Crayfish
  Bluefin tuna
  Bottlenose dolphin
<u>Ocean floor:</u>
  Oysters
  Scallops
  Lobsters

The projected loss of wildlife resulting from this disaster will be devastating. Some species may never recover and simply pass into history. Those that survive will take years to replenish. The fishing industry in the Gulf will be crippled, if not destroyed.

Pure Earth – along with a number of other environmental organizations and a growing majority of voters in the United States – are demanding that the President and Congress immediately act to stop the expansion of oil exploration and drilling in all environmentally-sensitive areas.

In addition, the operating and safety requirements for existing drilling rigs and oil pumping platforms, as well as those that apply to the shipping of crude oil, must be reviewed in detail, and changes imposed as appropriate. We have no choice but to tighten all safety procedures to avoid future disasters.

We must all act now to stop the irreparable damage we are causing to our earth.

CHAPTER 26

Two days before the scheduled progress meeting of Zara, Jet and Akrum, it was cancelled by Jet in an encrypted email to Zara. She tried several times to contact both Jet and Akrum, using their established, secure, procedures.

She received no response from either man, which was both unusual and unsettling. Zara was already unsettled and extremely curious about the explosion, fire and oil spill – it was still gushing out of the Gulf floor – involving the American PERL I. As it was to everybody, the incident remained a complete mystery to her, and she was not use to being in the dark.

Deep in her stomach, Zara feared what she would eventually learn about the incident. For now, she was most interested in talking with Jet and her father to decide what to say to the cartel members. All nine of them, she knew, had already begun demanding answers and assurances that she and Akrum were not behind the American PERL I disaster.

The presumed loss of life, the injuries, the volume of oil still spilling, the environmental damage and – last but certainly not least – the cost of the incident were all unacceptable. They had begun hammering on her when they did not receive responses from Akrum.

Most of their encrypted emails were also demanding an immediate meeting of the cartel. The members were scared and Zara was losing control of the situation. She was not used to the feeling of lack of control, any more than the feeling of being in the dark.

She used her encrypted cell phone to call each cartel member that day.

Zara explained – as calmly as she could, given state of near-panic she sensed from the members – that this was not one of her facilitations and probably was a true accident. She reminded them – as if they needed it - that deep-water drilling is a risky business and that each of them had experienced similar problems, although perhaps not of this magnitude, in the past.

And Zara agreed to schedule a cartel meeting immediately.

It was not until the next day that Jet called her back.

"Where the hell were you yesterday and why did you not answer your phone or respond to my emails?" she demanded without preamble.

"I've been on another assignment for the past several days and was not able to communicate," he responded calmly.

"I hope to God it was not the *American PERL I* catastrophe."

"No, of course not. I heard about that just last night. I was in a different part of the world, and like I said, I was out of touch."

"We must meet immediately to consider where we are at the moment. The cartel members are scared and furious. How soon can you and Akrum be available?"

Jet paused as if considering his schedule. "I can meet you the day after tomorrow, and I'll check with Akrum but I think he'll be able to as well."

"Do you know where he is?" she demanded fiercely. "He has not returned my calls or answered my emails, either."

"I'm not sure where he is, other than that, as far as I know, he's in the States and should be able to join us."

"Find him!" she demanded loudly. "We will meet in the Continental Airlines VIP Club at George Bush Intercontinental at 10:00 a.m. the day after tomorrow. No cancellations, no excuses. We have very serious problems and I want to resolve them immediately."

"We'll be there, Zara. I'll find Akrum and we'll see you there."

Zara read something in Jet's voice that went beyond the words he spoke. She felt that thing in the pit of her stomach again.

Zara, Akrum and Jet were all on time and were shown into a conference room of the Continental Airlines VIP Club promptly at 10:00 a.m. Zara began by again chastising Jet and Akrum about being out of touch, not answering cell phone calls or emails, then got down to the business at hand.

"We have serious problems with every one of our cartel members," she said. "I spoke to each of them the day after the *American PERL I* incident. They all believe we arranged it. They do not believe it was an accident because its proportions were just too big for it to have been one. They think we were involved, even though I assured them we were not."

"Of course we were not involved," Akrum responded immediately. "I believe it truly was an accident and that American Energy and PERL Oil are looking for a scapegoat for something for which they are responsible."

"I agree with Akrum," Jet said. "It had to have been an accident. I think PERL and American Energy want to pin it on us so the other seven members of the cartel will have to share in the cost of the clean-up and other liabilities that will follow."

Jet paused before continuing.

"However, I must say that it should have a significant impact on public opinion and the resulting pressure on the President and Congress to act."

"The members should be rejoicing instead of complaining and accusing us of something for which we were not responsible," Akrum said. Jet nodded in agreement.

"Well that is nice, but it is not the case," Zara snapped, the now-familiar feeling in the pit of her stomach coming back. They are demanding a cartel meeting as soon as possible, but certainly no later than 30 days from now. If we try to rush it too soon, PERL and American would not be able to be there. They must stay in their offices until the leak is stopped and the investigations are fully underway.

"When we meet, it will be entirely up to us to convince them that we were not involved with this disaster." She looked pointedly at Akrum and asked, "Will you set up the meeting as soon as all nine members can be scheduled?"

Akrum nodded. "I will start immediately." He knew his daughter well and he knew the look on her face meant she would brook no delays.

"I want to put the oil pumping platform facilitation on hold for now," Zara continued to the next item on her agenda. "What is its current status?"

"We're still in the planning stage," Jet said. "As you know, I turned the detailed planning over to the Huff twins and sometimes their planning takes a while. However, I have no problem with putting it on hold because I don't think we'll need another incident to cause a change in the open drilling policy. The *American PERL I* should do it."

"Okay, then take this as an order," Zara responded icily. "You are to immediately cease all planning of the oil pumping platform facilitation."

"I'll contact the Huff twins this afternoon and tell them to discontinue all planning on it until further orders," Jet said affably. "And I'll instruct them to shred any plans they have on paper. If they have set in place any implements of our work – which I don't think they have – I'll instruct them to retrieve and dispose of them."

The meeting adjourned and Akrum and Jet hurried to catch a flight to Washington, D.C. Zara had reminded them both that she expected them to be available to her at all times, either by cell phone or by email.

When they were airborne on the way to the nation's capital, Jet asked Akrum, "Do you think Zara suspects we were involved with the *American PERL I*?"

"Zara always suspects everybody and everything, especially when things go astray from what she planned or expected. We would be wise to continue to be extremely cautious."

CHAPTER 27

HENDERSON, NEVADA
THREE WEEKS LATER

Between 9:00 and 9:35 a.m., ten sleek, white business jets with no markings save their tail numbers touched down at the Henderson Executive Airport, just east of Las Vegas. The al-Kahtanis and the nine cartel members were met at their planes and whisked to a conference room in the terminal.

While Akrum al-Kahtani exchanged strained greetings with the members, Zara al-Kahtani moved quickly around the room discretely waving a small device the size of a cigarette pack, confirming that there were no listening devices. Then she too, greeted each member of the cartel. Those exchanges were strained, too.

Nobody expected that this meeting would be cordial.

Akrum opened the meeting at 10:00 a.m. and quickly turned the meeting over to Zara. After doing so, he slipped quietly to the back of the room.

Zara quickly got to the point. "We all know why we are here today," she said in a firm voice, "to discuss the *American PERL I* disaster. I want to start by assuring each of you once again that this disaster was not of our making. In fact, we were in the final planning stages for an offshore oil pumping platform facilitation.

"We would never have even considered a deep water drilling rig. The risks of human casualties, and of unacceptable environmental damage, would be too high – as was underscored by what actually happened."

Robert Beck of Royal Energy asked, "Which pumping oil platform did you select?"

"It was the *Monarch I*, a Mazurka Oil property, but that facilitation has been cancelled. I don't believe that any additional action on our part will be required, given the magnitude of the *American PERL I* tragedy."

Nods around the table were punctuated by the simultaneous comments of Fleming Worthy and Rodney O'Connor, "I should hope not."

Zara coldly stared around the room, but focused on Worthy and O'Connor before she answered. "Evidently, you did not hear me or perhaps you did not understand me. Let me repeat, slowly, so that there is no misunderstanding, that this was not – I repeat not – our doing. Neither I nor any of our people were involved in what happened at the *American PERL I*." She paused to let her anger simmer down. It took a full minute.

"I believe that once all the investigations have been completed, it will be determined that the *American PERL I* was an accident. I heard and understood your orders in Scottsdale with regard to casualties. A target such as the American PERL I was out of the question for the reasons I stated earlier."

Akrum, sensing the tension level had risen to a critical point, suggested a coffee break.

During the break, O'Connor approached Zara and asked if he could speak with her outside for a minute or two. When they were outside, O'Connor said quietly, "Zara, if you tell me you were not involved in the *American PERL I* disaster, I believe you. But I do not believe it was an accident. Somebody sabotaged that rig."

O'Connor opened his briefcase and pulled out a small electronic device. "One of the supervisors on the drilling rig found this in a trash barrel and picked it out before the rig was abandoned," he said. "My security people tell me the purpose of this device is to send out a signal. It could be used to set off a detonator. In addition, another supervisor saw three men jump from the rig right after the initial explosions. All three were wearing wet suits with diving tanks on their backs."

Zara examined the electronic device in silence. Finally, she asked in a very low voice, "Have you told anyone about this – about what you have just told me?"

"No, I have not, because I thought this was one of your facilitations," he replied in the same low voice.

"I will say it again," Zara said, "I had nothing to do with it, but I think it is in our best interests perhaps to investigate what this device is and who the men in wet suits were. The best way to prove we were not involved is to see if we can find out who was involved. If you agree, I do not believe you should go to the authorities with this until I have a chance to look into it."

O'Connor agreed.

"I would like to take some photos of this device and if you got a statement from your employee who saw the divers jump overboard, I would like a copy, if I may," she said.

"When we leave today, I will leave this briefcase behind for you. The device will be in it, along with the man's statement and a photo he snapped with his cell phone of the divers jumping into the water."

Zara formally reached out to shake O'Connor's hand. "I will do my very best to investigate this matter and will keep you aware of my progress."

O'Connor shook her hand and said, "Then perhaps it's time for us to rejoin the others." They returned to the conference room. As she made the rounds of the room, she managed to get a few private words with many of the other members before she called the meeting back to order.

Akrum stayed in the back of the room. It was becoming increasingly clear to all who was now in charge.

Zara began, "My efforts will now focus on working with the environmental and conservation organizations that have been most vocal in their reactions to our facilitations, since, as I said earlier, I do not believe any further facilitations will be required. Working through others, of course, I will encourage these organizations to continue the pressure on the President and Congress to reverse the open drilling policy and reinstate the ban on drilling in sensitive areas."

The nine cartel members let out a synchronized sigh, as if directed to do so by an orchestra conductor.

Zara continued, "I think all that has happened, both our work and the recent accident, will result in the ban on open drilling being reinstated fairly soon. Meanwhile, I will apply myself and my associates to conducting our own clandestine investigation of the *American PERL I* disaster. It affected two of our member companies very seriously, and I think we all owe it to them to find out what really happened."

There were murmurs of ascent around the table and she continued. "It may have been a tragic accident, but it may have been sabotage; what you in the West call a 'copy-cat' thing. I will do everything I can to find out."

She looked around the table, and nobody moved to speak.

"If there is nothing else, your planes have been refueled and are available whenever you wish to depart. Thank you for coming and have a good day."

As the cartel members filed out of the room and toward the flight line and their aircraft, Mark Mazurka whispered to Dan Mirza and Kristina Vandam, "It was damned interesting that Akrum sat in the background and didn't have a thing to say, once he introduced Zara." The others nodded.

All in the cartel had known from the beginning that they had no options but to stay with the cartel and Zara, and today had reinforced that in spades. Once in, there was no way out, they all realized with varying degrees of trepidation.

All of Zara's finely-honed instincts were on high alert after the cartel meeting. Something was not right about the *American PERL I* incident, and something was not right about her father's lack of involvement in the cartel meeting. He was almost completely disassociated.

Perhaps he had been fearful of a rebellion in the ranks, she thought, and that the members would be less likely to revolt with her leading the discussion and making the report. But Zara had never known Akrum al-Kahtani to be afraid.

Careful, yes, but that was quite different from fear.

They were going to have their chartered jet take them to San Diego, but she would leave Akrum there and fly on to Houston to start her investigation. She had one of the pilots stow Rodney O'Connor's briefcase in the forward baggage compartment, to be offloaded in Houston.

For the time being, she would conduct her investigation alone, and she would not tell Akrum, or Jet, about O'Connor's briefcase or its contents.

Once the jet had stopped in San Diego to drop Akrum off and had taken off on its three-hour flight to Houston Hobby Airport, Zara got on her secure cell phone and called the Huff twins. Tweeter answered the cell they shared. Zara told him she wished to meet with them in Houston and she did not wish for either Akrum or Jet to know they were meeting.

Tweeter, of course, agreed and told her they were then on Interstate 10 just east of New Orleans. They had checked out of their most recent motel and had their luggage with them. They would simply stay on the highway and, God and traffic willing, be in Houston in between four and five hours. Zara told him she would check Hobby Airport hotels and get back with him about where she would be.

Zara knew she could trust the Huff twins. She had formed a bond with them that she was certain was stronger than the bond between Jet and them, even though Jet had brought them into this operation.

When she arrived at Houston Hobby Airport, Zara surveyed the lodging and rental car call center on the baggage claim level of the terminal. She selected the Marriot Houston South and picked up the direct-connect phone. She secured two rooms, one in her name and one in the Huffs' and asked for an airport shuttle.

When she had checked in at the Marriot, she called the Huffs' cell phone. This time it was Slump who answered. She told him where she was and the address. Slump reported that traffic through Beaumont was "a bitch," and estimated it would be three more hours before they arrived.

Zara unpacked in her room and hurried back downstairs to the pool to spend some precious time by herself in the Jacuzzi. Without her Arabic dress, of course.

As she sat in the swirling, pulsating water of the Jacuzzi, Zara closed her eyes and thought about the last – very strange – month. Zara was used to being in control, and she had not been in control as the events surrounding the *American PERL I* incident and the cartel members' reactions unfolded around her.

While Zara prided herself on being emotionless and controlled, a myriad of emotions overwhelmed her and she felt close to tears, something she had not given in to since her mother had died when she was a little girl.

Her emotions ranged between anger, frustration, bewilderment and sadness. The suspicion that would not go away, that somehow Akrum and Jet had betrayed her, caused all four emotions to sharpen. How could her own father and Jet, her long-time associate, do this to her, she wondered. This was the most financially-rewarding facilitation any of them had ever been involved with.

And she wondered - if it was true they had betrayed her – whether they had sold themselves to others with the same goals in order to double dip or did they just go off half-cocked on their own.

She knew that if her suspicions turned out to be true, her relationships with both men were over. More to the point, if her suspicions turned out to be true, she might find it necessary to destroy both of them.

The realization that she had moved herself back from self-pity to the offensive – a much more familiar state of affairs for her – she felt better and relaxed, soaking up the soothing throb of the Jacuzzi.

The Huff twins arrived at the hotel four hours later; the traffic had been a bitch through eastern Houston too, and after checking in and calling Zara, went to her room to meet with her.

After greeting them and thanking them for making the drive to Houston on such short notice, she got right to the point. She did not ask them to speak in Arabic, as she often did for confidential conversations because she had swept the room with her little electronic marvel when she had first checked in, and again after she had returned from the Jacuzzi.

"I need you to do some investigative work for me," she began. "I do not want anyone to know about this assignment, and that includes, in fact, it especially includes, Akrum and Jet. "Do you understand that?"

Both Huffs nodded their understanding.

"I mean; do you really understand?" she persisted. "This is very important. I want what we are going to look into to be kept from Akrum, Jet and anyone else until I decide differently."

"We understand, boss," Tweeter said and Slump nodded to indicate his agreement.

"I know you are both aware of the tragedy involving the American PERL I, the explosion, fire, leaked oil, injuries and deaths and environmental damage," she said. "I suspect – but I do not have any direct knowledge at this time – that this was not an accident. Many in the cartel that is paying us believe, even after my disclaimers to them, that it was one of our facilitations."

Zara took a deep breath before continuing.

"Specifically, I suspect that Akrum and Jet might have been involved with the disaster. I do not make that statement lightly because I know you two have been friends of Jet's for a long time."

The Huff twins looked at each other, surprise clearly showing on both of their faces. The looks morphed from surprise to shock when Zara asked her next question.

"Were you involved in any way – even on the periphery – with *American PERL I?* In any way at all?"

They answered in unison and with equal force, "No way!"

"Did you notice anything unusual in your contacts with Akrum or Jet in the last couple of months?" she asked. "Anything that you think could connect them to *American PERL I?*"

Tweeter's eyes were wide as he glanced at Slump. "Why don't you tell her?" he said.

"Yes, please tell me, Slump," Zara said.

"Several things," Slump began. "First of all, you told us to report only to Jet on the facilitation we've been working on."

"Yes?" Zara responded. "Go on."

"We finished our planning for the *Monarch 51* oil pumping platform facilitation weeks ago," Slump said. "We both thought it was a relatively easy and fairly straight-forward operation and was a pretty simple plan to execute. But Jet would never approve it and kept sending us back to tweak this and that. We both thought Jet seemed pre-occupied and was just stalling us."

"Is there more?" Zara asked.

"Yeah, there is," Slump said. "You remember Sandy Agria, of course."

Zara nodded and gestured with her hand for Slump to continue.

"Well, Sandy is now working for Pure Earth, as you wanted her to, and she told me she saw Jet and an Arab-looking man meeting with Pure Earth's executive director, a guy named Klenner. She told me she didn't know what the meeting was about, but it seemed to be highly-secretive and she said it would accomplish a major goal of Pure Earth."

Zara felt stunned but then realized she really wasn't. "Did Sandy tell you anything else?" she asked.

"Yes, she said that she had found out that Pure Earth has been wiring what she called significant amounts of money to tax havens and charging it to pollution research and stuff like that, with no detailed accounting of what the money was used for."

"Why did you not tell me this before?" Zara demanded hotly.

"You told us very specifically to deal only with Jet. We assumed the Arab-looking guy was probably Akrum, so we assumed their meeting with Pure Earth was connected to this whole thing."

Zara was frustrated, knowing that she had brought this communication breakdown on herself. "Well, that was my fault, but from this point forward, you are only working with me, as we discussed earlier." She was firmly convinced that Jet and Akrum had worked with Pure Earth to stage the *American PERL I* incident. Now she needed to prove it.

"Here is what I want you to do now," she said. "I need to know what arrangement Jet and Akrum had – or have – with Pure Earth. I need to know about the so-called secretive project. I need to know how much Jet and Akrum are - or were - paid and where they were paid. And I need the details on the Pure Earth wire transfers for this so-called pollution research, including the final recipient of that money. And I need all that information right now."

This time, Tweeter spoke up. "We'll start by seeing if we can get Sandy Agria to help us. If she will, that will get us basic information on Pure Earth's operations and access to its computer system. And we've got a computer and finance guy we've used before that's a wizard at tracking money from wire to wire. But he'll be expensive."

"I will wire your account $250,000 tomorrow morning," Zara replied, her determination clearly exposed on her face. "And there is one other thing I had not focused on earlier. I was unable to contact – by cell phone or email - either Jet or Akrum during the days prior to the *American PERL I* incident. Find out their locations during this time period. You should be able to track their movements via the GPS in their cell phones.

"And, finally, please give me an update at least daily – more often if possible or when you learn anything major – on your progress."

After assuring Zara of their complete understanding of her instructions and the fact that she could count on them, the Huff twins left Zara's room and returned to their own to start making plans and phone calls.

Zara remained in her room, silent and brooding. She felt great sorrow at the same time she felt great anger, bordering on rage. She was unsure how events of the next few weeks would play out, but she was convinced, as always, that she would come out the winner.

CHAPTER 28

NEW ORLEANS, LOUISIANA
A WEEK LATER

Zara flew in a private jet to meet the Huff twins in New Orleans.

She had been receiving daily updates, but wanted a full sharing of news. She had been busy with the investigation herself. The Huffs had spent the first three days in Houston but had now set up shop in New Orleans, which was closer to that ill-fated drilling rig. And farther from the Pure Earth headquarters.

Zara's plane landed at the New Orleans Lakefront Airport, taxied to the general aviation terminal and stopped. As she deplaned, heading for the executive conference room in the terminal, the ground crew was already attending to the plane and its refueling.

When Zara walked into the conference room, Tweeter and Slump were already there, and as was often the case, she could not tell them apart.

"I have some interesting information on the *American PERL I* incident, but first I would like to hear what you have," she said in Arabic as she sat down.

Slump – or maybe it was Tweeter – responded in Arabic, taking Zara's lead. "We haven't found out anything new about Pure Earth yet, but we're working on Sandy Agria to join our efforts. I don't think she's happy at Pure Earth, but she's nervous, which I understand. Still, I think she'll come around and when she does, we'll get computer and password access. Our computer wizards are on standby if needed."

Tweeter – or maybe it was Slump – added, "But we were able to trace Akrum's and Jet's general locations before and after the drilling rig explosion." Zara nodded and gestured for him to continue.

"Most of the time, they were both in this area – Southern Louisiana. Jet was in and out of touch, which most likely means he was out in the Gulf."

"What is the range of a cell phone?" Zara asked.

"It depends on the relay towers," Tweeter responded. "But with a tall tower and flat terrain, 30 to 45 miles, depending on other factors, like weather conditions. The *American PERL I* was about 35 miles offshore."

"How sure are you of the location data you have for them?" Zara asked.

"We're 99 percent sure we know where their cell phones were throughout the period we searched," he responded. "Whether their cell phones were with them at all times is another matter."

Zara nodded with a wry smile. She opened the briefcase Rodney O'Connor had given her and handed the small electronic device to the twins without saying anything.

They both examined it quickly.

"Have you ever seen or used one of these before?" she asked innocently.

"Several dozen times, at least," Slump said.

"What is it used for?"

"Usually to send a signal to a detonator to set off an explosive charge. And this is the brand and model we've used in the past." Slump paused. "Where did you get this? We never leave these things behind after we've used one. We take them with us."

"This one was found in a trash can by a supervisor on the rig not long after the explosion." Zara handed them the statement of the supervisor and a photo of three men in wet suits and wearing air tanks who were jumping into the water.

The Huff twins read the statement together, then stared at the photograph. They were silent as they did so.

Zara broke the silence after the Huff twins looked up at her, stony looks on both their faces. "Do you believe, as I do, that we now have enough information to support the idea that the *American PERL I* explosion was not an accident?"

The twins both nodded grimly. Zara knew that, despite their absurd nicknames and quiet demeanor, both were intelligent and perceptive. One could not survive – even qualify for – service in the SEALs without being so. The bumpkin image they projected to some was but a clever deception.

"And it would appear," she continued, "that there is a very strong possibility that Akrum and Jet were engaged by Pure Earth to cause the incident." They nodded again, and she continued, "In which case, it is critical for us to gain total access to Pure Earth's computer system immediately."

Tweeter replied for both when he said, "It will be our top priority. We'll return to Houston tonight."

"Do you need any additional money?" she asked.

"No, we still have most of the money you wired us," Tweeter said, "but we may need to offer Sandy Agria a job – after she gets us into Pure Earth's computer, of course – to get her on board quickly. Like Slump said, she's nervous and letting her know we can get her another job, or some money at least, will help."

"That will not be a problem," Zara said. "Do what you must and keep me posted as you have been. We must get access to that computer as soon as possible, in fact immediately!"

Zara was tired and had already decided to remain in New Orleans for the night. The Huff twins went back to their motel, checked out and started the long drive back to Houston.

Sarah Cotton, coincidentally, was in New Orleans at the same time, gathering information on the *American PERL I* disaster and feeding it back to Boone Malory.

Sarah called to check in with Boone, and Suzy Dillinger answered the phone. After exchanging greetings, Sarah asked for Boone.

"He's doing an interview with Channel 8," Suzy said. Channel 8 was the NBC affiliate in the Monterey/Salinas area. "What have you found out about the spill?"

"Not much more than what's been in the news," Sarah said. "Oil is still leaking and nobody knows when they'll get it fixed. Where is Boone's interview?"

"It's a live interview in the studio," Suzy said. "You know how nervous he gets over any interview. He was a wreck this morning. He was walking around the office mumbling things like, 'Where the hell is Sarah?' and stuff like that."

"Oh, poor Boone," Sarah said sincerely. "Tell him I'll be home soon to relieve him. Did he wear a tie?"

"I had to threaten him with bodily harm and then when I also threatened to tell you, he agreed and he did."

"Thanks, Suzy. That's important to our image, and it compares us favorably with some of the crazies like Greenpeace and Pure Earth, who like to dress like twenty-first century hippies."

"One more thing before you go," Suzy said. "Amanda called and said that she's located the Captain of the *Mar Ascensor* – you know, the tanker in that Alaska oil spill a few months back – and he's agreed to an interview with her."

"Wow, that will be a scoop for her," Sarah said. "When is she going to interview him?"

"She said she's already met and talked to him once and she's meeting him again. Sometime next week, I think. Probably after her weekend with her secret lover." Sarah had hoped that Amanda's affair with Win Mifflin would have been more of a one-time event than a long-running epic.

"Well, tell Boone that I'll call him at home tonight," Sarah said, and they rang off.

Sarah liked that she now had a place that truly felt like home, as well as someone she wanted to be with at home. This was a new feeling for Sarah Cotton.

CHAPTER 29

MONTEREY, CA
THREE DAYS LATER

Sarah Cotton's email to Boone Malory read as follows:

"Be home tomorrow. Nothing new on American PERL I. It's still leaking massive amounts of oil and there appears to be no quick fix to cap it. No word yet on the 15 missing crewmen, other than they are still missing and presumed dead, either from drowning or as a result of the explosion and fire. I plan a couple of days in Monterey to catch up with you and the office and then off to D.C. for a little arm twisting. I think the President is on the run and has little choice now. We're getting close to celebration time. I'll be on the US Airways flight from Phoenix at 11:15 a.m. See you then."

After she clicked on the "send" key, she thought once again how nice it was to refer to going home. She also realized, not for the first time, that she really missed Boone and was looking forward to seeing him.

Sarah's plane arrived at the Monterey Peninsula Airport on time and as it taxied to the gate, she called the office. Suzy Dillinger answered. Even with the new people they had been able to hire, Suzy was reluctant to give up answering the phones unless she was in a meeting or out of the office. She thought that hearing who was calling for whom kept her in touch with the pulse of the office.

Sarah told her she had just landed and would be at the gate shortly.

"We're all glad you're back, Sarah," Suzy gushed. "Especially Boone. I don't think he asked more me than six or seven times this morning to call

US Airways and check your flight status. He's been out running errands but I'd be surprised if he isn't standing right outside the security area right now waiting for you."

"Thanks, Suzy," Sarah said. "I'll see you shortly."

As a matter of fact, Boone was at the exit from the secure area, inching forward so far that he had attracted the attention of a grossly overweight TSA watcher, who told him twice to stay behind the line. Sarah, in her usual lobbying uniform, strode toward him in a businesslike way, but Boone was obviously not thinking about business. He embraced her in a powerful hug, several kisses that were passionate enough that they bordered on the inappropriate for a public place, and, as they wheeled and walked toward the parking lot, his hand managed – several times – to caress her thigh and her derriere.

Sarah did not know whether the heat in her face was more from pleasure or embarrassment, but she definitely wished that Boone could be there to meet her like that every time she got off an airplane.

As Boone's pulled his car out of the airport, Sarah asked him if they could go straight to her apartment first so she could change into Monterey clothes and drop off her luggage. On the drive, they talked about the *American PERL I* and their next moves on Washington.

Boone carried Sarah's suitcase up to her apartment. She unlocked the door and when Boone walked past her she kicked the door closed with her foot as she tossed her blazer on the couch. Boone hesitated, wondering where Sarah wanted him to drop the suitcase.

She took the luggage from him, then grabbed his arm and pulled him toward the bedroom.

"I think I need help changing into something more comfortable," she said, her voice husky. Unlike at the airport, this time she was rubbing his butt. Boone did not resist. Indeed, he slipped down the zipper on her skirt as they moved toward the bed, and she reached for his belt buckle.

"Am I changing into something comfortable, too?" he asked.

"Uh-huh," she whispered as she started nibbling on his ear.

Almost an hour later, an exhausted Sarah asked an exhausted Boone if he thought Suzy was wondering where they were. Boone told her she probably knew where they were, but they should probably think about getting dressed and heading for the office. First, they showered together and watched each other put their clothes on.

They were holding hands when they walked into the office. There was little use, both had concluded, in trying to be coy about it in such a small office. By now, everybody knew about them being an item and they both concluded it would be insulting to the others to treat them like it was a big secret.

Suzy jumped up when they entered and hugged Sarah tightly, telling her how good it was to have her back. The other women in the office did the same, but were more restrained in their hugs.

As Suzy followed Sarah back to her office, she whispered, "God, Sarah, you sure look relaxed. You're absolutely glowing!"

"It was very nice getting to stop at my apartment to change clothes," Sarah whispered back, and Suzy thought, *bullshit!*

Instead she said, "It certainly took you long enough to change clothes."

"I've always been a very slow clothes changer," Sarah responded with a smile. *It sure is good to be home,* she thought again.

Boone just walked past them and into his own office, shaking his head. *It sure is good to have her home,* he thought again.

After a quick review of her email in-box, Sarah went into Boone's office, as she had told him she would do while they were still undressed in her apartment. They needed to get on the same page quickly regarding her upcoming trip to Washington and Boone, of course, had agreed.

When she walked into his office, she mentioned she also wanted to map out their media strategy for the next couple of weeks regarding the *American PERL I* incident, which, because it seemed to resist all efforts to cap the leak, was devolving rapidly from a disaster to a catastrophe.

"I don't see that we really need new releases or statements," Boone said in response. "It's dominating the news every day and unless there is something new – a significant event or disclosure – it seems to me anything we say in public will just be background noise."

Sarah was again impressed with Boone's media instincts, despite his own personal aversion to dealing with reporters. She agreed that one of the things that set CFRG apart from the noisier – even hysterical – Pure Earth, Friends of the Earth and Greenpeace, was that CFRG's statements were seen as thoughtful and even scholarly by comparison.

She wanted to keep it that way.

Boone continued. "I think it might be a good idea for us to issue a weekly statement, commenting on the latest in the *American PERL I* situation, which will also serve to remind the media that we're available for interviews." Sarah nodded and Boone went on. "And we need to keep giving regular updates to Caldwell Jones at ERIN, since they're our primary moneybags."

Individual contributions had begun arriving at CFRG headquarters on a regular basis since its visibility had risen, but they still amounted to parking meter change compared to ERIN's checks.

"Good point," Sarah said. "Do you think it makes any sense to send one of our people, maybe Suzy, down to New Orleans to snoop around and keep an eye open for anything new or unusual?"

"Again, I don't think that's really necessary," Boone said, then quickly added, "unless you can see some benefit that I can't. There are a bazillion reporters and camera crews down there covering it every way from Sunday. It seems to me we'll hear about anything as soon as it happens and if it came out we had someone down there snooping I think it would be seen as either interfering or grandstanding, or both."

Again, Sarah could find no fault with Boone's logic. "We'll need to make sure we're monitoring developments closely though, and keep sending a daily synopsis of the situation to our email subscribers and posting it on our web site."

Boone nodded. "And of course, keeping you available for interviews." Sarah smiled, knowing he was positioning himself to stay out from in front of cameras.

"And your trip to Washington might be a better place for news coverage, since you'll be in the capital trying to accomplish our goal rather than hanging around here whining about the latest spill," Boone added. "I can't believe the President and Congress would even think of dragging their feet now."

"I think there's a very good chance for a speedy reversal of the President's order," Sarah agreed.

"I don't know politics like you do," Boone said, "but it seems to me that with all that's happened since the President's order – Santa Barbara, Anacortes, Alaska, Galveston and New Orleans – it would be a no-brainer in terms of public support and votes."

"I would hope so," Sarah said, "but there are always other considerations for those in public office."

"How are you going to approach it?" Boone asked. "Are you meeting with your targets as a group or separately?"

"Some of each. My old friend, "Good" Deeds, has assured me he's got a meeting set up with Congressmen Schaefer, Siedler and Piergallini. They're friends of his and usually go along with him. All will be helpful in calling for a reversal by the President and, failing that, convening a Congressional hearing on the subject. I've talked with each of them before, so they know our position and support it.

"With them, we'll be talking strategy, not philosophy. I think each of them has just been waiting for the right circumstances and the *American PERL I* incident, I have no doubt, is the last straw for them."

"Do you think they would introduce the legislation we need?"

"If they need to, but I think first they'll work with the White House to get it done more quickly."

"What about the Senate?" Boone asked.

"I've already confirmed appointments with four of them, individually, and I think the situation is the same in the Senate as in the House. They've been waiting for the right circumstances. And right now, we've got the perfect storm."

"Do you need any help?" Boone asked. "Would it help any if I went back with you?"

Sarah sat back in the chair and stared at the ceiling as she thought out her answer, and Boone began to wonder if he had made a mistake asking about going to her turf with her.

But she said, finally, "You know, the more I think about it, the more I think that would be a great idea. You would be my expert witness, so to speak, answering the technical questions and strategic implications of restricting exploration and drilling, as well as the benefits to the environment."

Boone smiled and Sarah added, "I would think that everything you say should be coldly factual and delivered without any emotion or hype."

"That's good," Boone said, smiling again. "That's how I'm most comfortable, anyway, and that's the way I've prepared my information package."

"Good. Then let's plan on going to D.C. together. We should go next week, so you'll need to get your comments prepared and our information package finalized."

"I've already done both," he said, leaning back in his chair with the satisfied smile of a cat with a mouse's tail dangling from the corner of its mouth. "Suzy is finishing assembling the package today, or tomorrow at the latest."

Sarah smiled. "I've been set up by you two again, haven't I?"

"I might put it a bit differently," Boone said. "I'd call it being properly supported by the home office."

"Thank you for the always-efficient home office support," Sarah murmured as she got up and left Boone's office. She was glowing, happy for more than one reason that Boone would be going to Washington with her.

She hoped that nobody in the office noticed next month when expenses were processed and paid that there would not be a hotel charge for Boone. No way was she going to let him stay anywhere except in her condo.

With her.

CHAPTER 30

The US Airways Airbus 320 touched down at Washington Reagan Airport a few minutes early at 3:49 p.m. The US Airways flight was full, but Sarah had used frequent flyer points to upgrade herself and Boone so they did not feel as crammed in as they had on the regional jet from Monterey to Phoenix.

When they deplaned and were walking past a newsstand, a headline caught Boone's eye and he stopped to buy *The Washington Post*. The headline screamed:

GULF OIL STILL FLOWING

"It is estimated that 40,000 barrels of oil per day are still pouring out of the critically damaged American PERL I, the Gulf of Mexico drilling rig that suffered a catastrophic explosion recently.

"The well's owners, American Energy and PERL Oil, currently estimate that a relief well will intersect with the damaged well in approximately three weeks. The relief well will pump cement into the damaged well and, it is hoped, seal it. Current estimates put total oil leakage to date at over 2,000,000 barrels."

"This headline should help us," Boone observed drily, handing her the paper.

"Yes," Sarah mused as she glanced at the story. "Good timing by the Post."

Trailing their carry-on bags behind them, Sarah and Boone walked to the Metro station, where they boarded the train that would whisk them into the city and her condo.

Sarah's condo was less than a block from a Metro station, the location at least partly selected so she could avoid cabs if she wished. It was on the second level of a four-story brownstone which had been converted to condos and Boone carried the suitcases so Sarah could manipulate the alarm remote on her key ring.

Before opening the front door, she told Boone to wait while she ducked inside and shut off a back-up alarm system. She quickly entered and grabbed what appeared to be a television remote, punching in four numbers in sequence.

Then she called out, "You can come in now. All is secure. Just put the bags in the bedroom."

"Yes, Ma'am, I'll do my best," he replied with a touch of playful sarcasm in his voice. He dropped the bags on the floor of the first room he came to that had a bed in it and joined her.

"Let me give you the tour," she said, smiling. "It won't take long. There's not that much to it." She motioned with her hand as she started walking. "This is the living room – which is seldom used – and the family room, my office, my – our – bedroom, the bathroom and the kitchen. The kitchen, you'll notice, is pretty much in its virgin state. Much like me until I met you." Now her smile was wicked, and Boone smiled back, sure that he was blushing.

He said, "Well, maybe while we're in Washington, I can defrock the kitchen. I'm a pretty good cook and I love defrocking things." Sarah's heart almost stopped. Was this the same reserved man she had met not all that long ago? She decided to play along and see where this battle of wits ended.

"And I must say you're quite good at it," she said.

Boone could not think of a response. His tongue felt glued to the roof of his mouth and Sarah took pity on him.

"Why don't we unpack and go get an early dinner. Maybe buy some groceries on the way back," she asked.

While Sarah was unpacking, Boone walked around the spacious condo, taking his time and getting to know the place. It was nicely decorated and everything seemed to his untrained eye to be quite well coordinated.

Boone noticed a wall-mounted television in every room except the living room. There was art on all the walls, mostly numbered prints signed by artists he did not know. The kitchen was modern, complete and looked entirely unused.

But there were no photographs. None of Sarah, none of family, not even of any friends. Boone found that curious. And there was something else he found curious.

"Why is the closet door in your office locked?" he asked as he walked into the bedroom, where Sarah was in the final stage of unpacking.

"My goodness, you're observant," she answered lightly. "It's locked because I have a safe and two filing cabinets in the closet and a lot of very confidential client files of both current and past clients."

"Do you have a file on me and CFRG?" he asked.

"I'm sure I do, but it would be one of the smaller ones, since CFRG was never my client. In fact, not only are you not my client, but I am your employee, so you must have a file on me." She kept up the tease, enjoying the skirmish with this man for whom she felt so strongly.

"Yes, I do, and it's very complete," he said, his voice teasing as well.

"Can I see it?"

"Oh, no, that wouldn't do. It's very confidential and I keep it under lock and key in my office." He bumped her shoulder in a joshing way. "Should I unpack now?"

"I've already unpacked your stuff," she said. "Your clothes are hung up in the closet, and I cleaned out the second drawer in the dresser for you to use. I put your toiletries on the sink in the bathroom. You can arrange them the way you like."

"Thank you," he said. He was moved and a bit overwhelmed by the latent domesticity implied in her unpacking his suitcase. "Then why don't we go get something to eat and go over our meeting with Deeds and his pals tomorrow."

As they walked down the stairs, Boone asked, "I never even asked you if you have a car."

"Oh, I have one," she said off-handedly, "and a very nice one. I thought I had to have one. But I never drive it, other than when I used to go out of town for a weekend or something like that. The parking rates in this town make cabs far more economical. And as you could see earlier, the Metro is quite convenient."

"What kind is it?" he asked. They were now on the sidewalk and Sarah had gestured in the direction she wanted to walk. They were both wearing short-sleeved casual shirts, but the late July heat and humidity was still oppressive. With Washington's reputation for closing down during August and the fact that the Congress was already in recess for the month, Boone had been impressed that Sarah had found as many Congressmen and Senators to meet with as she had.

"It's a black Chevy Tahoe, two years old and less than 5,000 miles on it." Boone smiled appreciatively. He'd never been able to afford to keep something like that in gasoline.

Soon, they arrived at a small but well-appointed restaurant two blocks from her condo that was a favorite of Sarah's. The owner, a diminutive man with Mediterranean features and coloring, greeted her and asked where she had been.

"I've been out west for a few weeks," she said vaguely as he seated them at a private booth in the rear corner, long her favorite booth. "Marco, let me introduce you to a dear friend of mine, Boone Malory. We've been working together out on the coast. Treat him well if he comes in alone." She paused before adding, "But don't serve him at all if he's with another woman."

The men shook hands as Marco chuckled and Boone blushed. Marco handed them menus and waved a waitress over to take their drink orders. It was not yet 6:00 p.m., so the dinner crowd had not arrived in full force and the restaurant was very quiet. They asked for wine and studied the menus.

As they sipped their wine, Sarah went over again for Boone her plan for the meeting with Congressman Deeds and the other three, who they would be seeing at 9:00 the next morning in Deeds' office.

"Why are they still in town?" Boone asked. "I thought everybody left for August, and it's almost here."

"Most do, and my guess is that all four of them will be heading for home before long," Sarah said. "But most members are in and out of town during the month, unless they're on a three-week 'fact-finding' junket to some hell-hole like Tahiti or Majorca.

"In any case, Congressman Deeds told me that at least two of the others who'll be at the meeting made sure they stayed especially to hear what we have to say, so we'll have a receptive audience.

"I'll introduce you to them, then give a brief summary of CFRG's position – which they know all too well, but it's pro forma – and then turn to you to outline your estimate of the damage done to the environment by the accidents and spills over the last year or so.

"Again, you should approach this as an expert witness with no stake in the outcome. Just recite the facts as we know them, and hit the *American PERL I* hard, including the fact that it continues to leak oil at the rate of 40,000 barrels a day. Then hand out your reference material and ask if they have any questions."

"Why wouldn't I hand out my packet of materials before I start talking?" he asked.

"Because then they'll be reading instead of listening," Sarah said firmly. "I want them focused on you. They can read it later."

"Okay, but I also thought about telling them, assuming they support CFRG's position, we'll publicize their comments and support in our newsletters and web site," Boone said.

"Great idea!" Sarah said. "Of course. And tell them we'll support them during their next re-election campaigns."

Their entrees arrived and they dove in, both realizing they were hungrier than either had realized. Boone asked the waitress for two more glasses of wine as well.

When they were both almost finished with their meals, Sarah asked, "You're not nervous, are you?"

"A little," Boone admitted.

"You shouldn't be. Just remember tomorrow we're helping them as much as they're helping us, and all four of them know it. This is a perfect case of mutualism."

Boone just smiled at that. He'd never heard of mutualism before.

Before going back to Sarah's condo, they stopped at a small market a block in the opposite direction and bought some basics. The simple act of grocery shopping with Boone as he talked about defrocking her kitchen made Sarah feel warm and as contented as she could remember.

When they were back in Sarah's condo and had put the groceries away – Boone had bought mainly breakfast fixings – Sarah opened a bottle of wine.

They sat together on the couch in the family room. The TV was on and CNN was re-running the endless loop it used all day unless something came up that qualified as breaking news. In this case, thankfully for Sarah and Boone, the loop included lots of chatter about the latest Gulf oil spill. The sound was low and they had heard it all several times previously.

Sarah turned to Boone and held her glass up in toast. "Here's to a successful trip for us and for our environment," she said. They clinked glasses and sipped their wine.

"This is a very nice place you have," Boone said. "Do you use it much for entertaining?"

"Do you mean for lobbying purposes or for, let's say, relationships with persons of the opposite sex?" Sarah asked coquettishly.

"Well, in reality, I guess both," he answered a bit nervously.

"I've used it on very rare occasions in conjunction with my lobbying," she said. "Like once a woman who works for one of my clients arrived in town during peak season and could not get into a hotel, so I put her up here for a night. And once I had a little wine-and-cheese party to help a new associate meet some people when he was new in town."

"And the other?" Boone persisted.

"Boone, you may or may not believe this, but it is the truth," she said, looking him in the eye. "You are the first man who has ever set foot – or anything else – in my bedroom."

Boone just looked at her, not quite believing his ears but somehow glad he had heard it.

Sarah explained, "I consider this place my sanctuary. It is my private place and you are the first man I've ever wanted to share it with."

Boone felt his face get hot.

Sarah leaned over and brushed his cheek with her lips, then whispered, "Drink your wine. I may not have told you, but my bed is a virgin, like my kitchen, and I want to rectify that."

Boone raised his wine in a toast. "It seems that this will definitely be a good trip for us as well as for the environment. But it's early. Can we have another glass of wine? I haven't found myself in this position for a very long time and I'd like to savor the moment."

Sarah smiled brightly, bounded from the couch and topped off their glasses. They made small talk and exchanged not-so-small kisses for the next 30 minutes, then, when their glasses were empty, Boone stood, bent down and scooped Sarah into his arms.

As he carried her toward the bedroom, he muttered, "About time that nice big bed lost its virginity."

He laid her gently on the bed and they began shedding clothes. "Hard to believe a beautiful place like this and both the bed and the kitchen are virgins," he said playfully. "How about the owner?"

"Two out of three ain't bad, is it?" she teased and pulled him over on top of her.

Afterward, as they lay spent on the bed, Sarah turned to Boone and said, "You know, I really like being with you, Boone, both in bed and out. I like our relationship very much. And, if you'll forgive my being so forward, I honestly cannot ever remember being as horny as I am around you."

Boone was again amazed at the bluntness and openness of this gorgeous creature.

And again words failed him. "Me, too," he said simply. Soon, they were both sound asleep.

Boone was up first the next morning and started the coffee. After shaving and showering, he woke Sarah, who was still sound asleep. As she showered, she thought to herself how unusual it was for her to sleep this late, but she also marveled at how good it had felt to sleep next to Boone all night and decided she could get used to it.

After drying and brushing her hair, she put on Boone's shirt from the day before, which he had hung over the back of a chair in the bedroom. His scent still lingered in the shirt. When she walked in and sat at the kitchen table, Boone was just setting down two plates with poached eggs, grapefruit and toast.

When they finished breakfast, they dressed – Boone in a conservative charcoal suit and Sarah in her typical lobbyist uniform - and took a cab to the Rayburn House Office Building to meet with Congressman Deeds and his three colleagues. They entered Deeds' office exactly ten minutes before the appointed time.

They were shown into the office of Deeds' executive assistant, a stout woman named Mary O'Hanlon, who had come to Washington from Illinois with Deeds when he was first elected to Congress. Sarah introduced Mary to Boone, then handed her three loaves of San Francisco sourdough bread she had had shipped in the night before on Federal Express. Sarah knew Mary loved San Francisco sourdough.

"I hope they're fresh," Sarah said as Mary beamed and squeezed the bread to confirm it was fresh. "And here's a bottle of Martha's favorite California wine," she added as she produced the bottle from the same canvas bag which had held the bread.

"And remember it's for Martha and not the Congressman," Sarah said in low, conspiratorial tone.

Mary nodded and smiled knowingly. She thanked Sarah profusely and Boone knew he was getting a lesson in why Sarah was such a successful lobbyist.

Promptly at 9:00, Congressman Deeds buzzed Mary on the intercom to let her know he was ready for his visitors and Mary escorted Sarah and Boone through her side door directly into the Congressman's spacious office. Sarah hugged Deeds and introduced Boone. She was allowed to hug him because she knew the other three Congressmen would not join them until 9:15. Deeds had arranged it that way so he could have a quick briefing from Sarah and Boone before they arrived.

"I trust Martha is well," Sarah said. "Please give her my best."

"I will," Deeds responded jovially. "In fact, she's in town. You should call her at the apartment. And I hope you thought to bring a bottle of her wine with you. She's down to her last half bottle of it."

"Mary has it," she responded with a smile.

When they were seated at the conference table and Deeds had

gestured for Sarah to go ahead with her briefing, Sarah began. "I plan on a brief summary introduction and then turn it over to Boone to summarize the damage from the incidents we've witnessed over the last year and to expand on CFRG's position on the matter."

"There's no question that the damage we've seen in the last year is unacceptable on any level," Deeds said. "And I think Jim Schaefer, Sam Siedler and Tim Piergallini will agree with me that we've got to reverse the President's open drilling policy, whether by pressuring him to do so or by getting the Congress to over-rule him."

Just then, the other three Congressmen were ushered into the room and after a quick round of introductions by Deeds they sat around the table.

Sarah opened the conversation with a very generic overview of the dangers of the open drilling policy, as demonstrated by the incidents of the past year. She also stressed what she saw as the political upside for each of them that would result from leadership roles in reversing the President's policy, including polling that showed the extent of public support for reversing the policy and the campaign contributions and manpower help they could expect from CFRG and other environmental organizations.

She then turned the meeting over to Boone. She had not expected him to be as relaxed around four Congressmen as he seemed. As she had urged him, he took a positive approach in describing CFRG and its goals, stressing its desire to be a reasonable voice in environmental debates.

"Not like those bastards from Pure Earth and Greenpeace," Piergallini muttered quietly and Boone nodded. "Exactly," he said.

Boone took the men quickly through his assessment of the environmental damage of the incidents of the past year, concluding with a gloomy summary of the *American PERL I* incident, which he described as on-going, noting that 40,000 barrels per day still leaked into the Gulf as a result of that catastrophe. He also mentioned the loss of life from the *Mar Ascensor* and the *American PERL I*.

"We as a nation simply cannot allow this kind of environmental damage to continue," he summarized. "We have an obligation to protect this planet for future generations." He concluded by reiterating Sarah's point about political and campaign help for those who help reverse the

President's policy.

He passed out the information packages he and Sarah had prepared and sat back in his chair.

Sarah, who had conducted or sat through countless such briefings, was unabashedly proud of the job Boone had done. He had been factual, sincere and brief in his appeal for their help.

Deeds thanked Sarah and Boone for dropping by today, as if it had been for a game of bridge. He said, "Let us talk it over among ourselves and see what we can come up with as strategy for moving forward. There's no doubt we all agree with you, and we surely do appreciate your offer of campaign help next go-around."

Sarah and Boone arose, made their way around the table shaking hands and thanking each man for being there and for his assistance in the fight. They left the office and, after Sarah used Mary's phone to call Martha Deeds, bid farewell to Mary and they made their way to the elevators.

They were lost in their own thoughts as they rode down in the half-full elevator, and their thoughts were almost exactly the same. They were both impressed at how well they had done with their team approach.

It was just after 10:00 a.m. and their appointment with Senator Gilchrist was not until 11:00, so they walked to the Hyatt Regency, which was fairly close to the Dirksen Senate Office Building, and ordered hot tea in the coffee shop.

When they had their tea, Sarah said, "I've already discussed the issue with Senator Gilchrist, and told him I beleive that he'll have no problems with the oil companies. They won't oppose lifting the ban. All these incidents in the past year have created a lot of animosity toward them in the electorate. What they may or may not do is important because he's from Texas. I'm sure he's been in constant touch with them."

"Do you think he'll be a strong advocate for our side, or will he just agree not to be obstructionist?" Boone asked.

"I'm not sure," she said. "He's a reasonable guy, but he's got a lot of oil interests to answer to, and not all of them think alike. If it comes to a vote, I think he'll vote our way, but I'm not sure how far out front he would be in calling on the President to reverse his policy."

They arrived in the office of Senator Gilchrist five minutes early, and at 11:00 a.m. sharp were shown into his private office. Boone wondered if all visitors got such prompt treatment.

Gilchrist looked like a Texan. He was tall, slender and wore a western-cut suit with cowboy boots. Sarah knew the clothes and boots were an integral part of his persona. When he greeted them, his speech was clearly Texas as well. "Howdy," he said. "Glad to see y'all."

Sarah and Boone went through the same shtick they had earlier that morning and it seemed to work well again. The Senator had just two questions.

"First, why do y'all think the oil industry will support renewing the ban on open drilling? And my second question is why don't you tell me something about where CFRG gets its money from?"

"I'll let Sarah respond to the first question, but let me tell you about our funding," Boone said. "Originally, our primary benefactor was a man named Heimer Myerhoffer. However, in recent years, Mr. Myerhoffer has experienced some unfortunate health and financial problems, so his role has diminished.

"As a result of that, we have had to turn to a more broad-based funding strategy, and I'm proud to say that we have attracted an impressive list of individual and corporate contributors. And recently, we have attracted the attention of a foundation called Environmental Responsibility International, or ERIN. ERIN found CFRG attractive because they believe in our reasonable and realistic approach to environmental issues, and the foundation has made a significant commitment to us."

Sarah immediately jumped in to address the first question, not wanting to get into a more detailed conversation about ERIN or into any specificity about other donors.

"To answer your first question, Senator," she said, "I really don't anticipate that the major players in the oil industry will fight the reversal of the President's policy. They won't support it, but they won't fight it, at least aggressively. In my view, they'll just let it happen.

"As you know, the industry has taken a beating because of the accidents they've experienced in the last year or so, and an aggressive stance in favor of the status quo would backfire on them in the court of public opinion. They would be playing defense for years to come, and I think they know that.

"Quite simply, Senator, from their standpoint, reversing the President's policy is the lesser of two evils." She sat back, her eyes riveted on the Senator's.

"Very good synopsis of the situation, young lady, and I happen to agree with your assessment," Gilchrist said. At least he hadn't called her "little lady," as he'd done on occasions in the past. "Like my valued constituents, I'll support reversing the President's policy, and if necessary I'll even vote to make it happen.

"I happen to agree the stakes are too high, given all the things that have happened recently. I'll also promise you this; I'll make my position known to the members of my party caucus and encourage their support of a vote to reverse if the President doesn't reverse it on his own."

Sarah was stunned. She had not thought Gilchrist would come around that completely. She realized he must be getting beaten up by Texas voters – especially those along the Gulf coast – and was looking for cover.

Gilchrist thanked Sarah and Boone for droppin' by and walked them through his reception area until they were through the door and in the hallway.

Sarah suggested they take in a couple of the Smithsonian museums that afternoon. Boone had mentioned previously that he had never seen any of them. They settled on the Air and Space Museum on the Capitol Mall and the Museum of American History.

After their museum visits, they hailed a cab back to Sarah's condo at 6:30 p.m. Boone asked if they could go back to the same restaurant they had been in the night before. They had both lunched only on hot dogs from the museum snack bars and both were famished. The restaurant served hearty portions and that sounded very good to Boone.

During their walks around the museums, Boone had expressed surprise that they had secured commitments from all those they had met with so easily. Sarah assured him they all basically agreed with reversing the President or they would not have met with them. "They were pre-sold," she said simply.

They showered and changed into casual clothes, then walked to the restaurant. The owner was beside himself, seeing Sarah on successive nights. Sarah was thrilled that Boone liked her quiet little restaurant. She was serious about avoiding kitchens herself, often telling friends that her kitchen utensil of choice was a can opener, and that what she made best for dinner were reservations.

The next morning, Sarah had arranged consecutive meetings with Senators Robert Harrington of Michigan, Doug Pifer of Ohio and Lee Lansing of Alaska. All three meetings, choreographed like the ones the day before, went well, and the senators all indicated support for reversal of the President's policy by whatever means.

Lansing, they knew, had a particularly difficult balancing act. Like Texas, Alaska was heavily dependent on the petroleum industry, but Lansing's constituents were also heavily invested in protecting the environment, which was critical to its fishing and tourism industries. But in the end, Sarah and Boone had been able to supply him with enough talking points and to promise him enough support and political cover that his fears were allayed.

Clearly, they both thought, Sarah and Boone made a great team, playing off each other with a skill that belied the fact that this was their first venture into team lobbying.

Sarah had scheduled a late lunch with Martha Deeds. The last appointment – with Senator Lansing – was scheduled for 11:00 a.m., so she and Martha had agreed on 1:00 p.m.

Boone had assumed he would head back to Sarah's condo and rest for a while, but Sarah insisted – almost to the point of stamping her foot – that he come with her. "You'll like Martha," she said. "She's a real authentic down-home character."

"Do you ever stop lobbying?" Boone asked in resignation.

Sarah squeezed Boone's hand, which she had been holding as they strolled out of the Hart Senate Office Building, where Lansing's office was. "Almost never," she whispered as she pulled him closer. "But after this lunch, it'll strictly be personal time the rest of the day."

True to Sarah's promise, Martha Deeds was great company and, much to his surprise and delight, Boone found himself enjoying himself a great deal. He thought he was sitting with what Central Casting would have sent if he had ordered up a heartland farm girl in her late 50s.

Martha liked Boone immediately and thought he might be the one for Sarah. With her finely-tuned instincts, it took her less time than it took them to be seated in the restaurant to decide they were more than working colleagues. She felt the large jolts of electricity that seemed to pass between them when they looked at one another.

She regaled Boone with stories about certain congressional wives, mostly from the coasts, and Boone laughed so loud on two occasions that other diners were craning their necks to see what the floor show was.

When lunch was over, Boone was almost reluctant to say goodbye to Martha Deeds. Sitting in the back of a cab as it maneuvered through Washington traffic toward Sarah's place, Boone said, "You were certainly right about her. She is a character. And that bit about the California Congressman's wife and her physical therapist was priceless. I'm glad you asked me – actually forced me – to come with you."

Sarah smiled and squeezed his hand harder.

Later, Boone made sandwiches for them and they packed and went to bed early. Their return flight was the next morning at 7:00, which would put them into Monterey around noon, with a short layover in Phoenix. Sarah set the alarm for 4:00 a.m. and lay back next to Boone. She fell asleep almost immediately, thinking what a good trip it had been, for CFRG, for Boone and for her. Boone was already asleep.

CHAPTER 31

Win Mifflin had called Amanda Baines on her cell the day before and confirmed their rendezvous at the Embassy Suites in El Segundo, just south of Los Angeles International Airport. She was anxious for Saturday afternoon to come.

She and Win would have two nights together, and on Monday morning she was to meet a story source at the airport and fly down to San Diego to look over a ship that was in dry dock.

Amanda called Win as soon as she stepped off the plane, pulling her carry-on behind her. "I'm here," she said when he answered. "Are you in town yet?"

"I'm already checked in, Amanda," he responded. "Can't wait to see you. Take a cab to the Embassy Suites and we're in room 237. I've got a bottle of wine icing down and a back-up just in case I need to ply you with liquor."

"Only two bottles?" Amanda laughed. "Am I that easy?"

"Or maybe I don't need the wine," he said.

"You don't, and I think you know that. But a little wine does sound good. I'll be there shortly."

As she rode in the back seat of the cab, Amanda thought idly about how unusual this whole thing was. To go off on one or two-day flings with a man she hardly knew was new to her. She had always preferred closer and longer-term relationships, had always been a bit repulsed by casual sex. But she recognized, of course, that this arrangement with Win was just something to satisfy her physical needs, which seemed to be getting more demanding now that she was approaching her mid-thirties.

What were her 40s going to be like, she wondered with some alarm.

When she knocked lightly on the door of room 237, Win opened the door wearing a white silk robe and a black Lone Ranger mask. He held out her glass of wine and took the handle of her carry-on from her.

"Wine is served, my dear," he said when they were in the room. He raised his glass in a toast and hugged her as hard as he could, considering they were both holding wine glasses.

"Thank you, my dear," she said almost mockingly, and after taking a sip said, "If you don't mind terribly, I'll start with a shower to wash the airplane smell off me and get into something more comfortable."

Win smiled and pointed at another white silk robe that was lying across the enormous bed. As she turned to head for the bathroom, she flicked Win's mask with her finger and said, "Be right back, whoever you are."

Amanda came out of the bathroom in the white silk robe – loosely tied – and handed her empty wine glass to Win. "More wine, please," she said. Win refilled both glasses and, raising his, said, "Here's to an enjoyable 36 hours together."

Amanda thought her heart would jump out of her chest, it was beating so hard as she sipped her wine. She knew that the start of their 36 hours together would be quite memorable.

Sunday morning, Win took his Lone Ranger mask off.

"Oh, it's Win Mifflin," Amanda squealed. "I really didn't know who I was with last night." She snuggled up and kissed him. He responded, as she knew he would.

They decided on an early swim in the hotel's pool before breakfast, which was complimentary in all Embassy Suites and was served in a large cabana-style building that opened onto the pool area.

Amanda could not help noticing what a powerful swimmer Win was, as he effortlessly lapped the pool several times.

As they sat together on one of the steps in the pool, Win leaned close and asked, "Are you okay with this arrangement we have?"

Amanda was caught a bit off guard and hesitated before answering. "I certainly enjoy parts of it," she said, "like last night and this morning in particular. But to be brutally honest, I don't know that I really like it." She paused in thought and noticed a faintly hurt look on Win's face.

She put her hand on his cheek and said, "But I really don't want it to end. It's just that every 30 or 60 or 90 days, we have a very satisfying fling, and then it's over until I hear from you again."

"I too, enjoy our time together," Win responded softly. "I look forward to being with you, but I'm just not in a position where I can manage anything more than what we have now. I don't want to end this relationship, or whatever it is, either. I really like being with you, but my work makes a full-time relationship impossible."

Amanda sat thinking for a full minute. Then she kissed him on the cheek, slapped him on the butt and said, "Let's go in and get some breakfast." The rest of the day was delightful for both of them.

The terms of the arrangement were not brought up again.

Early Monday morning, as they were packing, Win gave Amanda her white silk robe and his Lone Ranger mask. "Here, you've earned these," he said playfully.

"Damned right I have, and then some," Amanda said, smiling. Win just nodded.

Both were quiet on the cab ride to the airport, neither of them knowing when they would see each other again.

If ever.

They were both flying on American Airlines, but Amanda had no idea where Win was going. In any case, she was to meet the man who would accompany her to the San Diego dry dock at the American Airlines ticket counter. Win's flight was scheduled to leave an hour before hers, and he was in a hurry. They embraced briefly, and he said, "Until next time."

From behind her, Amanda heard her name being called. She turned to see Captain Randolph Aglee wave and start toward her. Suddenly, he stopped, wide-eyed. At the same time, Win saw Aglee and when he did he abruptly turned and, with nothing more than a pat to Amanda's arm as a farewell, hurried toward the security checkpoint, quickly blending into the crowd. He'd said nothing further to her.

Aglee hurried toward Amanda, ducking and dodging around other passengers, who were milling about every which way. Even more than other times, Monday mornings at Los Angeles International were a beehive of activity.

Aglee was out of breath when he reached Amanda, and he had a startled – or maybe it was disbelieving - look on his face.

"Who was that man you were with?" he demanded.

Now Amanda was startled. She had met with Aglee not that long ago, and he had been courteous, even courtly, in his manner. She had never imagined him raising his voice like that to her. "His name is Win Mifflin," she said. "He's just a friend of mine." She knew she sounded defensive, and she felt defensive.

"He's also the missing oiler from my ship that we thought was dead," he said. "How the hell did he get off my ship, only to turn up here with you?"

Amanda turned around and searched the crowd for any sign of Win, but he was nowhere to be seen. She knew that, as much as he traveled, he must qualify for the expedited security line available to frequent travelers, so their chances of spotting him were next to zero.

"Let me call him and see if he can come back," Amanda said lamely, knowing in her heart he would not. Sure enough, Win did not answer his phone and the message option did not come on.

"He saw that I recognized him," Aglee said furiously, "and that's why he ran off so fast."

"I don't think so," Amanda said, not really believing it. "He had a plane to catch and was just in a hurry to get to the gate."

"Do you know where he was going?" Aglee asked.

"No, I don't," she said. "In fact, we've never discussed his travels or anything else personal about him. We just get together when our schedules intersect."

Aglee thought sourly, *typical sailor – a girl in every port.*

But he had liked Amanda when she had interviewed him earlier and it galled him to think that a nice girl like her would be one of those girls.

"Do you have any pictures of him?" Aglee asked.

"No, Win never wanted pictures. We don't have that kind of relationship."

She paused a moment, then blurted, "Oh, wait. I did sneak a couple of shots with my cell phone that I don't think he knew I was taking." She pulled out her phone and scrolled to Photos. Once she found what she was looking for, she handed the phone to Aglee.

"That's him, alright," he said, not able to disguise the disgust in his voice. "That's my missing oiler." He looked closer at the photos and added, "Look, he even has that watch that I remember him wearing. It's a real big, fancy diver's watch. There's no doubt that's him." He handed Amanda her phone.

She was confused. How could Win and the missing oiler be the same person?

But it was time to get through security and to the flight to San Diego. Once on the flight, Aglee peppered Amanda with questions about Win. The roles had reversed, she realized. She was the reporter and she was supposed to be interviewing him, but the opposite was now occurring.

As Aglee's questions kept coming, Amanda was struck with the reality that she knew nothing about the man she had enjoyed repeated sex with for the past day and a half except that he was some kind of consultant who had worked for Sarah Cotton before she had joined CFRG.

She was forced to admit to Aglee that she had no idea what he really did for a living, where he lived, whether he had any family, where he went to school.

Nothing at all, except those dark, dashing good looks, the fact that he claimed to have been a Navy SEAL and the unmistakable aura of self-confidence.

The American Eagle regional jet touched down in San Diego on time and Amanda and Aglee hailed a cab to take them to the dry dock where the *Mar Ascensor* was undergoing repairs.

The shipyard foreman they tracked down was reluctant to let them near the massive ship, but Aglee's PERL Oil credentials and Amanda's plea about the human interest story she was working on convinced him to call PERL Oil for approval.

He relayed to the PERL executive he got on the line that Amanda was writing a story relating the Alaska incident, the fact that Captain Aglee was retiring and that it had been the last voyage of the *Mar Ascensor* as a PERL Oil ship. He put Amanda on the line and she assured the PERL man that she intended the story to focus on the record of the ship, the experience of the Captain and the freakishness of the incident.

The PERL man quickly checked with the public relations department and approved the idea, but forbad any photographs. They were to be shown only the exterior of the ship and to limit the tour to 30 minutes.

The foreman got them hard hats and led the way to the ship. He would, of course, accompany them so they did not walk into any dangerous areas.

Aglee told him he would like to look at the starboard side, where the initial damage was done by the ice floe, or so he assumed.

When the party reached the rip in the hull at about the waterline, Aglee stopped and stared, his mouth agape. The rip was not from an ice floe. Rather than being caved in, as it would have been from a collision with ice, it was bowed outward, indicating the damage had been done from within the ship. That explains the fact that it sounded more like an explosion than a collision, Aglee thought to himself.

He inspected the rip more closely, and noted that it ran in almost a straight line.

Amanda seemed not to notice the anomaly, but the foreman, noticing Aglee's expression, nodded in understanding. He had obviously been told about the incident and what was supposed to have happened. He wasn't buying it either, but he kept his mouth shut. He was a shipyard foreman, not an investigator.

Higher on the hull, and just forward of the rip was the larger hole made by the explosion that killed the two crewmen who were being lowered to investigate the original, unknown damage and one crewman on the deck manning the winch. The foreman was hailed by one of his assistants, who had a question for him.

While he was thus distracted, Aglee asked Amanda to shoot some clandestine photos of the damage. Soon after she snapped the fourth photo, the foreman returned and told them that, regrettably, he would have to cut the tour short and return to his duties. Aglee assured him that they appreciated the time they had and that he had seen what he most wanted to see.

As they walked away in the direction of the shipyard gate, Aglee turned and took another long look at the rip at the waterline.

"Well, Captain, what do you think now?" Amanda asked as they rode in a cab back to the airport.

"I'm not sure I know what I think," he said, and turned and gazed out the window, signaling her that the conversation was over for the time being.

They were on another American Eagle regional jet, bound for Los Angeles, before Aglee spoke again.

"May I see the photos you took?" he asked.

"What are you looking for?" she asked in return as she handed him the phone.

"I'm not sure. Just trying to piece it together. I'm confused about my missing oiler, about you showing up with him, and how all of it relates to what happened on the *Mar Ascensor.*"

"Believe me, Captain Aglee," she said contritely, "I'm as interested – both professionally and personally – in finding the answers as you are."

He stared at each of the photos in turn, and decided to open up to her and see where that took him.

"As you could see, the long tear in the hull at the waterline is not caved in, like it would be if it had struck an external object, such as an ice floe. Instead, the skin of the outer hull is protruding, as it would be if the source of the damage came from within the ship. And it's virtually a straight line, and right at the water line.

"Remember I told you during our first interview that Rabbit – my first officer – and I both heard what sounded more like an explosion than a collision. It looks to me like this damage was caused by a shaped charge placed inside the outer hull. No significant damage was done to the inner hull or to the ribs of the outer hull."

"What about the other hole?" Amanda asked. "The one that killed the crewmen."

Aglee flipped to the single photo of that hole she had been able to take before the foreman had returned. "You can see clearly from this that, once again, the damaged skin of the hull is protruding outward and that this one involves both the inner and outer hulls. I'm not an explosives expert, but I think this came from a much larger circular explosion that caused the oil leak and the deaths of three men, who died an agonizing death, burned alive on the deck."

"Yes, I can see that," Amanda murmured, eyes darting from the photo to her notebook. Aglee could see that she had already made a lot of notes.

Aglee continued, "Now, as we discussed last time, all power to the ship was lost mysteriously, then just as mysteriously restarted not long after the explosions. Add to the mix that my chief engineer was found slumped over his control console, dead, supposedly of a heart attack, and my replacement oiler just disappeared, personal belongings and all. Then he turns up, in the company of a reporter in whom I have previously confided, and who I was meeting at LAX.

"Nothing could have been tampered with in the dry dock, because as you saw, access is very restricted, so what we saw was as it was when the *Mar Ascensor* came out of the water."

"It doesn't sound good, does it?" she said quietly. But something about her manner convinced Aglee that she was not working in concert with the missing oiler, or whomever he really was.

"Amanda, I'm going to be honest with you," Aglee said. "I do not believe the *Mar Ascensor* had an accident at all. I believe it was sabotaged for some reason, and I believe your friend played some role – maybe the key role – in the sabotage." He took a deep breath and let it out before adding, "And murder."

Amanda did not respond right away. She was confused, baffled, and upset. She had given herself to the man Captain Aglee was accusing of sabotage and murder.

"Captain, are you absolutely sure that man you saw at LAX this morning was your missing oiler?" she asked, looking intently into his eyes. "I mean, you've had a lot of men on your crews and I'm just asking if there's any chance you could be mistaken."

"I'm absolutely positive," he said. "I would swear to it in a court of law. And if there was any doubt of my recognizing him, I could see the fear and panic on his face when he saw me this morning. If he were not my oiler, why would he have reacted that way?"

Amanda sighed, and Aglee asked, "Why don't you tell me what you do know about him?"

Amanda sighed again and began. "I met Win up in Anacortes, Washington, last New Year's day. He was having dinner with a friend of mine, Sarah Cotton. I was up there on assignment."

"The oil spill at Anacortes?" Aglee interrupted, thunderstruck.

"Yes. The *Royal Bearing II* was unloading up there at the Royal Energy refinery when the ship became disconnected from the unloading pipeline for reasons they still haven't determined. *The Chronicle* sent me up to cover the story and that's when I ran into Sarah and Win."

"Do you know what the relationship is - or was – between this Sarah what's-her-name and this man, Win?"

"Sarah – her last name is Cotton - told me that Win worked for her on various assignments from time to time. It was all very vague, as I think about it now. I still don't know what Win does, except consulting, and that can cover a lot of ground."

"What does your friend, Sarah Cotton, do?" Aglee could feel the connection between the *Mar Ascensor* and the *Royal Bearing II* in his bones and he was determined to pursue it. It might clear his name, now tarnished in retirement after a lifetime of a perfect safety record.

"Sarah was a very successful lobbyist in Washington, D.C. who's now working for Citizens for Responsible Growth, which is run by an old childhood friend of mine, Boone Malory." Aglee wrote the name in his notebook.

"What is Citizens for Responsible Growth?" he asked.

"It's a small environmental organization that promotes a reasonable approach to dealing with environmental issues."

"Why would someone leave, as you say, a very successful lobbying career to join a small organization that I can't imagine would be able to pay that well?" he asked. "I've heard those D.C. lobbyists rake in the money."

"I can only tell you what she told me when I first met her. She had made good money and she decided she wanted to do something for mankind, something that wasn't solely motivated by greed."

Aglee nodded, his face clouded with skepticism.

"Sarah has also become a good friend of mine," Amanda continued. "And she did warn me after she found out that Win and I had spent the night together to be careful of him. She said he could be dangerous – her word, not mine."

"You spent the night with this guy when you had just met him?" Aglee asked, incredulous. He was just old-fashioned enough to find the idea repugnant. At least with a nice girl like he thought Amanda was.

Amanda blushed, and her eyes were downcast when she went on. "Not my finest hour, I admit," she said. "It was late and we'd been drinking more than we should have. And he can be a real charmer." She was tempted for a moment to tell him about the Lone Ranger mask but quickly discarded the idea.

They sat in the clouds of their own thoughts for the rest of the flight. When they deplaned, Amanda suggested they find a quiet place to grab a sandwich and continue the conversation. She had already concluded that her relationship with Captain Aglee had changed from reporter/interviewee to investigators looking into a conspiracy that might be quite sinister.

"We have some unusual and questionable circumstances to think through," Amanda said when they were seated in an airport restaurant and had placed their orders. Aglee motioned for her to go on. "We've got the incidents involving the *Mar Ascensor* and the *Royal Bearing II* and whether – or how – Win Mifflin and Sarah Cotton relate to them. And how Win and Sarah relate to each other."

"Are you suggesting that we team up to investigate this ourselves?" Aglee asked.

"Yes, I am," she said. "I feel like I may have been used by someone I would not be proud to be associated with. And I feel very bad that your reputation may have been damaged by something that was criminal activity rather than incompetence, or even an accident."

"How do you propose we proceed?" he asked.

"I'd like to start by talking with Boone Malory. Like I said, he's a childhood friend and I think he'll be very straight with us. Then I'd like to talk with Sarah."

"Where do we find them?"

"The CFRG office is in Monterey. We can fly up there this afternoon."

"And what if we turn up more on this sabotage? Do we take it to the authorities? What if your friend, Sarah, or your friend, Boone, is involved?"

"No chance Boone's involved," she said flatly. "None at all. He's too straight-arrow and like I said, I've known him for too many years to have any doubts about that. I just don't know about Sarah. Or Win. I really don't know either of them very well, I guess."

As it turned out, the next flight to Monterey did not leave until 4:15 p.m. Amanda called Boone and asked if he could meet them – alone. Boone picked up on the alone and asked if that meant she did not want Sarah to join them.

"I'm just turning up some interesting stuff, Boone, and I'd really like to talk to you alone, then to Sarah."

Boone, who knew and trusted Amanda as he did nobody else on earth, agreed. He told Sarah and Suzy that he had some personal stuff to take care of that afternoon and left the office at 4:00.

He was waiting for Amanda and Captain Aglee when they stepped off the plane. Aglee seemed almost jaunty, so anxious was he to move forward with the investigation with his new partner. His new partner was not looking forward to it as much on a personal level, but her primal reporter's instinct told her this could be the story of the year. Maybe of a lifetime.

The word Pulitzer kept ringing in her head.

CHAPTER 32

Amanda introduced Boone to Captain Aglee when they walked into the terminal. Boone suggested the airport coffee shop would be a good place to have their conversation. They went to a table along the back wall and ordered coffee. Boone looked at Amanda and nodded, indicating she should start.

"As you know, Captain Aglee was the captain of the *Mar Ascensor* when it was involved in the incident in Prince William Sound a few months ago," Amanda began. She smiled and added, "It was the last voyage for Captain Aglee before he retired and it was to be the last voyage of the ship under PERL Oil colors before she was sold.

"The *Mar Ascensor* supposedly hit an iceberg, or at least a large ice floe, which ruptured her hull and caused an oil leak. But there was a mysterious explosion and fire aboard at about the same time that killed three crewmen, possibly caused a fourth to have a fatal heart attack and a fifth man was missing and presumed dead."

Boone nodded, recalling every detail, and Amanda continued.

"Then, you'll remember I was sent up to Anacortes last New Year's to report on that oil spill and ran into Sarah, who was vacationing in the area at the time."

"I remember," Boone said.

"When I ran into her, she was having dinner with a man she introduced to me as 'an associate' or 'a former associate' – I don't remember exactly – whose name was Winter – or Win – Mifflin. He drove me out to the refinery pier where the incident had taken place. Well, to tell the truth, since that time, Win Mifflin and I have been having an affair of sorts."

"You what?" Boone asked, his voice rising. "That's not like you, Amanda."

"I know. I told the Captain it wasn't my finest hour. But this is where it gets interesting. Win and I were both flying out of LA International this morning – different destinations, of course – and I was meeting Captain Aglee there to fly down to San Diego to look at the ship. Then, when the captain saw me from across the terminal and called out to me, and Win and I turned, the captain froze for a second and then started in my direction. At that point, Win, without a further word to me, turned and disappeared into the crowd. The captain identified Win as the missing crewman from the *Mar Ascensor*, a man he thought was dead."

"I tried calling Win but he'd switched his cell phone off. I told the captain that I honestly do not know a lot about Win, who was always secretive and didn't like having his picture taken. But I've managed to snap half a dozen photos over time with my cell phone. The captain identified him positively." She held out her phone to show Boone one of the photos.

"All of this man's personal possessions were also missing when we assumed he'd fallen overboard," Aglee added. "He was a replacement oiler we had just picked up in Valdez. We had no idea what happened to him, but assumed he fell overboard during all the chaos of the explosion, loss of power and so forth."

"The captain and I flew down to San Diego this morning," Amanda put in. "The *Mar Ascensor* is in dry dock undergoing repairs down there."

"Go on," Boone said.

Aglee picked up the story, filling Boone in on the straight-line tear at the starboard waterline, the fact that it was protruding rather than bent inward. He told him his theory that the damage had been caused by shaped charges, and filled him in on the larger explosion that had ruptured both hulls and caused the spill.

"My first officer and I both heard an explosion – muted like it was not a very big one – rather than the kind of crushing sound you'd expect from an ice floe," he said. "The second explosion – the one that killed my men – was louder, more powerful and higher above the water line."

Amanda showed Boone the photos she had taken with her cell phone.

Boone looked at Aglee and asked, "You believe this was an arranged accident and that your missing oiler – Amanda's friend, Win – played a role in it?"

"Absolutely," he said with surety. "And I would call it what it is – sabotage and murder – rather than an arranged accident. I think there's a lot that's fishy here, and Amanda and I have sort of teamed up to get to the bottom of it. That's why we wanted to talk with you."

"And don't forget, Boone, that I met Win at the site of another oil spill," Amanda put in.

Boone shifted uncomfortably, remembering how Sarah just happened to be in that area on vacation – at a time of year nobody vacations up there – and that she just happened to be at a conference in Galveston when the incident down there had happened.

Amanda continued, "Win was not available to me by phone during the time of the *Mar Ascensor* incident, nor was he around the time of the most recent incident down in the Gulf."

All three sat silently for a long moment.

Amanda decided it was time to say the words she dreaded saying. "Boone, I have to tell you that there seems to be a reasonable possibility that Sarah is involved in all this, somehow." She paused, watching for a reaction from Boone, whose face was as if carved from stone. When there was no reaction, she went on.

"There has been a rash of oil spills since the President opened up exploratory drilling, starting with Santa Barbara and they all have had a lot in common. They have all been in sensitive areas, they have all generated huge media coverage and they have all resulted in minimal damage, with the exception of this last one. Sarah has been on site at several of them and has been responsible for a lot of the media attention."

Boone just nodded, and the now-stricken look on his face told the story. He was a smart man and he could not fail to connect the dots.

Amanda took another deep breath and continued. "We both think the coincidences are too much to ignore, but before we decide where to take this we wanted to talk to you, and to Sarah, first."

"When you say where to take this, what do you have in mind?" Boone asked.

"Captain Aglee wants to clear his name," Amanda said as Aglee nodded vigorously, "so I think he's inclined to take what we have to the authorities and let them run with it. As for me, Boone, you know I'm a reporter and at some point I have an obligation to *the Chronicle* to report what I know."

"I have a college buddy who's with the FBI," Boone said quietly. "So if need be, I'll call him."

"I told Captain Aglee that," Amanda said.

After a pause, she went on, "I also told him that you're a good man and no matter your relationship with Sarah, if it appears she's been involved in things that are illegal or would harm CFRG, you'll do what's right."

Aglee's eyes were alight. He was a man on a quest. He desperately wanted to retire with honor, not with the stain of failure, of environmental disaster and dead crewmen.

Amanda and Boone desperately hoped Sarah was not guilty of anything more than being lucky at having been at the right place at the right time, and of having an acquaintance who might be less than savory. To them, Sarah was, variously, a friend, a lover and an extremely valuable employee.

"When do you want to talk with Sarah?" Boone asked, resignation in his voice.

"As soon as possible," Aglee said. "The more time that goes by, the farther away this Win character gets and the colder any evidence gets."

"Can you call her now, Boone?" Amanda asked.

Boone pulled out his phone and hit a speed dial number for her direct line at the office, hoping she would still be there. Sarah answered on the first ring.

"Hi, Sarah," Boone said. "I'm with Amanda Baines and Captain Aglee of the *Mar Ascensor* and there's a situation we'd like to talk over with you as soon as we can."

"You sound so serious, Boone," she said with forced cheerfulness. "Is anything wrong?" Alarm bells were clanging loudly in her head.

"Sorry about that, but it is rather serious," Boone said evenly. "We can be back at the office in 20 minutes or so. Can you wait for us?"

"Of course, but can you give me a clue?" she asked.

"We'd rather go over it with you in person," he said. "See you in a few minutes."

"Okay," Sarah said, and hung up.

Sarah sat back in her chair, thinking. She knew that if Amanda and the captain of that ship had an issue to discuss, Win Mifflin must be involved. And she also knew that she could very well be in a lot of trouble.

It was after 6:00 p.m. when Boone unlocked the front door of the CFRG office and ushered Amanda and Aglee inside before relocking it. Sarah came out of her office when she heard the front door open and Boone introduced her to Aglee. Amanda gave Sarah a hug, but it was noticeably more tentative than those Sarah had become used to.

They went into Boone's office and, though nobody else was in the building, he shut the door. They sat in a circle around the small conference table in his office. All seemed to hesitate, wondering how to start.

"You were saying something about a serious situation," Sarah finally said, trying but not quite succeeding to put lightness into her voice.

"It has to do with events on the *Mar Ascensor*, a missing crewman and your friend, Win Mifflin," Boone said. "Perhaps, Captain Aglee, you would be good enough to fill us in on what you know."

Aglee recounted the sequence of unusual and unexplainable events on the ship, the loss of power, the so-called collision, the explosions, the dead crewmen – including the chief engineer – the missing oiler, his missing personal belongings and the fact the missing oiler was a replacement hired on the spot in Valdez.

He then described his and Amanda's inspection of the hull damage and his spotting of his missing oiler, in Amanda's company and known to her as Win Mifflin.

"And you were with Win when the Captain saw him?" Sarah asked.

"Yes," Amanda said. "We both had flights out of LAX this morning and I was meeting Captain Aglee for our inspection trip to San Diego."

"And when I called out to Amanda, you should have seen the look on his face when he recognized me," Aglee added. "And I recognized him right away, but by the time I got to Amanda he had blended into the crowd and disappeared."

"And you're sure he was your missing oiler?" Sarah asked.

"I was sure of it when I first saw him," Aglee assured her. "But Amanda has some shots of him on her cell phone, and there's no doubt of it. I don't even know the bastard's name, but I know it's the same man."

"And Captain Aglee even recognized that unique diver's watch he wears," Amanda said. "Win is the missing oiler, Sarah." She showed Sarah one of the photos on her cell phone to emphasize the point, and Sarah nodded, acknowledging the fact.

"Amanda tells me you introduced her to this man in Anacortes and that you told her he was an associate of yours, Sarah," Boone interjected. "Can you tell us in what ways he was an associate of yours?"

"He handled specific assignments for me on behalf of some of my lobbying clients," Sarah answered vaguely. She knew she was stuck, that her legendary luck had run out. Now she was in damage control mode.

"What kind of assignments?" Boone persisted.

"I'm not at liberty to discuss them, Boone," Sarah said. "Client confidentiality is still in play here."

"Amanda told me you were in Anacortes on vacation," Aglee added.

"Yes, I was taking some time off and had heard the area is beautiful," she responded.

"And damn near uninhabitable that time of year," Aglee barked.

Sarah did not respond to that, so Aglee persisted, "And she said you were in Galveston when that incident took place a few months ago as well."

"I happened to be attending a convention when that happened," Sarah answered defensively. "It was pure coincidence. Ask Boone. I got a lot done on behalf of CFRG at that convention." Boone nodded but said nothing.

"Too many coincidences, Sarah," Aglee growled. "I've always distrusted coincidences."

The tension in the room had become as thick as New Orleans humidity. Amanda told Sarah that Captain Aglee had wanted to go to the authorities after he had inspected his ship, but that she had dissuaded him from doing so until they had a chance to talk with Boone and her and see what they had to say.

Sarah looked at Boone. He was clearly uneasy and had difficulty meeting her eyes. Sarah had no trouble reading his conflicted feelings. She remained quiet for a minute, using her considerable skill as a negotiator to evaluate the situation.

Finally, she turned to Boone and said, "Are you still in touch with that college friend of yours in the FBI?"

"Yes, he's in special investigations in the D.C. headquarters, but I haven't talked with him in a while," he said.

"Good. I would like three days, starting tomorrow morning, to try to find out what I can about the recent incidents, then I will go with all of you to meet with your FBI contact and I promise I will cooperate fully with them. Can you set that up, Boone? To meet with us in four days?"

Boone looked at Amanda and Aglee, both of whom seemed agreeable, then answered, "Why don't I wait until you get back with us, whether that's in three days or less." He looked again at the others, who nodded again.

"Thank you, Boone," Sarah said. "Captain Aglee, it was nice to meet you – and to see you, Amanda – even though I'm sure we all wish it were under better circumstances. Now, if you'll excuse me, I had better get started."

Sarah rose to leave, then almost as an afterthought turned to Amanda and said, "Remember that, as a friend, I warned you about Win." I knew that relationship would lead to trouble, she thought to herself as she left Boone's office and went into her own, closing the door softly behind her.

Boone drove Amanda and Aglee to an airport hotel. It was too late for them to catch flights out that night. Aglee was going back to Los Angeles and Amanda was going to San Francisco. Both had agreed to meet back in Monterey in three days.

While Aglee went in to arrange for two rooms, Boone asked Amanda, "Are you alright?"

"Aside from having my recent sexual activity become everybody's favorite topic, I'm fine. But I'm worried about Sarah. She knows more than she's saying. I just can't see how she's not somehow personally involved in at least some of these oil spills. And I'm concerned that a lover – a former lover – of mine could have been involved in sabotage and murder."

"I'm worried about Sarah, too," Boone confessed. "She may have been too clever for her own good. I couldn't help noticing how calm she was while we were talking back there. As damaging as it must have sounded to her, she didn't crack. She just sat there thinking through the situation. She never really answered any questions or put forward any facts or mitigating circumstances in her defense. And then she offered to go with us to the FBI. How do you figure that? She's amazing."

"She certainly is," Amanda agreed. "And you love her." It was a declaration, not a question.

"I do," he confessed simply. "And I don't have any idea how to protect her. She's always protecting and helping me, and this is so atypical. I just don't know what to do."

"She's been very good for you, Boone," she said quietly. "I'm sure you haven't noticed this in yourself, but I can see that you are back to the Boone I used to know."

"So what can I do to help her?" he pleaded.

"Hopefully, we'll find that out when we get back together in three days," she said.

Boone drove slowly to Sarah's apartment, sure that she would be home by now and almost hoping she wouldn't be. He was as uneasy as he had ever felt, as helpless as he had felt when he had lost his wife and son.

He knocked softly on her door and when she answered it, she greeted him with a hug and a peck on the cheek. She held his hand as she led him to the couch.

"This has been a day full of surprises," she said softly, "and none of them particularly pleasant. But it will all work out." She gave his hand a squeeze.

"How can you be so calm and confident?" Boone asked.

"I'm not sure," she said, "but I've got three days."

"I still don't know how you can remain so calm." He turned and looked deeply into her eyes. "Sarah, you are a very special person to me and I hope you know I'll support you however I can. I don't want to lose you, so tell me what I can do to help."

Sarah smiled broadly and said, "You've just given me the help I needed most right now."

Boone fixed a Caesar salad with sautéed scallops for dinner and after that they showered and went to bed, holding each other as they fell asleep.

Early the next morning, Boone drove Sarah to the airport. She did not tell him where she was going and told him she would not be in touch. She would just see him in three days.

CHAPTER 33

The Huff twins, Tweeter and Slump, had been waiting in the Aero Premier Jet Center at New Orleans Lakefront Airport just over twenty minutes when the sleek jet rolled to a stop, shut down its engines, and discharged Zara al-Kahtani.

She walked briskly to them, exchanged perfunctory greetings and followed them to their rented Chevrolet Suburban. It was a short ride to the St. Louis Cemetery, where they were to meet Sandy Agria of Pure Earth.

True to her word, Sandy was waiting for them at the Wall of Tombs. She had driven, carefully checking her mirrors all the way, from Houston to New Orleans early that morning. Zara walked up to her and introduced herself before either of the twins could do so.

"The work you did for us a few years ago was first rate and I appreciate it," Zara said. "It is nice to put a face with a name, is it not?"

"It's not always an asset in my position," Sandy responded.

Zara nodded in understanding, and Sandy said, "Tweeter and Slump tell me you have an interest in Pure Earth and its role in the *American PERL I* incident."

"Yes," Zara said, "and I am also quite interested in the relationship, if there is one, of Akrum al-Kahtani and Jet Jamieson to Pure Earth."

"I am sure there is a relationship there," Sandy replied. "How soon do you need whatever I can find?"

"I need it just as soon as possible," Zara said.

She was staring hard through her veil at Sandy. "And I need it to be accurate. Accurate enough that we can reasonably expect that it can be documented later."

"Documented by whom?" Sandy asked.

"By whomever I select to document it," Zara replied coldly.

"I see," Sandy said, a slight smile on her face. She was getting nervous again. She excused herself, stepped away from Zara and the Huffs, and used her mobile phone to send a text message. Zara wondered who the recipient was. In less than a minute, Sandy's phone pinged, indicating an incoming message.

After reading and deleting the message she had received, Sandy announced, "I can have information in your hands in 36 hours. But it will be expensive."

"How expensive?" Zara asked, a wry smile hidden beneath her burka.

"Fifty thousand," Sandy said.

"I will pay you one hundred thousand if I have the information I require in 24 hours," Zara said without hesitation. "I will wire $25,000 now to wherever you want it and the balance when you deliver the information and I have reviewed and approved it."

"I would prefer cash," Sandy said.

Zara laughed. "Of course you do," she said, "but we would all be fools to carry such amounts of cash on our person, especially in New Orleans."

Sandy accepted the inevitable and gave Zara her bank information. Zara recognized the wire routing prefix as a Cayman Islands account. Sandy was not stupid, that was for sure.

They all agreed to meet back at the Wall of Tombs the next day at noon.

Zara and the Huffs drove to their hotel and set up their laptops in Zara's suite.

They spent the afternoon and much of the evening trying to contact, or at least locate, Akrum al-Kahtani and Jet Jamieson. Zara called both men, using both the secure cell phones they had for cartel business and their personal cell phones. None of her calls were answered and she left urgent messages demanding a return call immediately.

Her tone of voice was not calculated to indicate this was a casual call for purposes of gossip.

Meanwhile, the Huffs spent their time scouring databases for airlines, rental car agencies, aircraft and boat rental and leasing firms and hotel chains. Zara had even shown them how to hack into the computers of the customs, immigration and passport control functions of the U.S. Department of Homeland Security.

After two hours of searching the passport control records, Slump turned up an indication that Akrum al-Kahtani had departed New York's Kennedy International Airport two days before on an Emirates Airways flight to Dubai.

When he reported this discovery to Zara, she slapped the table angrily and said, "Going to hide in Saudi Arabia, the son of a goat." She was disgusted and sickened as it became increasingly apparent that her own father had betrayed her, then turned and ran like a dog.

But five hours of trying by three different people searching dozens of databases provided not a single record of Jet Jamieson nor of the alias Zara knew he sometimes used. It was as if he had ceased to exist.

Finally, seemingly out of options, Zara consulted the contacts record in her personal cell phone and pushed the call button. A woman answered on the second ring with a cheery, "Hello, Zara."

The woman was a psychic who went by the unlikely name of Tuesday Monday. Zara was not, by nature, a woman who believed in the metaphysical. Until she had met and reluctantly worked with Tuesday Monday some years before, she had thought that psychics, mystics, fortune tellers and palm readers should be banished to the Croatian mountains where they could live among the gypsies who believed in such bullshit.

But she had delivered for Zara that first time, and on three occasions since. Now she had nothing to lose in turning to her another time.

"I feel that you need my services again, Zara," Tuesday Monday said in a cheerful and reassuring tone. "You seek to locate someone or something you have misplaced or mislaid. And I sense that your need is urgent."

As usual, she had sensed correctly, and Zara was again amazed that the unexplainable appeared to work.

"You are correct that my need is quite urgent," Zara confirmed. "I would like to meet with you as soon as possible. I am tied up until tomorrow afternoon, but can meet you wherever you are soon after that."

"I'm in Sedona, Arizona," Tuesday Monday said. "I'm attending a small gathering of men and women who share my calling."

Zara was familiar with the small mountain town set amid some of the most beautiful red rock scenery. She made a quick mental calculation and said, "I can be there by 6:00 tomorrow evening. As I recall, the Sedona airport closes at nightfall, so I must get there by that time. Is that convenient for you?"

"I'll look forward to having another session with you, Zara," she said and gave her the name of a small lodge within walking distance of the airport. "You make the reservation, but I'll check you into a room and be waiting for you if I get there before you."

"I appreciate your flexibility," Zara said.

"Can you give me any information on who or what you wish to find?" the psychic asked.

"There are two men. The names are Akrum al-Kahtani and Jet Jamieson. I will email you background information on both men, along with photos, tonight," Zara said. "And please use all of your considerable powers to help me find them. The need, as I said, is quite urgent."

"I will," Tuesday Monday said confidently. "See you tomorrow."

Zara called the lodge in Sedona and reserved a room for the following night, telling them that a friend would be checking in prior to her arrival. Then she remembered to wire $25,000 to Sandy Agria.

The next morning, Tweeter drove the Suburban as the three of them headed back to St. Louis Cemetery. They arrived at 11:00 a.m., hoping Sandy Agria would be early, but mostly hoping she would come at all. On the drive, Zara called the flight service and told them to have her small jet serviced and ready to be wheels up by 2:00 that afternoon.

Sandy walked up to them at the Wall of Tombs just after 11:30 a.m. She looked tired but confident.

"I have found some things that I think you'll find very interesting,"

Sandy said.

"Did you receive the wire transfer?" Zara asked.

"I wouldn't be here if I had not," Sandy said, a bit of defiance in her voice. She sat on a bench, opened her laptop and clicked on the file she had for Zara. She passed the laptop to Zara and patted the bench beside her.

Zara sat down and started scrolling through the file, which she had copied from Pure Earth's restricted files.

As she scrolled, Sandy provided a verbal synopsis. "You'll find proof of a relationship between Pure Earth and the *American PERL I* incident and of the roles of Akrum al-Kahtani and Jet Jamieson in the planning and implementation of that incident. You'll find a trail of disbursements over the past year from Pure Earth to both men.

"You'll also find several visits by both men to Pure Earth's headquarters, as recorded on security cameras. But I didn't have time to look into whether Pure Earth was involved in any of the previous oil incidents."

Zara read through the entire file. It took her most of thirty minutes, and she asked a few questions as she read. When she finished, she asked Sandy, "Can you get for me the original documents for some of these transactions?"

"No, these electronic records were all I could find," Sandy said. "The originals are either stored in a secure vault or have been fed into the shredder."

Zara was not surprised, so she thanked Sandy for her efforts and assured her she had found most of what she had hoped for, and certainly enough to get the job done for her.

"I'm glad you're pleased," Sandy said. "I'll email this file and mail you a back-up thumb drive once I get the balance of my fee."

Zara opened her laptop and emailed instructions to her bank.

Three minutes later, Sandy was able to confirm that her account had been credited with another $75,000. She smiled, emailed the file to Zara and reached into the pocket of her jacket and handed two thumb drives to Zara.

Zara stood. When Sandy stood up too, Zara offered her hand and thanked her for the prompt response.

"Thank you for the nice fee," Sandy said. Then she paused in thought and added, "Oh, there's another thing. I almost forgot. I came across some additional information you might be interested in, but it will take a lot more work and more money, but if what I suspect is right, it will definitely be worth it to you."

Zara asked the Huffs to take a walk, but to keep her in sight. Then she looked at Sandy and nodded for her to continue.

"I'm not sure," Sandy said in a low voice, "but I saw some things that led me to the feeling that there may be a longer-term relationship between Pure Earth and Akrum al-Kahtani than just this one incident."

"What led you to that suspicion?" Zara asked, her heart rate quickening.

"I found that, in the months before last year's election, Pure Earth made some large disbursements to unusual people and organizations. Ones not on normal payables records of Pure Earth."

"How long will it take you to pin that information down?" Zara asked. "And what fee are you thinking about?"

"I think a week or ten days at the most would do it," Sandy responded. "And I think we can settle on a fee once we know what I'm able to find. If it's what I think it will be, it will be very valuable to you, and I know you'll be fair with me."

"I'll make a $50,000 down payment on it today," Zara said quickly, "and we'll agree on a fair price when we see what you can find."

They shook on it. Then Sandy had another thought. "Say, I remembered last night as I was looking for things connecting these guys to Pure Earth that your last name is al-Kahtani, too. Is Akrum a relative of yours?"

"He's my father," Zara said quietly.

Sandy did not look as shocked as Zara expected her to be. "We've all got relatives that we wish we didn't, but your father? My God!"

Zara waved the Huffs back and said to Sandy, "Please contact either Tweeter or Slump when you have anything new. I will be leaving New Orleans in the next hour, but they will remain here or in Houston and are available to help you in any way they can."

Sandy smiled warmly at the twins. It was clear she liked them. "I'll keep them posted," she assured Zara.

"One additional matter before I leave," Zara said to Sandy. "Do you have the ability to delete - or I should say destroy - specific files in the Pure Earth system?"

"Yes," Sandy answered, caution in her voice. "But it would be very risky and I would need to be protected with more money."

"That is not a problem" Zara said. "So as you search through the data files for the next week or ten days, I think you should work out a plan for destroying some of them."

Sandy nodded her understanding and they said their farewells as Zara hurried the Huff twins toward the Suburban for her ride to the airport. They got to the airport just before 2:00 p.m. and Zara bought a box lunch and boarded her jet. The Huffs returned to their hotel.

The jet went wheels up at 2:05.

It was a three-hour flight to Sedona's picturesque little mountain-top airport. Zara ate the egg salad sandwich, chips and fresh apple that were in the box lunch, washing it all down with a bottle of spring water she found in the small refrigerator on the airplane. She used the rest of the time to study the file Sandy Agria had supplied.

She used the air phone to try Akrum and Jet again, but got the same result she had the afternoon before. Zara was furious.

When the small jet landed at Sedona – using the entire runway to get stopped and turned around – she deplaned and walked to the lodge. Tuesday Monday had not arrived yet, so she checked in and went to her room and waited for the psychic to arrive.

As she waited, Zara reflected. She was not religious nor had she ever held anything but scorn for psychics. But she often used meditation and other techniques to delve deeply into her subconscious to extract strength and wisdom as she needed it. Tuesday Monday had been recommended to her by a college friend and she had been reluctant to try her. Then on an occasion where she was absolutely vexed by something that at the time was of critical importance, she had tried the psychic. She had been amazed.

Now, she looked forward anxiously to Tuesday Monday's arrival. Something told her the woman would conjure up the answers she desperately needed.

The psychic arrived just after 5:30 p.m.

As usual, Tuesday Monday gave Zara a long, firm hug. She had told her in the past that doing so helped her connect with Zara and her needs. Releasing the hug, she unfolded and set up her small reading table and placed a chair at each end.

"Before we begin," Tuesday intoned, "is there anything else aside from the location of Akrum al-Kahtani and Jet Jamieson for which you would like me to summon the guidance of the spirits this evening?"

"Yes, as a matter of fact," Zara said softly. "I have a feeling – intuition, perhaps – that Akrum, an organization called Pure Earth International, and others may have controlled transactions and events that have, or might have, a major political effect on the world."

"Can you be more specific?" the psychic inquired.

"Not really. I just sense something more besides creating oil spills."

Tuesday directed Zara to a chair and asked her to sit. Zara knew the routine: sit up straight, both hands palms up and open on the table before her, and take slow, deep breaths with her eyes closed. Tuesday sat opposite her.

She instructed Zara to relax, continue taking slow deep breaths and slowly roll her head. It was almost like Zara was preparing to be hypnotized, and in many ways it was the same thing.

Tuesday gently told Zara to continue relaxing, to feel a bright white light penetrating her body from her head to her feet which would bring with it peace and further relaxation. Zara could feel the tension leaving her body, the feeling sensuous.

When Tuesday sensed Zara was totally relaxed, her breathing deep and regular, she slid a photo of Akrum under Zara's right hand and one of Jet under the left.

She said softly, "I will now hold your hands and I want you to think only of Akrum and Jet." She intoned a quiet chant, then implored the powers to guide them to the location of Akrum and Jet. After repeating the chant and the request for ten minutes, she became silent.

Minutes later, Tuesday spoke again, very quietly. "I feel Akrum is very far away, in a different country, maybe at home, a large – very large – house in a warm climate, a very comfortable setting for him."

She went quiet for another minute before speaking again in that same low tone.

"I see Jet far away, too, but not as far as Akrum. I feel sex is in the air with Jet. He is in a warm place by the ocean that is familiar to you. I feel you have been there many times."

Tuesday was quiet again and continued to hold Zara's hands, her thumbs making circular motions in Zara's palms.

"I see Akrum involved in a campaign. No, he is involved in an election, an important election, with money – lots of secret money – involved. The others involved are diverse and are unrelated, not aware of each other. I do not see Jet in this picture, but rewards or money comes to Akrum. Lots of money. I feel money very strongly."

She was quiet and still for several more minutes before unclasping Zara's hands and telling her she was free to open her eyes. Zara did so and sat deep in thought.

"Thank you, Tuesday," she said at length. "As usual, you have been very helpful to me."

Zara poured two glasses of wine and they visited for a while before Tuesday left for her hotel. Zara handed her a large wad of bills as she left.

Early the next morning, Zara checked out and walked to the airport coffee shop.

The call from the Huff twins came as she was eating breakfast.

"We're in Washington," Tweeter said. "We figured since Akrum left we'd check out his apartment. Both the doorman and his limo driver are of the opinion that he went back to Saudi Arabia, so the airline info we got off the Internet was apparently right."

"Can you get into his apartment?" Zara asked.

"We will be able to next week. We gave the doorman and the driver some spending money, and the doorman told us the next scheduled cleaning service is at that time. It was bad timing for us. The service was just there day before yesterday. We've contacted the cleaning service and will join them when they clean the place next."

Zara was puzzled. How would the cleaning service just let them join in? She asked Tweeter that question.

"Slump went to see the owner, who's Middle Eastern himself. Slump had ICE credentials which he showed the man. When he asked for the

I-9s on his employees, the guy shit himself. When Slump explained that the Immigration and Customs Enforcement Service suspected Mr. al-Kahtani of human smuggling from the Middle East, the guy fell all over himself cooperating."

Zara laughed out loud. "I want to be with you when you search the apartment. Also, make sure you stay in close touch with Sandy Agria and make sure the quality of the information she is getting from Pure Earth meets our needs. I'll be busy for the next two days, but I will see you in Washington the day after that."

"Do you know if Akrum has a vault in his apartment?" Tweeter asked.

"That is a good point, Tweeter. Yes, he does, so you will need to find someone to accompany us who can open it. And I do not care whether we have to damage it to open it." Her meaning was clear. If an explosive charge became necessary, so be it.

Zara finished her breakfast and walked to the jet that awaited her.

CHAPTER 34

MONTEREY, CA
TWO DAYS LATER

Sarah walked up to the CFRG office at 12:30 p.m. The door was locked and the "Back in a While" sign showed 1:00 p.m.. They were all obviously out to lunch, so Sarah let herself in, relocked the door and went to her office, where she checked her mail and started to print documents she expected she would need in the coming days.

Suzy was the first of the staff to return, and was surprised to find Sarah in her office, busily working on her computer.

"Sarah, what a surprise!" she exclaimed. "Are you okay?"

"I'm fine, Suzy," she replied. "How are you?" Suzy could not believe how relaxed Sarah looked.

"I just thought that under the circumstances, you would look a little more stressed out," Suzy said. Boone had obviously given Suzy at least an abbreviated version of what was going on. That did not bother Sarah, who felt Suzy deserved to know anything that affected the operation of CFRG.

Sarah smiled and said, "I'm not stressed out at all, Suzy. Everything will be worked out soon. And by the way, here are my comments on the new articles for the web site you emailed me." She handed Suzy several pages.

"How long will you be here?" Suzy asked. "Boone will be back at 2:00. He had some errands to run and will want to see you as soon as he can, I know."

"I'll be here," Sarah said. "But for now, I've got some calls to make." Suzy nodded, somewhat in awe at how cool Sarah was. As she backed out of the office, she closed Sarah's door.

When Boone walked through the door, his first question to Suzy was "Have we heard from Sarah? This is the third day."

"She's in her office working and she gave me these revisions for the website articles," Suzy replied, smiling widely. Boone just shook his head as he walked to Sarah's office, knocking softly when he got there.

Sarah jumped up, unlocked the door and gave Boone a fierce hug and a kiss that was somewhat more than a friendly hello. "It's good to see you, Boone," she said, her voice husky. "I've missed you."

"I've missed you, too," Boone responded quietly, as amazed as Suzy had been as Sarah's poise under the circumstances.

Sarah got right to business. "Boone, can you call your FBI friend right away and set up an appointment for late tomorrow afternoon?"

"I'll try," he said. "What's up?"

"I'll explain later, but I also need you to call Amanda and Captain Aglee and get them here by 6:00 tomorrow morning. I have a private jet to take us back to D.C. If we need for it to pick up Amanda or the Captain, we can do that. But the three of you need to be at the Monterey airport at 6:00 a.m." Boone made notes on a pad from Sarah's desk and nodded. "Tell them I'll brief them on what I've found to date on the flight back. We'll have five hours. I'll brief you tonight over dinner. That is, I will if you're free for dinner."

"Of course I am," he said quickly.

"But for now," she went on, "I need some time to finish preparing and I want to go work out." They agreed to dinner at 6:00 p.m. and Sarah grabbed her laptop case and hurried out of the office.

Boone called his friend at the FBI. He had briefed him in general terms two days before, and the man agreed to a 4:00 p.m. meeting. Boone had no problem getting the agreement of both Amanda and Captain Aglee to be at the Monterey Peninsula Airport no later than 6:00 the next morning.

Sarah got back to the CFRG office at 5:30 p.m., not surprisingly finding Suzy and Boone still at their desks, although Suzy was tidying up in preparation for her departure for home and whatever she and Sergeant

Preston had planned for the evening.

Walking into Boone's office, Sarah asked, "Is everything set for tomorrow?"

"Yes, ma'am," Boone said, smiling smugly.

"Perfect. Then why don't we go get some dinner and get home early?"

"Yes, Ma'am," Boone said again, his heart racing suddenly. He had not, quite frankly, expected to be home with Sarah that night.

They went to one of their favorite spots on Cannery Row, where they ordered a bottle of wine to enjoy while they talked. Sarah wanted to talk before dinner.

"I have some very interesting information," she began. "Some of it still needs corroboration, but I believe that Pure Earth International orchestrated and funded the *American PERL I* incident. The leader of the group that actually sabotaged the rig is a man named Akrum al-Kahtani, who is a Saudi Arabian national. In fact, he was once the Saudi Oil Minister and more recently an Ambassador at Large.

"He used a man named Jet Jamieson – alias Win Mifflin – to plan and execute the incident. I have been trying to locate both men, without luck. I also strongly suspect that Pure Earth has been behind many, if not all, of the other recent oil spill incidents. But I need more time to document all of this and complete my investigation."

She extracted a bound file from her briefcase and handed it to Boone. He had been listening intently, marveling again at this woman. He sipped his wine as he carefully reviewed each document in the file, not noticing that the waitress was standing there, waiting for their orders.

Sarah ordered dinner for both of them.

"This is pretty convincing stuff," he murmured. "How much time do you think you need to wrap it up with all the evidence you'll need?"

"I think no more than a couple of weeks." He nodded, flipping back and forth through the documents. Their meals arrived.

It was a quiet walk to Sarah's apartment. As they walked in the door, Sarah grabbed Boone and gave him a very long kiss. Boone was getting excited, but Sarah pushed him back and said, "We need to talk some more, but first I need to change clothes. While I'm doing that, why don't you open another bottle of wine. I need another glass and I think you will, too."

As he watched her disappear into her bedroom, Boone reflected once again on how unpredictable Sarah could be. Just when he thought he had heard everything at the restaurant, she came home wanting to change clothes, have more wine and talk some more. But he opened the wine and filled two glasses.

He was sipping one and the other was sitting on the coffee table when the bedroom door opened. Out walked a woman wearing a niqab and an abaya, her entire body covered in black cloth except for a thin slit for her eyes. She walked over to Boone and sat beside him.

"You look unsettled, Boone," Zara al-Kahtani said with a noticeable Arabic accent. "Were you expecting, perhaps, Sarah?"

Boone was silent. He was actually dumbstruck, and not a little fearful. What the hell? was all he could think.

"It is time for me to tell you that I exist as two different people – Zara al-Kahtani and Sarah Cotton. I have used the identities – and the personalities that go with them – as the situation requires. Zara is the more cunning and aggressive and Sarah is more the charmer." She almost laughed, watching Boone's expression turn from fear to complete befuddlement.

"Both are my real names," Zara continued. "I hold dual citizenship – the United States and Saudi Arabia – although my true loyalty is, and always has been, to the United States. My mother was an American who married Akrum al-Kahtani. Her maiden name was Cotton. I was born in the U.S. Now, shall we have a sip of wine?" She pulled her niqab from her face so she could sip from her glass, raised it in toast, and said, "To us."

"Please continue," Boone said, finally able to find his voice.

"My mother and younger brother died in a fire when I was nine," she said. "As is normal in the Arab world, my brother was my father's favorite. I was raised by my father, who was distant to me, and by relatives, until I was college age and then Sarah went to Trinity College.

"I sometimes work with my father, but he will only deal with me as I am now, Zara. He does not acknowledge Sarah. My father is completely and totally untrustworthy and you must remember that. His only loyalty is to himself and he will sacrifice anyone and anything for his own benefit. We are not close as father and daughter."

Boone sat staring at her, nodded for her to go on.

"I prefer being Sarah over Zara. And I must tell you that Sarah is more than very fond of you and her relationship with you is very close to her heart."

Boone was still silent.

"I will not disclose my existence as Zara to the FBI tomorrow," she continued. "It will be all Sarah tomorrow."

Boone was still silent. Finally, he picked up the wine glasses and handed Zara hers. He said as he raised his glass, "Here's to all three of us." When they had returned the glasses to the table, he grabbed her and pulled her very close. He kissed her lovingly and she returned it.

They drank their wine in silence and Boone got up to refill their glasses. She joined him at the counter were he had sat the wine bottle. He was regaining his composure and said, "Well, Zara, since Sarah seems to be away for the night, I think we need to take advantage of the situation. I won't tell if you don't."

"I agree," Zara said quietly. "And I most certainly won't tell." Boone reached out and pulled the entire abaya over her head. He was not surprised that she was completely nude underneath it.

"Please don't tell Sarah," Boone teased.

"She will never know," Zara replied, her Arabic accent having disappeared somewhere in the course of the conversation, and she pulled Boone down on top of her on the couch. Sometime later, they moved to the bed.

The alarm was set for 4:30 a.m. A 6:00 rendezvous with Amanda, Captain Aglee and a private jet awaited them at the airport. After shutting off the alarm, Sarah rolled over and draped her arm across Boone's shoulders.

"What time did you come to bed last night?" she asked, still in the teasing state they had entered the night before.

"It was late," Boone grinned. "I was visiting with an old friend of yours."

"Oh?" Sarah asked. "And how did the two of you get along?"

"Very well," he said. "I think we both enjoyed getting to know one another."

"Should I be jealous?" she asked coquettishly.

"No, I don't think so," he said. "Well, maybe just a little."

Sarah swatted Boone's butt as he jumped out of bed and headed for the shower. She was close behind him.

CHAPTER 35

Sarah and Boone walked into the executive aircraft terminal at the Monterey Peninsula Airport at 6:15 a.m. Amanda and Captain Aglee were already there. They were in casual clothes, but Sarah was in her lobbying uniform.

"Sleep in this morning, kids?" Amanda chided sarcastically.

"No, we needed to make sure we had all of Sarah's documents organized correctly," Boone said, more defensively than he intended.

Sarah just gave Amanda a glowing smile and Amanda thought, *Documents, my ass.* They bounded up the stair door of the jet and it was soon airborne, headed for Reagan National Airport. Amanda asked Sarah how she had managed to arrange for – or to afford – a private jet. Sarah smiled and told them she had stashed a comfortable sum from her years of a lucrative lobbying practice and since she had gotten them all into this, she felt she owed them some comfort and convenience.

After a breakfast of coffee, orange juice and banana nut muffins – which Amanda thought were the best she had ever tasted – Sarah began her briefing. Amanda and the captain listened attentively, and Amanda literally jumped when Sarah got to the part about Jet Jamieson, alias *Winter Mifflin*. Aglee shot her a glance that had *I knew something about that bastard was wrong* stenciled all over it.

Sarah told them she did not know whether either was his real name, but that he had used the Jamieson name in his dealings with Pure Earth.

Amanda sighed in relief. Captain Aglee asked a lot of questions, especially about the oil spill that had involved him and the *Mar Ascensor*. And his missing oiler.

He asked whether she had determined that Jet Jamieson, or *Win Mifflin*, or whatever other name he might have used, was his oiler.

"I just don't know yet," Sarah said. "I don't have everything yet. I need time to complete my investigation." She paused, then continued. "But I would bet that when I am finished, I will find that Pure Earth, Akrum al-Kahtani and Jet Jamieson were all involved, and that Jet was the oiler who disappeared."

"What, exactly, do you expect to accomplish with the FBI today?" Aglee asked.

"I need to buy more time, Captain," she said. "I need to buy two weeks. I'd like them to issue arrest warrants on both al-Kahtani and Jamieson. But I don't want a warrant at this time for Kirk Klenner of Pure Earth."

Aglee nodded. "Do you think the FBI will agree?" he asked.

"Yes, I do," she said. "I have worked with them before and have a good idea of how they operate."

Aglee and Amanda were surprised – or stunned – by Sarah's answer. Boone had already learned not to be surprised with anything that had to do with Sarah.

In truth, Sarah knew she could probably have just handled all this through the FBI's San Francisco Field Office, but she needed Boone's support and involvement, and going to his old friend in Washington was the surest way to ensure that. She also suspected that Captain Aglee would be more convinced of the seriousness of her efforts if they were working with the headquarters in Washington.

They were all quiet for several minutes, each lost in his or her own thoughts.

Then Sarah leaned toward Captain Aglee and asked, "May I ask, Captain, why you ordered your crew members over the side to inspect the starboard side of the *Mar Ascensor* after the unidentified impact? I mean, is that a normal procedure in that circumstance with a ship that size?"

Aglee was surprised – and more than a little offended – by the questions. "Are you now second-guessing my actions as a ship's captain?"

he asked, the offense he felt evident in his voice. "May I remind you that, until the last voyage, I had maintained a perfect safety record throughout my career?"

"I meant no offense, Captain," she responded in her most calming tone of voice. "But my instinct is always to question what seems unusual. It just seems very risky to me to send an inspection team over the side of a ship that size when you were unsure of what had happened."

Aglee glowered at her. "In hindsight, it was beyond risky," he said. "As you know, it turned deadly. But keep in mind that at the time the ship was virtually dead in the water, so the risk was not the same as it would have been if she were underway."

Boone and Amanda sat staring, both uncomfortable with Sarah's questions.

"Captain, I realize that, in hindsight you regret what you did," Sarah persisted. "But you did not answer my questions."

Aglee sat back in his seat. "As captain, I am responsible for the actions of my crew at sea," he said. "I accept full responsibility for their actions. In this case, I ordered an inspection of the starboard side of ship, and that is all I ordered. The seaman in charge of the inspection crew made the decision to lower two men for a closer look."

"Thank you," Sarah said. "I understand now, and I will mention none of this to anyone else."

It suddenly struck Boone that Sarah had already known the answers before she asked the questions. *But what the hell is the significance of the inspection party?* He wondered.

Amanda jumped in her seat, and Sarah noticed. Amanda had been reading her emails on her I-Phone. Sarah looked at Amanda inquiringly.

"Win – or maybe I should say Jet - just emailed me," she said in a low voice, but Boone and Aglee heard her and looked at Sarah, who waved her hand as if to tell Amanda to continue.

"He said he's going to be in San Francisco and wants to get together," Amanda said. "How should I answer?"

"Don't say anything yet," Sarah said. "Let's wait until after our meeting this afternoon, then we can discuss what you should do on the flight back to California." Then Sarah booted her laptop out of sleep mode and fired off an email.

Boone could not help noticing Sarah's sudden change in expression, and the change is her tone of voice.

Sarah had arranged for a limousine waiting for them when they deplaned at Reagan National and in less than 20 minutes it pulled up to the curb in front of the J. Edgar Hoover Building at 9th Street and Pennsylvania Avenue. The four passengers walked into the public entrance of the headquarters of the Federal Bureau of Investigation.

Boone told the fit young man at the reception counter that they had an appointment with Patrick Moblox of the Criminal Investigative Division. They were asked for photo IDs and after signing in, they were issued visitor badges.

Two minutes after the fit young man had called Moblox, the agent pushed through a closed door with an electronic reader next to the knob and rushed up to Boone, shaking hands and embracing him warmly. They had known each other in college and had been in the Navy together as well.

Boone introduced the other members of his party and Moblox ushered them through the door – after swiping his ID in front of the reader – and to a bank of elevators. When they got to a conference room, another man was waiting for them, and Moblox introduced the man has his supervisor in the CID, Clyde Peed. Boone quickly introduced the others and briefly summarized the reason he had asked for this meeting, then turned to Sarah.

Before she could begin, Peed asked, "Didn't you work with us on a case involving radical Islamists a few years back?"

"Yes, I did," Sarah answered, "but it seems longer ago." She knew from his question that Clyde Peed, if not Patrick Moblox as well, knew about Zara.

"You provided information that allowed us to take out a radical cell before they could blow up the Capitol Building, if I remember right, Sarah," Peed said.

"You have an excellent memory, Clyde," she responded.

"Please just call me Peed. Everybody does."

"I will," she said, passing a file to Peed and a duplicate to Moblox. "Thank you. Now, if you'll indulge me, let me begin by going over some strange events of the last few weeks." She began with Captain Aglee recognizing Win Mifflin when he saw him with Amanda at the airport in Los Angeles. She filled them in on the *Mar Ascensor* incident and the curiously missing oiler.

She then went over the *American PERL I* incident and the damning information implicating Pure Earth International and Kirk Klenner in its planning and funding. Finally, tying it all together, she filled them in about Akrum al-Kahtani and Jet Jamieson, alias *Winter Mifflin.*

She told them she was positive of their collective involvement in *American PERL I* and had every reason to believe they were behind the *Mar Ascensor* and very probably the other recent incidents as well.

Both FBI men asked a lot of questions and studied the documents Sarah had provided.

"As I said earlier," Sarah continued, "I strongly suspect that Akrum and Jet arranged some, if not all, of the recent oil-related incidents, and that they did so under an agreement with Pure Earth. However, I need more time to check everything out and try to get the documentation necessary to make the case. And, of course, I need to locate Akrum and Jet. Fortunately, I do know where Kirk Klenner is."

"Do they know you're checking up on them?" Peed asked.

"I doubt that Klenner has any idea. Akrum and Jet almost certainly suspect, since they know Amanda and I are friends.

Moblox spoke up, directing his question at Amanda. "Have you seen Jamieson, or Mifflin, if you will, since your encounter with Captain Aglee at LAX?"

"No," Amanda said, "but he sent me an email. I haven't responded to it."

"Is there any reason the FBI should not issues arrest warrants for these parties right now?" Peed asked, directing the question to Sarah. As soon as he asked, Sarah knew with certainty that the FBI was prepared to cooperate with her.

"If you issue warrants and attempt to arrest them now," she said, "all it would do is ensure that records get destroyed. You'll have Pure Earth for only the last oil incident. And most importantly, you'll never locate, let alone arrest, Jamieson or al-Kahtani."

She paused to let those statements sink in before continuing. "But if you'll agree to give me two weeks on my own, you'll get much more – probably the whole ball of wax. If I am not able to deliver, you've still got what you have today, and you're just out two weeks."

"Why are you doing this?" Peed asked.

"For many reasons," Sarah said with a casual shrug. "But one of them is for the integrity of the conservation movement."

Peed had a slight smile on his face when he said, "Sounds like a plan we can live with." He looked at Moblox, whose left hand was tightly gripping his right wrist, and added, "Oh, and would you mind wearing an electronic tether?"

"Why?" she snapped.

"Let's just say it's for the integrity of the conservation movement," Peed said wryly.

"I will not wear an ankle monitor," Sarah said firmly. "But now that you mention it, I would be willing to carry an electronic tagging device so you'll always know where I am. But I'd want it clearly marked as FBI property." She paused in thought. "And I'll also need two additional monitors that I can activate as I need to."

"Who would those be for?" Peed asked, thinking he knew the answer.

"If all goes well, for Mr. al-Kahtani and Mr. Jamieson." She smiled.

Peed smiled. "I like your thinking," he said, and Moblox nodded.

"I assume I'll be working directly with the two of you," Sarah said and the FBI men nodded in unison. "In that case, I'd like to get your 24-hour contact information. If I need your help, it may not be during normal working hours."

"Of course," Peed agreed. "We'll give you all our phone numbers as well as our restricted email addresses, and we'd like the same for you." He paused and looked around the table. "Hell, all of you," he said, waving his arm at them. "I'm assuming you're all in this together."

Then he turned and directed his attention to Amanda. "What, exactly, was the nature of your relationship with Jamieson, or rather Mifflin?"

Amanda felt her face burning, knew she was blushing furiously. "We are, or were, having an affair, I believe is how you would classify it. We were lovers, occasionally. I haven't seen him since that morning at LAX."

"But he's left messages or emails?" Peed persisted.

"Just the email this morning. I had not heard from him, otherwise, since he rushed off after seeing Captain Aglee."

"Does he know where you live?" Moblox asked.

"He has my address, but he's never been there."

"Please add your home and work addresses to the phone numbers and email addresses you leave for us," Moblox said to all of them.

Peed said, "Sarah, in your estimation, is this Jamieson-Mifflin character dangerous?"

"I've known him for a long time," she said softly. "He's cautious and ruthless, which I think classifies him as at least potentially dangerous."

Amanda felt a rush of uneasiness, but then said bravely, "Win would never hurt me. We were too close, and I think he cared very much for me."

Sarah's look of concern, directed toward Boone, was picked up by Peed.

"Amanda, I would suggest that you take Sarah's assessment of this man to heart until all this is straightened out," Peed said. "I would not respond to his email, and if I were you I would be very careful around home and work both." Amanda nodded her understanding.

All exchanged their contact information and Sarah said, "Thank you, gentlemen, for taking the time to listen to us and for your willingness to work with us. We're leaving right away to get back to Monterey and get to work on this."

Peed handed Sarah the electronic trackers. Only hers was activated, and he showed her how to activate the others.

Boone and Patrick Moblox talked about old times as they all walked out of the FBI building. When they were separated from the others, Moblox asked Boone, "What's your deal with Sarah?"

"Well, she's an invaluable member of the CFRG team – almost a co-director with me – and much more than a close personal friend."

Moblox knew what Boone meant by that. "Are you living together?"

"Mostly," Boone admitted.

"I figured. I suggest you stay as close to her as possible during this. She'll need the support, but she may also need protecting. Try to be cautious, old buddy. And don't break the law." Moblox's voice was firm as he said the last.

"I'll stay close to her," Boone said, gratitude in his voice. "And we won't break the law. And, Patrick, thanks for helping me with this."

Moblox said goodbye to each of the four as they piled into the limo. On the way to the airport, Sarah reminded Amanda and Captain Aglee to be alert, careful in their movements, and make sure they keep all doors locked at all times. She told them to call her immediately if they saw any signs of Jet – or Win – and make no contact with him, as Peed had advised. His email to her would go unanswered.

As the party was exiting the limo at the airport, Sarah pulled Boone aside. "I need to stay in D.C. for another day at least," she said.

"Do you need my help?" he asked.

"Yes, and when you get back, please take Amanda to my apartment for tonight at least. I'm very concerned for her safety. I have to get something done here in Washington and then I'll be able to get someone to guard her."

"You really think she's in danger?"

Sarah nodded. "I'll be back in Monterey as soon as I can, then we can figure out what to do next."

"Should I be worried about you here in Washington?" he asked.

Sarah just smiled, kissed Boone, then patted him on the butt as she pushed him toward the airplane. "Protect Amanda and avoid any contact with Jet," she ordered.

"Yes, ma'am."

CHAPTER 36

When the others were on the aircraft and it was spooling up for its return to Monterey, Sarah got back in the limo and gave the driver the address of Akrum al-Kahtani's apartment.

The Huff twins were parked in a white van with the markings of Pristine Cleaning Service on its panels outside of Akrum's building when the limo drove up. She told the driver to park a block up the street and wait for her call. She jumped into the back of the Huffs' van and quickly changed into a Pristine Cleaning uniform. Only when she was changed and ready did she notice there was third man in front with the Huffs. That would be the box man, she reasoned.

They all jumped out of the van, the Huff twins carrying the cleaning equipment. Sarah saw that one of them – especially in those uniforms, she could not tell them apart – now had a full beard and other's uniform was emblazoned with the word, "Manager," on his right breast pocket.

They entered the apartment building through the service entrance and the twin identified as the Manager held up two keys to Sarah, indicating that everything was set. Soon, they were in the apartment of Akrum al-Kahtani and the bearded twin punched in the code to disable the alarm.

"Good job," Sarah muttered to the twins and she led the box man – she did not know his name and had no interest in learning it – to where Akrum had his vault hidden in a bottom kitchen cabinet. The man set to work while the twins and Sarah started searching everywhere else.

She had by then determined from their voices – which had tiny differences in the inflection of some words - that the Manager was Tweeter and the bearded one was Slump.

Sarah went to Akrum's desk while the twins started going through closets, cabinets and nightstands. They even looked under the beds, sofa and chairs. Sarah was not surprised to find Akrum's desk unlocked. *The bastard always thought diplomatic immunity would protect him*, she mused.

The only interesting things she found in the desk were telephone bills for his home phone, bank records for an offshore bank account – *why the hell would he have a printed record of a bank account he dealt with only online and by telephone?* – and an address book.

The box man soon announced in a loud whisper that he had the vault open, and Sarah hurried in to join him. Her eyes fell immediately on an unfolded document which was laid across the top shelf of the vault. As she studied it, she saw that it was a typewritten list of 25 or so foundations and political organizations with handwritten notes of dollar amounts and dates next to each entry. The notes were in Akrum's handwriting, no doubt about it. She felt herself getting more excited.

Then she set the document aside and peered back into the vault and was astonished at what she saw. Stacks of tightly-wrapped bills were topped by what appeared to be four large bars of gold bullion. She handed the gold bars to the twins, who set them on the kitchen table. Then she started handing them bundles of cash, which seemed all to be in $100 bills.

Tweeter had found a large empty plastic storage container in one of the closets. Setting it beside the table, they counted out the money in one bundle, then started stacking it in the container, keeping track of the number of bundles. When it was all stored, Tweeter looked up at Sarah and said, "Jesus Christ! One million dollars!"

"Plus the fucking gold!" Slump added.

There was nothing else in the vault and the box man closed it and shut the cabinet door that hid it. Sarah put the documents found in the vault and in Akrum's desk on top of the gold and cash and closed and latched the lid.

As they were preparing to leave – they were close to the limits of the plausible period of time a cleaning crew would be in an apartment, in case any of Akrum's neighbors had noted their arrival – Sarah had another thought and asked, "Did anyone think to check the refrigerator and freezer?"

"Yes, I did," Slump answered. "Nothing in it except two ice cream containers in the freezer. Nothing at all in the fridge."

"Did you check the ice cream containers?" she asked.

"Yep, just ice cream," Slump responded.

On an impulse, Sarah decided to check for herself. There were two one-gallon containers, a size which was unusual enough that she set both on the kitchen counter and found a large serving spoon. She had barely dipped the spoon into the ice cream before the spoon hit something solid. She scraped a half inch of ice cream off the top and found a quart-sized glass jar. When she removed it and wiped it clean, she could see sparkles inside.

When she unscrewed the lid, she could see that the jar was full of what looked to her untrained eye to be expertly-cut diamonds of various sizes ranging from medium to gigantic. A similar glass jar in the second ice cream container was revealed to be full to the brim with gold Krugerrands.

"How did you know?" Slump asked.

"Akrum doesn't like ice cream," Sarah replied simply.

"Son of a bitch had quite an emergency fund here, didn't he?" Tweeter muttered. The box man looked to Sarah like he might soon go into shock. He was an experienced safe-cracker, but clearly he'd never seen a haul like this. But she knew the man had settled on a flat fee of $50,000 in cash, and he would settle for that. He had no choice.

As they left the building, Tweeter detoured to the lobby and handed the doorman an envelope and said, "Pristine Cleaning Service appreciates your help."

Sarah changed out of her cleaning uniform in the back of the van and called the limo driver to come pick her up. When she got out of the van, she told the Huffs to meet her in the general aviation terminal at Reagan National at 7:00 the next morning, and to check in with her by phone when they were on their way in case of any late changes of plans. But first, she had them load the plastic container in the trunk of the limo.

She removed and kept the documents with her.

She told the limo driver to take her back to Reagan National and then he could go home. He nodded and hurried off. Sarah put up the divider behind the driver and called Peed on his FBI cell phone.

"Good evening, Peed," she said when he answered. "This is Sarah Cotton and I wanted to tell you to let your boys know that I'm on my way to Reagan National in case they lose me in traffic."

"Thank you, Sarah," he said. "I'll let them know."

"And when I arrive at the airport," she went on, "will you have them meet me at the limo I'm in? I have a package to give them for safekeeping."

"What kind of package?"

"Cash, gold bullion, gold coins and diamonds, I believe."

"How much?" he asked. "And who does it belong to?"

"I think the cash alone is about a million, and I don't know the market value of the other stuff, but I'd guess it's two or three times that, maybe more. As to your second question, for the time being let's just say it relates to the matter we discussed this afternoon. You're better equipped than I to hold onto it until this all plays out."

"A little unusual, but I'll have them pick up the package and take it straight to headquarters and sign it in as evidence in a case under my name. That'll keep it secure."

Sarah started to sign off, but Peed had another question. "Just tell me one other thing. Is there anything illegal about how you came into possession of this package?"

"To the best of my knowledge, I have never done anything that you would find illegal."

"Just wanted to confirm," Peed said. "Thank you." Peed liked people who got the job done, and it sure seemed Sarah was moving very quickly.

When the limo pulled into Reagan National Airport ten minutes later, the FBI car was directly behind them. The limo pulled to the curb and the car followed. Sarah got out of the limo and walked back to the FBI car and asked for identification from both men in it. Then she called Peed again, read him the names and confirmed they were his men. Peed was impressed with her attention to detail.

The FBI men loaded the plastic box in their trunk and drove off.

Sarah grabbed her bag from the trunk and sent the limo driver home with her thanks and a $100 tip.

Sarah went inside the terminal, found the bank of courtesy phones that would connect her to any of the numerous airport hotels that provide shuttle service and called one. She needed rest. It had been a long day, and they would be leaving early for the flight back to Monterey.

An executive jet identical to the one that had carried Boone, Amanda and Aglee to California was waiting when the hotel limo pulled up to the executive terminal the next morning. An Avis Rental Car shuttle had dropped the Huff twins in the same spot eight minutes earlier. At 7:25, the jet lifted off and banked along the Potomac as it gained altitude, headed for Monterey.

The three passengers were going through the documents they had found in al-Kahtani's apartment. Sarah asked Slump to contact Sandy Agria and ask her to look for any transaction between Pure Earth and any of the organizations on the list she had found in the vault, and to see if she could match any Pure Earth transactions to Akrum's bank statements.

"Why don't we just turn this thing and go to New Orleans now?" Slump suggested. "That may save us some time."

Then he called Sandy as Sarah was telling the pilots about her requested change in flight plans.

Sandy Agria was waiting for them at the executive terminal at the New Orleans Lakefront Airport when they arrived. Sarah repeated to Sandy what she wanted her to look for.

After some discussion, it was decided that Slump would remain in New Orleans to work with Sandy, and to watch over her, while Sarah and Tweeter would continue on to Monterey. Having him work with Sandy would give her a sense of security and increase their chances of finding what they needed. Slump would get a commercial flight to Monterey later that day or the next.

After using the flight operations copy machine to make three copies of all the al-Kahtani documents, Sarah and Tweeter boarded the plane and Slump left the airport with Sandy.

CHAPTER 37

Sarah had just turned her cell phone on after landing in Monterey when it rang. It was Boone.

"Sarah," he said, "I'm with Amanda at her apartment in San Mateo. We just drove up here."

"I just arrived in Monterey," she told him. "How is she?"

"She thinks someone has been in her apartment. Nothing seems to be missing so far, but she's sure that things have been moved around, rearranged."

"Any sign of a forced entry?" she asked. She was alarmed but projected a calm voice. She didn't need anyone on her team to panic.

"No sign of it," Boone answered. "But she found a message on her answering machine from 'Win' that he's planning on being in San Francisco tomorrow and wants to see her. She's acting pretty calm and all, but she's scared."

Sarah thought about that as she and Tweeter were deplaning, then said, "Have her call him back and tell him she'll meet him at her apartment tomorrow night. Whatever time she'd normally meet him, it doesn't matter."

"You really want her to do that?" he asked, almost incredulous. "Won't that be dangerous?"

"Probably. But Tweeter and I will drive up there as soon as we drop some stuff off at my apartment and pick up some things. Then we'll plan for Jet's – Win's – visit."

Boone gave her directions to Amanda's apartment and they said goodbye.

They rented a car at the airport – Sarah still did not have a car in Monterey– and drove to her apartment, where she dropped off her dirty clothes and picked up some fresh clothing, as well as some equipment they thought they might need. On the way to Amanda's, they made a couple of stops for additional equipment they might need.

"Do you think he'll actually show at Amanda's?" Tweeter asked Sarah.

"I doubt it," she replied, "but he or someone else is probably watching her apartment, maybe via some hidden cameras. But in any case, I think we have to play it out, just in case."

"What do you want to do with him if he does show?" Tweeter asked, and edge of menace in his voice.

"I don't want him harmed," she warned, "unless he gives us no choice. He has information I need. And I'd like to give him a bit of guidance about his future."

Much to her surprise – even shock – 'Win' answered his phone when Amanda called. Without much in the way of an exchange of pleasantries, he said, "Glad we finally connected. I'm going to be in San Fran tomorrow and was hoping we could get together tomorrow night."

As she had been coached by Boone, she said, "I'd like that very much. It's been awhile."

"Great," he said. "I'll call when I know what time I'll be free."

"Win," she blurted, "did you get my message when I tried to call you after you left me at LAX."

"Yeah, I did," he said dismissively.

"I wish you'd called me back. Captain Aglee was positive he recognized you as the man who went missing from his ship after that incident in the Gulf of Alaska."

"I didn't bother calling back because that was total bullshit. He was mistaken. I remember clearly that I heard about that oil spill when I was in New Orleans. And I can assure you that I have never even been on an oil tanker. So with that behind us, I can't wait to see you tomorrow. I'll bring the wine. Dress appropriately."

"I can't wait, either, and I will," she said.

Amanda was disgusted with herself. The man was treating her like a sex-crazed slut. *I'll bring the wine and you dress appropriately – meaning wear nothing – and I'll just waltz in, pour a little wine down your throat and then fuck your brains out.* See you whenever it next suits me. And most frustrating to Amanda was that she could feel her panties dampen even as she was talking to the son of a bitch. *Jesus Christ! Am I nuts?*

Sarah and Tweeter arrived in the early evening and had some difficulty finding a visitors parking space. Sarah called Amanda to let her know they were there, and when she knocked on the door, Amanda flung it open and hugged her, then greeted Tweeter with a tentative hug as well.

"I talked with Win this afternoon and he's coming by tomorrow night. I recorded the call so you can listen to it."

Sarah told her that Tweeter would be serving as her 24-hours-a-day bodyguard for a while, then sat down next to Boone to listen to the call. While she listened, Tweeter used an electronic device to search the apartment for listening or video recording devices.

After listening to Amanda's recorded phone call, Sarah told the group that she thought they should all remain in the apartment until the next night as they wait for Win – if he kept the date. She said she wished Amanda had not mentioned the run-in at LAX, but it could not be undone so they would live with it.

Amanda was a nervous wreck after her phone call and her moment of self-realization as a result of it. She was now thinking of herself as a slut first, a reporter second and a part of this investigation third.

And she became more nervous when Tweeter began setting up hidden video cameras and voice recorders in the living room, kitchen and Amanda's bedroom. Then he began laying out his weapons and Amanda began sobbing.

Boone pulled out his cell phone and told Sarah he was going to call Aglee and keep him up to date with what was happening. Sarah told him that was a good idea. It was important to keep him on their team. And

Amanda's mention of him in her call to Win made it advisable that Aglee be extra-careful as well.

Amanda pulled Sarah into the kitchen and told her how she was feeling. "I can't believe how I behaved with Win," she said, tears leaking from her eyes. "He treated me like nothing more than a sperm receptacle and I kept going for it. And the sick thing is I really enjoyed it all, even though weeks would go by without any contact. What the hell is wrong with me, Sarah?"

Sarah held her friend's hand and said, "Amanda, you're not the first woman – or man either, for that matter – who has let lust over-rule good judgment. You're a good person, Amanda, so all you can do is learn from it and move on."

Time passed slowly, and after watching television mindlessly for a couple of hours, they all went to bed. Sarah and Boone shared the guest bedroom and Tweeter bunked on the couch in the living room.

The next day, time passed even more slowly. Amanda offered to cook breakfast for them when they had all got out of bed. Nobody was hungry and coffee and toast was enough for them.

Time continued to crawl by. Tweeter rechecked his cameras and voice recorders, cleaned and checked his weapons. Boone thought he had been in Amanda's apartment for a year.

Four o'clock came and went, with no word from Win.

Six o'clock came and went, still no word from Win.

Sarah asked Amanda to call Win. She did. There was no answer and she left a message asking if he knew how soon he'd be there, that she was anxious to see him. She disgusted herself again with the coquettish tone of voice she was able to summon in a desperate attempt to appeal to the scum-sucking son of a bitch.

Eight o'clock came and went. So did nine, then ten. No word from Win.

"Fucker must have seen Sarah and me arrive," Tweeter observed. "Or a watcher reported it to him."

It was clearly time to call it a night. It was decided that Sarah and Boone would head back to Monterey, even though they would get in quite late. They had work to do the next day. Tweeter would stay, sleeping in the living room again that night, and changing the locks, adding double dead bolts and having an alarm system installed the next day.

"Is all this necessary?" Amanda asked, although in her heart she knew the answer.

"Damn right it is," Boone said forcefully.

As they drove down Highway 101 in the direction of Monterey, Boone asked Sarah, "Do you think we'll be able to find Win – or Jet?"

"In time, but I think something - either yesterday or earlier – spooked him and he's deep under cover. I just don't know if we'll find him in the two weeks we have." Sarah made a number of phone calls and sent several emails on the drive to Monterey. They drove to Sarah's apartment and fell immediately into bed, too exhausted to think of anything else.

In the CFRG office the next day, Sarah continued her quest. She reviewed all the documents she had and checked with Slump, who had stayed overnight in New Orleans to continue working with Sandy Agria. They had matched some things that were interesting, but were not finished, he told her.

Late that afternoon, Sarah stood up, walked into Boone's office, grabbed him and, using both her mouth and her hands, let him know she had plans for him. Soon.

"Let's go home now. We're still exhausted and we need some time together."

Boone required no further encouragement.

As they walked to Sarah's apartment, Boone asked her if she had had any luck in finding Jet/Win.

"Not even a decent lead," she admitted with a sigh. "Let's not think about it anymore tonight, though. Maybe a little wine, some time to relax and other things we'll find to occupy ourselves and my thinking will clear up."

Boone opened a bottle of wine and poured two glasses. He started to hand the wine to Sarah, who had been behind him, but she was not there. He walked into the bedroom, where he found her, already undressed and in bed. He handed her a glass and raised his in a toast. "Here's to relaxation and a clearer mind."

Sarah took a sip, set her glass down and pulled Boone down on top of her, almost causing him to spill his glass. "How do you plan to relax me and clear my mind with your clothes on?" she whispered. In a remarkably short time, Boone's glass was on the nightstand, his clothes were draped over a chair and he was in bed with her.

After a little more wine, a couple of naps sandwiched between repeats of the relaxation and mind-clearing procedure Boone applied with intense dedication, Sarah suddenly shot up in bed and exclaimed, "I've got it! I know where he is." Then she laid back on her pillow.

Boone smiled and said, "See, I seldom fail in my duties as relaxer-in-chief. Now, are you going to tell me where he is?" She did not answer and when he looked over he saw that she was already asleep. He draped his arm around her waist and was soon asleep as well.

When Boone awoke, Sarah was already out of bed and he could smell the coffee brewing. He walked into the kitchen, hugged her, and was about to ask again where Jet was when she announced, "We're going to San Diego today."

"You think he's in San Diego?" Boone asked, surprised. He had assumed Jet would have left the country.

"Yes. I think he's at the Del Coronado," she said, referring to the most famous and stately old structure in the San Diego area.

"If he's hiding, why in the world would he be in such a public place?"

"Because he thinks that's the last place I'd look. Haven't you ever heard of that old saying, 'hiding in plain sight?'"

Her voice was smug and had the tone of certainty to it. She asked Boone to start breakfast while she made some phone calls. After breakfast, they dressed, retrieved Boone's car from in front of the CFRG office and left for the airport. Boone had been surprised to see Sarah when she emerged from her bedroom. She was dressed in an abaya.

Once again, Sarah had become Zara.

CHAPTER 38

MONTEREY, CA
THAT MORNING

Sarah had a small jet on standby for the two weeks of her FBI-sanctioned investigation window.

Thus, ShareJet was waiting, crew in place and fueled, at the Monterey Peninsula Airport when Zara and Boone walked up to it. Boone was surprised to find one of the Huff twins already aboard when he entered the cabin.

"Hi, Slump," Zara greeted him. "Do you have everything we talked about?"

"They're right here," he said, patting two large briefcases. Zara nodded.

"Boone, you remember Slump, do you not?" Zara asked. She had slipped into her more formal manner of speech with the transformation to the Zara persona.

Boone put out his hand to shake Slump's. "I thought it was Tweeter and that he'd abandoned Amanda."

"No, he's still sitting on her," Slump assured him. The image of the literal translation of that statement amused Boone greatly.

"Just before I left New Orleans last night, I got some good news," Slump announced triumphantly. "The *Sealer* is docked at Coronado."

"What's the *Sealer*?" Boone asked.

"Jet's boat," Zara answered simply. When they were airborne, Zara picked up the air phone and called the Hotel Del Coronado. Over many stays at the hotel, she had developed a friendship with its Assistant Director of Security, who – despite his mainly Aryan features – Zara knew to be a Kuwaiti native.

An hour after takeoff, they were pulling up to the general aviation terminal at Lindbergh Field in San Diego, where a Lincoln Town Car awaited them. While on the aircraft, Zara had made sure that Slump briefed Boone on the use of a Taser stun gun and both men carried one when they got in the car. Carrying it made Boone more nervous than he was already.

Zara told them again that if Jet did anything to her, they were to hit him with the Tasers. She told them not to worry about her, that there was no way Jet would be armed or wearing any body armor. Their job was to put him on the ground if he tried anything with her.

When they pulled up in front of the hotel, the Assistant Security Manager was waiting for them. Zara spoke with him for a couple of minutes and he disappeared through the front door. She turned to Boone and Slump and said, "He's out on the deck having mimosas with a young lady. Slump, you go around and approach the deck from the south and Boone and I will go the other way. Jet is supposed to be facing south. You both just stand at each end of the deck as I approach them. Questions?"

"Only a comment," Boone said. "I'm nervous." He was not smiling.

Zara patted him on the arm and said, "You'll do fine. Just Taser the bastard if he does anything stupid."

Jet, sipping his mimosa, tore his eyes from his very striking and very young companion when he noticed a man standing at the south end of the deck watching him. The man looked familiar, and suddenly he realized it was one of the Huff twins.

At that same moment, his friend, whose breasts were fighting a fierce battle to remain covered under a bikini top with less material than a medium-sized bandage, leaned forward and said, "Like, what the hell is an Arab woman with all that shit on doing out on a sun deck?" His mind now on full alarm, Jet whirled around just as Zara reached their table. There were few others on the deck, which Zara considered very fortunate. The sun was bright, but the temperature was comfortable.

"Hello, Jet, or Win, or does it really matter?" Zara asked as she hovered over him, only her cold, piercing eyes visible. "How nice to see you again after all this time. May I join you and your friend?" Without waiting for an answer, she sat down and nodded to the girl. "My name is Zara. What is yours?"

The girl looked like she might faint. Surely this Arab was not some old girlfriend, or an ex-wife. "Tiffany," she said faintly at last.

"What a nice name," Zara said, sarcasm dripping from her voice, "but Jet and I need to talk a few minutes, so why don't you just go to your room and slip into something more comfortable?"

"We don't have anything to discuss, Zara," Jet said but his voice lacked conviction. Zara handed him a sealed envelope and suggested he open it. He saw a wanted poster with his photograph on it and a $1,000,000 reward advertised.

"Great photo of you, don't you think?" Zara asked teasingly. "And the fingerprints and DNA information is a nice touch, don't you think? Did we miss anything?"

"Can I see your picture?" Tiffany asked. She pronounced it "pitcher."

"Tiff," Jet said quietly, perspiration now flowing down his face as if he was under a shower, "why don't you go wait for me in the room? This is business and I need to talk to her privately."

"Why," Tiffany whined. "I want to stay!"

Jet got up and lifted her up from her chair and somewhat roughly pushed her in the direction of the hotel doorway. She stalked off in a huff.

Zara looked at Jet, her eyes showing disgust. "Where do you find these bimbos?"

He ignored the question, instead asking, "Is that Tweeter?"

"No, it's Slump, although I guess it could be Tweeter. He's here to make sure you don't do anything stupid." She nodded her head to the north and added, "And the other one watching you is Boone."

"What do you want?" he asked, all his senses on alert. Zara realized at that time that he knew he had gambled and lost. She slid one of the FBI ankle bracelet monitors toward him, turning it on as she did so.

"You disappointed me, Jet," she said, a touch of sadness in her voice. "I believed you were loyal and could control your innate greed. I knew I could never trust Akrum when money was involved, but I gave you more credit than that. Now, you have put me in, shall we say, an unstable position; one however, that I will resolve."

She paused and stared at him, her eyes now back to the icy hardness that made men fear her, and continued. "As I see it, you have only two options today. The first is arrest, which will certainly be followed by a trial and a long time in jail. The second is to cooperate fully with me. If you do so, and I get the information I need, you have a reasonable chance to remain free. And just so there will be no misunderstanding on your part, if you try to leave before we have finished our discussion, you will be disabled by 50,000 volts of electricity by one of the gentlemen who are watching us, and after that you will be placed under arrest for multiple counts, including murder in the first degree."

Jet was looking down at the ankle bracelet. "You're working with the FBI?" he asked bleakly.

"With a team in the Hoover Building in Washington, headed by Chief Inspector Clyde Peed. In your line of work, I thought maybe you were familiar with the name. Are you?"

Jet nodded. "I have heard people say that 'you don't want to be Peed on by Clyde.'" Despite his misery, Jet managed a weak smile. Now he was certain that he was screwed. He remained silent as he stared at the bracelet and took a sip of his mimosa. But he had to hand it to Zara. She was one cool cookie. Never sought revenge; her only goal was to stay in the game and keep winning.

Finally, after a deep sigh, he said, "You can call me Mr. Information today."

Zara did not change her tone of voice or the look in her eyes. "Good," she said quietly. "First, tell me about Akrum's deal with Pure Earth and how you were involved."

"He had two deals with them," Jet said. "The first was to arrange the oil incidents. Pure Earth and Akrum both – for different reasons, of course – wanted to force the President to reverse his oil drilling policy. You know what the goals of the incidents were. Then, after they reached their agreement, Akrum came up with the idea of forming the cartel and getting you to head it. It was a designed double dip from the beginning, and neither Pure Earth nor the cartel – you – were to be aware of the other."

"Who was Akrum's contact with Pure Earth?" she asked.

"He worked with Kirk Klenner himself," he said. "Nobody else."

"I presume Pure Earth was not as concerned as the cartel over any injuries or deaths in the course of the facilitations." Jet smiled at her use of her old term.

"Not at all. They almost encouraged them. Thought they'd get a bigger bang for the buck if workers were killed."

"When did you become involved?" She was ticking questions off from the notebook in her head.

"From the day Akrum first presented his plan to Klenner. Day one, in other words."

"Where is Akrum now?"

"I believe you would find him at his home in Saudi Arabia. And, incidentally, I think it's safe to say he has no plans to return in the near future. I think he gave up the Ambassador assignment a couple of years ago so he'd have the freedom to get out of Dodge quickly if the need arose."

"You mentioned a second arrangement."

"It was called Vornado. I wasn't involved with it, but I heard bits and pieces about it when I was with Akrum and Klenner on the other stuff. Vornado was a political deal. A super-pac or whatever you want to call it. It was to slip secret money to candidates for office. Donors to those super-pacs are anonymous and they can give unlimited amounts of money. I understood that the money came from just a few parties."

"Who?"

"I don't know where Pure Earth got its money for Vornado, but I had the feeling all the dough Akrum put in it was from Middle Eastern sources, primarily Saudi Arabia."

"What candidates did they support? Do you know?"

"It was my impression that in the last election, all the money went to one candidate."

Zara was stunned. "Are you talking about the current President of the United States?"

"I am," Jet replied solemnly.

"As far as you know, was there any documentation kept about Vornado's contributions?"

"Shit," he snorted. "Klenner is a paperwork freak. He wanted documentation for everything. Every fucking cent we spent on gear for our facilitations had to be accounted for. I told Akrum he was nuts for doing that, but what the hell. I'll bet every damn bit of it is in the Pure Earth computer system somewhere."

Zara sat in thought and Jet sipped again at his mimosa.

"Jet," she said finally, "you have seven days, then the FBI will track you down and arrest you. The warrant has already been issued, and all airports, ports and border crossings have been ordered to detain you if they find you and hold you for the FBI. You're being given the seven days to see if you can be any more help to me, but Peed told me that if I found you to tell you the only way they will give you those seven days is if I put that monitor on you."

"Do I have to put this on?" he asked.

Zara stared hard at him. "You can if you like, but it may serve you better just to carry it, if you get my meaning. And remember, Jet, seven days."

Jet understood what she was saying to him. "Thanks, Zara," he said, sincerely grateful.

As Zara rose, she added, "And Jet, for the next seven days, please answer your cell phone if I call you."

He nodded as he rose from the table. "Sorry this didn't work out."

"Greed and lust are difficult instincts to overcome," she said without rancor. "Now, why don't you go back in that nice hotel and service that stupid bimbo? And I hope in the future you will come to realize what a prize you had – and threw away – in Amanda." She paused and decided to ask one last question. "By the way, what is your real name?"

"Win or Jet are good enough," he muttered as he walked off toward the hotel. "It really doesn't matter."

Zara motioned for Boone and Slump to join her and they walked back to the car and the ride to the airport. The jet was waiting to take them next to New Orleans.

Once airborne, Zara went into the rear of the cabin, pulled a curtain across the aisle and emerged as Sarah. "I think I'll put Zara away for a while," she announced to the bemused smiles of Boone and Slump.

Then she called Tweeter to make sure all was still okay with Amanda. She briefed him on her conversation in San Diego and suggested he be extra vigilant for a couple of days. She knew that was a waste of breath as soon as she said it. The Huff twins were always vigilant.

Sandy Agria was waiting again at Lakefront Airport when they landed in New Orleans. Sarah told Boone and Slump that she wanted a private word with Sandy and they walked off to get sandwiches.

Sandy handed Sarah a thumb drive and said, "This is the information you asked for. It covers all Pure Earth records regarding al-Kahtani, Jamieson and the five oil spill incidents. I think you'll find it's all there: selection of incident targets, payments to both men, itemized lists of equipment needed for the incidents, Klenner's involvement and – I couldn't believe this stuff was in the system – memos from Klenner to both men."

"Will these records still be available on the computers when they are subpoenaed?" Sarah asked.

"Absolutely," Sandy assured her. "I've made it very difficult for them to be completely deleted from the system and I've backed them up in three different ways."

"I'd guess you should be prepared for that investigation to come to Houston very soon," Sarah said.

"I'll be ready," Sandy replied, smiling broadly.

"What about the other issue – the political deal? If my information is correct, its code name was Vornado."

"I've found a lot of unusual transactions involving a hell of a lot of money," she said. "Big amounts coming into Pure Earth's accounts and being quickly shipped back out to a group of 20 or 25 organizations, none of which I've seen in our finance system before."

"Do you know what these funds are used for by these organizations?"

"Not yet," Sandy said, "but I think Pure Earth controlled all of them. They may just be shells. The Vornado name might help. I'll keep looking."

Sarah held Sandy's forearm tightly and said, "Sandy, this is extremely important and time gets more critical by the hour. I need to find out about Vornado in the next two or three days, maximum."

"I've recruited some help and we're working virtually around the clock," Sandy assured her.

"I appreciate what you've done so far, Sandy. Keep me posted and don't forget, if Vornado turns out to be what I think it is, I'll want it permanently deleted from their system once you've run it for me." Sandy nodded and hurried off. She did not understand why the stuff they had on al-Kahtani, Jamieson and Klenner needed to be secured so it could be found in an investigation but Vornado should disappear after being copied, but she knew Sarah always had a reason for what she wanted.

Sarah found Boone and Slump in the snack bar and they headed back toward the plane and the flight back to Monterey.

Once aboard, Boone said, "You look pleased."

"Oh, I am," Sarah said. "Pure Earth, Klenner personally, Akrum and Jet are all tied into the planning and implementation of all five oil spills that have occurred since the President has been in office."

"Will this be what the FBI needs?" Boone asked.

"Absolutely," she said. "Mr. Kirk Klenner will be in for a real surprise."

"What about Akrum and Jet?"

"I suspect Akrum will remain in Saudi Arabia and because of diplomatic immunity – he still holds a diplomatic passport - he'll walk." Jet will most likely just disappear before the FBI can find him."

"And Pure Earth?"

"Finished. They'll never recover. Klenner will go to jail for a long time and nobody will touch the organization, except for lawyers for the oil companies that have suffered losses, not to mention the families of those killed in the incidents."

"When will we turn the information over to the FBI?" Boone asked.

Sarah noted with significant satisfaction that Boone had used the plural, "we."

"Sandy still has some work to do for me and I want to wait until she's finished," she said.

"What about?" Boone asked.

"Just more of Pure Earth's slimy activities that may be connected."

Slump's seat was reclined and he was sound asleep. It had, indeed, been a long day already and Boone took Slump's lead. Sarah spent the rest of the flight looking through the contents of the latest thumb drive in detail.

It was after midnight when they landed in Monterey. Slump left immediately for San Mateo to relieve Tweeter on the Amanda watch. Boone and Sarah went straight to her apartment.

For the next two days, Sarah worked hard to review, organize and catalog the information on the thumb drive. She wanted it in good order before she presented it to Peed.

Three days after the encounter with Jet Jamieson at the Hotel Del Coronado, Sarah was scanning online newspapers when a Los Angeles Times article caught her attention.

PLEASURE BOAT COLLIDES WITH OIL TANKER

Long Beach – A 45-foot pleasure boat exploded and sank about one mile outside of Long Beach Harbor after colliding with a large oil tanker. The tanker, Prince, a Royal Energy vessel, was inbound to Long Beach when the collision occurred in clear weather.

The pleasure boat was identified by a piece of the fantail as The Sealer. The Times has been able to confirm that The Sealer was based in San Diego and was owned by Mr. Jet Jamieson.

Sources at Royal Energy told The Times that the pleasure boat failed to take evasive action as it approached the Prince at high speed and collided with the tanker in the stern area of the ship. Those sources indicate that the pleasure boat exploded and burst into flames following the collision, sinking almost immediately. No bodies were found.

The Prince immediately radioed the Coast Guard, which was on the scene in minutes. A Coast Guard spokesman in Long Beach confirmed the pleasure boat's identity and told The Times that only scattered debris was left in the area, including the piece of fantail, a life preserver and several pieces of charred clothing. A heavily-damaged jacket found at the scene contained items that identified it as belonging to Mr. Jamieson, according to the Coast Guard.

In addition, the Coast Guard found several thousand dollars in charred currency, mostly $100 and $20 bills, was found on the surface *around the crash site, leading to speculation the boat may have been involved in the drug trade.*

An employee at the fueling station in the San Diego marina at which the pleasure boat was registered reported to the Coast Guard that Mr. Jamieson fueled the boat earlier in the morning. He reported that Mr. Jamieson appeared agitated and drank three beers while his boat was being fueled. He reported that Mr. Jamieson appeared to be alone on the boat, and seemed in a hurry to leave.

Attempts to reach Mr. Jamieson by the Coast Guard proved futile. He is being classified by the Coast Guard as missing at sea and presumed dead.

After reading the article, Sarah – who was not surprised by it – called Clyde Peed at the FBI. Patrick Moblox was in Peed's office when the call came in, and Peed put the call on speaker.

"I assume you've heard about the collision between Jet Jamieson's boat and the oil tanker down in Long Beach," she said.

"We heard," Peed confirmed. "We had one of our people out there. Choppered her from the Los Angeles Field Office out to the first Coast Guard cutter on the scene. She reported that nothing of substance was found except for our ankle monitor; as you may know they're made to float, specifically for circumstances like this. It was damaged but recognizable from its serial number. And it had Jamieson's blood on it."

"What does your agent have to say about it?" Sarah asked. Boone walked into her office just then, having seen the online story, too. She put her phone on speaker.

"The working theory at this point is he was trying to leave the country. Why he ran from San Diego up to Los Angeles is anybody's guess, but we're assuming he was going to pick somebody up before turning around and heading for Mexico. His boat had a hell of a fuel capacity."

"Did she find any documents or anything like that – a thumb drive in any of the clothing that was recovered, for instance – that might tie him to al-Kahtani and Pure Earth?"

"Nothing. No documents could have survived the explosion and fire unless they were thrown free on impact, like some of the clothes. The fire was apparently pretty intense. The fueling guy in San Diego told us that Jamieson had two auxiliary fuel tanks jerry-rigged in the boat. We're trying to run a trace on the money we found. But if he was rabbiting, it's natural that he'd take as much cash with him as he could."

Sarah looked at Boone, whose shrug told her he had no additional questions.

"I should have my investigation into the Pure Earth matter wrapped up in another three days or so," she said. "What I have so far clearly supports the conspiracy between Pure Earth, al-Kahtani and Jamieson. I'll bring it all to your office as soon as I have it."

"Thanks, Sarah. Keep me posted on your progress," Peed said, then added, "and your whereabouts."

"My whereabouts?" she asked incredulously. "You know where I am as well as I do. I'm keeping that monitor on me at all times. That was part of our agreement." Her face was flushed.

"Keep in touch," Peed said again and disconnected the call. She was left to wonder what that was all about.

"Are they certain Jet is dead?" Boone asked her.

"They believe so. His boat was loaded with fuel and money and he was running, racing through busy shipping lanes at an unsafe speed."

"Do you believe he's dead?" Boone asked in a low voice.

Sarah thought a moment, then said, "For our purposes, I believe he is dead."

CHAPTER 39

MONTEREY, CALIFORNIA
LATER THAT DAY

Not long after Sarah talked with Peed and Moblox at the FBI, her computer pinged, indicating a new email. She saw it was from Sandy Agria and opened it immediately.

"Bingo," it said. *"Call me."*

She did.

Sandy was breathless. "You need to come back here as soon as you can. I've got a lot of data for you to look at. The code name you gave me, Vornado, was the key. It was like 'Open, Sesame.'"

"Is it complete?" Sarah asked anxiously. "Documented?"

"Absolutely," Sandy said. "That idiot Klenner is a stickler for complete, detailed records."

Sarah looked at her watch and said, "We should be able to get there by about 4:00 this afternoon, your time. I'll call you en route to confirm arrival at Houston Hobby."

Not much over an hour after her call to Sandy, Sarah, Boone and Slump Huff – who had turned Amanda back over to Tweeter - boarded the ShareJet, which had still been sitting at the Monterey Peninsula airport when she had called them. Once airborne, Sarah called Sandy to confirm their expected arrival at 3:35 p.m., and Boone called Moblox at the FBI to tell him they would like to meet with him and Peed the next morning. Moblox checked quickly with Peed and the meeting was set.

Sandy Agria was again waiting when the jet taxied up to the executive terminal at Houston Hobby Airport. Sarah asked Boone and Slump to review once more the information they had for the FBI while she talked with Sandy, who looked both tired and excited.

Sandy handed Sarah another thumb drive and said, "You'll be very pleased, I think, with what's on this."

"I could use some good news," Sarah said. "Let's see what you have."

They found an empty conference room, went in and closed the door. Sandy put the thumb drive in her computer and booted it up. It was all there. The Vornado plan was outlined, with amazingly precise documentation.

The flow of money began with detailed recordings of the flow of money from Saudi banks to ERIN – *What the hell?* Sarah thought when she saw that name – to Pure Earth's offshore accounts to 25 other entities to political action committees and super-pacs and finally to one individual candidate.

Sarah sat back, stunned by the enormity of it all. "Wow!" she said. "This is much more than I expected. This could be the basis for a textbook on how to buy an election."

"I was surprised myself," Sandy admitted. "Especially that it was so well-documented and still in the Pure Earth computer system."

"Can you permanently delete all traces of these transactions?" Sarah asked.

"Already done," Sandy said as she handed Sarah two back-up thumb drives.

"What about any paper documents?"

"They've all been scanned into the computer system and shredded." She handed Sarah two additional thumb drives, these of a different color so Sarah would not get them confused.

"All of the records on these drives have been deleted from the system?" Sarah asked. "I just want to confirm in my own mind that when the FBI investigators start looking, they won't find any of these files."

"Not a one," Sandy confirmed. She wondered why Sarah did not want the FBI to find these, but she was being paid very well and would defer, of course, to Sarah's judgment.

"Great job, Sandy," Sarah said with a sincere smile. "You're good. I'll wire the rest of your money now, with a bonus for your hard work."

"Thank you, Sarah."

"Do you think you're in any danger now at Pure Earth?" Sarah asked. "Or from Klenner personally."

"I don't think so, depending on how the FBI handles it," she said. "But I gave my notice last week."

"Slump will stay here and stay close in case you need help," Sarah said.

Sandy left with Slump. Sarah asked a man at the flight operations desk if there was a post office and a secure storage facility nearby. He told her the post office was about four miles away and a secure storage facility about six miles away. He gave her directions to both. Sarah and Boone took a cab to the post office, asking the driver to wait. She mailed one small package, registered mail, to a post office box in Washington, D.C.

The cab then took them to the storage facility where Sarah rented a small secure storage room, purchased a fire-proof lock box and paid in cash for three years' rent. The cab then drove Sarah and Boone back to the executive terminal at Houston Hobby Airport.

On the ShareJet, now bound for Reagan National, Boone looked over at Sarah, who was busy studying the new information she had just received. "You look very pleased with yourself," he said. She had been hearing that a lot in the past few days.

"I'm feeling better," she admitted. "It was touch and go for a while, but I think things might work out for us."

"Are you going to tell me about what Sandy gave you today?"

Sarah leaned across the aisle and gave him a kiss on the cheek. "No," she said firmly. "It relates to something else entirely that's more, let's say, lobbying-related. But more importantly, I think it's safer for you if you don't know what's on these drives."

Boone leaned back, disappointment etching his handsome face. "Oh, hell. What am I going to do with you?"

"Just love and tolerate me," she said softly.

After landing in Washington, they took a cab to Sarah's condo and went through their final plan for the FBI meeting the next day.

Patrick Moblox was waiting for them in the lobby of the FBI building when Sarah and Boone stepped out of the cab. He whisked them through the sign-in process and up to the same conference room they had used before, where Clyde Peed was waiting for them.

After quick greetings, Peed got right to business. "What have you got for us?"

Sarah handed Peed a thumb drive. "Everything on this was downloaded from Pure Earth's computer system, and is still on the system so your folks can find it for themselves. You'll find details of their agreement with Akrum al-Kahtani, and through him, Jet Jamieson, to plan and execute the five recent oil incidents".

Peed put the thumb drive in the port of his laptop and spent five minutes reviewing it.

"This is a gold mine," he said as he looked to Moblox, who was peering at the screen as well. Then to Sarah, "This should make an easy case, I think, against Pure Earth, Klenner personally, al-Kahtani and – if we need it – Jamieson."

"We thought so," Boone said.

"Why the hell would they keep stuff like this on their computer?" Peed asked Sarah.

"According to my source, Klenner is a real records freak and insisted on everything being recorded in detail," she said. "But I'd suggest you move quickly on this, before their records get destroyed."

"Why?" Peed asked. "Is there any indication they might we wise to this?"

"Just that with al-Kahtani out of the country – let's assume permanently – and Jamieson dead, Klenner might get nervous and realize how much at risk he is with these records around," she said.

Peed paused, then asked Sarah a question out of the blue. "You sometimes use the name, 'Zara al-Kahtani,' do you not?"

"Why are you asking a question that we both know the answer to?" she responded dryly.

"I'll take that as a 'yes'," Peed said. "The next question is why?"

"Both are my names," Sarah said, defiance in her voice. "In some situations, and with some clients, the Zara persona fits better and in some the Sarah persona works better. As you're undoubtedly aware, Akrum al-Kahtani is my biological father, although we've certainly never had what you would call a normal father-daughter relationship."

Moblox looked at Boone and asked, "Were you aware of this?"

"Yes, I was," he answered in an unapologetic tone.

Peed still stared at Sarah. "Now I must ask this: did you – or Zara – have any involvement with al-Kahtani and Jamieson in relation to any of these oil incidents?"

Sarah did not hesitate. "Akrum is my father and, as you would imagine, I have been in periodic contact with him – before, during and after the incidents. Jet is someone I have engaged a few times over the years to provide research and investigative services on behalf of my clients. But as far as Pure Earth and the oil incidents are concerned..."

Just then, her cell phone buzzed and she glanced at the read-out. "Excuse me, this call may have a bearing on this case."

She hit the 'talk' button and said, "Yes, Slump, what is it?"

She listened and said, "What happened? Go over that slowly." More listening. "When?" More listening. "Is she okay?" Then: "How much damage? Is there security there? Any other injuries? Okay, thanks. Talk with you later."

But then, the three men at the table were looking on in some alarm.

"Gentlemen," Sarah intoned, "it seems that someone has tried to set fire to the Pure Earth computer room. When one of the employees saw the fire, she pulled the fire alarm and activated the carbon dioxide fire suppressant system." She looked around the table, saw that she had everyone's complete attention.

"She was then attacked," Sarah continued, "and beaten by one of the intruders – there were two of them – but one escaped. Actually, Slump Huff, who works with me, ran him off after he heard the commotion and intervened. Slump said the employee left some bruises and fingernail scratches on the intruder, so she'll have his DNA under her fingernails."

"What about the other one?" Peed asked. Moblox was already on the phone to the Houston Field Office.

"The second one is dead," Sarah said. "Apparently suffocated when the fire suppressant system went off. He was locked in and unable to get out of the room in time. The injured employee is in a hospital."

She stared at the FBI men, waiting for a response. When none was immediately forthcoming, Sarah said in a heated voice, "Then, gentlemen, I'd suggest we've exhausted this discussion, so let's break it up and you can get off your asses and get your agents in Houston over to the Pure Earth headquarters. And put some protection around the injured employee."

Peed and Moblox looked at each other, shocked to speechlessness. People did not talk to FBI agents like that. Finally, Peed asked her if she knew the identity of the injured employee. She told them her name. "Sandy Agria."

"Do you know this woman, by any chance?" Peed asked. She nodded in the affirmative.

"What's your relationship with her?" he asked.

"Goddammit, Peed, you're starting to piss me off. I know a lot of people and have worked with a lot of people over the years. Now, I've just solved the case of a career for you and instead of moving, you're still sitting here asking dumb questions. Do the job this country hired you to do and go arrest Kirk Klenner."

"You get off your high horse right now, Sarah," Peed said, clearly angry. "Patrick has already talked with our field office and they've got agents on the way already. You can believe this or not, but we're pretty good at connecting the dots, so it's not hard to figure that Klenner set up the fire to get rid of the evidence on the computer. For that reason, our best electronic forensics expert in Houston is on his way, too."

Sarah gathered her papers and started to rise.

"Where are you going?" Peed asked. Sarah sat back down and gave him her coldest, most intimidating stare for a good half minute.

Then she said, "We're going to Houston before heading back to Monterey."

"Is there room on your plane for us?" Peed asked. "It would be faster than trying to arrange for a Bureau plane."

Sarah smiled and nodded her head. "Yes, but we're leaving now."

"I understand," he said. "Can you give us ten minutes to gather what we need? We'll have a Bureau Suburban take us to the airport."

"Sure," she said, quietly now.

Peed stuck out his hand. "Partners again?"

"Deal," she said.

Ten minutes later, they were on their way to Reagan National.

The jet was met at Houston Hobby by two FBI Suburbans. One took Peed and Moblox to the Pure Earth offices while the second took Sarah and Boone to the hospital to visit Sandy Agria.

On the way to Pure Earth, Moblox said to Peed, "Sarah didn't answer your last question, whether she had any involvement in any of the spills. Her phone call changed the subject for her."

"I know," Peed said.

"There's more to Sarah Cotton than we know, I think."

"Yes, much more," Peed acknowledged. "But now's not the time to press it. Maybe later. For now, this case is the priority. She may be right. This could be the case of a career."

Meanwhile, Sarah and Boone arrived at the hospital and found Sandy Agria in Room 413. Slump and an FBI man were posted in the corridor outside her room. It looked like Slump had made his peace with the FBI man. The Feds were known not to like working with amateurs.

Sarah and Boone took quick stock of the young woman they saw on the bed with a collection of tubes sticking out of her. She had a broken right arm, what appeared to be a broken nose, plus numerous scrapes and contusions. She was happy to see them.

"Hi!" she exclaimed, with some effort. "I'm surprised to see you, though."

"How are you doing?" Sarah asked.

"It could have been a lot worse."

"What happened, if you can talk about it now?"

Sandy took a few breaths before she spoke. "I went to the computer room to make sure everything was okay after I came back from lunch. Slump was in my office. There was a man in the room with two big gas cans. I'd guess they were three gallons each, at least. He was pouring gas directly onto the computers and on the floor around them. When he saw me through the window in the door, he emptied the first can and lit it. I saw him coming toward the door, so I locked it from the outside and hit the fire suppression system and alarm."

She paused and took some more deep breaths, then continued. "As I was backing away from the door, I was grabbed from behind by someone else, who I assume was with the guy inside. He hit my arm with a bar of some kind, and it turns out he broke it.

"But I was able to get in some licks and I think I hurt him. I scratched him across the face, and may have got one of his eyes. He sure screamed like I did. That's what Slump heard and he came running. I guess my self-defense classes paid off. Anyway, I assume the one in the room suffocated from the carbon dioxide."

"That's what we're told," Sarah said. "As far as we know, he hasn't been identified yet."

"Well, the important thing is that the fire suppression system works very quickly, so the computer files should be salvageable," Sandy said.

"Did you recognize the one who attacked you?" Sarah asked.

"I didn't get a look at him but I'd be willing to bet it was Kirk Klenner. I haven't told the police that yet."

Sarah called Peed on his cell and told him where they were and what Sandy had just told them about her attacker, stressing the word, think.

"Is our agent there yet to guard her room?" Peed asked.

"Yes, and an associate of mine – a man well capable of taking care of himself – is with him."

"We'll be there shortly," Peed said and hung up without waiting for a response.

Sarah looked down at Sandy and asked her if there was anything she needed.

"Just time," Sandy sighed. "But I'll be fine. Don't worry, and I do appreciate you coming by."

Sarah told her to be prepared for a lot of questions, some of them relentless and possibly brutal, especially regarding their past relationship. She told her to stick to the documentation of Pure Earth's involvement in the oil incidents. She reminded her that Peed had copies of the thumb drives.

"If he's got questions about anything but the oil incidents and what you found about Pure Earth's involvement, tell him you don't remember," Sarah said. "Or tell him he'll have to ask me." She reminded Sandy that

Peed and Moblox did not know about the second set of thumb drives, the ones dealing with the political money trail.

Finally, she told Sandy, "If he gets too aggressive and you think you'd like an attorney, tell him that and let me know. I'll be in touch, but we have to be careful at this stage. Peed has been cooperative, but he's still the FBI and he's on the scent of something big, so think your answers through carefully."

Sarah lightly hugged Sandy, Boone shook her hand and they left her in the room with her guards outside.

CHAPTER 40

During the flight back to Monterey, Sarah studied the last thumb drive Sandy had given her, reaching across the aisle from time to time to rub Boone's arm.

"It was nice of you to visit Sandy," Boone said. "And to leave Slump guarding her."

"She's loyal and did a hell of a job for us on this," Sarah said. "Remember the old saw about taking care of good help because it's hard to find." She poked Boone in the ribs.

"If you meant what I think you meant, I'm not sure who's working for whom," he said in rejoinder. "Most of the time, I feel like I'm working for you." But he was smiling.

"Boone Malory is the name on the bottom right corner of my paychecks," she said slyly. "That must mean I'm working for you."

Yeah, right! Boone thought to himself but remained silent.

Sarah returned her gaze to the screen of her laptop.

Suzy Dillinger was glad to see Boone and Sarah walk through the door the next morning. She had become the de facto office manager and had become perfectly capable of running the office by herself, but she was always happy to have them back.

They had arrived in Monterey the evening before and gone to Cannery Row for dinner. After their second glass of wine, Sarah had reached across the table and grabbed Boone's hand.

"I just want you to know that your support and concern really have helped me through what could have been a much more difficult time. I don't want to lose you."

Boone had almost choked. "I don't want to lose you, either." In truth, the thought had occupied his mind, off and on, continuously since Amanda and Captain Aglee had talked to him about Sarah's possible involvement in the oil incidents in the airport coffee shop.

After the dinner had arrived, he said, "This has been a tough month, hasn't it?"

"Yes, but I think we're making progress and the next couple of weeks will tell the tale." She had paused, lost in thought for a moment. "You know I love to win, but maybe even more I love playing the game, and I really want to stay in the game."

"What, exactly, are the details of the current game?" he had asked thoughtfully.

"Not tonight. I'll fill you in as the pieces start to fall into place. For tonight, I just want to go home. I'm full, a little tipsy and, like our friend, Amanda, a little horny."

"You mean you want to go to your apartment?"

"No, I mean I want to go *home*."

Boone had liked the sound of that – a lot.

And Sarah had been right. She had been horny.

The following morning, after greeting Suzy and the other staffers, Sarah went to her office. She intended to spend the next two days alone there, reviewing the massive list of documents on Sandy's last thumb drive. This one had information that she did not intend to share with Boone, Suzy or the FBI.

She took a call on her cell phone from Sandy Agria, who happily reported that the FBI men had not presented as much of a problem as she had been afraid they would. They grilled her about the workings of the Pure Earth organization and had a number of questions about Kirk Klenner. They had not asked about how she and Sarah had come to know each other. They had seemed sensitive to her medical condition and her need to convalesce, for which she was grateful.

Meanwhile, Boone spent his time pressing his campaign to reverse the President's oil exploration policy. His computer spit out a steady stream of media releases, newsletter articles and other public pronouncements.

Boone and Sarah were having breakfast in her apartment on their third day after returning to Monterey when Sarah said, "Boone, I need to talk about the next step I have in mind."

"I was wondering when you were going to start sharing what you've been working on," he said, just a shade sharply. That it had been gnawing at him was quite clear, however, and Sarah was not surprised by that. She was most surprised at the depth of Bonne's patience.

"I will need to resurrect Zara once more," she said, "and you'll need to accompany me to Scottsdale for a meeting."

"Okay," he said guardedly, "what are we doing?"

"I'll fill you in later, as soon as I've worked out the details and schedule. For now, I need more coffee."

Boone just sighed, got up and poured her more coffee.

Once in CFRG's office, Sarah called Clyde Peed and asked him if he would share with her the latest on the FBI investigation. From his tone of voice, he seemed to be in a very good mood.

"What you gave me on Pure Earth and its role in the incidents was golden," he said. "Totally accurate and corroborated by data on the Pure Earth computers. The fire didn't have any real effect on the system. Sandy Agria is almost certain Kirk Klenner is the one who attacked her – Mr. Huff also identified him from a photo line-up - but we haven't been able to locate him yet. Sandy's been very helpful, as you said she would be, and as soon as we locate Klenner, we'll file charges and put something out to the media."

"How is Sandy doing?"

"Seems to be fine. She's been released from the hospital and has gone to New Orleans, where she'll feel safer for a while. You friend, Mr. Huff went with her."

"That's great," Sarah said. She made a note to call her and Slump Huff as well. Then she remembered to call Amanda and Tweeter to check in on them. With Jet only reportedly dead, she was not yet ready to pull Tweeter's protection from Amanda. Still, she was almost positive that, whatever Jet's true status, Amanda would never hear from him again.

"Sarah," Peed continued, "Patrick and I really appreciate the work you did putting this case together for us, and I'm sure you'll get an official letter of appreciation from the FBI, too."

"No need for that," she said.

"One other question: Have you heard from Akrum al-Kahtani?"

"No, and I don't expect that I will," she said. "He's undoubtedly in Saudi Arabia and will stay there under the cover of diplomatic immunity."

"We'll keep watching for him. We've alerted all our field offices and U.S. Embassies around the world to keep an eye out for him." Peed appeared ready to ring off.

"Will you call me when you find Klenner?" she asked. "And before you put anything out to the media?

"I'll do that," he assured her. They hung up.

CHAPTER 41

The next morning, Sarah noted that Boone did not appear engrossed in anything important and walked into his office.

"What's new?" she asked rhetorically in greeting.

"I've just been wondering about something," Boone said, a bit uneasily. "Tweeter is still up in San Mateo, guarding Amanda, but Jet's been dead for a week. What's he guarding her from? I know he's your guy and all, but I'm just curious why you still have him sitting on her."

She was far from certain that Jet was dead, but Boone could not know that. Jet had always been the master of deception, of misdirection, and the fortunate timing of his demise seemed far too convenient, somehow manufactured. Still, she no longer thought Amanda was in danger. She could not testify against a dead man, and she would only become a threat to Jet if he were still alive and happened to be discovered.

"That's a good point, Boone," she said at length. "With everything else that's been going on, they just slipped my mind. I guess I could send him to New Orleans to help Slump with Sandy Agria."

"It would seem Sandy's the one in danger right now," Boone agreed. "But how about you? With Akrum at large and Klenner on the lamb, how can you be sure Akrum hasn't filled Klenner in about you? Klenner probably attacked Sandy. What's to keep him from coming after you?"

Sarah admitted she had not even considered that possibility and reluctantly conceded that Boone had a good point. She went to her office to call Amanda.

Amanda sounded hurried – or harried – when she answered her cell, and the background noise told Sarah that she was not in her apartment.

"I'm in the office," she said when she heard Sarah's voice. "When Tweeter heard about Win – Jet – he saw no reason I couldn't come back to work. I'm waiting to get into my editor's office to see if I can get turned loose to follow the Pure Earth story. Once the FBI is in a position to release what they have, it could be huge." She sounded excited, almost giddy.

"I didn't realize you were back at work," Sarah admitted. "Tweeter didn't tell me, and I thought he would have done that."

"I don't know why he didn't," Amanda said with what to Sarah's practiced ear sounded a false cheeriness.

"Well, I'm going to need him down here in the next day or so, so it's just as well you're back to your normal routine," Sarah said.

"In the next day or so?" Amanda asked, the cheeriness – false or otherwise – now gone from her voice.

"Is that a problem?" Sarah asked, her senses alerted.

"Uh, no," Amanda stuttered. "I suppose not. Oh, Sarah, can I call you back? I'm being called into the editor's office. Bye."

Sarah sat, wondering what was bothering Amanda. She called Tweeter and told him she would need him in Monterey the next day, that she was convening a cartel meeting in Scottsdale and she needed his help with the arrangements. She told him she had talked to Amanda, and would be talking with Slump, who would have to bring Sandy Agria with him unless Klenner was nabbed first.

"Tomorrow?" Tweeter asked, a bit bleakly.

What the hell is going on? The question roared in Sarah's head, but she said, "Yes, tomorrow. You can drive down in the morning. Meet me in my office when you get here." Tweeter acknowledged his orders and hung up.

The question kept roaring in Sarah's head, and she took a walk to see if that would clear her mind. Somewhere along Cannery Row, it hit her.

That goddamn Amanda is now getting it on with Tweeter. It was difficult to contemplate, but as she thought about it, it made a kind of sense. Tweeter was a big, good-looking, good-natured – most of the time, at least – guy. They had been thrown together for days in her apartment. Hormones had kicked in. Jet – Win – had betrayed her, then had died. At some level, at least, she could grasp it, although she wondered whether a midlife crisis had hit Amanda early and hard.

Tweeter appeared in Sarah's office late the next morning, greeting her and closing the door behind him. The roaring question in Sarah's head had not subsided. She stood over Tweeter and demanded, "How long have you been screwing Amanda?"

Tweeter blanched. He was speechless. Sarah had never talked to him like that. To be sure, she had used the same demanding tone of voice when she had confronted Jet, Slump and him after the crew deaths on the *Mar Ascensor*. But she had never shown any interest in his private life.

"Jesus, Sarah," he said, his voice almost plaintive. "It's not like that."

"It's not like what, exactly?" she asked. "Are you or are you not?"

"Uh, yeah, I guess we're involved. But you make it sound like rape. It's not like that at all."

"Tweeter," Sarah said, addressing him as if he were a disruption in the first-grade class she was teaching, "I sent you to San Mateo to guard the lady. The man she'd been fucking until very recently presented a danger to her. So what were you protecting her from, falling ceiling tiles?"

Tweeter jumped up, stunned, his face red and fists bunched. Sarah knew him and knew she was not in any danger, but she was at that moment very glad he was on her side. "Jeez, Sarah!" he said heatedly, "It just happened, that's all. I feel sorry for her, the way that shit Jet treated her. I like her and I guess she likes me. It just happened, and it was more than some goddamn mercy fuck."

"What, are you in love now?" Sarah asked, more quietly.

"I don't know," he said, more meekly, as he sat back down. "I've never been in love before, so I'm not sure what it's supposed to feel like. Why don't you tell me? You and Boone seem to be getting pretty tight. Are you in love?"

Tweeter's words startled Sarah into silence. Suddenly, she saw how infantile her rant must have sounded to this man, who had survived who knows how many near-death experiences while a SEAL, and since.

"Point taken," she said simply. "I'm sorry for my outburst."

"No problem," he mumbled.

As if the conversation had never taken place, she brightened and asked, "Now, can we talk about the cartel meeting?"

They moved to her conference table.

"I've called a meeting for next Tuesday," she said when they were seated and had note pads in front of them. Tweeter wrote Tuesday's date on his pad.

"It will be at the Scottsdale Airport again," she told him. "I like the facilities and there's enough corporate jet traffic that this wouldn't attract much attention. I've notified the cartel members – CEOs only this time – and reserved the meeting space at the same center we used last time. Would you give me a hand by calling ShareJet and arranging for the jets?"

"No problem," he said, happy to be on familiar ground again with Sarah.

"Let the company know the meeting will start at 11:00 a.m.," she said, "and they'll tell you when the members will need to be wheels up at their respective airports to arrive by 10:45 a.m. Then use my email address to send those times to the members."

"No problem," he said again. Sarah knew it would be handled. She pointed Tweeter toward the hotel where she had reserved a room in his name. It was the one she had stayed in on her first two visits to Monterey and was an easy walk.

CHAPTER 42

During the flight from Monterey to Scottsdale, Sarah changed into her abaya and became Zara once again. Boone had been very curious since Sarah had mentioned the meeting in Scottsdale a few days before, but she had told him every time he had asked that she would have plenty of time to brief him on the flight down.

Now she did. Tweeter was already asleep in the seat nearest to doorway where the legroom was greatest.

"We'll be meeting with the chief executive officers of nine of the largest energy companies in the United States," she said. "I'll meet with them first myself, to set the stage for introducing you to them. You can wait in another room with Tweeter, Slump and Sandy Agria. Slump is bringing her along because they haven't caught Klenner yet."

"Why am I meeting with them?" he asked.

"Unless I miss my guess, they should be making you a job offer," she said slyly, "which you should accept."

"What?" he said, jarred. "What about CERG?"

Zara patted his knee across the aisle. "Be cool, be open-minded and let's see what happens."

At that moment, Zara's cell phone buzzed. She saw on the display that it was Clyde Peed.

"We found Klenner," he said without preamble.

"Where?" she asked.

"He rolled his car and was ejected when he was running from a Louisiana State Police trooper, who was chasing him for speeding just after he crossed over from Texas. He was dead on the scene."

"Are you sure?" she asked quickly.

"Positive ID," Peed confirmed. "And there were scratches on the right side of his face, which would seem to confirm he was the one who attacked Ms. Agria. And he had a briefcase full of cash in his car. The amount hasn't been confirmed yet."

"So I guess all that's left is to file charges against Pure Earth as an organization," she said. "When do you plan to do that? And make a public statement?"

"Tomorrow morning, 10:00 eastern time."

"Thank you very much for the heads-up," she said and they disconnected.

Zara looked at Boone and said, "Well, that was perfect timing." She filled him in on what Peed had said about Klenner's death, the scratches, the cash and the fact that charges would be filed the next morning.

"I'm glad they got the son of a bitch, but I'm not following the bit about perfect timing," Boone said.

"You will," Zara said and sat back in her seat. The plane was on final approach into Scottsdale.

The nine cartel members were already in the conference room, talking to one another and sampling the delicious array of fruit and pastries that were laid out on a draped table at the back of the room.

Slump and Sandy Agria were waiting in a smaller room across the hall from the cartel's meeting room when Zara led Boone and Tweeter in and briefed them all on Klenner's death.

Sandy sagged into a chair when she heard the news, tears of relief evident. Once they were all settled, Zara put on her niqab, the veil that covered her face except for her eyes, and walked across the hall and entered the conference room, closing the door softly behind her.

The cartel members stopped their conversations and hurried to their seats when Zara strode to the head of the table.

"Greetings," Zara said, affecting her Arabic-accented English.

"Thank you for your attendance, especially on such short notice. I have some new and extremely interesting information that may, in fact, amaze you. And I have a new opportunity to discuss with you". None of the members said anything.

"So, to begin, you have probably noticed that Akrum al-Kahtani is not here for today's meeting."

"I was just going to ask where he was," Rodney O'Connor said, and others nodded.

"Mr. al-Kahtani has returned to Saudi Arabia, and in all honesty I must tell you that his departure is related to an investigation by the FBI that might have resulted in his being declared persona non grata. He could not, of course, be prosecuted for crimes in this country because of diplomatic immunity."

She paused to let the alarmed looks and the buzz at the table die down.

"And his operations man, Jet Jamieson, of whom you have heard previously, is dead. Ironically enough, he was killed when his boat struck the Royal Energy tanker, Prince, just outside Long Beach Harbor." The members had all heard of the incident but had not focused on the name of the man reportedly killed.

For a full minute, there was total silence in the room, the only sound seemingly the accelerated heart rates of nine oil executives.

After this silence, Dan Mirza of Mossy Oil, who, like the others, looked visibly shaken, asked in a halting voice, "So where does that leave us?" The sweep of his arm made it clear he was referring to those seated around the table.

Zara stared around at the faces before her gaze settled on the table in front of her. "My information is that the FBI will file charges and make a public statement about the five oil incidents tomorrow morning."

The smell of fear hung in the room as the eyes of the cartel members darted from one to the other. Zara was playing them very well, she realized. Then she continued.

"The charges will be filed, according to my information, against the environmental organization, Pure Earth International, Akrum al-Kahtani and Jet Jamieson. Charges will not be filed against the executive director of Pure Earth – a man named Kirk Klenner – because he was killed yesterday in an automobile crash resulting from his attempt to evade the Louisiana State Police. As I said, Mr. Jamieson is presumed to have been killed in the boating incident, but since his body has not been recovered, he is being charged, just in case.

"Mr. Klenner, it turns out, was trying to avoid a traffic stop with good reason. He had tried to destroy Pure Earth's computer system and injured a Pure Earth employee who was attempting to save the computers." She stopped, looking around as if inviting questions.

Kristina Vandam of Prime Oil said, "Let's get back to Dan's question. Where does that leave the nine of us? Are we next?"

"Prior to Akrum al-Kahtani's formation of this cartel, he and Jet contracted with Klenner and Pure Earth to do exactly the same thing this cartel was formed to do," she said. "The only difference is that Pure Earth did not impose the restrictions you did about avoiding fatalities and injuries. To put it quite bluntly, this group was simply a double dip for them.

"I became suspicious of them after the *American PERL I* disaster. As I told you during our last meeting, I undertook an investigation of that matter, at the conclusion of which I provided my information to the FBI, and I have been working with the Bureau since then to resolve this matter."

"God!" Mirza exclaimed. "You've been setting us up, then." The usually mild-mannered man was clearly agitated.

"On the contrary," Zara replied evenly. "You – all of you – are home free, as you Americans like to say. As am I, I might add." The scowls at the table turned to relieved but still-wary smiles, as if they all expected the other shoe to drop at any time.

"Except for one continuing matter," she said and paused while still more alarmed looks were shared around the table. She smiled and said, "No, not anything bad. I just have a new idea to run by you that I think you will agree has great potential benefit to all of your companies."

Zara circled the table, handing a leather-bound binder to each of the participants.

"Before going into the details of this idea," she said when she had resumed her place at the head of the table, "I think I can safely say that this cartel, as we have known it, no longer exists, and therefore before we leave here this afternoon, I will collect the laptops and cell phones we have been using to communicate with each other. We will have no more use for them."

Nine smiles of relief greeted that statement.

"My proposal," Zara plunged ahead, "involves starting and funding a new organization. I have given it the working name of 'Do Good for America'". Several chuckles around the table were not unexpected to her.

"I know," she continued. "It is corny. I love that American term. And it is meant to sound corny, to denote a group of people and companies who truly care about their country and want to protect it from environmental devastation caused by politically expedient but ill-advised policy decisions.

"As you know, the cartel has had indirect ties over the past year or so, via its funding through ERIN, with Citizens for Responsible Growth, but I think that name implies a narrower scope of interest than what I have in mind. CFRG is a fine organization with a visionary leader and I would suggest our new organization incorporate CFRG under its umbrella.

"But I see Do Good for America also taking a world-wide lead in such things as research into economically-feasible alternative energy sources."

By then, the nine executives at the table were becoming animated. Kristina Vandam, who seemed to immediately grasp the potential of Zara's idea, said, "I like the sound of that. The 'economically-feasible' part, in particular. The problem with all the programs in place now – for solar, wind, biofuels and so forth – is that they only work because of Federal subsidies or tax breaks, so we in the petroleum industry are having to compete with both arms tied behind us." Heads nodded vigorously.

"Exactly," Zara said. "But if an organization with the right leadership, especially one financed by the nine of you, came up with alternative sources or technology, and you controlled it, you would still be the leaders in the energy industry. Only the energy you have to sell would then consist of a full menu of options, not just fossil fuels."

"I like that," Vandam said with enthusiasm. She looked around the table and saw that her opinion was the general consensus. "So let me ask a couple of questions," she continued, looking at Zara. "First, would you propose to run this new organization?"

"Absolutely not," Zara said firmly. "I am a facilitator. I am not, by background or temperament, a manager. And frankly, my ethnicity would be a detriment to many people."

"Second question:" Vandam went on. "You said CFRG had a visionary leader but we would absorb his organization into ours. Would he stand for that?"

Zara, had her face been visible, would have been showing them a very wide smile. She was playing them perfectly. "I have taken the liberty of inviting my choice as executive director to this meeting, and he is waiting in another room. And, Ms. Vandam, I think you will find that my choice eliminates the need to get the leader of CFRG to agree. His name is Boone Malory, and he is, indeed, the executive director of CFRG."

"My goodness," Kristina Vandam exclaimed. "You are a facilitator, aren't you?"

"I try," Zara replied simply. "Now, are there any further questions before I ask Mr. Malory to join you? I think Ms. Vandam can chair the meeting until you finish talking with Mr. Malory and start to create the structure of Do Good for America."

Rodney O'Connor spoke up. "Before we leave the, ah, let's say, previous business of this group, may I ask a couple of questions?"

"Of course," Zara replied evenly.

"Am I mistaken, or is Akrum al-Kahtani not your father?"

"He is."

"When do you expect to see him?"

"Only if I go to Saudi Arabia," Zara said. "And I have no plans to do so. My father and I have worked together on occasion, such as on this cartel's previous endeavors, but we are not close in what you would define as a normal father-daughter relationship."

"Thank you," O'Connor said. "And what about ERIN, which we've all put a lot of money into?"

"Good question, and I apologize for failing to cover that issue," Zara said. "My plan is to have it disbanded, to cease all activity immediately. As it turns out, the funds you provided to ERIN were only used to fund CFRG, and the funds remaining on its books will be transferred to Do Good for America, so your money will still be used to support your new organization. "In addition, on the subject of wrapping things up, we will finalize the accounting of the costs of the various incidents and apportion the assessments as agreed. As I see it, my contract with you will cease to be effective as of the end of the accounting period. Of course, the profit-sharing portion of our agreement will remain in full force.

"I have done everything possible to eliminate any remaining risk to any of you, and I think once the accounting is complete the work of this group, as it relates to my services, will have come to a conclusion. And I believe the primary goal of this group will be achieved in the very near future. I expect the President to reverse his open drilling policy within a matter of weeks."

Robert Beck asked, "Are you sure nothing will ever come out about this group?"

Zara paused, then responded, "If this group ever comes to light, it will have to come from someone in this room, and I do not think that will happen because you have shared culpability, and therefore a shared interest in seeing that nothing ever comes out. As it stands now, the FBI is very confident it knows who the guilty parties were. All matters, as regards this group, should be closed."

That seemed to satisfy everyone, so Zara continued. "I do not think I need to say this, but Mr. Malory is unaware of the past activities of this group. His resume is included in the information I distributed. I will give you thirty minutes to discuss this in general among yourselves before Mr. Malory joins you. During that time, I will brief him on the broad outline of why you are here and why you wish to meet with him."

"Thank you, Zara," Vandam said. "As always, you are very thorough."

Zara went into one of the small rooms to brief Boone. She told him she had worked, during her lobbying days, with the petrochemical industry briefly, and had maintained contact with several of the lobbyists and a couple of CEOs. One of them had contacted her on behalf of a group who wanted to form a non-profit to deal with environmental issues, alternative energy and related issues in a realistic way.

The idea was to show the world that Big Oil could be a good corporate citizen.

They had asked her, she told Boone, to help them think the idea through and to recommend a staff leader – whether they called that person the executive director or president – and she thought Boone was perfect for it. She thought CFRG could be rolled into the new group, and that ERIN would be disbanded and all its remaining funds transferred to the new organization.

Funding would be assured, she told him. The nine companies had convinced her they were all in for the long haul. He could base the organization in Monterey if he wished but the money would be there for a full-time office in Washington, too.

Boone was speechless. "I'm not ready for this meeting," he muttered.

"Neither are they," Zara said firmly. "Just wing it. You'll do fine. I've sold you to them on the basis of your vision and understanding of the issues. There will be plenty of money for people to handle the lobbying, bookkeeping and all the things you're uncomfortable with."

"Lobbying?" he blurted. "Aren't you going to be part of it?"

"I am, for now, but there may be another opportunity soon," she said mysteriously. "And if that happens, believe me when I tell you that I'll be even more help to you than I am now. But I can't say any more about it until it happens." She squeezed his hand. "I'm going to be in your life, Boone, one way or the other. I've waited a long time for you to come along and I'm not letting you get away from me."

Kristina Vandam knocked on the door to the smaller room and stuck her head in. Zara jumped up and, very formally, introduced her to Boone Malory, who followed the woman across the hall and into the room where the cartel members were waiting.

CHAPTER 43

Zara locked the door, removed her niqab and placed a call on her cell phone.

"Congressman Deeds," the voice answered.

"Sarah Cotton, Congressman," she said. "How are you?"

"Sarah, it's always good to hear from you. Are you in town?"

"No, I'm in Arizona," she said. "And I need another favor. I know I'm always asking you for something, and I apologize for that."

"You've done plenty for me, Sarah," the Congressman said jovially. "How can I help?"

"I need a meeting with the President." She waited a beat for that to sink in.

"Oh, is that all?" Deeds asked brightly.

"No, not quite," Sarah replied carefully. "It needs to be private – very private. Just him and me. No staff, no recorders, and I need to meet with him just as soon as possible."

"Can you tell me anything about what you want to talk with him about?" Deeds asked warily.

"I'm sorry, Congressman, I can't," she said. "Just that what I need to discuss with him affects him directly – both personally and politically."

"That sounds ominous," he said, "but it doesn't give me much to go on."

"If you can talk to him personally," she said, "tell him it concerns environmental issues, specifically as they relate to an organization called Pure Earth International and two men named Kirk Klenner and Akrum al-Kahtani." She spelled both names for him and he carefully wrote them down.

"Got it," Deeds said when he was finished writing.

"But, Congressman, let me stress that you should only mention those names to the President personally, and not relay them through his staff. That's important."

"I'll try my best, Sarah," he said. "And if I can get you the meeting, maybe someday you'll be able to fill me in on what this is all about. Meanwhile, stay flexible with your time. This is a hard order to fill and you may not get much advance notice at all."

"I'll be available whenever he is, Congressman," she said gratefully. "And thank you very much."

"I'll get to work on it immediately, Sarah. Take care of yourself." With that, he hung up. She hoped it was to make his first phone call for her.

The niqab was back in place when Zara unlocked the door. Not more than thirty minutes after walking into the conference room, Boone returned, smiling.

"That was quick," Zara said and moved to close the door behind Boone.

"That Kristina Vandam is one organized lady," he said. "She said they wanted to move forward with the organization as you outlined it for them, and hired me. I'll be President and Ms. Vandam will be Chairman of the Board.

"I have 30 days to develop an initial plan, goals and funding requirements. They're wiring $1,000,000 to CFRG for organizational and start-up costs to keep us rolling until the ERIN money comes in and the permanent funding plan is developed and approved."

"How about your pay package?" she asked.

"My total desired compensation package is to be part of my plan. I'll present it to them in thirty days. I'm to be in Kristina Vandam's office in Los Angeles, and most of them will be tied in by video conference. I'm to email everyone the plan two days before the meeting."

"Did you accept?" Zara asked, a hint of mischief in her voice.

"I didn't think you left me any choice."

"Good boy. You're learning." Zara walked over and entered the conference room.

Kristina Vandam was smiling broadly. "Excellent recommendation, Zara," she said. "Most of us had heard of him from the CFRG reactions to the oil spills, but we liked what we saw – and heard – in person."

"He just told me you are all basically agreed," Zara said. "He will serve you well in all respects. And for the record, the only goal of this group has just been met. That is, this group was convened for the sole purpose of discussing and, if agreed, creating the non-profit, Do Good for America." All at the table understood the subtext of what she had just said and beamed.

"And now," Zara concluded, "I believe all of our business is concluded. Please leave the laptops and cell phones on the table and I will have them destroyed. Have a good flight home and do not forget to watch for the FBI statement tomorrow."

Zara stood at the door and shook hands with each of the executives as they filed out of the room and headed toward their waiting aircraft. She pulled Kristina Vandam close as she shook her hand and congratulated her for taking the lead in the meeting.

Without exception, the CEOs were happy to board their planes and leave the cartel in the dustbin of history.

In the small room, Zara pulled off her niqab and burka and became, once again Sarah. "Let's put Zara away and get back to Monterey," she said to Boone. "You have a lot of work to do and I need some rest."

Relieved to be with Sarah again, Boone replied, "I'm not sure what you do – or did – when you were Zara, but it seems to be working out. And under your criteria, you still seem to be in the game."

"I am still in the game," Sarah agreed happily.

Slump Huff got on their chartered jet with Sandy Agria. Sarah had told him to go ahead and accompany her back to Houston. It was her home and she would now be safe there. Tweeter gathered up the laptops and cell phones and loaded them on the ShareJet that would take them back to Monterey. He would spend the next day or two downloading all the information on the devices before he had them destroyed.

CHAPTER 44

After an early breakfast, Sarah and Boone sat transfixed in front of the television, which was tuned to Fox News. Sarah knew nine oil company CEOs who would be tuned into the same thing. The director of the Federal Bureau of Investigation, with Clyde Peed standing just behind him, opened the news conference by reading a statement:

"Agents of the Federal Bureau of Investigation, working with state and local law enforcement agencies in Alaska, Texas, Louisiana, California and the State of Washington, have uncovered a massive conspiracy to cause five recent incidents involving the oil industry."

He outlined each of the five incidents, beginning with the barge off Santa Barbara and concluding with the *American PERL I* off New Orleans.

"The conspiracy was the work of a non-profit organization espousing environmental protection, Pure Earth International, based in Houston, Texas, and in particular of that organization's executive director, Mr. Kirk Klenner, now deceased. The chief of the Bureau's Criminal Investigation Division led the investigation and has uncovered evidence that Pure Earth International engaged Saudi Arabian diplomat, Mr. Akrum al-Kahtani.

"We have further evidence that an associate of Ambassador al-Kahtani's, Mr. Jet Jamieson, was personally involved in all five cases of sabotage of the ships, barges and platforms targeted in this conspiracy. Ambassador al-Kahtani is believed to have returned to Saudi Arabia, and the Attorney General is working with the Administration to have Mr. al-Kahtani declared

persona non grata.

"*Special Agent Peed, chief of our Criminal Investigation Division, is with me today and would be happy to answer any questions he can.*"

One of the early questions regarded the current whereabouts of Jet Jamieson.

"He is missing at sea following a boating accident off the coast of Long Beach, California, and he is presumed to be deceased," Peed said in his best FBI jargon.

Peed was then asked how they got wind of the conspiracy.

"We got lucky, to tell you the truth," Peed said. "As so often happens, a conscientious citizen tipped us off to start with, then worked with us to develop key information about Pure Earth International, which led us to Ambassador al-Kahtani and Mr. Jamieson."

The news conference droned on for another hour but nothing new came up. The questions were repeated – sometimes with a little rewording and sometimes not – so that each of the reporters could be seen asking astute questions by their own cameras.

Boone, knowing Sarah intended to stay in her apartment that day, walked to the CFRG office, where he and Suzy Dillinger started planning Do Good for America. They quickly agreed that CFRG would become part of the new organization. Suzy was beside herself with joy that she would never have to worry about fundraising or looking for checks in the mail again.

The next day, Fleming Worthy of PERL Oil flew into Monterey. Sarah had asked Captain Randolph Aglee to fly up, ostensibly to receive a full briefing on the final results of her investigations. Worthy had agreed to come to Monterey after hearing Boone explain over the phone the story they had uncovered about the *Mar Ascensor* incident.

Sarah and Aglee were sitting in her office, sipping coffee and making small talk, when Suzy came in and announced that their other guest had arrived and was in the Board room.

"Mr. Worthy, I am Sarah Cotton of CFRG and we appreciate your accepting our invitation today," she said as she strode into the Board room, and introduced Boone and Suzy. When Aglee walked through the door she continued. "And I believe you are acquainted with this gentleman."

Captain Aglee stepped through the door, stopped and turned toward Sarah, shock on his face at the sight of his former boss. Suzy and Boone were also in the room, Boone with a video camera and Suzy with a digital still camera. Boone had the video rolling.

Worthy took a step forward and cleared his throat. "It is a great pleasure to see you again, Captain Aglee." He turned to Sarah and recited – for the record, as it were, since Boone's camera was picking up the audio – the relevant facts. Worthy was speaking as if to an audience. "Captain Aglee, as you know, is a master mariner with nearly three decades as a captain of PERL Oil tankers. Nearly three decades, I should point out, with a perfect safety record. That record was apparently stained on his last voyage before his planned retirement.

"We now have incontrovertible proof that his ship was sabotaged by a radical environmental organization, and that there is nothing Captain Aglee could have done to prevent it. Therefore, Captain, it is my pleasure and honor to tell you that your perfect safety record has been officially restored."

He shook Captain Aglee's hand again before continuing. "I have three things to present to you, Captain." First, he handed him a framed certificate attesting to the years of his career as a ship's captain and his perfect safety record. Captain Aglee's eyes were tearing. Sarah Cotton had clearly not told him what was coming when she asked him to travel to Monterey on a chartered jet and he was in shock.

Next, Worthy handed the captain a diamond-encrusted gold Rolex President, engraved on the back with his name and years of service at sea.

"And finally," Worthy intoned, "I would like to present you with something verbal. It is a promise of a job, now or any time you are ready to abandon retirement, as a consultant and safety instructor for PERL Oil. The pay will be the same as you were earning as the captain of a VLCC. This is a lifetime offer, Captain, and the job is available any time you're ready."

He turned again, and this time enveloped Captain Aglee in a bear hug. Sarah was in tears, too, and the captain's knees were so weak he wondered about his ability to continue standing. Suzy was sobbing so hard she was having trouble holding the camera steady to get her still shots memorializing the occasion.

Sarah thanked Captain Aglee for coming to Monterey and escorted Fleming Worthy to the front door, where a cab waited to whisk him back to the airport. Worthy and Sarah felt almost as good as Aglee. A wrong has been righted.

As it turned out, Sarah largely stayed in her apartment for next two days, relaxing. She had put Zara and her abaya and niqab away, tucked tightly into a corner of her closet. She thought often how at home she felt now, here in Monterey. And with Boone. The thought of a quiet, mostly-relaxing life, was becoming more appealing to her, and she wondered if the day would ever come when she would need to bring Zara out of her closet once again.

Late the third afternoon, her cell phone rang and she almost jumped when she noted that it was Congressman Deeds.

Wasting no time, Deeds announced, "Sarah, you have an appointment with the President at eight tomorrow night. It will be just the two of you and he assured me there would be no recordings. Do you have something to write with?" She did and he gave her a phone number. "Call that number at six tomorrow night and let them know where you are and the Secret Service will send a car to take you to the White House."

"I can't tell you how much I appreciate this, Congressman," she said. "I knew you could do it if anybody could. I owe you a big one."

Deeds brushed the compliment off. "It was easier than I thought it would be, once I got the President on the phone personally. Once I mentioned the names you gave me, he almost insisted on the meeting."

"Thanks again, anyway," she said and they rang off.

So much for the peaceful life in Monterey, Sarah thought to herself as she arranged with ShareJet to have a plane ready for an early departure from Monterey to Washington. Then she called Boone.

"I need to go to Washington tomorrow morning, and I'd like you to go with me. We can spend a couple of days there and maybe start planting the name of Do Good for America with some of the right people."

"Why do you need to go to Washington?" Boone asked.

"I have a meeting at eight tomorrow night," she said without elaboration.

"What kind of meeting? Or is that another of those 'I'll tell you later' deals?"

"It's a later deal, Boone," she said. "But we're getting close to when I can lay it all out for you. And thank you for agreeing to come with me."

"I haven't agreed," he protested.

"Yes, you did," she said, an innocent sweetness in her voice. "And let's plan an early dinner so you can pack. We'll leave at six in the morning."

Sarah called Clyde Peed, and he answered his cell immediately. "Great news conference," she said. "And getting the director to make the statement was great!"

"I thought you might like that," Peed said.

"It will look good in your personnel file."

"How can I help you, Sarah?" Peed asked. He didn't think Sarah was calling to blow smoke up his ass.

"Just tying up loose ends," she said. "That cash and gold I turned over to your guys? And the diamonds?"

"Yes?" Peed wondered what shoe was going to drop, but as it turned out, he was surprised.

"Just keep it," Sarah said, "and apply it to the national debt. It was Akrum's blood money and I don't want to touch it again, even if I could."

"The U.S. government thanks you," Peed said, "although in all honesty it will be like adding a small glass of water to a swimming pool and expecting to see the water level rise."

"And, Peed, if things go as I think they will, we may be working together again."

"Oh? How so?"

But Sarah just said, "Thanks again for your help" and hit the end key on her cell phone.

Peed looked at Patrick Moblox and said, "That was strange. Sarah Cotton congratulated us on the news conference, gave us all that money and gold, and said we may be working together again. I wonder what the hell she means."

"Are you going to look into her previous activities any further?"

Moblox asked.

"Who knows? Maybe later. Let's see how this plays out."

CHAPTER 45

The ShareJet was waiting for Sarah and Boone when they arrived at the Monterey Peninsula Airport early the next morning.

They landed at Reagan at 2:35 p.m. local time.

This trip, they eschewed the Metro and took a cab to Sarah's condo. As they walked in, Boone asked her how long she planned to keep it, now that she was living in Monterey.

"For a while," she said. "It's paid for, so all I have to keep up with is taxes and insurance. And we can use it when we come to Washington. Who knows how much we'll be coming here in the future, with the new organization and all."

They unpacked and walked to the same little restaurant they had enjoyed so much on their previous trip. She got the same effusive greeting when they walked in and they were led to the same dark table in the rear. Halfway through their salads, Boone asked, "Are you going to tell me why we had to come to Washington, or is it still later?"

Taking Boone's hand, Sarah said, "It's still later, but not by much. I'll be able to explain it all after my meeting tonight."

"Who are you meeting with?" he asked.

"Later, my dear," she said and squeezed his hand.

Back at her condo, Sarah showered, washed her hair and dressed for her meeting. Of course, it was the same uniform she always used in her lobbying mode, and she wore high heels rather than pumps. She had, as

Congressman Deeds had instructed, called the Secret Service number at 6:00 p.m. sharp and given them her address. The efficient-sounding man on the phone confirmed she would be picked up in front of her condo at 7:40 for the short ride.

At 7:57, Sarah was escorted through a private entrance into the West Wing of the White House and to the President's private working office just off the Oval Office. Her purse had been checked by one of the Secret Service agents on the ride over.

As the agents escorted her down the hall, Sarah's heels made a low clicking noise on the marble floor. One of the agents knocked softly on the door and the President's response could be heard from inside. The agent opened the door and waved Sarah through, closing it softly behind her. The two agents took up posts at each side of the door.

"Mr. President, my name is Sarah Cotton and I appreciate you making the time to meet with me, especially on such short notice."

"Please sit down, Sarah," the President said genially. "It is Sarah, is it not? I'm told that sometimes you use another identity. Zara, is it?" The question jolted Sarah. He had not simply taken the word of Congressman Deeds. He had had her checked out. The FBI had obviously been one of the agencies that he had checked with. As far as she knew, it was the only agency that was aware of her dual identity.

"Yes, sir," she said with a bow of her head, "it's Sarah tonight."

The President smiled broadly, enjoying the repartee. "I assumed it must be Sarah, since you aren't wearing your abaya and niqab."

"You have done your homework, Mr. President," she said, "but the abaya and niqab, in my case, are just a costume."

"I understand," he said. "Now, my good friend, Congressman Deeds, said you have something urgent to discuss with me." His face had lost its good-natured look and had been replaced by his famous business face. "He mentioned, specifically, the names of Pure Earth International and two gentlemen named Klenner and al-Kahtani."

"That's correct, Mr. President," she said, but she was now glancing around the room.

"There are no audio or video recording devices in here, Sarah," he said in a mildly-annoyed tone of voice. "I assured the Congressman that I would abide by that request. That's why we're meeting in here. This is my working office and there is no need for such devices in here."

"Thank you, sir," she said. "Then let me begin, and I assure you I will make it as quick as I can. I know your time is precious." The President nodded and gestured for her to continue.

"I believe, sir, that in most instances our goals are the same, even if our methods to achieve them might be different in some cases. I would like to discuss current and future relationships and events. But the real purpose of wanting to talk with you is really not to talk about Pure Earth, Mr. Klenner, Mr. al-Kahtani, or the rash of recent oil spill incidents, including the most recent disaster off Louisiana."

"I am told that Mr. al-Kahtani is your father," the President interrupted.

"He is."

"Have you been in contact with him recently?" Sarah knew the President had almost certainly been told that Akrum had fled to Saudi Arabia and he was fishing.

"Not since well before he left the country," she said firmly. "In fact, not since before the Louisiana disaster."

"Did you have any involvement in that disaster?" he asked pointedly.

"No, not at all, but I do know who organized and executed it. It is substantially as the FBI has reported it, sir."

"So you're the informant who put the case together for them?" he asked. He had done his homework.

"I am," she replied simply.

"But what you wish to discuss tonight is unrelated to that disaster?" he asked.

"Not directly, sir," she said. "But there is a tangential relationship that affects you and that's why I wanted to meet privately with you."

"Before we get to that," the President interrupted again, "I'd like to know how you got the information you provided to the FBI – and presumably whatever it is you wish to share with me tonight."

"From computer records," she said. "Pure Earth's and Mr. al-Kahtani's. And some hard files of Mr. al-Kahtani's."

"I'm curious. How did you get access to all that?" he asked.

"I won't answer that," she said, "and I believe that, in your position, you don't want to know the answer." She smiled.

The President smiled back, inclining his head. Clearly, he appreciated her response and wished some of the people in his employ were as astute.

"Do they know you have this information?" he asked at length.

"No," she said, shaking her head firmly. "But Mr. Klenner is dead and Mr. al-Kahtani is hiding in Saudi Arabia." The President sat in thought for a moment.

"Okay," he said, "let's hear what you have."

Sarah handed him two thumb drives. "Two other sets of these exist," she said carefully. "But here's a synopsis of what you will find proof of on those: Pure Earth International and a certain Mideast oil-producing country desired a permanent restriction on new oil exploration and drilling in this country. They decided to focus on the politically-acceptable environmentally-sensitive areas as a stalking horse for all oil exploration.

"Those areas, in fact, hold most of our known significant reserves anyway." The President nodded, his brow beginning to furrow.

"Go on," he said.

"The plan was really quite simple. First, provide unlimited campaign contributions – obviously done anonymously – via Internet contributions and by funding independent expenditure campaigns to a presidential candidate who they know to be an opponent of expanded exploration and drilling but who would agree to open up the existing restrictions upon being elected for political reasons.

"Second, a series of incidents involving offshore oil drilling or transportation would be arranged and financed. And finally, given the political fallout over the incidents, the President would have the cover to permanently reinstate the previous restrictions on exploration and drilling. These permanent restrictions would be a boon to the environmental organization – Pure Earth – and to the Mideast oil country."

The President's face was now set in a grim scowl. He did not move – seemed not even to blink – for a full minute. Finally, he asked, weakly, "Do any other copies of these exist?" He opened his hand, which had been locked around the thumb drives in a death grip.

"No," Sarah said, almost jauntily. "Just the two other sets of those drives that I have, and they are in very secure places."

"What do you plan to do with those copies?" he asked. "This is very unpleasant stuff."

"I was hoping – in fact, my real goal in coming here tonight – was to see if we could join forces and move forward," she said. "As I said earlier, I think that, at heart, we share many of the same goals, especially when it comes to the environment. If we do decide to move forward – to join forces, as it were – I will destroy my copies and nobody outside this room will ever know the information on them ever existed."

The President nodded, took a deep breath, and relaxed in front of her eyes. She glanced at her watch. It was approaching 9:00 p.m. and she expected to be told he would think about it and be ushered out of the White House.

Instead, the meeting continued for another two hours as the two discussed details. The President wanted to know everything about her background, her environmental concerns, and finally her interest in joining his Administration. She had cast another line and once again, the fish – this time the biggest fish of all – had bitten.

Just before 11:00 that night, the two Secret Service agents ushered her back into the black Suburban and drove her back to her condo. Sarah felt exhilarated as she bounded up the stairs to her door. She could hardly wait to tell Boone everything. That is to say, almost everything.

The next day, Sarah and Boone took in two more of the Smithsonian museums. In the course of the day, she fielded no fewer than five calls from the President and one from Interior Secretary Jackson Delamater, asking her to set up a lunch with him as soon as her arrangements had been put in place.

Of course, Sarah could not tell Boone the truth about who these calls were from. As far as he was concerned, most were from former lobbying associates, or from Sandy Agria or the Huff twins.

The following morning, Sarah sat at the breakfast table with a satisfied smile on her face as she watched Boone – mouth agape – read the headline story at the top of page one of *The Washington Post*.

DRILLING BAN FOLLOWS OIL DISASTERS

Washington, D.C. – *In a move expected by Washington insiders after a series of oil-related incidents, near misses and the recent major disaster off the Louisiana coast, Interior Secretary Jackson Delamater announced a permanent ban on oil exploration and drilling in environmentally-sensitive areas, including all coastal areas.*

This is a reversal of the President's action of last year, when he lifted the ban, stunning environmentalists, who had previously considered him a staunch ally.

"The rash of oil spills and disasters our country has endured over the past year can no longer be tolerated, Delamater said in a statement. "They have caused great environmental damage and unacceptable loss of life."

In a related development, the President moved to strengthen his White House staff and reassure disaffected environmental groups by adding Sarah Cotton to his staff as a Special Advisor with a broad portfolio, including domestic and international issues.

Ms. Cotton has been a successful lobbyist for over ten years and most recently worked at Citizens for Responsible Growth, a conservation organization which played a leading role in pressing for the reversal of the President's order lifting the ban on oil exploration and drilling.

The President noted in his statement that Ms. Cotton has worked on several special projects for him since he has been in office, and that he is looking forward to working with her on a daily basis. The President's statement noted that she would start immediately and would report directly to him.

(Continued on page A5)

www.ingramcontent.com/pod-product-compliance
Lightning Source LLC
Chambersburg PA
CBHW020254030726
47499CB00001B/196